The Lost Blade

K. L. Tate

For my friends and family

The Lost Blade

Prologue

The screaming could be heard throughout the entire city, echoing from beyond, past the gates that few dared to cross. It rattled the buildings, waking children from their beds, worrying lovers as they held onto one another, reminiscence of what they'd done earlier in the night. Perhaps it was a ghost, haunting them, scaring the wits out of every living soul. Or maybe it was a dying animal, though there was only one kind of beast that survived in The Wry. Maybe it was nothing but a call on the wind, a reminder from their god not to act out of line, for if they did, they could end up banished from the city as so many had before.

As the young lord was pulled from sleep, jarred so thoroughly that as he sprang out of bed, he slid right off of the mattress, he couldn't help but suspect the worst. He heard the scream, the same as everyone else did, and he was prepared to ignore it if it wasn't for the feeling in his gut, some sort of strange tether.

He walked over to the window, as if he could see beyond the walls from there, but all he saw was the moon-filled sky, and the sprawl of buildings beyond. And then he could hear footsteps, echoing down the hall outside of his door. He wouldn't have thought it unusual—perhaps it was just the guards changing shifts—if it wasn't for the murmuring, the hushed whispers, though he could still hear everything. And then the door to his bedroom opened, strange men entering, accompanied by his father, the Lord of Mortefine himself. They were dressed in their nightclothes, with armor and

1

weapons holsters thrown over them, and looked disheveled from sleep.

"Come," his father said, his voice as cold as ice. He went to move for the door, his father holding a hand up to halt him. "Bring your weapon." And so he did. He slid on his belt, and connected his sword to its holster. It was a small, skinny thing, which he would outgrow within the next few years. He wasn't much old enough to wield it even then, but like any young man, he needed to learn to protect himself.

They left the estate, a dozen guards flanking them, and walked across the city to the gates. It was eerily quiet out, some houses lighting candles as they passed, as if to get a look at what was happening. They, no doubt, could hear the screaming as well.

And that scream continued, as it had for almost the past thirty minutes now. A scream that indicated the greatest evils of the world. A scream that almost seemed like it couldn't have possibly come from a human. But perhaps something much, much scarier.

The night was cool, much cooler in comparison to the scorching temperatures of the daytime. The moon shone brightly above, full, filling up much of the sky. On and on they went, the closer they got, the louder the screaming became.

To pass the time, his father decided on lecturing him, which wasn't unusual, but didn't often happen in the middle of the night, when they were on the cusp of danger. But then again, they didn't really face much danger trapped behind the walls of Mortefine. *It is important for you to see how unexpected situations get handled,* his father had told him, *so one day, when you are lord, you can handle them without my help.* He would never admit this to his father, he never could, but he didn't particularly want to become the next Lord of Mortefine. He had little interest in what it entailed, though he didn't have a choice in the matter.

His first thought, of whatever this situation was that they were handling, was a banishment. He didn't think he could stomach watching it happen, though he had before. It was a barbaric practice—a fate worse than death. Those who faced the sentence did not survive. Or perhaps, this screaming, it was coming from a person who had been banished, someone who had returned to the city. Though something like that was unheard of.

When someone was banished, it usually came after a tremendous amount of torture. The exact manner of that torture was always different, depending on what his father felt like inflicting at the time. He'd seen fingers and toes cut off, some hands and feet. He'd seen wrists and ankles shackled. Brands inflicted. Poisons administered. Unimaginable things. After all of that, when the actual banishment was commenced, the criminals are brought up to the wooden platform atop the wall and dropped thirty feet down into The Wry. If they didn't die upon impact, which was a mercy, to say the least, there were far worse things in The Wry that would soon claim their life.

It never mattered that these criminals were guaranteed entry back into the city, should they accomplish the task set by the lord to earn their freedom. It was always a meaningless and impossible task, meant to give false hope to criminals and be rid of them with little difficulty. After seeing it happen again and again, always forced to watch as his father dragged him along, the boy swore to himself that he would never continue the practice once he became lord, and if that was the only good thing that came out of his reign, then so be it.

They continued towards the gate, the screaming louder now than he could have thought imaginable. He grew anxious for what awaited, not knowing what he would see, what he would be forced to do. Perhaps it was only someone that had completed their journey through The Wry, and hoped to enter the city, but that didn't explain the screaming. Surely if they had the right papers and documentation then the guards would have let them in. They could have come from elsewhere, with the right protection and equipment, of course. There were places beyond their guarded city, none of which the boy had ever seen before. Most people don't consider the risk of leaving worth it, especially not his father who had left only a few times during his own lifetime, often to answer the king's summoning.

At last, they made it to the stairs at the gate that led atop the wall surrounding the city. The boy's palms were sweaty, his legs wobbling slightly beneath him. Thankfully, his father was too preoccupied with the other matter at hand to notice. The gate was barred shut, so there was no doubt at all now where the screaming was coming from.

The boy tried his best to move around the guards as they made it to the top of the stairs, into view of land beyond. He surveyed the vastness in the distance, but he did not look up closely. He did not look at the faint outline of something that could be seen at the foot of the gate. In every direction as far at the eye could see, and even beyond that, lay a desolate wasteland. Land that supported no life, gave no shelter, and took the spirit of those who dared to pass through it. It was formidable, infested with vile creatures that hailed from the Otherealm itself, with one purpose: to kill. People called it The Wry, but the name did no justice for how dreadful it really was.

The boy had to cover his ears now to keep out the screaming. He feared his ears might start to bleed, as the sharpness of it made his head dizzy. His father was pointing to the ground below, and while he could not hear what was being said, he knew what his father wanted. *Look*, his father mouthed. *See*. So the boy finally turned his head, looking below, and gasped, nearly falling backward when he saw what it was.

A girl. A small child. Younger even than the boy himself. Her hair was matted and tangled, and even in the moonlight, the golden hue of it could be made out clearly. Her skin looked tanned, though the boy suspected that it was only because of the layer of dirt covering her. Her clothes were torn, her delicate feet blistered and bare. She held both hands to the sides of her head as she screamed and screamed and screamed, letting out heavy cries, streaks of tears running down her cheeks.

The boy wondered how she had gotten outside of the city, past the gates. He considered it for a moment, his father assessing him as if to ask for his opinion. But then he saw the truth. Past the girl, farther into The Wry, were *footprints*. They were faint, barely visible, but they were there, and they were coming from the wrong direction. The girl had come from The Wry. From the world beyond.

The boy didn't know what to do or say, he didn't know if he was expected to at all, but from the way his father was staring at him. He thought it was some sort of test. Deciding to let this girl in or not.

She did not belong to their city, his home, but she had made it out there, alone, with nothing but the clothes on her back. Something like that was thought impossible. It was a week's trip at least to the nearest town, and even longer to the coast. If she had survived, then there must have been something about her, she must have had help or there must have been some reasonable explanation for how she had survived.

The boy's mind strained to piece things together. He thought hard, more than his child's mind was generally capable, but then something caught his attention. Or rather, the lack of something did. It was silent. The screaming had ceased. He ran to the edge of the wall, a guard grabbing onto his arm as if to keep him from falling down. He pulled away from them, surveying the girl. She was still there, but had fallen over. Passed out. Her eyes were closed, her legs tucked under her in a strange position, her hands still limply holding her head. The boy would have feared her to be dead if it weren't for the rising and falling of her chest, so faint, but even he could see it.

The boy turned to his father, falling to his knees. "Help her," he begged. "Please." He watched the expression on his father's face, like he was considering every one of his options before he made the final call. "Please," he repeated. The boy

5

had no reason to care for her. He didn't know her at all, but he knew helping her was the right thing to do. It had to be. If it wasn't, then what sort of world did they live in?

"Open the gate," his father said, sending a chill down the boy's spine. "Bring her to my estate. I don't want a word of this getting out." Then he turned back to his son. "From this point on, she is your responsibility. You made the call, so you can take care of her. And if she turns out to be a nuisance, you will be the one to get rid of her as well, do you understand that?"

The boy nodded, unsure of why tears were starting to fill his eyes. He looked back down, seeing the guards now lifting the girl's limp body, carrying her like a corpse. He flew down the stairs, meeting them at the bottom, shocked to see that the girl was much more beautiful up close. He reached his hand out, interlacing his fingers with hers, leaned down, and whispered, "Everything will be okay now."

Chapter 1

I often wondered if it was usual for me to feel this way, every single night. I dreamt how I thought others did, but my dreams always took me to dark, terrible places—places that I feared one day I could not return from. As I slept each night, there was a coldness, which left behind a sad and hopeless feeling. It followed me out of my dreams, into the light. Recently, it followed me through every waking hour of the day. I did my best to ignore it—to push it deep, deep down—but it seemed to always find some way to creep back up on me. It tore me apart, taking what little energy I had, like it was trying to take me over—take control of my soul—or just rip it out entirely. Perhaps it was just my fear of night, creating something that wasn't really there. It was a reminder of that night so many years ago. I often awoke in fear—hopeless, alone, terrified.

It seemed that the only thing that could revive me was the waking of the sun, letting me know that I was alive, and that the evil had not taken me over entirely. Of course, there were those reminders throughout the day, in the shadows I passed, or in the dark corners of the rooms I entered. I did my best to ignore it, as well as that voice I sometimes heard whispering.

Even now, as I felt the sun, inviting me back to the surface, out of that dark place and once again into what I could hardly consider a satisfactory life. I knew it would never leave me alone. It would never stop until it got what it wanted—I just needed to figure out what exactly that was.

Warmth flooded my skin, and I could feel the sun seeping in from the window, from the curtains that were half drawn, when I failed to close them the night before, stumbling half-drunk into bed after a night out. With every second it arose, I could feel its light dancing across my face, burning as it finally made its way to my eyes. I dared to open them, finding the glowing orb barely past the horizon, working its way up and up to illuminate the sky. It was early. Too early considering that today was a holiday, and that I had the day off from work. But I had errands and preparations to do, like everyone else in the city today. Or, more accurately, everyone in the country.

I slid out of bed, opening the curtains completely and flooding the room with sunlight. Beyond my window I could see smoke rising from nearby houses, families already cooking breakfast to celebrate the day. I could do something like that for myself, but I would be eating enough later, so I wouldn't bother. Especially considering that there was nobody here for me to celebrate with.

Even though I've never really had a place in the world, things seemed to have been getting worse and worse lately. The days have become harder to get through. The nights even harder. I have a life, a rather happy one, but there's a big part of me that's missing: I don't know who I am. Thirteen years ago, I came to Mortefine, when I was around five or six years old. I had no recollection of it. They say I walked straight out of The Wry, completely unharmed, having completed the impossible. They say I screamed in terror until it made me pass out—that I scared the city into thinking they were under attack. But I remember none of it. Not a thing. My memories began with waking up inside of the city, surrounded by strangers. I don't know how any of it happened. I don't know where I came from. The only trace of my past is the amulet around my neck, a round piece of gold with strange carvings on it, and on the back, there was a name inscribed. My name.

Kara, never forget, it read. I always found that funny, what the amulet said, because I had in fact forgotten, whatever it was. But there was no one to ask or confide in. Nobody who knew me—who claimed me. I was alone, and at the mercy of the lord of this city. I still am, really, and I think I always will be.

I stood next to the window in my bedroom, sliding it open and then taking a deep breath of dry air. Something spicy filled my nose, no doubt what was being used to season roasted meat nearby for the celebration tonight. My townhouse overlooked the city, standing two stories high at the top of a hill. The street I lived on was crowded, packed with other residents, but from the windows I had a breathtaking view. And then there was the roof. From the roof, on a clear day, you could even see beyond the walls, and out into The Wry. I've always looked, hoping to see something other than dead land, but my attempts have always been unsuccessful, like even the sand serpents don't want to visit us anymore. This was my home, and I did the best that I could for myself here. But one very important thing was missing. Or should I say, one very important person.

My friend Nola. But I would consider her more of a sister if I had any say in it. Some would even suggest us as lovers, though if they were brave enough to accuse me, I laughed in their faces. Nola and I were close. There was a bond between us that nobody else could understand, so I let them say what they wanted about me, but in the end, it would never matter. She had been gone for nearly six months, on orders to the capital, fulfilling her duty as the lord's delegate. Her arrival back to Mortefine was set for two weeks ago, yet she still had not returned. There could have been several reasons for her delay, some of them harmless, yet I couldn't help but fear the worse.

Anyone who left the city would be a fool not to take the necessary precautions. And leaving the city means going through The Wry. Mortefine is a desert, but The Wry is much, much worse. Nola left with about a dozen guards, all ordered by the lord to protect and defend her, to make sure she made it safely to and from the capital. Beyond the walls of the city, nothing grew, no water fell from the skies. The sun could melt your skin during the day, and at night, you would freeze to death before the moon had fully risen. Some say it was cursed by our god, punishment for some long-forgotten sin that had been committed.

It takes at least a week in any direction before reaching any type of civilization beyond the city. The safest choice would be to go north, where you could find passage to one of the bordering towns along the Alanah Sea or sail to Kraxoth. Going east or south would take you to the coast, to the ocean beyond the land. But the most dangerous choice would be to head west. That would take you straight to the Sandsaal Mountains, that mark the boundary of The Wry, which was a death sentence all on its own. Nola would be returning from the north, which is the safest and quickest way to and from the capital, Vatragon City, without going over the Sandsaal Mountains, or heading very far out of the way.

I'm certain Nola will make it back to Kraxoth—back to The Wry—but I fear that they won't make it back to Mortefine from there. Because of the sand serpents. They're vicious beasts that roam the wasteland, destroying everything in their paths. Some have been known to grow over fifty feet long, with fangs longer and sharper than a sword that can rip you apart in seconds. People who travel through The Wry should bring at least a dozen guards, or more, with them as they travel. No single person fights one and lives to talk about it. They run, and they pray to Drazen that they make it away. There are few left alive that have encountered them, which means few left alive who could tell you how to kill them.

Which was another reason that Nola needed to be alive. I didn't know what I would do if she wasn't. Spending this long without her had already taken its toll on me, so I couldn't imagine a lifetime of that. She was one of the only people there for me when I first came to the city. She welcomed me as a friend when everyone else chose to be afraid. She accepted me for everything that I was, even though I couldn't tell her exactly *who* I was, because I didn't know. People always had their suspicions about where I came from—

theories that somehow led them to fear me—but Nola never did. And neither did Hiran, but that's another issue entirely.

Nola was an orphan, the same as me. Her parents died of a flu when she was barely a babe, so she never had a chance to know them. The two of us grew up at Lord Rendal's estate, under his protection and in the company of his son, Hiran. The three of us lived together, trained together, studied together. We were inseparable, of course, until Hiran became lord. A lot of things changed then.

Now, Nola and I live in a townhouse a few blocks from the lord's estate. We moved out a few years ago, after everything happened, keeping mostly to ourselves until Hiran begged us to come work for him. I'm one of his advisors, the youngest, the only female, but certainly the most favored. Nola is his delegate to the king and queen, which requires her to often travel to the capital and speak on the lord's behalf. It's quite unusual for two nobody females to hold such high positions with the lord, but it certainly did not happen because of the lord's generosity. Hiran always has an ulterior motive, and with this decision of his, I had yet to figure out what it was.

I would usually be getting ready to head to the estate by now, and get started on the day's work, but today was special. It was Rebirth Day—the anniversary of the day our god Drazen was reborn as a dragon from a man. All of the lords found some way to celebrate it, and in Mortefine, it was usually celebrated with a ball at the Rendal estate. Every year, on this night, city folk were invited into the estate to celebrate. Only the upper-class citizens, of course. Hiran wouldn't degrade himself to partying with peasants. But it was usually fun, with all the drinking and dancing. It's supposed to be a happy day, but I knew it wouldn't be, not with Nola still gone.

When I finally left my room, after having stood like a statue and stared straight out the window for probably too long, I walked down the empty hall, stopping outside of Nola's closed bedroom door. Six months. That's how long her room had remained vacant—untouched. I was too much of a coward to enter on my own while she was away. The door handle was cold as I lifted my hand and carefully wrapped my fingers around it, twisting, hesitating, and then finally opening the door. The air from inside poured at me through the crack, smelling like it had been sitting for a while. I could see a faint layer of dust coating the furniture as I walked further into the room. I looked into the corner, finding a potted plant that had long ago died, remembering that I promised Nola I would water it while she was away. Part of me wanted to cry looking into the empty room. Another part of me felt sick.

My feet were moving before I had another second to consider, walking backward, out of her room, slamming the door shut as I exited. I didn't like being in there, not for one second, and I wouldn't do it again. But some stupid part of me hoped that I would open the door and find her asleep in bed, waiting for me to greet her. Someday soon, perhaps.

I walked back to my room, rummaging through the closet to find clothes for the day. I didn't need to wear the usual jacket designed for me as the lord's advisor, so I settled on a simple pair of black pants and a green tunic, as well as my leather boots. I fastened my sword holster across my back, the hilt of it poking over my neck. Fangmar was its name—a gift to me from the late Lord Rendal. I always knew it was likely a meaningless gesture on his end, but the weapon suited me well. The blade was long and thin, light enough to easily wield. The hilt was golden, with a black jewel welded to the bottom. I certainly knew how to use it. Even before I received it as a gift, I had enough training to consider myself familiar. Nola and I would practice, or I would find a guard. Years ago, Hiran had been my sparring partner of choice.

It felt good on my back, reassuring, though I knew there would be little trouble in the city today, when everyone was already in high spirits because of the holiday. I left my room, headed downstairs, ate some leftover bread from the night before and then headed out into the city.

It was quiet, the sun still having barely risen. There were hardly any people out, aside from others headed to the market, whether to buy or sell. It was on the other side of the city, but I didn't mind the long walk at all. The air was warm at this hour, and it would only be getting warmer as the day progressed—better to get the shopping over with now before I have to worry about passing out from heat exhaustion.

I needed to buy some food, the usuals, as well as water, maybe a treat to celebrate the holiday, and pick up my gown from the tailor. The fabric had to be specially ordered from the western part of the continent, which then took months to be put together. I didn't really care how I looked at the ball—showing up in a tainted nightgown would have satisfied me—but the lord insisted that his most trusted advisor should look like a good representation of his power. I made sure to send the bill his way as well, considering that I would not at all be able to afford the luxury, even with the hefty pay I receive every month.

I surveyed the sky as I walked—not a cloud in it. It hardly ever rained, and if it did it was never for more than a few minutes. Dirt blankets everything, so we have to be careful about what we do outside. In the heart of the city lies a large underground water reservoir, accessible by a well, which is fed by an underwater river that travels all the way across the country, all the way from the Alanah Sea itself. It couldn't be accessed by the general public, so they had to resort to buying water from vendors, at an insanely expensive price. But without that water, nobody would survive. Whatever price was asked, they would continue to pay it. It's simple: the more money you have, the more water you can access. It wasn't uncommon for lower-class citizens to die from dehydration in the heat of summer. While the upper class filled ponds with it or used it to water luxurious gardens.

Unfortunately, I was a part of that upper class. Not that I had a pond or a garden, but the house I lived in was nice, and the people I surrounded myself with weren't exactly struggling to get by, like so many others. But for me, it wasn't my choice. I can't say I'm not grateful for all that I have been given, because that would be incredibly selfish of me, but it's not fair to everyone else. It's not fair that some people get to go to balls and dinner parties, while others constantly fight to live another day. It's not fair to the parents that have to watch their children die when they can't afford to feed them. But that's just the way things were in Mortefine, and how they always would be.

Going to the market always set my mind at ease, giving me a break from all of the nonsense on the other side of the city. It allowed me to surround myself with decent people— ones that I could actually bear to be around. There was no need to uphold my reputation as the lord's advisor or as the child who crawled out of The Wry. I was just me. And even if people did recognize who I was, they never made a big deal about it.

I continued down the main road, observing the tall and skinny palm trees that sporadically lined the sandstone road, peering into the windows of families just waking up for the day, exchanging gifts if they could afford them. Most of the homes had dried up gardens and shrubs, while others had freshly planted flowers, orange and red in honor of Drazen. There was no telling where those came from, or who was lucky enough to grow them here.

It was hard enough to grow fruits and vegetables, let alone flowers. Most of the food in Mortefine was imported: grains, nuts, tea, fruits and vegetables preserved in glass jars. Fresh foods were very hard to come by, especially anything that came from livestock. Families were lucky enough if they could afford to keep chickens, but richer families were even known to keep cows or pigs. Food and water were the most valuable resources in the city.

I continued on my way towards the market, my stomach now grumbling with hunger. I assumed that most people were sleeping in for the day, those who were lucky enough not to have to work. But I offered a friendly wave to the occasional person I passed.

The market was nearly empty when I made it there, half of the vendors not even set up yet. I walked up to a familiar older woman, purchased two rolls of bread, stuffed them into my satchel. A younger many sold me a dozen eggs, which one of was already cracked so he offered me a discounted price. But I refused, feeling generous because of the holiday. I passed by other stands, some selling special items for Rebirth Day, though I had no interest in those. There were three women at one cart selling bakery items, to which I could hardly resist, practically dragged over by the delightful smell. I bought a pastry, filled with what looked to be some kind of preserved berries. They offered it to me for free for the holiday, but again, I paid anyway.

I passed by another woman selling pottery, which I had no interest in purchasing. She asked me how I was celebrating the holiday, and I hesitated before explaining that I would be with friends later. It was a lie, of course. There would be no friends with me later. She informed me that her family would enjoy a meal of roasted chicken, the first they could in months. The feeling of guilt struck me like a punch to the gut. I then purchased a plate painted with flowers, which I had no use for, but I just needed to buy something. I paid twice what she'd asked for, then watched her eyes widen in disbelief and gratitude. When she started to lower herself to the floor, to kiss my feet, or do whatever else, I stepped away, suddenly horrified. I offered her a kind smile before I turned and walked away.

That was certainly enough of the market for one day. I headed in the direction of the tailor, which was a few blocks over.

There were a few other women in the shop when I entered, most of them looking my age or younger. The woman that ran the shop, who I recognized, walked out from the back with two hideously colored gowns. Those were most definitely not mine. She smiled when she saw me, handing the girls their gowns and sending them on their way. They could barely contain their excitement as they left the shop, giggling quietly to one another, likely also attending the ball tonight. The tailor went to the back and returned a minute later with another gown. This, I knew, was mine. It was my signature color—emerald green. I knew I would look fabulous in it, but I hated the idea of turning so many heads. I wished it could be for my eyes only, but it didn't work that way. The tailor wrapped my gown in a special cloth bag, and I headed on my way.

The sun was welcoming, touching me as a soft caress as I walked back to the townhouse—no hint at all of that usual darkness. It was such a relief to have the day off, even though I would still be at the Rendal estate later, I wouldn't be working. I had several hours left until I needed to be there, which meant I would go home, and curl up on the couch with a novel.

The walk seemed quicker on the way back, even with the food, pottery, and clothing I now carried. My arms were full, but I felt lighter than ever. Maybe even happy, which had happened so little in the past six months. I turned the corner onto my street, more people out now than there had been before. The townhouse came into view, and I smiled a little as I saw it, my home. Until I came closer into view and saw the two men standing directly outside the front door. I kept walking until I could see that they were guards, the lord's men, either keeping me out… or keeping someone in.

"What do you want?" I asked as I approached, my voice tired yet there was a demanding coldness to it. I asked neither one in particular, and my eyes darted back and forth between them, waiting for an answer. "Did you hear me? What do you want?" I repeated.

"His lord requests your presence," the man on the left said, and I couldn't help but notice that his hand grazed the pommel of his weapon, as if he was poised to pull it free and use it on me.

I flashed him a wicked grin. "Does he now?" The guard opened his mouth to speak to me again, but I cut him off. "Unfortunately, you'll have to ask the lord to summon me some other time. Has he forgotten what day it is? I'm supposed to have today off."

16

"Would you disobey a request from your lord?" the man on the right asked, giving me a frown that made him appear twenty years older than he probably was.

"I would never disobey," I smirked. "Just—delay. Or you can tell him to deal with whatever it is without me." I tried to squeeze past them into the townhouse, but they held firm. They glanced at each other wearily, before stepping aside, giving me room to enter. I opened the door, sticking my tongue out at them, and then slammed it shut in their faces. But before I could set anything down or even move away from the door, a voice spoke from inside of my kitchen.

"Kara," the voice said. "That was *very* rude."

Chapter 2

My stomach dropped to the floor as I turned into view of the man sitting at my kitchen table, feet propped up, smile plastered on his face. His clothes were fine, clean, though they would have been any day. His dark hair was washed and brushed back; the usually crazy waves tucked behind his ears. And his eyes, as blue as a diamond held up to the sky, were staring straight at me. Hiran continued to grin as he stood from the table and moved toward me.

I stepped back a little, instinctively, and if Hiran noticed, he was good at hiding it. "What are you doing here?" I asked, not bothering at all to sound kind. I looked up to him, as he stood at least a head taller than me, his hands in his pockets, not a weapon in sight, and he leaned down to brush a kiss against my cheek. He always did that because he knew that I hated it.

"It's nice to see you," he told me. "I was feeling rather sad that I wouldn't get to see you today. Well, not until tonight, at least." His eyes moved to the items I was still holding—to the dress carefully wrapped. "Is that your gown for the ball?" He reached out a hand. "Let me see it."

I yanked it away, stepping a few more feet back from him. "You can see it on me later, as everyone else will."

He laughed softly, his eyes roaming over me, lingering on my most intimate parts. "Oh, I hope to."

"I thought I didn't have to work today," I said, ignoring him and moving into the kitchen, putting away all of the food that I purchased. When I turned back, he was still standing in the same spot, still staring at me. "Are you going to tell me what you want or just keep standing there like a freak? I don't have time for this, Hiran."

"Something came up, Kara." He said my name slowly, drawing it out, as I had just done with his own name. He was frowning now, like he was disappointed with my attitude. I debated telling him to kiss my ass. Bothering me on my day off, who does he think he is?

"Can you just tell me why you're here?" I said, my voice lower, as if I had been defeated. This always got him, somehow. While he didn't have a shred of decency for anyone else, he seemed to care for me in his own morbid way.

He took a long breath, sighing as he exhaled. "The delegate has returned from the capital."

I froze from where I had been fumbling around in the kitchen, my back turned to Hiran, but he seemed to have paused as well. I had just grabbed a glass out of the cabinet, was about to fill it with water, but it slipped out of my hand, crashing onto the floor beneath. "What?" I said.

"Nola is back," he confirmed, not a hint of a smile or any sort of affection for her on his face. He seemed almost disappointed by it.

"When?" I whispered.

"Just this morning," he told me. "They're still at the gate, awaiting my welcome. I thought I'd come and get you before I head over there."

"Oh." I didn't know what else to say. So many thoughts were running through my mind, but mostly the excitement of Nola actually being back in the city. She was here, waiting for me. "Well, let's go," I told him, already moving for the door so we could leave.

"There's something else," he cut in, halting me in my tracks. "They were attacked. A lot of people died." He almost sounded... remorseful, which was terribly confusing. Hiran didn't care about anybody but himself.

"By what?" I said, finally turning back to him. But I already knew. There was only one thing in The Wry that could have attacked them. Only one monster dwelled in those lands. "Sand serpents."

His confirmation nod was answer enough, setting me into action and out the front door where the two men were still standing guard. Hiran followed after me, the guards behind us, and we set off to the gate.

"Is she okay?" I asked him.

"As far as I know," he said. "The reports say there's only a handful of men left, but they succeeded in keeping Miss Westchase safe."

I turned to him, looking him straight in the eyes. "Thank you—for bringing me with you."

He didn't answer, just turned away, like it was as painful for him to receive my thanks as it was for me to give it. That's how it has always been between us, since all those years ago, since he became Lord of Mortefine. We used to be good friends, more than friends, even. But our relationship now was strictly professional.

As children, when I first came to the city, Hiran was the person that took me in. His father allowed me to live at their estate, as if I was his own child. Hiran showed me a kindness in those early years that nobody else did, not until Nola came along. The only reason I am skilled with a sword is because he insisted that I be allowed to train with him. The only reason I have a decent education is because he asked for me to learn with him. Nola too. The three of us did everything together. They were my friends, and they taught me how to be happy. With them, I learned to accept that even though a part of me was missing, I could still have a life worth living.

As children, we would run around the city together and explore forgotten places. We would hide until the sun went down. We would wreak havoc, getting in trouble with the lord, but not caring because of how much fun we were having. I wish I could still think about those years and feel happy, but at least Nola and I still had each other.

When I was sixteen years old, Hiran eighteen, he finally confessed his feelings for me. We started what seemed like a long-awaited relationship, and I was genuinely happy. Until a few months later when his father died. The former Lord Rendal was killed by sand serpents on a trip to the capital. Hiran's mother had passed many years before, long before I came to the city, which left him an orphan. I remember thinking that maybe I could offer him my help, because I had gone through something similar, but he made it clear very quickly that he did not want my help.

When his father died, it was as if a new part of him took over. Or maybe it was there all along and I just never noticed. He was no longer my childhood friend, or the boy I came to care for. He was Lord Rendal of Mortefine, appointed by King Daemien and Queen Felisa of Vatragon, the inferno continent under the watch of the god Drazen. Hiran's childhood ended abruptly. He no longer had time for friends, which was understandable, but the cruelness and the tormenting personality was not. I knew there was a harsh reality to being part of such a powerful monarchy, but he let it take him over. He let it consume who he was, turning him into a terrifying authority figure—a bad man.

I can remember the exact moment Nola and I realized what he'd become. We were still living at the estate, about two years ago. The lord was meeting with advisors, all his father's former men. Nola and I were seated towards the back of the meeting room, unsure of why we were even there in the first place. Somebody brought up an issue that needed dealing with, that several people in the south part of the city, the poorer part, had fallen ill from drinking contaminated water. The others urged him to fix the issue, but he refused. I'll never forget the words he said at that moment. *Why should I care about them?* The words of a foolish man, barely more than a child. I wish I could say that now he has changed, that he wouldn't do something like that again, but that would be a lie.

A few days later, at another council meeting, a man had been arrested for speaking out against the monarchy—against the king and queen. The man claimed that the royals lied about being descended from the god Drazen, that they were frauds and imposters. While it wasn't usually a severe crime to speak one's mind, even if it was about the royal family, Hiran gave the man an unusually cruel punishment. I don't think he cared much about the exact words the man said, but rather he felt the need to prove a point, to show the people that he wasn't just some weak boy, that he was better than his father had been. He ordered the man's tongue to be cut out, leaving him to bleed out, forbidding him from going to a healer. It was entirely undignified, but it surely would not be the last time I saw Hiran do something like that.

It was clear to me then that whatever Hiran thought being lord meant was an abuse of power. I wanted no part of whatever he had planned, so Nola and I left as soon as we could, buying a townhouse with what remained of the money the former Lord Rendal left us. I could only imagine the horrors that took place in the time we spent away. But of course, he came back to us. He didn't come to make amends or to apologize for the agony he put us through, but to ask us to work for him. I became his advisor about a month after I turned eighteen, Nola his delegate. Hiran still was not the boy we knew long ago, which I didn't expect him to be, but he had lightened up just a bit. Just enough for me to agree to work for him.

I don't know how much advice I actually gave him. Usually he asked for my opinion, pretended like he was going to agree, and then did something else instead. I knew it was all part of whatever wicked game he was playing. There's no way I could ever trust him, but I saw the position as a way for me to keep an eye on things in the city, to make sure Hiran doesn't destroy it entirely. Though I think what Nola does is far more important—and interesting. She has more sway when it comes to controlling the city.

But the generosity that Hiran showed me now, with coming to get me before he went to meet Nola, it was very confusing. I'm certain it wasn't him attempting an act of kindness, I just need to figure out what.

22

Hiran's hand settled on my lower back, keeping me close to him as we continued to walk. I did my best to ignore it, to fight the urge to pull my weapon free and stick it against his neck. I turned my head faintly to peer at him, to get a read of his face, but all I saw was coldness, boredom. When he saw me looking, he shot me a faint smile, to which I returned a frown.

"Don't be so glum," he told me. "You should be happy, your friend has returned, and on a holiday. I would say that's a sign from Drazen himself, but I know you aren't the religious sort."

"And you are?" I shot back. "Hiran, don't act like it's not true that you haven't visited the temple since we were children."

"I have bigger problems to worry about than making sacrifices to a god that has never once given me help in my entire miserable existence. Forgive me for speaking ill on this day, but I think we can at least agree on that, Kara. Don't you think?" I knew he was looking at me, but I refused to meet his eyes.

"Yes," I said as I continued to walk. We could agree on that.

We made it to the base of the stairs, Hiran taking my hand to help me up before I had a chance to refuse. I debated yanking my hand away, but that wouldn't really look good to the people that were gathered nearby. We made it to the top, the sun now hot enough to scorch, not a bit of shade anywhere to be seen. I ran my palm across my brow, removing any trace of sweat.

I absolutely hated being atop this wall, especially because a few feet away was the banishment platform. While it's been years since I've seen it in use, I could never forget the times before. A banishment was a punishment sentenced by the Lord of Mortefine, dropping them thirty feet down from atop the wall, into The Wry, leaving them utterly alone and defenseless. It was a terrible punishment, one that Hiran, thankfully, had done away with since he became lord. It doesn't matter the manner of crime committed; a banishment was the same for them all. No food or water, no weapons, and utterly alone. Some would die just from the fall to the ground, while most made it far enough away from the city that we didn't have to see their body when they perished.

Those who were banished were sent on an impossible quest in which their crimes could be erased if they completed a task ordered by the lord. It could entail bringing back the fang of a sand serpent, or a diamond as big as a grapefruit. It was always impossible to complete—a trick—a clean but not merciless way to end somebody's life.

Hiran had never banished anyone, for his own reasons. But I suspect it is because he thinks it lets criminals off too easily, that they should suffer more before the end.

I averted my eyes as we walked past the banishment platform, roped off and unused for so many years. Hiran didn't seem to want to look at it either, slowing down and turning to me only when we were long past it. Further down the wall, I could see a small group of people gathered. I couldn't make out their faces, but I could see a long braid of auburn hair, tan skin, a woman with her sword still in hand.

My feet moved without thinking. I almost ran straight for her, until Hiran lashed out, grabbing onto my wrist, and stopping me in my tracks. "Calm yourself," he said to me, and then I took a breath and matched his leisurely pace.

As we got closer, Nola finally recognized me, her eyes widening and a grin spreading across her face. "About damn time you got here, sister," she said to me, and then to Hiran, "My lord." She bowed at the waist, the other men with her joining in. When we stood only a few feet away, I could see the blood and dirt covering every one of them, and the blood still clinging to Nola's sword.

"Are you okay?" I asked, unable to find any other words.

She nodded. "Yeah, I'm fine. I can't say the same for everyone else that was with us." She was attempting a joke, to make light of the terrible situation, but there was a tiredness to her voice that she couldn't hide. She must have been exhausted.

There were four other men resting behind her, what I assumed to be the remaining guards that she traveled with. I scanned their faces, recognizing none of them. They all looked just exhausted, just as beat up as Nola.

"This is all who made it back?" Hiran asked. He didn't wait for an answer as he said, "Remind me, how many did you leave with?"

"There were twenty of us," one of the men said. A trail of dried blood covered him, starting on his neck, and traveling all the way to his feet. Sure enough, just beneath his ear was some sort of puncture wound, just starting to scab over.

"My god," I whispered. "I can't believe it."

"Son of a bitch sand serpent," Nola spat angrily. "The bastard *hunted* us like livestock. First, it came for the horses, leaving us with no way to get away, and then it came for us. For three days it kept coming back, picking us off one by one. We barely made it out..." She trailed off, her dark eyes glistening in the sunlight.

"How did you escape?" I asked, and Nola whipped her head to me. There was a look of terror on her face as she likely recalled the events. She said nothing. "What happened to the sand serpent?"

"She killed it," one of the guards said, pointing to Nola. "Stabbed it through the head, with that tiny sword. Can you believe that? The tiny woman, that *we* were supposed to be protecting, ended up saving our asses. The beast was distracted tearing someone in half. She ran straight up to it, fearlessly, and brought her sword down upon it, with the might of a god."

"You killed it?" Hiran asked Nola, in utter disbelief. He was unconvinced, until he looked at the sword still in her hands, the dried blood gleaming from it.

"She did," another guard confirmed when Nola didn't answer.

That seemed... impossible. Sand serpents could be killed, maybe, with enough bolts pelted into it from a distance, but it was unheard of for one to be killed in such close proximity, one-on-one, with a sword, and only a moderately strong female wielding it. Perhaps I underestimated my friend's abilities.

I turned to Nola again, her eyes locking with mine. "I wish I could have been there to see that," I admitted, the two of us smiling at one another faintly.

Her smile remained as she said, "No, you don't."

Hiran interrupted. "I'm relieved to see that you made it back in one piece, if only because it means I don't need to hire another delegate."

She frowned at him, puckering her bottom lip out. "Is that your way of saying you missed me, Hiran? I didn't think you were one for sentimentality. But if it's any consolation, I missed you too." She grabbed him by the shoulder, then placed a kiss on the tip of his nose. He looked disgusted but made no move to reprimand her. I didn't expect her to do anything like that with me, especially not with Hiran right there. She would wait until later when we were alone in the privacy of our townhouse.

"We should head back to the estate," Hiran said to me and Nola. And then to the guards, "Well, since Miss Westchase has done your jobs for you, you are dismissed from your positions as guards of my city. You're lucky I'm letting you live at all after the dishonor you've done me."

The four guards looked stunned, utterly in shock. None of them dared to retort. Nola, still at Hiran's side, said, "Do not undermine their abilities, Hiran. We saved each other out there, not the other way around. If you want to dismiss them, well, I know there's nothing I can do about that, but at least do it honorably. I would not be here right now if it weren't for them."

Hiran's eyes turned to her, assessing. "I'll reconsider my decision after you give me your report, Miss Westchase." Then he dismissed the guards, sending them on their way. I knew he didn't plan to reconsider anything. I offered them a thanks, if only to unnerve him, for getting Nola back in one piece.

Nola locked her arm through mine, turning away from Hiran and then dragging me down the walkway, back towards the stairs. She greeted other guards as we passed, men who were happy to see her back as well. While Nola was a fierce warrior, she had a kind heart. Everyone adored her. Even after we descended the stairs, walking along the now crowded city streets, she greeted the citizens with smiles and hugs, though some of them turned away when they saw her disheveled appearance.

"Why is the city so bustling today?" she asked.

I gave her a wide smile, showing my teeth. "Well, today is Rebirth Day. You made it back in time for the holiday."

Her mouth quirked to the side, and she held on to me tighter, both of us aware of Hiran walking behind us. "I hate to say it, but I really missed this city. I missed you, Kara."

There was so much I wanted to say to her. So much I wanted to ask her. But that could wait for later. We would have all the time in the world after tonight. So for now, we headed towards the Rendal estate, and I never thought I could feel so relieved. I never thought I could be this happy.

Chapter 3

As we walked up the long dirt drive, to the large doors of the estate, Nola looked around like she was seeing it for the first time. She ran her hands along the flat-trimmed bushes, bending down to pluck a flower from one, bringing it up to her nose and inhaling. I suppose it's a gentle reminder for her, after spending so long out in The Wry, of how beautiful the earth can be.

The guards standing post opened the doors for us as we approached, Hiran still directly behind us. We walked in, and I saw that the place was completely different. There were servants decorating for the ball tonight, clearing out the great hall just to the right of the entryway. The usually dark interior had lightened up a bit. Colorful flowers sat in vases along every wall, ribbons hung from the ceilings, the chandelier was being cleaned of dust, fresh candles were placed for tonight. As we passed the kitchens, wine glasses were being set out, food prepared. I'd never seen so many people in the estate all at once, but something about it I found oddly comforting.

"This place cleans up well," Nola said, turning back to glance at Hiran. "If I didn't know any better, I would have thought you did all this for me." She shot him a wink, turning back ahead towards the stairs.

"You won't be expected to attend tonight," Hiran told her. "Unless you want to."

Nola gasped. "I would *never* miss it."

I leaned in towards her, whispering. "Don't worry. We can just drink all of his wine and go and sit in the corner to entertain ourselves." We both broke into laughter then,

28

turning to look at Hiran's face and then laughing even harder from how annoyed he seemed.

We walked up the stairs, stepping as far to the side as we could get because of the servants that were hauling down a velvet couch from one of the upstairs rooms. When we made it to the second floor, Hiran brushed past us, walking towards his study, pulling a set of keys from his pocket. We walked for a minute until we reached the door, then Hiran unlocked it, and allowed us in.

"Expecting intruders?" Nola asked him, likely commenting on the fact that she had never seen him lock the door to his study before. "Or just paranoid?"

"I'm a private person," Hiran said. "And you can never take too many precautions." Once we were in the room, he shut the door again, turning the lock to keep anyone else from interrupting. "Sit," he told us, his eyes flashing to the couch. He moved for his desk, pulled out the chair, and then sat down facing across from us.

I plopped down on the couch, allowing myself to relax, knowing that my presence was only required here so I could listen to what Nola had to say. Nola remained standing, like she didn't want to dirty the couch with her tainted clothes, though she set her sword down on the table.

Hiran crossed his hands atop his desk, scooting some documents aside. "What news do you bring us, Miss Westchase?"

She was silent for a moment, like she didn't know how to start, which was strange because she just needed to repeat to him what the king said to her. Finally, she raised a brow, smiling. "They were pretty pissed that you sent me—again," she started. "They want to speak to you personally about setting up a trade agreement with Orothoz, preferably within the next year."

Hiran's nostrils flared. "What do they think we have to trade? Buckets of sand?" He paused, like he was waiting for Nola to answer. "Besides, it's impossible to get to Orothoz.

We'd be losing more men and money than it would be worth."

I recalled the city, Orothoz. It was south of the capital, on the other side of the Sandsaal Mountains. You could technically travel south to get there, to the coast, and then sail to the Southern Bay, but it was too much of a risk to travel through The Wry for so long, and then to sail even longer. It did seem weird that the king would want Mortefine to trade with Orothoz, but I must admit I know very little about such things.

Orothoz, like Mortefine, was one of the five ancient cities of Vatragon. Yet they were the only one not ruled by a lord or lady, or the king himself. They used to be, years ago, but the family in power were all murdered in the middle of the night. I couldn't really recall the story, after never having heard it all myself. I overheard a guard once talking about it, but if I asked about it during my lessons as a child, they would never give me a straight answer, like everything surrounding the incident was a mystery. So now, Orothoz was a free city, and likely did not need to rely on a trade agreement with a distant city to keep them afloat.

"It's not *impossible* to get there," Nola explained to Hiran. "We could go south, to the coast, then sail around the Sandsaal Mountains—"

"And are they going to supply me with men once all of my guards have been killed?" Hiran cut in. He scoffed a laugh. "Do they even know how much danger this would put us in? Do they know how vulnerable we already are, with as little traveling we currently do through The Wry? Maybe I should inform him of what happened to your envoy as you made your way back from the capital, see if he still wants it to happen then."

Nola leaned against the far wall, peering out of the window, arms crossed over her chest. "It's what they've requested of you. I'm only the messenger." Her tone could not have been more carefree. "He wants you to send a letter detailing exactly when he should expect you in the capital.

And for all of our sakes, let me say that I will *not* be joining you on that trip."

"It's not going to happen," Hiran said. Nola just waited. "If there's no other news, then I must ask you to give me and Kara some privacy." His eyes were on me as he spoke to her. "I hope to see you at the ball tonight, Nola."

"You can count on it," she said, more quietly, as she retrieved her weapon and then walked to the door. I noticed for the first time that there was a slight limp in her left leg as she walked. She flipped the lock and then strode out, not looking back at all.

When it was just the two of us, I turned to Hiran, scowling. "Why would you refuse to go to the capital?" I asked him, but he ignored me. "Are you afraid... because that's how your father died? I know it's dangerous, obviously we know that, but you can't defy what the king has ordered of you. I'd be happy to come with you," I offered.

"No," he answered, too quickly. "No. I wouldn't ask you to come, even if I was going myself."

"Hiran," I said softly, grabbing his attention. "Are you afraid? You can tell me if you are."

His gaze held on me, but he remained silent. For a second, his mouth parted, as if he would say something, but then it closed again, and he averted his eyes away, towards the window where we could see Nola leaving the estate grounds and reentering the city.

"Can you just take this one piece of advice from me?" I asked him. "As your advisor."

"No," he shot back. It was a violent, angry, and assertive no, that told me to keep my mouth shut. I had enough of whatever game he was playing. I stood from the couch, moving to walk for the door, but Hiran halted me. "Sit down." But this, it sounded less like a demand and more like a request, so I obliged, if only to keep his temper from flaring any more than it already had today. "Have you discovered anything else about the lost blade of Sazarr?"

I cringed a little, clenching my fists at my sides as I walked towards his desk and leaned against it. "Here I was, thinking I had the day off, and then you had to bring up that god damned artifact."

Recently, as his advisor, Hiran had tasked me with helping him search for it. It supposedly belonged to Sazarr, The God of the Otherealm. The serpent god. There was little information about it anywhere, and I wasn't sure that it even still existed. But Hiran wanted to find it, for some reason. He thought perhaps it could ward off sand serpents from the city, keeping us safe from them, but I suspect it was something more than that.

I gave him a shake of my head. "I've been reading, but everything seems like a dead end. It's been forgotten for hundreds of years." And that was a damn lie if I ever told one. I had read something, in one of the books I found in the archives, which I had been keeping hidden from Hiran at the townhouse. The blade was last seen in Kraxoth, nearly five hundred years ago, in the hands of the leader of some failed rebellion. It was said that the blade disappeared when he was killed, but if I were to bet, I'd say Kraxoth was a good enough place to start searching for it. Which meant I could never tell Hiran about it.

"We need to keep looking," Hiran said to me. "Things are getting worse out there, as we've seen with Nola's recent journey through The Wry. It's the only way to ensure our safety."

"I know," I said.

But he didn't seem to think I was convinced. "Kara, I'm doing this to keep the people of this city safe. Isn't that what you want? I know you didn't agree to become my advisor because you enjoyed my company, it's because you care about these people, as insufferable as they are." He sounded genuine enough, but I still didn't trust his motives.

"And you care about them as well? You, who would sooner let the peasants die of thirst before you freely give them a drop of your precious water?" If I thought there was

32

any way to find the blade, and use it to keep the sand serpents away, then I would more than happily agree. It would make traveling to and from the city much easier. But the blade was only a myth, and the myth of its abilities seemed even more unrealistic.

"Do not make me out to be a monster, Kara. Find the blade." I knew this was him dismissing me without him having to say anything else. Though he was only a few years older than me, he always spoke like I was a child, like I was so naive of things.

"I've been looking," I told him. "I'll keep looking."

He dipped his head at me, not saying anything else other than, "I'll see you at the ball later." And then I exited his study. I shut the door on my way out, then leaned against the wall directly outside, running my hands over my face, taking deep breaths to calm myself. A servant girl walked by, pulling me out of my stupor, sending me walking toward the stairs. I descended, ignoring all the people setting up for the ball tonight. I held my breath the entire time, until I was outside again and back on the streets of the city. There was a carriage parked nearby, which I recognized as Hiran's. I found the driver waiting, no doubt to take Hiran somewhere, and I ordered him to take me home, feeling too faint to walk the entire way. I slipped him a coin or two for his troubles.

I peered out the window at the afternoon sun, listening to the horse hooves clank as they trotted towards my townhouse. I knew all this artifact nonsense would be bothering me for the rest of the day now, as my mind continued to linger on it even when I tried to push it away with thoughts of Nola's return. Hiran seemed so desperate to find it—too desperate. Even if it could guarantee our safety from the sand serpents, I did not want it to end up in Hiran's hands. It was the weapon of a *god*. The god of evil and darkness. Something like that should not end up in the hands of a mortal, especially one so likely to give in to violent impulses. Wherever it was, I knew it needed to stay hidden. At least until I could guarantee that it would only be used with good intentions.

When I walked back into the townhouse, after having dismissed the driver and thanked him for taking a little detour to drop me off, Nola was in the bath, the familiar scent of her soap greeting me. Cherries and cinnamon. I could hear the splash of water from what I could only guess was her wringing out a washcloth. After all of that mess with Hiran, it was a relief to know that she was here. That she was safe.

I went upstairs, looking into the open door of Nola's room, unable to believe that just this morning I was in there, wondering if I would ever see her again. The curtains were open, the dry desert breeze blowing in. The dust had also somehow been removed from everything, in such short a time. It almost looked like she had never been gone, except for the dead plant. I saw her open closet, some dresses pulled out like she was deciding on what to wear tonight. I supposed I could just let her borrow something of mine, so she could at least wear something she never had before.

I went into my room, hung up my own dress, and then picked out a few that I thought Nola would like. I set them on her bed, and when I heard the water from the bath start to drain, I went back downstairs and into the kitchen, looking around for something that we could eat. I hadn't planned on cooking, but, well, Nola was back now. I couldn't very well make her cook herself something.

I took out a pan, spreading what little oil I had left in it. I lit a match and then turned on the stove, the already warm room becoming much hotter in an instant. I cracked a few eggs into the pan, listening to them sizzle as they started to cook. When they were done, I separated them onto plates for us, adding pieces of bread as well. I poured two glasses of water, and then set everything on the table, cringing as I remembered Hiran with his feet propped up there earlier.

As if on cue, Nola walked downstairs, a robe slung over her body, her hair wrapped in a towel. "That smells delicious," she said to me. She walked up to the table, pulled

34

back a chair and then sat down. She brought her arm up to her nose, smelling. "I missed my good soap. Well, I missed any soap at all, really."

"You do smell divine," I told her, picking up my fork to start eating.

"Why, thank you." She shot me a smile, picking up her fork to eat as well. "I would have told you not to bother with all of this trouble," she said, gesturing to the food, "but I'll just assume that this was for the holiday as well."

I shrugged, and then dug into my food. "Did you see the dresses I left out?" She nodded. "I know I've worn them all before, but I think the maroon one would look divine."

"Yes, I think I'll wear that one," she told me, smiling, though I could still see the sadness in her eyes. She was trying to hide it, but she was never very good at hiding things.

"You don't have to pretend like everything is okay," I told her. "What you went through... it was horrible. We can stay home tonight, get drunk by ourselves, relax. I'll tell Hiran to kiss our asses."

"It's okay," Nola told me. "I think it would be good for me to go out. It will remind me that I'm not still—out there."

"Does it haunt you that much?" I asked, though she didn't answer. I reached for her hand, the one she was not using to eat, grabbing onto it softly. "I missed you," I told her. "So, so much."

"I missed you too," she said, still not looking at me. "I thought I was going to die out there. I thought you would be stuck here with Hiran forever."

"Am I not already?" I asked, trying to force some amusement.

Nola huffed a laugh. "Not in a way that I think you understand."

I was about to ask what she meant, but she finished eating, stood from the table, and then walked back upstairs. I wouldn't push her, not yet. I knew she needed rest, which I would give her, until she was ready to talk. There seemed to be something odd about her most recent trip, something that she didn't want Hiran to know. Or maybe even me.

A few hours later, I was curled up on the couch with a book, though not one I really wanted to be reading. It was one of the history books I borrowed from the archives, specifically on the history of Kraxoth. I hoped to find clues in it on the blade, but my hope was misled, because there was absolutely nothing helpful in it.

I heard footsteps upstairs, which meant Nola had awoken from the nap she was taking, and they neared, eventually coming down the stairs to join me. I looked away from the book, finding her rather disheveled.

"Kara," she said, her voice soft. "There's something very important that I need to tell you."

"Okay," I said, closing my book and sitting up straighter.

She just stood there, her hands gripping the railing of the stairs. She said nothing, and I couldn't tell if she was hesitating or if she just couldn't find the words for whatever it was she needed to say.

I was suddenly aware of how quiet it was, hearing only the faint ticking of the clock. I looked over at it, gasping out loud because that could not have possibly been the time. The ball was only an hour away, and I had not yet started getting ready. "Shit," I said, standing up from the couch. "We're gonna be late." And then I was running up the stairs, pushing past Nola.

"Kara," she said, a warning.

"Can't you just tell me later? We don't have time for this now." I put my hands on her shoulders, turning her around so she was facing upstairs. "Go. You need to get ready, too."

"I suppose that's fine," she said, but my mind was already on other things. I ran up the stairs and into my room, shutting the door so I could start getting ready. I couldn't believe I let time slip away from me like that.

I sat down at my vanity, my reflection staring back at me. The girl I saw there, I almost didn't recognize her. She wasn't a girl at all anymore, but a woman. My cheekbones had gotten sharper, my jaw more angular. I'd always had a larger nose, but now it seemed to fit well with the rest of my face. I traced charcoal along my eyes, bringing out their vibrant green color, emerald, so dark that they almost looked black. I painted my lips dark red, almost identical to the color of blood. I let my golden hair fall in waves down my back, braiding two pieces and connecting them into what looked like a crown. Then I slid on my gown.

I knew the sight of me would be turning quite a few heads tonight. The dress that took so many months to make, and cost so much money, it was sheer silk—emerald green—just a little darker than my eyes. The top dipped into a low V-shape, revealing the outlines of my breasts. It flowed to the ground, exposing my legs with two large slits down each side. I strapped on a pair of golden sandals and decorated myself in an array of golden jewelry—including the golden amulet with my name carved onto the back. I left my sword strapped to my back, feeling safer with it, though I was sure I wouldn't need it.

Nola wore the maroon gown, opting for silver jewelry, and her lips were painted a color darker than the gown itself, almost black. She looked like a lady of darkness. She was taller than me, but the gown still fit her well, showing some of the black heeled shoes she wore. While her hair was longer than mine, she pinned it back so it fell only to one side, showing off one of her ears that held a giant diamond earring.

Both of our eyes widened at the sight of one another.

"Woah," she said.

"I know," I grinned. "We look good."

She grabbed onto my hand, interlacing our fingers. "Let's try not to get into *too* much trouble tonight."

Chapter 4

The sun had already started to set as we made our way outside. I could feel things in the shadows, scary things, but the presence of Nola at my side mostly took my mind off of it. I didn't dare to glance into the shadows, afraid that I would see something glancing back at me.

The carriage that Hiran sent for us was already waiting outside, the driver smoking from a pipe as he waited. We climbed in and then headed off, neighbors watching as the expensive transportation rolled by, wondering exactly who was inside. Too bad it was only us.

A few minutes later, and we were there, lifting our skirts as we exited to keep them from dragging through the dirt. There were dozens of other carriages lined up, women in every colored gown stepping out, plain-looking men trailing them.

We walked up the long drive, a familiar guard dipping his head in Nola's direction in greeting. "You look lovely this evening, Miss Westchase," he said to her. She offered a friendly smile in return. Not a word to me, though I hardly needed the validation.

The estate was always more beautiful at night than during the day. It was one of the few places in the city able to grow a grass lawn and maintain a large array of plants. There were lily pads in the fountain, vines growing up the shutters along the front of the house. It was quite a sight to see. I used to love wandering and exploring the gardens as a child, though I haven't gotten the pleasure to in years. Perhaps I would have to, sometime. Staked on the other side of the yard were tall trellises with white blooming flowers snaking their way up them. The metal gate surrounding the estate was so tall, with pointed tips, that nothing got past it that the lord did not want to.

We watched all of the other women that walked up to the house, wearing thick layered gowns, their hair done up like they were meeting the king and queen themselves. Some wore thinner, more revealing gowns, like me. The fading heat of the day still lingered in the air, making me grateful for the lightness of my dress.

We reached the doors to the estate, and though I had just walked through them only hours ago, it seemed so different now, like this was not that same place. I took one last look up at the sky, to the fading orange that would soon turn to darkness. It made me shiver. As if she could sense my unease, Nola slid her hand into mine, and we walked inside together.

The inside was a mass of dancing, laughing, and bustling excitement. People were smiling, engaging in conversation, enjoying themselves as they celebrated the holiday. It was a good sight to see, and I almost smiled, until I remembered that much of the city could not celebrate like this, not even for one day of the year. I wondered if it made us selfish, to do this, even when I tried my best to help those other people in any way I could.

The grand hall had been emptied out of all furniture, save for a few chairs on the outside of the room. There was a podium, where a handful of musicians were set up, playing soft, melodic tunes. Even the dining room, which was usually saved for formal events, had been transformed into a sprawl of multiple circular tables, with a buffet table on the opposite side of the room.

I couldn't help then but smile—seeing everyone enjoy themselves, knowing that Nola was here with me. I wasn't always the happiest person, especially while Nola was gone for six months, but perhaps this meant change was coming. Perhaps tonight I could be happy as well.

A servant walked by, carrying a tray of glasses, to which Nola plucked two from, and handed one to me. It was red wine, sweet and fruity. I tilted my head back, drinking the entire thing in one swig. Nola smiled, and then did the same with hers, setting them back on the servant's tray and then retrieving two more.

We walked into the grand hall, staying mostly to the outside, before finally settling in the corner opposite the entrance. I sat down in a chair, and Nola perched on the edge. Neither of us were really the dancing type, so we silently agreed to just watch as song after song played, couples pairing and dancing to the graceful music. It always amazed me that people could memorize the motions, every step in rhythm to the music. But again, I could probably know them as well if I ever bothered to learn.

At some point, after consuming further glasses of wine, we drifted off into a peculiar conversation. See, we'd grown rather bored, so we were commenting on people's appearances.

"Look at her," I shouted, probably too loudly, pointing across the room to a woman who did her hair up in an unusual way. It reminded me of that rare, expensive breed of chicken, with the puffy feathers that stick out the top of their heads like a tall hat. The woman glanced my way, like she heard me, to which I slammed a hand over my mouth, while Nola roared with laughter.

"Look at that guy," Nola said this time, pointing towards the opposite side of the room. I squinted my eyes, trying to find them, but I couldn't. Because something else caught my eye instead, or should I say, someone.

Hiran was walking straight towards us, stumbling a little, his glass of wine spilling onto the floor, some of it splattering onto a woman's dress. He didn't seem to care or notice, not with his eyes set so intently fixed on us. I turned my head to Nola, to ask her what we should do, finding that she was no longer beside me. I scanned the room, looking everywhere for her, seeing if I could use her as an excuse to get away, but she was nowhere near me. In fact, she was already on the opposite side of the room, standing with a group of women like she was heavily engaged in conversation with them.

"Kara," Hiran's deep voice slurred from beside me, causing me to wince. I didn't turn his way, but sat as still as I could as I felt a cold hand brush the back of my arm, sending a shiver through me.

I finally looked at him, his eyes bloodshot, and dipped my head. "My lord," I said as way of greeting.

Hiran looked across the room, like he knew exactly where Nola was as well. "She got away quick, didn't she?" I couldn't make out the expression on his face. I didn't want to. "How rude."

I remained silent as I stood from the chair, across from Hiran, my arms crossed and a frown on my face. He was wearing all black, finely made clothes, the only color on him coming from the blue in his eyes. A few seconds passed, like he was waiting for me to say something, before he spoke again.

"That is a very beautiful dress," he told me, leaning in too close. "The wait was certainly worth it. And I see I've gotten my money's worth." The way he was smiling down at me made me rather uncomfortable. "I didn't expect something so... alluring. What a scandalous sight."

"Perhaps you should have me thrown out for scandalizing all of the husbands in attendance," I said flatly.

He laughed. "It was a compliment, Kara. A thank-you would have been appreciated."

"Thank you."

I went to move away from him after that, anywhere but this pathetic corner, but he tugged on my arm, stopping me in place. Across my back, Fangmar almost seemed to be vibrating, as if to remind me that it was there, aching to be used. I knew how unwise that would be, but it was pleasant to have the thought cross my mind.

"I want to talk to you," he said. The smell of wine seeped from his breath, hitting me in the face so strong that I had to close my eyes. "In private," he added after a moment. "Now." It wasn't a bad smell, just a dreadful reminder of how much wine I'd consumed tonight as well. Whatever he needed to *talk* to me about, it couldn't be good.

"Okay," I replied. I pulled myself out of his grip, stepping a good distance away. It really made me angry sometimes that such a waste of a man could have such a beautiful face. He was undeserving of it. Such a nice mouth. A mouth that had indeed been on my own before—on other parts of me. The drunken thoughts were indeed starting to take over. Sometimes I just wanted to break his nose or give him a big ugly scar, just to mess that face up. But that wasn't worth losing my life over. *He* wasn't.

We walked down the hall towards a sitting room, one that he had to unlock, though he didn't lock it back once we were inside. I remained standing, waiting for him to tell me whatever it was that was so important—that he needed to pull me from the party for.

"Why don't you sit," he said to me, gesturing to one of the many chairs spread about the room. The curtains were open, to where anyone in the yard outside could see into the room, though I couldn't see if anyone was watching. I stood tall and proud across from him, watching as he sank into a nearby chair, letting his legs hang over the edge. "That isn't very polite," he told me. "When your lord gives you an order, you should obey it."

I almost laughed at the absurdity of him. "What are you going to do, banish me if I refuse to sit down? Just tell me why you dragged me in here, Hiran, and then let me be on my way."

He gave a small, annoying chuckle in response. "Alright, you can stand." And I did just that. "The reason I wanted to talk to you is because... I want something from you."

For a second, I had no idea what he was saying. "I'm already your advisor. What more could you want?" But the moment those words left my mouth, a pit opened in my stomach. I realized that there was a lot more he could want from me, things that I'd been grateful he'd never asked for before now. Things I suspect he'd looked for elsewhere.

To my luck, he didn't answer that question. "A lot of people have been looking at you tonight," he said, his eyes tracing my body, lingering over my breasts.

My face heated. This was much, much worse. I crossed my arms over my chest, covering that hint of skin that could be seen through the fabric. I tried to keep my voice steady as I asked, "Would you forbid them to look at me?"

He flashed me a dangerous smile. "If you wanted me to. I would do *many* things, if you only asked." Why was he saying this to me? Why now, after so many years?

My heart began to race in my chest. "That's unnecessary," I told him.

"Don't be modest," he said, staring at me from where he was sprawled on the chair, like he was still waiting for me to take a seat. "I remember how you felt for me when we were younger. It was only a few short years ago. We could go on as if nothing had changed. Don't stand there and pretend like you don't still have those feelings."

But he was wrong. I didn't have those feelings, I hadn't for a while. I used to care for him, very deeply. I gave myself to him, in the most vulnerable way, and then he changed, and what we'd had was over. I would never put myself through something like that again.

Hiran stood from his chair and sauntered towards me, moving slowly, drunkenly. "I could protect you, if you would let me." He was still standing a few feet away, but it felt like he was sucking the air out of the room, suffocating me.

"I don't need protection, and especially not from you." I moved away from him, walking backward to keep my eye on him. I bumped into the wall behind me, but then he continued forward, not stopping until he was close enough to touch me. He raised a hand to my cheek, his fingers as cold as ice. I couldn't move. I couldn't do anything.

This was certainly the last situation I thought I would end up in tonight. I was very confused, not sure if I should just let whatever he was planning to play out, or run for the door and flee. The shared feelings between the two of us died a long time ago. He had never acted this way towards me since I started working for him. And he had to have an idea of how much I hated him, right?

"You must be very drunk," I whispered to him.

"I am," he laughed. "But I don't really care."

I didn't have the chance to move before his lips were on mine, kissing me the same way I remember he used to. I kept my mouth shut tight as he attempted to devour me, to seduce me with that charming tongue of his. His body was pressing me into the wall, keeping me from moving, his hands traveling over me like he remembered exactly what I liked. When I tried to pull away, he only pressed into me harder. When I tried to grab my sword, he interlaced his fingers with mine, pushing my arms above my head.

He pulled back, just for a moment, and looked into my eyes, studying me, reading me like a book. He looked just as confused as I felt, and I wondered then if he had planned this, or if he just couldn't resist himself after seeing me tonight. The thought of that sent a thrill of excitement through me, as dangerous as it was.

I didn't try to get away then. I think... I think I didn't want to. What I felt was not so much desire as it was curiosity. Did Hiran really feel this way for me again? Had he ever stopped after the first time? Because I never would have guessed it with the way he usually treated me, when we worked beside one another. But I was intrigued to find out what he was doing—where he would take this.

And I might have tilted my chin up, ever so slightly, an invitation for him to resume. He wasted no time before his mouth was back on mine, and I didn't resist this time, not at all as his tongue slid into my mouth, as I released soft noises against him.

The taste of wine on each of our tongues mixed together, from which we had both drank a lot of tonight. His kiss wasn't soft, but I didn't want it to be. It was demanding and possessive, as he took exactly what he wanted, and gave back exactly what he knew I needed. He slid his knee in between my legs, pressing into me, his hips moving in a way that one would have thought he was doing something else entirely.

We held the kiss for a while, pulling away for only a few seconds to gasp for air, and then pushing back together again. I was certainly falling under his spell, but it was very hard to care at the moment.

I hadn't even realized where his hands had drifted. One was gripping my backside so hard that his fingers were digging into it, where I knew there would be bruises the following morning. The other was inching its way under the front of my gown, running his hands over those breasts that were driving him crazy. That was more contact than I wanted from him, but I was desperate to see how far this would go.

I let his hands travel—let them explore. My own hands were tangled in his perfect hair, pulling on it. My legs had come up to wrap around his middle, which I hardly even realized had happened. It was some strange instinct, my body remembering the action he and I had done so many times before. But then one of his hands drifted lower, traveling up from the bottom of my gown. He ran his fingers over my thighs, and then even further inward, until I finally decided that it was enough.

I didn't tell him to stop. Instead, I reached behind me, attempting to pull Fangmar free, nearly having it released before Hiran pulled away, practically dropping me on the floor.

"Were you going to use that on me?" he asked, touching his lips as if he could still feel me there. I resisted the urge to touch my own. He didn't sound angry, but rather… enticed.

I knew I should have ended it there, but I said, "Would you like me to?" quirking my mouth to the side.

"That depends," he said, stepping back towards me, "on if you care to be restrained afterwards."

I laughed then, the most genuine laugh of the night. "Don't be ridiculous. You were getting a little too friendly, so I needed to change that."

He laughed then too, though his eyes were still on the sword in my hands. "I don't think anything about that was *friendly*."

I caved first, giving up whatever charade we were playing. "Why would you do that, Hiran?" I asked. I moved farther away from him, towards the door just in case.

He watched me move, and remained silent for a moment before he spoke. But when he did, his voice was kind. Sincere. "I had to, just one more time." His words hung in the air like a noose. I didn't say anything back. I just stood there, still in shock from what had just occurred. Hiran must have been extremely drunk, because he had never once even *hinted* at such feelings. And this... this was insane. "But at least now I know how you really feel about me."

"*What?*" I hissed. "How I feel about you? Believe me, one kiss does not mean I feel *anything* for you. You practically forced yourself on me." While I can admit that those words weren't entirely true, I can't admit to having any sort of feelings for him, other than hatred. He was an evil, controlling, manipulative man. Nobody could ever feel anything like that for him, not if they truly knew him. It was just a kiss, and one I could have shared with anyone, and have shared with others before.

"Don't lie to yourself, Kara," he said, his expression hardening into anger. "I gave you a chance to stop. You didn't. Now correct me if I'm wrong, but that seems to indicate that you wanted it."

I surprised myself by letting out another laugh, though I should have been scared of the way Hiran was talking to me. "I just wanted to know what you were up to. Haven't you ever faked it a little to get what you wanted? Obviously, you just want to use me in some way. Maybe you're trying to get me to like you. Maybe you're just lonely. If that's the case, then I'm sure one of those girls out there would gladly kiss you instead. I'm sure they'd come crawling straight into your bed if you only asked. If it's something else, well, then I suppose I don't really care either way."

"I remember now why I picked you as my head advisor," he said, his anger remaining though his words suggested otherwise. "That mind of yours, it truly is something else." Was he... trying to charm me? After everything we've just said. What was wrong with this man?

I couldn't help but wonder if I'd figured it out. If any of the things I suggested matched his reasoning for... kissing me. I just wanted to know what all of this meant. I wanted to peel away the top of his head and pick that brain apart, find out exactly what he was thinking. There had to be more to it than just any feelings he might have felt for me. It took me a few minutes, but I realized then how foolish it was for me to kiss him back. I let him think that I really wanted it—wanted him. Now I just needed to find some way to spin this to my advantage.

My mind swirled with an array of confusion. Hiran must have sensed this, because he moved for the door, straightening his clothes and fixing his disheveled hair. As he opened the door I heard the murmuring of people outside, and I stood there as the door closed and it grew silent again. I leaned back against the wall, letting my head hit it hard as I closed my eyes and contemplated what the hell I was doing.

Chapter 5

I never could have expected that my night would turn out this way. Never in a million years did I think *that* would happen. I doubted Hiran would just let me forget about it—no, he would find some way to spin it to his advantage. I could ask him to pretend like it never happened, but *I* know it happened, and I have to live with it. I don't know what he was thinking or planning, but I had no interest in finding out tonight. I needed to get out of here—to grab Nola and head straight home.

As I remained standing in the empty sitting room, my legs felt weak beneath me, so I finally sat in one of the velvet-lined chairs next to the windows. I could vaguely make out people outside, a continuation of the party that was happening indoors. I wondered if any of them had seen what happened, or if they would even care. I just needed a minute to think, to try and find some explanation, and then I would go and find Nola.

But as I sat there, not really thinking about anything at all, I heard footsteps nearing from the hall outside. My heart sped; my palms began to sweat. I thought Hiran was returning, maybe coming back for more. I should have left while I had the chance. But as the door opened, and a person walked in, it was not Hiran. It was just the person I wanted to see.

I sprung out of my chair. "Nola!" I said frantically. "Oh my god, am I relieved to see you." I walked across the room towards her, aware of the fact that something seemed wrong with her, but I didn't think that whatever she had to say could be more important than what I had to tell her. "You aren't going to believe what happened. Hiran asked me to come in here, then he—"

"Shut up," Nola hissed at me, getting right in my face and putting her hand in it. I jerked my head back, clamping my mouth closed. Was she… angry? "I don't really give a shit what happened. I mean… I *do*. There's just no time for that right now…" Her eyes were wide with exasperation. She looked scared and angry all at the same time. "I need to tell you something and it *cannot* wait any longer." She seemed so on the edge, her breaths uneven, small beads of sweat appearing on her forehead.

"What is it?" I asked, grabbing onto her hand and forcing us both to take a seat. "Are you okay?" Whatever she had to say, it seemed important, so I could wait to tell her about Hiran.

"I'm fine," she said quickly. "But this isn't about me."

"Who is it about?" I asked, suddenly terrified of what she would say.

Her bottom lip began to tremble, like she was afraid to say whatever it was. "I lied to Hiran—about what happened in Vatragon City." She sat still, studying me, waiting for me to show some sort of reaction. But I sat still as well, not speaking, not doing anything other than waiting for her to continue. "They don't want to set up a trade agreement," she told me slowly. "I made that up."

"What?" I asked her, unsure of what else to say.

"I lied," she said, "to Hiran. A crime that he could decide to kill me over if he learned the truth. But I only did it to protect you—from him. I only did it to keep him from learning the truth."

"What the hell are you talking about, Nola?" I wasn't bothering with sounding kind now. She just admitted to performing a criminal act, did she expect me not to react to it? "Did the king and queen want something else instead?"

"The… the king and queen have requested nothing of me," she explained. "They were disappointed that Hiran was not the one there, but they said they were satisfied with how he has been ruling." Well, if this had nothing to do with the king and queen, then what?

"Why would you lie?"

"I had to tell him something to distract him," she said. "So he wouldn't get suspicious about you."

"What about me?" I asked.

"What I'm about to tell you," Nola said. I waited, watching her carefully, extremely confused. "The king and queen didn't want anything, but the prince did. Prince Daenaron." *Prince Daenaron?* Why would Nola have business with him? And why did it need to be kept secret? And what did this have to do with me? "I found out who you are, Kara... who your family was."

Was?

"Your name isn't Kara," she continued. "It's *Karalia Havu.*" She gave me a second to think about that, like the name was supposed to mean something to me, but it didn't. I don't think I'd ever heard it before. "Karalia Havu was the daughter of the Lord and Lady of Orothoz, that was suspected to have died along with her parents thirteen years ago."

And then it all came back to me. *Havu.* That was the name of the family that used to rule Orothoz. I was their daughter? A... *lady?* That was impossible. My heart sank in my chest as I recalled that they had been murdered years ago. I was nobody's daughter. I was still an orphan.

"That's not me," I whispered to Nola. "If that were true... they're all dead. It means nothing."

Her eyes filled with sorrow. "Yes," she said. "Your parents are dead." She reached out a hand and rested it on my thigh. "But not your brother."

I quirked my head to her. "Brother?" I had a vague recollection of the Havu son, evading the attack that came to... me... and my... parents. What a strange thought. But if he lived, why was he not the Lord of Orothoz? They've been a free city since... since it happened. I couldn't start making assumptions about any of this, not yet. But if this were the truth, how had nobody realized it sooner? I had the name of a

50

supposedly murdered child that belonged to a ruling family. But maybe someone had realized it, and they've been keeping it a secret.

"Hiran knows," I whispered to Nola.

"I don't know," she admitted. "We suspect, but it's too dangerous to confront him about it."

"We?"

"Me, your brother, and Prince Daenaron," she explained.

"I'm an orphan," I said, more to myself than to Nola. I'd always considered myself one, but a part of me also secretly hoped that my parents were out there somewhere, alive, waiting for me to return. This just confirmed that they weren't.

"Kara, think about it," Nola said. "You came out of The Wry, a few weeks after the Havu's were murdered. You must have somehow escaped and crossed over the Sandsaal Mountains. The whole world has thought you to be dead this entire time, but you weren't. You were here. If that doesn't convince you, I have even more proof. From your brother."

"You spoke with him?" I asked.

She nodded, smiling softly. "He's how I realized it. The two of you look so alike. You have the same golden hair, the same eyes, though his are just a tad lighter than yours, but they're the same shape. And his sword, on the pommel there was a golden charm welded to it. the same exact design as your amulet." She poked a finger at where it hung across my chest. "I asked him what it was, and he explained to me that his mother had it made for him when he was a child, a matching one for his sister. His dead sister by the name of Karalia."

She gave me a moment to take all of that in. It still seemed impossible—hard to fathom. But it was also getting harder to deny the facts.

"At first I thought it was just a coincidence," she told me. "But then I told him about you. Your brother, Kadon." Her face began to lighten then. "He wanted to believe it. So badly. He asked me so many questions about you, and I was more than happy to tell him. I explained that you had no memories from before you came to Mortefine, that you didn't remember him. I told him how we grew up together at the estate, how we both work for the lord now."

"Is this real?" I said, finally allowing myself to smile. "Or am I dreaming?" There was almost desperation in my voice. "Are you sure?"

She laughed softly. "I am. We all are."

"So what does this mean?" I asked. "What do we do?"

"We get the hell out of this city, and never come back," she told me, her face more serious than I'd ever seen it before. "This is where Prince Daenaron comes in."

I considered it. Leaving. The thought seemed absurd. I'd never gone beyond the gate of the city, not since I initially came to Mortefine all those years ago. Could I go now? Could I leave behind this life, and go back to the one I unknowingly left behind?

"I know this is a lot," Nola said. "But we don't really have a lot of time for you to decide. Daen and your brother are good friends. He sent a group of soldiers here to help free you, and to escort us back to the capital. They traveled a couple of days behind us when we returned, so they should be here soon. The plan was for me to get you out of the city, quietly, but if that doesn't happen then the soldiers have orders to retrieve you. By any means necessary."

This was madness. A group of soldiers were coming to Mortefine? To break me out? To maybe kill a few people in the process?

"Did the king and queen order this?" I asked Nola. If they had, then perhaps this would be easier to fathom.

"No," Nola said. "They know nothing about this. Daen went behind their backs to dispatch the soldiers. And he doesn't plan to tell them until you are safely within the walls of their castle."

Well, that seemed a little excessive. Why couldn't the king and queen know? Why was I so important that I needed to be broken out of Mortefine? Couldn't I just leave willingly if I wanted to?

"This is treason," I whispered, not that I would ever turn Nola in, but just the whole idea of this was hard for me to fathom. "We would be criminals."

"I know," Nola said. "And if we got caught… it could be bad. The prince is the one who made the order, so maybe that gives us some sort of liberty over Hiran, but he could always decide to stop us."

"So I'm just supposed to trust these people that have come to *take* me away and leave with them to do what exactly?" How did I know that leaving would even be the best choice?

"You need to be anywhere but here," Nola told me. "It isn't right. You could have a better life in the capital, with your brother. I think Hiran knows the truth about you. He has to."

And maybe that meant that I couldn't leave willingly. Maybe that meant that I've been kept here, locked up, lied to for all these years. If I really am a lady, then shouldn't that mean I can leave without going behind Hiran's back? Or without the prince going behind his parents' backs?

The realization hit me like a punch to the chest.

"You're right," I said to Nola. "Hiran has to know. He knows who I am, his father probably did as well, and they kept it from me. Why would he let me leave if he's kept the truth about who I am hidden?"

Nola silently agreed, giving me a slow nod. That had to be it. That had to be why Hiran and his father before him have kept me so close all of these years. But what did it matter to them? What did *I* matter to them?

"I think Hiran suspects what's going to happen," Nola told me. "He said something strange to me earlier, so I couldn't wait any longer to tell you the truth. I fear he's going to do something to try and stop us."

But Nola didn't know that he had done something already. Did he think that kissing me would somehow make me want to stay? That it would make up for the truth he withheld from me my entire life?

"When do we leave?" I asked her, my voice strong, surer than I ever have been before about anything. I needed to be strong for whatever came next.

We formulated our plan, hoping to slip quietly from the party, pack our things at home, and then leave the city while everyone else still drank and celebrated the night, unaware of us entirely. I wanted nothing more than to leave the estate, and never return, but Nola ordered me to stay in the sitting room. She had me lock the door and remain silent as she made sure things were okay on her end. I wasn't to leave until she came back for me, and I hoped that wouldn't be too long. I didn't want to be alone right now, not with all the thoughts bubbling in my mind.

I sat there for nearly half of an hour, listening to the faint sounds of the revelers celebrating beyond, enjoying themselves while I contemplated the treason I was about to commit. I still wasn't calm. I sat up straight in the chair, bobbing my head slightly from side to side, trying my best not to start crying. This night just seemed to get worse and worse. First, what Hiran had done, which I still didn't understand. And then what Nola revealed to me. I didn't want to cry because I was sad, but rather because I was so overwhelmed.

There had to be some connection between Hiran's strange behavior and Nola plotting my escape. Surely I would get some answers eventually, I just hoped I wouldn't have to wait until we made it to the capital. I knew my brother was eager to meet me. He thought I was dead all this time, and now, here I am, waiting for him. And Prince Daenaron. I don't know why he was so eager to aid my escape, and I knew there had to be more to it, but again, the answers I sought would have to wait. Right now, I just needed to get out of Mortefine. Away from this gods damned party.

I never expected *myself* to be someone so… important. Maybe I should feel excited about that, but I don't. I can't. My parents are dead. Gone, as in, I will never be able to meet them. I have been locked up in this city like a prisoner, and now I might have the chance at freedom that I didn't even know I needed. Then I'm expected to go and do what? Become a lady? My life has never been perfect in Mortefine, but I was content living with Nola in our little townhouse. But now I have no idea what lies ahead, which is utterly terrifying.

How did I end up at the estate tonight in the first place? This stupid holiday, to celebrate our god Drazen. This day feels more like an excuse for people to misbehave and get away with it. Certainly, Hiran thinks so.

We celebrate our god on this day, but I don't think he watches over us at all. They say that long ago, he flew to the sun, where he now lives and keeps an eye on us from above. But the story, his legend, started long before that.

The legend claims that two mortal friends, Drazen and Sazarr, traveled the continent together. They came upon the keep of a powerful sorceress. She thrummed with powerful magic, and Sazarr betrayed his friend by trying to kill the sorceress and seize her power for himself. Drazen stopped him, saving the sorceress' life, so she gifted him with the power of immortality, and the ability to transform into a dragon. As punishment, she banished Sazarr to the Otherealm and cursed him to live forever in the form of a serpent.

And today marks the anniversary of the day Drazen was reborn as a dragon. Not literally, I don't think. Maybe he could just turn into the dragon at will, but he still looked like a man every other time. Everyone tells their own version of the story, with nobody really knowing the truth.

The legend of our god is so distant that some don't even worship him anymore. But anyone with an ounce of respect for the monarchy does. The Drazos family is said to be descended from Drazen himself. I don't think that claim could be proven. I mean, if Drazen was around at some point, then I'm sure he could have furthered his family line. But that was thousands of years ago. The Drazos family is said to have inherited some of his power. The power of fire. Every couple of generations, a lucky member of the family is born with the ability, and they are called *dragon blooded.*

Sazarr, too, is said to have descendants. The *serpent blooded.* However, the history books would claim that they died out years ago. It's another one of the many myths of our gods. I always wondered if the sand serpents were Sazarr's descendants, as those creatures surely could have come from the Otherealm.

I was starting to scare myself with all these thoughts of the gods, and whether they existed or not. More time had passed, and I sat there, wondering when Nola would return. I was so preoccupied within my own mind that I hadn't even noticed the shift in atmosphere outside of the room. The ball had gotten very quiet. Silent. No more music, no more laughing and talking and dancing. I should have just stayed in the room. I should have waited for Nola. But I needed to know if something was happening, if something had gone wrong.

I carefully crept to the door, pressing my ear against it to see if there was anything I could be missing. I heard distant footsteps, like everyone had walked off somewhere. Slowly, I unlocked the door, twisting the handle and opening it just a crack. I couldn't see anybody, so I opened it wider, sticking my head out, finding that everyone had gathered in the grand hall. Hiran was standing on the podium, like he was trying to get their attention. If he was making an announcement, then it would seem rather suspicious if his head advisor wasn't there.

I slipped out, walking quickly to the room, attempting to catch up as if I hadn't been missing at all. Nobody saw or even noticed me as I pushed into the crowd, except for Nola who had walked up to me out of nowhere, a hand around my arm. She was tugging on me softly, like she didn't want me to be there.

"I have an announcement to make," Hiran said to the room. He sounded almost excited, in a morbid sort of way.

Everyone's attention was on him, remaining silent for their lord. At last, Hiran said, "A crime has been committed."

Gasps filled the room, some people with worried expressions on their faces, like they thought they were in danger. I turned my head back towards the exit, finding a dozen guards standing there, hands resting on the pommels of their swords as if ready to attack at any moment.

Nola squeezed onto my arm harder. "We need to get out of here," she whispered. "Right now."

I hesitated—my eyes wide. It was already too late.

When I turned back to Hiran, his eyes were locked directly onto us, shifting the crowd's attention to us as well. He remained watching us as he said, "Nola Westchase, my delegate to the capital, has betrayed me. I let her into my command, trusted her in Vatragon City on my behalf, and she abused that trust."

People were scowling at Nola now, at me as well. I pulled her hand from my arm, only so I could interlace our fingers, keeping her tightly connected to me. If she was going down, I would as well. "Everything will be okay," I whispered to her, aware of everyone's eyes and ears on us.

She shook her head, the motion barely perceptible, and then whispered back, "When they arrest me, you need to run, Kara. Do you understand that? You need to get out of here and go through with the plan."

I was about to disagree, about to argue with her, when Hiran continued. "She has lied to me about the details of her most recent trip to the capital. She has been conspiring to abduct someone very important to me, thinking that I wouldn't find out. But I know everything."

My heart might have stopped. He already knew everything we were planning. He knew all of the truth. And now he was going to arrest Nola before it could happen, and prevent me from leaving. Nola wanted me to get away, to run, and I probably could, but I would not leave her there.

Everyone at the ball stood there in shock and silence as the events transpired. People were staring at us. We had seconds to act.

"Arrest her," Hiran said, and right as the words left his mouth, guards were already at our backs, like they had been standing there waiting for him to say the words. "Restrain her," he said next, pointing to me.

Nola and I looked at one another one last time, as if to say goodbye, before chaos erupted. There were two guards on her, each holding her by an arm, pulling them behind her back and sliding shackles over her wrists. She kicked her legs out, doing everything she could to try and break free, but she was not strong enough, not compared to those guards. They dragged her by her elbows, ankles sliding on the ground, over to where the lord stood.

Foolishly, I tried to run for her, but Hiran already predicted that, which is why he ordered me to be restrained. There was another guard behind me, and his thick meaty hands wrapped in my hair, pulling my head back so hard that I thought my neck would snap. I cried out, at the same time he kicked me behind my legs, forcing me onto my knees. Everyone who had been standing around us cleared away, some fleeing the room entirely.

I looked at Nola, who was still being held up by the guards, standing proud in front of Hiran, with no hint of fear on her face at all. She tilted her head back a little, and then let out a strange sound from her mouth. While I was across the room, I could see the shiny glob of spit that she just landed on Hiran's face, and I could see his own disgust as he wiped it away.

"You're a coward," Nola said to him. "And a fool. And you will die for it someday, Lord Rendal."

"Get rid of her," Hiran said, casually waving a hand to the guards as if the matter was the least important thing he'd ever had to command. You wouldn't think that the three of us were once childhood friends.

I thought the guards would pick her up and escort her away, but they didn't. One of them shoved hard on her back, pushing her face onto the floor. Then the other leaned down, ripping open her dress, bearing her back for the entire room to see. The guard smiled as he brought his foot down onto her back, stomping down so hard that Nola cried out in pain. The other guard grabbed her by the hair, drawing her head back before slamming her face onto the floor. When he lifted her head again, all I could see was a mass of red, her nose likely broken.

"STOP!" I screamed across the room. Hiran angled his head to me, acknowledging that he heard, but did not make the order to stop. The guard at my own back wrapped his hand around my throat, hissing at me to keep my mouth shut.

I watched in horror as those guards beat Nola to a pulp, kicking her, punching her, dragging her around the floor, leaving behind a bloody mess. About half of the people that had first been in the room were now gone, most of them women who could not stomach the sight. It was terrible, what they were doing. And there was nothing I could do.

This was Hiran. This was the monster who I used to care for. Who I now worked for. I knew he was capable of something like this, but I never thought Nola would be on the receiving end of it. She was going to die if he didn't stop it soon.

"HIRAN!" I called across the room. He looked straight at me. "Please, stop this."

But the guards continued prodding at Nola's near naked body, as she lay there limp, so much blood on her you could hardly see any skin. I was going to be sick.

The guard restraining me whispered into my ear, "This is for your own good. Don't do anything foolish and he might just show you mercy if you behave."

That enraged me. I was so beyond foolishness at the moment. My friend needed my help, and I was just standing there doing nothing. But at that moment, I remembered exactly what was strapped to my back. The weapon I carried.

Fangmar. They were the fools for not taking it from me. I needed to use it, at the right moment.

Hiran snapped his fingers, the guards finally backing off. She stopped screaming, but was now letting out quiet sobs, lying on the floor, helpless and afraid. The guards picked her up by her arms, dragging her from the room, leaving a trail of blood behind as they did.

It was so, so quiet, that I could barely hear it. But I could read her lips clearly as she said to me those final words. *I'm sorry, Kara.* That was the only thing that got me moving, that kept me from falling to the floor and sobbing. I couldn't give myself even a second to think.

The guard was still standing behind me, keeping me restrained. He was taller than me, so I had to jump a little as I drew my head back in one hard thrust, right into his race. He cursed, loosening his grip on me just enough that I could get away. He reached for me again, pulling some of my hair out, but I was already too far. I didn't dare turn back to look at him, to see how close he was. Fury guided me through the crowd, and I think some people even moved aside to let me pass.

I sprinted to Hiran, oddly agile even in a dress and sandals. Just before I reached him, I swung my right arm behind my back, my hand finding the pommel of Fangmar as if it was magically drawn to it. It was warm in my hand as I slid it free, just as I reached Hiran.

His eyes widened in fear, and he staggered back a little at the sight of me. I gave him a vicious smile as I drew that sword back and brought it down on his face in one swift motion.

Blood splattered. People screamed. All I could do was lunge for Hiran again, using all of my energy to try to finish him off. He had collapsed on the ground, clutching his face, unable to see me as I again approached. But before I could attack again, something very hard jolted me in the head from behind, and then there was nothing but darkness as I was swept away.

Chapter 6

I knew I was dreaming, yet it still terrified me. Wherever I had gone, this was no normal place. Darkness found me in the void that I drifted off to, a cold, terrible darkness. I didn't think that I was dead, but I knew this wasn't life. A coldness swept over me, chilling me to my core. There was nothing. I was no one.

For a while, I stayed there like that, stuck between what was and wasn't, waiting for something to happen. And then I felt a tug, this invisible tether, drawing me through the darkness, towards what seemed like the end of everything. I floated away, not really in my own body at all, perhaps not even in my own mind. Hours and hours could have passed, I wouldn't have been able to tell.

A dash of light in the distance caught my attention, like a sprinkle of stars in the night sky. But it grew larger with time, as I moved closer to it. It simmered, almost singing to me, seducing me, luring me in. I tried to hold my hand out in front of me, to reach for it, for the warmth I knew it would bring. But I couldn't. My presence reached it at last, and instead of warmth I only felt a piercingly cold sensation, right at the back of my head.

But then I felt something else behind me—something even more strange. It felt like something was watching me. I couldn't explain it other than the chill that went through me as I thought about turning around. It felt like something was urging me to look, while something else urged me not to. The air grew heavy and stale as the silence of this place felt louder now than ever. I didn't know if I was breathing, I didn't know if that was possible here.

Very slowly, my presence turned around, fighting every instinct to not look, and to not run as far away as I could get. I found a giant pair of eyes watching me, and because of their size, I couldn't tell exactly how far or close they were, only that they were watching, unblinking. And if that wasn't strange enough, the eyes were bright green, as if I were looking into my own reflection. But they were no human eyes. They had thin slits down the middle, like some sort of uncaged beast.

The eyes continued to bore into me, terrifyingly, moving slightly from side to side as if whatever body they belonged to was hovering in open air. They would move back a little, the darkness hiding the sight of them from me, but then they would move forward again, too close for comfort. It made me want to scream. I just wanted to be back in my own mind, in my own body, and back on my own two feet. I didn't like this lack of control.

As if my thoughts had willed it, those eyes blinked once, and then they were gone, consumed by the darkness that was also starting to fade. I was still drifting somewhere beyond my own reality as I heard a voice call out. It was soft, feminine, and oddly comforting. *Run*, the voice told me. *You have to run*. I don't know what the voice was, but I was certain it didn't belong to the same beast with those green eyes.

I tried to ask why, to ask who they were, but I had no mouth to produce words, silently choking as I swallowed them back down. The voice continued calling out to me, whispering now, so far away that it sounded like nothing more than a tune being whistled. It grew quieter and quieter as I finally neared the surface of wherever I was headed.

And then brightness flooded my vision, so blinding that it was followed by a pounding in the back of my head. I was in a lot of pain, my entire body sore and strained. My senses began to steady me, the spinning in my head slowing down, as if I'd just traveled a very long distance. And even better, I could feel my body again. I could feel the toes at the ends of my feet as I wiggled them. I could reach up and feel my face, touch my mouth, use it to produce words. The throbbing at the back of my head continued, and I dared to open my eyes, overwhelmed by the reality now in front of me.

That's when I remembered everything.

I expected to find myself locked in a cell of the dungeon, rotting away while I begged for anyone to let me see Nola, but I wasn't. I was in a soft, warm bed, the sheets smelling freshly cleaned, the pillows full and comfortable beneath my neck. My head was propped up, some sort of cloth wrapped around it, which explained the headache. Someone must have knocked me out.

After what happened last night... I didn't even want to think about it. Hiran and me in that room. Nola coming in later and revealing the truth to me, about who I was. Agreeing to get out of the city. And then even later, finding Hiran addressing the people, accusing Nola of betraying him. Watching on, unable to do anything, as those guards nearly beat Nola to death. Running towards Hiran. Attacking him. Darkness. And now, here I was, locked up in a room of the estate.

The sun was up, and I had no idea how much time had passed. If it was only the next day, or if it had been much longer. I was certain that I was still at the estate, as I recognized the bedroom, and the view from beyond the window, but where was Nola? Where was Hiran? Did he survive my attack? He must have, because I don't think I'd be alive right now if I murdered the Lord of Mortefine in front of over one hundred people.

I didn't realize it last night, mostly because I didn't allow myself to, but it was incredibly foolish to attack Hiran. Nobody could do anything to help me if I was a murderer. Though I would still argue that he deserved it, he deserved far worse for what he had done to Nola. Knowing where my fate likely ended now, I hoped at least Nola would be okay. Before my last dying breaths, I would do anything to ensure that.

I was awake for only a few minutes before I heard a knock at the door. An older woman walked in, not bothering to wait for my reply, like she didn't expect me to be awake. I could tell she was a healer from the worn brown robes she wore, and the satchel of medical supplies she carried.

She paused when she saw me awake. "Ah," she said, clicking her tongue. "The assassin awakes at last."

"I'm not an assassin," I told her, my voice hoarse from the dryness in my throat.

"You're lucky," she said to me, setting her things down on a nearby table and pulling out a piece of equipment. "You could have had permanent brain injury from that blow you were given to the head." She brought a pair of scissors over to me, raising them to my head, cutting the cloth that was wrapped around it. I sat there as she snipped away, waiting until she was done to speak again.

"Where is Nola Westchase?" I asked her.

"Who?" she said, not meeting my eyes.

"The other girl that was injured last night," I told her.

"Last night?" She let out a cruel laugh, turning away and setting down the scissors. "It's been three days now since your injury. And there's no other girl here that I'm treating. Only you, the lord, and the guard whose nose you broke."

"Hiran is alive?" I asked her.

She turned back to me, a frown on her face, likely realizing that she wasn't supposed to tell me that. She pulled out a fresh piece of cloth, wrapped it around my head, and then moved to leave the room. "Get some rest," she told me. "You're going to need it."

I didn't rest. I wouldn't allow myself to sleep, not another minute, if I had been asleep for three days already while Nola was elsewhere, awaiting my help. But if it had been three days... the soldiers from the capital should have made it here by now. I needed to speak to someone. I needed to know.

But nobody came in, and I knew the door was locked without even having to check. We were also on the third floor of the estate, so it would be suicide to climb out of the window. I thought about every way in which this could play out. For one, they could kill me. Well, they were probably already planning to do that, but it was more important that I figured out how to help Nola before it came to that. Hiran wasn't dead, but he might have been bedridden, unable to talk to anyone, unable to give commands, which meant that his other advisors would be in charge of deciding what happened. Which meant they wouldn't listen to anything I had to say, and would likely just decide to kill me anyways.

But Nola, they were probably planning to kill her as well, after Hiran told his guards to *get rid of her*. They took it quite literally. But she needed to be my first priority. If I could help her get free, get out of the city, she could find the soldiers from the capital, and ask them for help. And then maybe after, they can break into the city and free me next.

Who am I kidding? Why would they want to help me after they find out that I tried to kill the Lord of Mortefine? They would probably just leave me here to rot instead. That would be okay, so long as Nola got out, I could take care of myself after.

Sometime later another knock sounded at the door, and a guard walked in. I didn't give him much attention until I heard the second set of footsteps entering just behind him. My head shot to the door, and walking in was a man with his face covered in bandages. I could hardly even recognize him.

Hiran was most definitely not dead. He was standing right there, right at the foot of the bed. He seemed in perfect health other than whatever was going on with his face, courtesy of yours truly. The bandages wrapped around his head were similar to the one around the back of my head, but his covered the entire left side of his face, and some of his right. The only visible part of him was his right eye and the cheek beneath. The only part of skin I left unmarred.

Maybe my exhaustion had made me loopy, but the sight of him forced a genuine laugh out of my mouth. I had to slap a hand over my face to stop. It was hilarious to me—how ridiculous he looked. But I was also laughing at myself for

66

being so stupid, for being too weak to finish him off when I had the chance.

"Stop," Hiran rasped, glaring at me with one eye. At least he sounded like he was in pain, if he didn't look it. He moved closer to the bed, sitting on the edge of it, so close to the person who had just recently attacked him.

"I thought you were dead," I told him, keeping my tone neutral. Let him think what he wants about my feelings on all of this.

"You're lucky I'm not," he said, lifting his feet and resting his legs on the bed beside me. I raised a hand and patted his shin, if only to see what the guard would do. And to my satisfaction, the guard moved closer to us, a hand on the hilt of his sword. Hiran raised a hand to stop him. "Wait outside," he told the guard. "I'll be fine."

I laughed again, shaking my head. "You're so stupid," I told Hiran.

"Call me what you want," he said. "None of it will matter soon."

"Where is Nola?" I demanded.

"Don't you want to see my face?" he asked. "Don't you want to see what monstrous work you've done on me? The healer says I'll be scarred for the rest of my life, unable to see anything out of my left eye."

Curiosity got the best of me. I sat up in bed, realizing for the first time that I was still in my gown from the ball. "Let's see it."

He reached his hands up to his face, unfastening the bandages from behind. "You know, it's funny that you would do this to me, considering that I was the one who taught you to use that sword. It was my own father that gifted it to you, was it not?"

"And yet you did nothing to defend yourself," I said coolly. "You just stood there like a scared child." He watched me with his uncovered eye, still fumbling with the wrap. "You weren't the one who taught me to use that sword. That boy died a long time ago."

67

He paused, his hands lowering into his lap. "Is that what you truly believe? No wonder you think I'm a monster. I tried to show you that I cared for you, Kara, and you cut my face open for it."

Kara. Did he know that wasn't my name? Not all of it, anyway.

"You had Nola nearly beaten to death," I said to him, scooting away from the pillows and closer to where he sat. To his credit, he didn't look the least bit deterred. "And nothing you have ever done for me was because you *cared* about me. You care about nobody but yourself. You've been keeping me locked up here all these years, but now I know the truth."

He watched me carefully. "Are you referring to the truth that we found you, orphaned and alone, and took you in to save your life?"

"The truth about my family," I said to him, remaining unbelievably calm. "That I am Lady Karalia Havu. You knew that, didn't you? And you still didn't tell me. After knowing how desperate I was to discover my identity. After knowing how much I hated myself for not remembering."

Though I couldn't see much of his face, I knew he was confused. "We kept the truth hidden to keep you safe. There was nothing left for you as a Havu other than a sad, miserable existence. My father knew who you were from the moment you arrived here, and he ordered me not to tell anyone."

I ran a hand over my face. "You are such an idiot that I'm surprised nobody tried to murder you sooner. Your father is dead. It's been years since, and you still kept that secret from me. What harm would it have done, for me to know? Where would I have gone? To the brother that I don't even know?"

"I was afraid you would leave," he said, so quietly that I barely even heard it.

"Maybe I would have," I told him. "Or maybe not. But the chances of me wanting to leave got a lot higher when I found out you'd been keeping me here like a prisoner."

"I know," he said, not meeting my eyes. "I'm sorry."

"Do you even understand how important this was to me? My whole life, this part of me has been missing." I had to stop to take a breath, feeling the tears building. "And now that… now that I finally got the chance to know, you had to take it away from me. You arrested the one person who was trying to help me. Did you think doing that would keep me here, because let me tell you that right now, it won't."

"You speak as if it's still in your will to leave," he snapped at me. "Do not mistake why I have come to speak with you. I don't care about the lies I told you long ago. You tried to kill me, and that cannot go unpunished. Do you understand that?"

"Show me your face," I said again, having forgotten that he'd stopped.

His hands went back up to his face, to the bandages, sliding them off gracefully up and over his head. I was a little afraid of what I would see, of knowing the devastation I was capable of causing someone. But when I finally looked, I saw everything, and it revolted me.

There was one large gash, starting from one corner of his forehead, and ending on the opposite side of his jaw. The deepest part was in the middle, on his eyebrow, his eye, and directly below it. And his eye… what used to be blue… it was foggy and clouded over, the slice through it still visible. It wasn't nearly as bad as I intended. He just stood there, letting me look at him, reading the disgust on my face.

"I'm sorry," I said to him, and I could tell that he thought it was genuine. "I'm sorry that it wasn't a killing blow."

He winced slightly from my words, pulling away from me like I was an asp readying my attack. He scooted off of the bed, leaving the bandages forgotten, and knocked on the door, two times, signaling for the guard to let him out.

The guard looked shocked to see Hiran's face uncovered, and wasn't very good at hiding his disgust either.

"I will live," Hiran said, as if to reassure me. "But you… I'm going to meet with my advisors, so we can decide what's to be done with you."

He stepped through the door, and before it closed I yelled, "What about Nola?" but I got no response, listening as the door closed, and as the lock clicked shut.

Chapter 7

The healer returned a few hours later to check on my head. I didn't sleep. I didn't eat, as they had given me no food. I just sat there, moping in my own failure.

There had to be something I could do to pass the time—while I waited to see if they would execute me or not. Something I could do to keep me from doing another foolish thing, like trying to break out of here.

I got up to search the room, which proved unsuccessful, as I couldn't even find a spare sewing needle to use as a weapon. I would probably never see Fangmar again, or any of the other weapons I kept at home. I would never even see my home again, for that matter.

Pushing those thoughts aside, I continued searching the room, a book on one of the shelves catching my attention. It was a dark blue color, leather-bound, one that I used to read all the time as a child, living at the estate. It was no book of grand adventures or heroic tales, but just a simple history book, of our country. It was titled, *The Five Ancient Cities of Vatragon.*

I mainly used to use it to look at the drawings, but now... perhaps I could find something useful in it, if I was to be traveling throughout the country soon. I flipped it open, dust shooting out straight into my face, likely having gone unread for many years.

I flipped to the section on Orothoz first, never having known before that it was my birthplace. It was the southernmost of the ancient cities, along the Southern Bay, the easiest port to access the other continents from. There was an illustration of the bay, the waters turquoise blue, the shores covered with white sand. North of Orothoz was the capital, Vatragon City, and north of that, over the Indrun River, was Frystal. I'd never heard much about Frystal, other than that it was extremely cold and very hard to get to because of its location up in a small set of mountains. Those mountains were much smaller than the Sandsaal Mountains, which blocked off The Wry from the rest of the continent. East of Frystal was Kraxoth, on the northern edge of the Alanah Sea. I didn't know much about Kraxoth, either, other than it being a large trade center with even larger crime rates. It was not a place I felt particularly eager to visit. And then south of Kraxoth, over the sea, was the vast expanse of The Wry. And located in the very center of The Wry, was Mortefine.

There are other smaller cities and towns throughout the continent, but the five ancient ones have specifically designated lords to rule the surrounding territories. Except for Orothoz, where my father once ruled as lord, who had yet to have another lord reinstated.

I never once considered that I could have been the murdered Havu child. How could I have known? I didn't even know her name, or what she looked like, or that there was a chance she might still have been alive. I've always assumed that my name was Kara, because of the amulet, but I never thought that it could have been short for something else. Thinking about it now, it seemed like I was foolish for not having realized it. If I'd only been allowed to travel anywhere outside of this city, then surely the truth would have found me eventually. But that wasn't my fault, it was Hiran's, and his father's before him.

I knew that Nola needed to be the priority, with whatever came next. Whatever they planned to do with me, that didn't matter so long as Nola was safe. She had already made acquaintances in the capital. She could seek refuge there. But me, I didn't see the same path for myself. And I was prepared to beg for her life if Hiran had something different to say about it.

My stomach began to grumble, just as the door to the room opened, and I realized it was from the smell of food wafting in from the hall. It smelled so good, and I had gone so long without eating. I was expecting the healer again, or another servant, but it was Hiran. His still unbandaged face gave me a fright as he walked into the room, a tray of food in his hands. Why bother giving me food if they're going to kill me anyway?

"So, it'll be poison then?" I asked Hiran, watching as he set the tray before me on the bed, and moved across the room to sit at the small table in the corner. "It was nice of you to deliver it yourself."

I might have seen something like… a smile cross Hiran's face. "It's not poisoned," he said, his mouth definitely quirking up to the side. "That's not the usual type of punishment I give people. You should know that."

"Well," I said, not moving for the food yet. "I'm not the usual sort of criminal in need of punishing. Forgive me for being cautious."

"Because you tried to kill me?" he countered. "Or because I actually have feelings for you? My advisors wouldn't be happy if they thought I was going easy on my assassin."

I tried very hard to keep my face neutral as I responded. "Because I was your advisor. How many others in your employment have tried to kill you? I'll assume that I'm the first." I knew he didn't care about me. Even now, he was still trying to mess with my head.

He ignored that, propping his feet up on the table in the same way I found him the other morning, in my own kitchen. "The others want you dead." He stared, as if searching for my reaction, but I did not give him one.

"I figured," I told him, letting out a sigh. "What did you decide?"

"You should eat first," he said.

I rolled my eyes. "I'll eat when I find out if I'm dying or not."

"You will not die," he told me, but it didn't give me the relief I hoped for. "Not now, and not by my hands. But you *will* be punished."

"When you say it like that, it sounds so naughty," I told him, flashing a smirk. Joking about this was the only thing I could do at the moment to not fall apart—to not fall onto my side, curl up in a ball, and weep.

"This is serious," Hiran said, his voice growing louder. He dropped his feet from the table at the same moment he slammed his fist down on it. "The only way for you to make it out of this with your life is if you *listen*. I'm not playing any more games with you."

"Do enlighten me, my lord."

Hiran took a heavy breath. "You're going to be banished."

My breath caught in my throat, so quickly, that I began to choke. The guard waiting in the hall walked in to make sure everything was alright, and found me red-faced, a hand wrapped around my throat. "I'm sorry," I said. "I think I misheard you. I'm going to be *banished*?"

"Yes," Hiran said. "I have agreed to spare your life."

When the coughing finally subsided, I began to laugh. "Is this some sort of trick?" I asked Hiran. "You say I will not die, and yet you sentence me to a banishment. I will most definitely die out there, without a doubt."

"I think it's fitting considering you intended to kill me." He waited for me to say something else, but there were so many thoughts in my mind, I couldn't think of what to voice to him. "You have a better chance out there than you would here, if I sentenced you to a hanging, or a life in the dungeons. Do not mistake this kindness I am showing you."

"*Kindness*?" I imagined steam rising off of my head from how angry I was. "Did you show Nola any kindness when you had your guards beat her, after she was already restrained and in your custody? I don't think you even know what kindness means, as you've never shown it to anyone in your entire miserable life. You want to banish me? Fine. But you'd better banish Nola as well. I'm not leaving her behind here to rot."

It seemed like the best idea at the moment. If we could both get banished, we'd be free of the city, able to find those soldiers who were already out there waiting for us. But still, even if he didn't agree to that, I could ask the soldiers to come back, to help get Nola out before we headed back to the capital.

"Why would you want her to suffer such a fate?" he asked me.

"Is it any worse than what you're planning to do with her here?"

He eyed me carefully for a moment. "We haven't decided on Miss Westchase's punishment yet, as the matter of your punishment was more pressing, but I can assure you that we did not plan on banishing her."

"All I hear are lies, Hiran," I hissed at him. "That's all you've done your entire life. It's all you know how to do. And even after I die out there," I pointed out the window, towards the desert beyond, "you will still be a sad, pathetic, lonely liar. You'll regret this, maybe not until years later, but a time will come when you can't even live with yourself anymore because of the decisions you have made."

To my surprise, Hiran stood from the table, pure hatred in his eyes as he stormed over to me. He bent down, pointing a finger right in my face as he said, "I already want to die, Kara. And nothing you say to me right now is going to change that. So don't waste your breath."

I didn't understand what he was saying, but I wasn't going to ask him to elaborate either. If he was some suicidal freak, then that was his own problem. I couldn't exactly say he didn't deserve that. I waited for him to speak again, not sure of how to respond to that grand declaration he just made.

"You are going to be banished," he told me, more calmly now, backing up towards the table again. "Tonight. Nola is *not* coming with you. She will remain here, in my custody, at least for the time being, until you successfully complete your task and return to the city."

I'd forgotten about the gods damned task. Whatever he was about to ask me to do, I knew it was just another trick. "And what is my task?" I asked him sarcastically.

"I am ordering you to retrieve the lost blade of Sazarr," he said, as if that would be the easiest thing in the world. "You have the advantage here," he explained. "You've already been searching for it, for months, which gives you a lead I don't really think you deserve. But I'm desperate to find it, for the sake of our people, not that I think you have ever cared about them. You will have six months to find it and bring it back to me. If you fail to do so, Miss Westchase will be executed on the first day of the seventh month."

"That's not fair," I said to him. "You can't use her as an ultimatum. You can't give me my punishment and then pile on another punishment on top of it. That's not how this works."

"You could always just leave, and forget about saving your friend. I'm sure you could establish a happy life somewhere else, since I know you're so miserable here."

I balled my fists beneath the blankets of the bed. "You're a bastard."

"And you're a bitch."

I sighed. He could call me whatever he wanted; it didn't matter. While I *had* found some leads in my search for the blade, it was still impossible to locate. If those leads played out, it would take far longer than six months to travel to get it *and* return here on time.

"It's not fair," I repeated.

"You don't get fair," Hiran said, yelling again. "You tried to *murder* me. You're lucky I'm not sending your body to your brother in pieces. That would be a real homecoming present for him. He'd never forget it, I bet. It'd be worse than when your parents died."

"Do not talk about my brother. Or my parents. You have no right to speak of them."

Hiran walked towards the door, pausing before he opened it. "You have one hour to compile yourself, eat and drink as much as you can, and then we are leaving for the gate. I want this over with. It's happening tonight."

"At least let me talk to Nola before I go," I managed.

"No." It was all he said before he stormed through the door and then slammed it shut.

I closed my eyes as if to will the tears away, but it was too late for that. Hiran thought he had tricked me. He thought he was getting away with this decision. But he was wrong. It didn't matter whether he really believed that I could find the blade or not, because I wouldn't have to, not when I can get those soldiers to help me free her. But she would have to stay locked up, for a short time.

The next hour drew by slower than the past three days that I've been stuffed into this room. I should have been preparing myself, both mentally and physically, but hadn't felt the desire to, considering that my life was already a disaster.

I started by eating the tray of food that Hiran left for me, which I didn't really care if it was poisoned at that point. He was decent enough to leave me a glass of wine, which I hoped would ease some of my nerves, but there wasn't nearly enough for that. There was a bowl of soup, blandly seasoned, packed with chicken and vegetables, and a broth that should keep me hydrated at least for a little while. There was also some bread, which I dipped into the broth, and a dish of preserved cherries for dessert. A decent last meal, if I must admit.

A servant entered at some point, supplying me with items for the journey, which I hadn't expected at all, but again, it was greatly appreciated. They supplied me with clothes, a long pair of pants, a leather tunic, and thick boots, all my size. Being out in The Wry with my gown from the ball still on would have been quite a predicament. I was even more surprised to find my sword holster, with Fangmar in it, which

I strapped over my back. I left the amulet around my neck, removing all of my other jewelry, and tucked it beneath my top. The servant also left a satchel, which I found contained a full canteen of water and some dried foods to take along. All of it would only last me a few days, enough to get me away from the city before I died, but Hiran didn't know that I would be meeting up with others, who could hopefully supply me with more food and water.

It was dark outside now, the sun long having slipped beneath the horizon, but being out in the sun tomorrow, it would be formidable. Hoping that I wouldn't get caught, I slipped one of the pillowcases off and shoved it into the bag, to use as a shield from the sun, to keep my skin from burning too badly.

I expected Hiran to come retrieve me personally, but he didn't. Instead, two guards walked into the room, informing me that it was time, and they slipped shackles over my wrists before I followed them out. Finally, they were starting to make some smart decisions. With my sword across my back, I could cut them down and make a run for it.

But that thought died just as quickly as it had started when I left the room, walking down the stairs, finding many more guards waiting in the entryway to the estate. Still, no Hiran. The decorations from the ball had all been removed, the place back to its usual bitterness. I peeked into the grand hall, if only in fear that I might see the blood that had been spilled that night, whether it was from Nola or Hiran. But there was none. Everything had been cleaned and put back in order.

We stepped outside; the air long having chilled to a comfortable temperature. The moon was full above, another mercy to me, as it would allow me to see better once I was out of the city. The streets were empty, families long having gone to sleep, unaware of what was about to transpire. It was better that way, I thought, that they wouldn't see it happen. Maybe then they could just forget about me—they could forget that I abandoned them. A faint murmur of laughter sounded from a nearby tavern, revelers still celebrating the night, but most windows were dark, lanterns out, asleep in their little homes.

That all changed when we made it to the south part of the city. People were out and about, whether they were heading home from work, heading home from their after-work activities, or just socializing in the streets. Most of them minded their own business, likely because their minds were not their own because of how much alcohol they had consumed. But some people did look our way as they noticed the guards, and as they noticed the seemingly young and frail girl in shackles. Little did they know, I almost murdered their lord just the other day. I would have been doing them a kindness.

"What's happening?" an older man murmured as we passed, not asking anyone specifically. We were nearly to the gate then, and people began to whisper, some of them following along, ignoring the pointed stares from the guards. "I think she's getting banished," someone else said, getting into step behind us.

As we finally approached the gate, a sizable crowd had gathered, parents pulling their children out of bed, everyone coming to see the show. I looked around, finding some people wisely watching from the open windows of their houses, while others stood on the edge of the street.

"Make way," a guard shouted to the crowd. "Your lord approaches."

That got them even more excited. Hiran never came to this part of the city, so most of them had likely rarely seen him if at all. His father had come often, to commence banishments, but not Hiran.

They cleared a path, and that's when I saw him, face wounds on display for all to see, a silver crown atop his unworthy head. He didn't smile, he didn't even look at them. So he wanted to make an entrance, is that it? He wanted to show them that he was someone to be feared.

A guard nudged me forward, towards the stairs that led atop the wall, the very same ones I had climbed a few days ago to greet Nola. How different my life has become since then. I started to walk, but then paused when I heard Hiran clear his throat.

"I know you all are likely wondering what this is about," he said. "And as my subjects, it is your right to know. This woman here," he pointed to me, "my advisor, Kara. Three days ago, at the ball I held on Rebirth Day, in my own home, she attempted to assassinate me. On our most sacred day." The crowd remained silent, more eyes turning towards me. Not with hatred or envy, but with pity. "As punishment, she is to be banished from the city. If she succeeds in retrieving the lost blade of Sazarr, she will be granted back into the city."

It didn't surprise me that he was withholding most of the truth. He wouldn't tell them about Nola, what he was doing with her while he sent me on this foolish mission.

When he finished speaking, the guard pushed on me again, urging me up the stairs. I walked, until I heard a woman in the crowd yell. "*Sazarr save her!*" she said. I turned back, finding that she had stepped out of the bundle of people, revealing herself, moving closer to Hiran. "Let the serpent god protect this woman from the clutches of evil men. Let him poison her enemies and rip apart those who would stand in her way."

She finished her prayer, Hiran standing there, completely stunned. And then shouting erupted. Not because of what the woman had said, but because of Hiran. People started running towards him, pushed back by the guards, but the woman remained, standing before him as she smiled, like she would curse him herself. I watched as Hiran reached behind himself, into the back of his pants, and as he pulled out a large sheathed knife. The woman did not try to fight him at all as he pulled the knife free and slid it across her throat, ear to ear, and then her body collapsed to the ground, blood spilling onto the dirt.

"NO!" I screamed, but it went unheard because of all the other commotion. Tears welled in my eyes as I saw the woman's body, limp, being dragged away by a guard. Hiran

80

wiped the knife off before returning it to the back of his pants. This—I was going to kill him for this.

"Let me remind you all," Hiran shouted, his voice beckoning through the crowd, terrifyingly authoritative. "That *I* am your lord. You will not speak out against me. You will not speak out against the royal family. And you will not speak out against our god. Not unless you want to end up like her." He pointed towards the corpse. "Let us get on with this banishment."

I felt such a sense of pride when the crowd did not cower in fear from him. But wisely, they backed down, some of them looking afraid, others angry. They watched as Hiran turned to me, and I didn't need a push from the guard this time to keep walking up the stairs. I didn't stop until I was at the top, until I saw the banishment platform. Hiran walked to my side, and from down below I could hear more shouting.

You're no lord, you bastard. You'll burn in hell for this.

"Fools," Hiran spat onto the brick floor beside me.

I almost laughed at Hiran's arrogance, but I willed my face to remain neutral. "They only spoke the truth, Hiran. If you wish to punish them all for their insolence, then you'll be ruling a city of corpses." But I also wanted to cry, for the woman's life that he'd just ended. He'd killed people for less, but never by his own hands.

The rope sealing off the banishment platform had been removed, some of the rotted wood replaced. Yes, they'd certainly had time to prepare for this. They guided me towards it, my heart beating faster and faster every second.

I looked over the edge, the thirty feet down seeming more like one hundred. My body would surely break if I landed incorrectly. If they pushed me off, I would need to recover before I made it to the ground. But if I leaped myself, I could position my body to lessen the impact.

They removed my shackles, tossing them to the side. I rubbed my wrists where the skin had grown raw in just a short time, closing my eyes to finally accept what lie ahead. Things would only get harder from here. Finding out my true identity seemed inconsequential compared to the task that was now set before me. Which wasn't finding the lost blade of Sazarr, but saving Nola.

I turned around to look at Hiran, just one last time, as if I would see something different there, something new. But I didn't see anything other than coldness and despair. "Goodbye, Kara," he said to me, as if he was so certain he would never see me again. As if he had just made the call for my head to be removed or my throat to be cut. He might as well have.

And as I stepped onto the platform, so close to the edge, I made a decision. Once Nola and I were free from Hiran's grasp, once we were both safely away from the city, I would destroy Hiran. I would complete the murder I failed to the other night. I would come back to Mortefine, one last time, and let him suffer before his end. I would return to him the pain he has caused me and so many others. He would die for what he has done. That was a promise. I would sooner have let the sand serpents destroy him, if it weren't for the thousands of lives in the city, under his rule. I would find a way to save them, too. To free them from him.

"Goodbye, Hiran," I said, a large, taunting grin forcefully spreading across my face. Then without another word, I leaped from the platform, down the wall, and into The Wry.

Chapter 8

I thought I heard a bone crack, but perhaps it was only the guards cackling at me from above. I didn't dare to look back—didn't dare look to see if Hiran was still there. A sharp pain shot through my right ankle, all the way up to my knee. Something was definitely wrong. I'd landed on my feet, knees bent, as I'd intended, and then immediately fell onto my side, face-planting into the dirt. But other than that, I was okay. I survived the jump from the wall, now I just needed to start heading north, towards where I hoped the soldiers would be waiting for me.

Knees wobbly, arms weak, I managed to pull myself up into a standing position. I brushed the dirt off of my pants, off of my ass, and reached behind me for my sword, only to make sure that it was still there, as was the satchel strapped across my chest. I took a few steps to assess my ankle, limping slightly, but still able to move without extreme discomfort. I wasn't sure that I would be able to run, though, if the situation came to that.

I turned back to the wall, unable to see anything inside the city, finding a few guards watching me, Hiran nowhere to be seen. I couldn't hear anything. No more shouting from the crowd. No more proclamations from Hiran. Only the faint hum of The Wry, the wind blowing in the distance.

It was a comfortably cool night, not as cold as it could get sometimes, which meant that the heat of tomorrow was likely to be devastating. I would cross that bridge when I came to it.

There were still hours off from dawn, so I figured I'd better take advantage of the time I had now, and get moving. I knew the gate of the city faced south, so I walked the opposite way, what I assumed to be north, using my little knowledge of astronomy to guide me. It was easy to find my way with the city still in sight, but once I made it farther away, I would need to be more careful about my movements, using the sun during the day and the stars at night.

I just needed to find the soldiers. They had to be out here somewhere, coming from the north, hopefully their group large enough that I could see them from a long way off. Everything would be okay once I found them, and then I could beg them to go back for Nola. But a part of me also feared that they wouldn't, considering that they came all this way for one purpose. Once they had me, there was no reason for them to risk going to Mortefine.

All it would take is a few strong men, some decent weapons. The walls of the city are designed to keep out sand serpents, not people. They could be easily climbed with the right equipment. If we could sneak in, undetected, and free Nola, there'd be no reason for me to complete that ridiculous task, no reason for me to even come back to Mortefine after that. Except maybe to end Hiran's life.

If the soldiers refused to free Nola, then I would go with them to wherever it was they were ordered to take me, and I would come up with a better plan along the way. Even if that meant having to find the lost blade, I would do it. For Nola, I would do anything.

But right now, right at this very moment, I just needed to find safety. So I willed my feet to move, one-by-one, ignoring the pain, as I walked away from Mortefine, and into the unknown.

I did not stop once throughout the entire night. Not to rest. Not for a drink of water or a bite of food. I kept walking, even when my body screamed at me to stop. I could have slept, probably should have, but I knew I needed to make it as far as possible without the sun bearing down on me.

Dawn had barely started to creep over the horizon, to my right, which was good because it meant that I had stayed on the correct path, that I hadn't veered off somewhere in my fit of exhaustion.

My feet ached terribly; my ankle having long gone swollen. I just needed to find the soldiers, then I could rest. I turned to look behind me, finding that Mortefine was no longer in my frame of view. That was good because it meant I had traveled a great deal. But it was also scary because it was the farthest I had traveled from Mortefine in a very long time.

The dry dirt beneath me cracked as I walked over it, land that had once been lush and moist, long having dried to nothing. Not even a shrub or a tumbleweed could be found out here. Nothing grew. Nothing survived. Other than the sand serpents, which I wasn't really sure if they were alive at all, or if they were cursed to live that way.

I continued walking, on and on, until something caught my eye. I could barely make it out because of how much I was squinting, even with the sun barely having risen, but I saw it. It seemed to be a set of footprints. Or multiple sets of footprints, from a few people. They were barely visible, probably left no more than a week ago, almost brushed away completely by the wind.

I knew they had to be from Nola and the few guards that made it back with her. They would have traveled this way back to Mortefine, even after they were attacked. And then I saw the bright red color—small droplets of blood scattered next to some of the footprints, likely from an injury. And the steps were far enough apart that I could tell they were moving fast, maybe even running.

I decided to follow the footprints, knowing that they would take me where I needed to go, hoping that perhaps the soldiers had been following them from the other direction as well. Then I remembered that they would also likely take me to the scene of a bloody and violent massacre. But I could also find it useful, the supplies and food left behind from those who had perished. I could use any help I could get my hands on, even if it was from a corpse.

That seemed like a good enough idea to me, so I continued traveling alongside the footprints, the sun rising higher into the sky with every passing second. I knew what the sun could do, how it could dry me out, so I made sure to drink water, if only it was a few small sips. Luckily, my clothes covered most of my skin, and I had the pillowcase to put over my face. I could cut holes in it for my eyes if I grew desperate enough. My lighter skin could turn to blisters even after just an hour in these conditions.

I kept walking for a while longer until the smell of something foul hit me abruptly, like a gust of wind had shot it straight towards me. I must have been getting close. It smelled sour and rotten like death, with hints of something metallic, like the scent of blood.

And as I walked even farther, I could see the faint shape of something standing out against the rest of the flat desert. Some more walking, and I could see the massive and slender body of a dead sand serpent. It must have been twenty feet long.

I approached the crime scene, a bloody mutilated mess, holding my breath as if the serpent would come back to life and attack me as well. Its head was pierced right through the center, courtesy of Nola, and just beneath it was a large pool of dark blood, long having dried into the dirt. The smell caused me to gag, like nothing I'd ever experienced before. It was terrible.

The serpent was tan, to match the sand, with bright yellow eyes, sharp fangs. There was something sticking out of its mouth, and when I peered closer to see what it was, I gasped, falling back onto my ass in shock. It was the upper half of a human body. And a few feet away, torn in half, was the lower half of that body, lying in the sand. Their sword was still in hand, still reaching for the serpent as it devoured them, and a permanent look of fear held his cold, dead face. The color of red spread about stood out harshly against the rest of the tan desert.

There were a few other bodies spread sporadically about, left there to rot. On one of them was a shiny metallic canteen, which I carefully slipped over his body, only in the hope that it might contain water. The man had large gapes in his lower torso, the wounds that had killed him. Bite marks. Once I had the canteen pulled free, I carefully set him back down.

To my great satisfaction, the bottle was full. And it was not water that was contained within it either, but wine. I pulled off the lid, tossing it aside, and then poured the warm liquid into my mouth. It was sour, like it had spoiled, but I drank it anyway. It was so refreshing—like life was being poured right back into me. I would save my water for later, for when I grew more desperate.

I didn't find anything much else of use at the attack site, so I hurried away from the destruction, willing the sight of what had occurred out of my mind. If I encountered another one of those beasts, a live one, I don't think I would get as lucky as Nola did.

I traveled even farther throughout the day, partly thanks to the wine. I had no idea how long it had been or how far I had gone, only that the sun remained high in the sky, never seeming to pass that threshold and start to lower again.

The dry air burned my chest—my lungs inside. My lips began to harden, stinging as I ran my tongue over them. It never felt this hot in Mortefine, because out here there was no shade. There was nowhere to escape from it.

My stomach grumbled from hunger, which was easy enough to ignore, but I wouldn't risk stopping to eat, not yet. My need for hydration was more prevalent. I tried to go at least an hour each time in between sips of water, though there was really no way for me to tell time. I drank just enough to moisten my tongue, and to get one cool gulp down. It did nothing against the pounding in my head, and the dizziness starting to blur my vision. I knew what it meant—what was happening to me.

My legs were so exhausted that they must have gone numb at some point. My feet too. It felt more like I was floating, which was strange, but it made walking easier. More tolerable.

I could rest tonight. I could rest when the sun went down and I didn't need to worry about shielding myself. I would need to, whether I wanted to or not. Too much more of this and I think I might have collapsed onto the ground and passed out. It had been almost a day now since I'd slept, and forcing myself awake much longer than that would be just another thing taking a toll on my body. Even just a couple hours of sleep would replenish me enough to get up and continue on my way.

Finally, after what seemed like hours and hours of mindless walking, the sun began to set. It was such a relief, to feel the heat of the day begin to fade. If I could see myself, what I looked like, I'm sure there would be burns on my skin, dirt in my hair. It would be an unpleasant sight.

Once the sky had turned to darkness, and the air began to chill, I finally stopped for rest. The lower temperature was refreshing at first, until it got colder and colder, until my fingers and toes went numb for an entirely different reason than before. I sat down in the dirt, removed my sword as well as the satchel, setting them to the side. I pulled out some food, dried fruit, and ate a few bites, taking one sip of water, before I turned onto my side and fell asleep.

It was still dark when I awoke, my things spread about around me, my knees tucked into my chest to keep warm. The air was even colder, and I wondered how I had slept at all considering how hard I was shivering. It was too cold. I couldn't sleep like this. My body needed to get up—to get moving.

I felt only a tad replenished, and I did my best to ignore the millions of warning signs my body was currently giving me. But when I tried to get up, to stand, I couldn't. My body was either too weak, or there was something wrong with me, but I just couldn't move. *More rest,* it seemed to say. My feet still burned and the muscles in my legs were weak. I guess I would be getting more rest whether I wanted it or not.

It had only been one day since I left Mortefine. Just one day. But it felt like it had been ages. I knew it could take weeks to make it out of The Wry, so I was depending on those soldiers to save me. I wouldn't last weeks, not even a few days out here on my own.

There was a part of me that thought I would never see another person again—that I would die out here and that would be the end of it. No grand heroic act of me saving Nola. No revenge when I got to kill Hiran. Just me—in this desert. Those thoughts kept me from getting up, kept me curled up in a ball in the dirt, like a pathetic child. I drifted back to sleep, hopeless and alone. *Just a little longer.*

I only awoke the following day when the sun began blistering down on me. I supposed it was a relief—sleeping all that time without having to feel the pains of thirst and hunger, the aches of my body. I sat up, feeling slightly disoriented, though fresher than ever. It was time to get up and get moving.

As I gathered my things, somewhere off in the distance I could have sworn I heard… screaming. I straightened, stilling, listening for it again, but there was nothing. I surveyed the surrounding area, finding nothing but the expanse of desert in every direction. Perhaps it was my mind playing tricks on me—the lack of water in my body creating hallucinations.

It was enough of a startle to get me moving again. The day went by in a blur. I couldn't tell how fast I was walking or how far I traveled, only that my feet continued to move beneath me, kicking up dirt as they dragged over the earth. The dizziness began to blur my vision at some point, making it hard to see even a few feet in front of me. If there was any food left in my stomach, I would have thrown it up.

I thought I might have glimpsed something in the distance at one point, shiny and reflective like water, but as I neared, I found that it was only a mirage. My mind could be playing tricks on me, and I would be far too exhausted to care.

My body became used to the feeling of thirst, of being deprived of water. I think that meant that it was starting to accept the fact that it would never get enough of it again. I was saving the last bit of water I carried for when I really needed it, which still was only a few sips. The food I had more of.

When night came at the end of the day, I collapsed to the ground and immediately fell asleep. The coldness didn't even bother me anymore. Nothing did.

The next morning, I did not get up.

There was nothing left in me. I didn't feel the pain as it consumed me, but I didn't feel anything else either. I had no will to keep going. My thoughts no longer made sense. There was so much sand in my eyes I couldn't even open them. The dizziness prevented me from standing. I no longer felt thirst or hunger or pain. I just wanted to sleep—to drift away. That would make everything better.

More time had passed as I lay there, questioning if I would make that final pass into the Otherealm. If Sazarr would come to claim my soul, and end my suffering. Was it minutes? Hours? I couldn't tell. The sun was still out, that much I did know. The rest of reality was no longer comprehensible. I was wasting away.

But then I began to feel something—a faint vibrating sensation. I put my palms flat on the earth, feeling, then put my ear against it, listening. There was a humming. The winds seemed to quicken, blowing my hair around and whipping it into my eyes. Was this real? It took so much strength for me to lift my head and look around.

But as I did, the pure shock of what I saw completely revived my body. My eyes widened, my breath catching in my throat. I knew there was a storm coming, though there were no clouds in the sky above. This was no usual storm, but one made of sand. In the distance I could see the massive plume of dust and dirt and darkness, rising up into the sky. A sandstorm was brewing, coming from the east, headed straight in my direction. What would happen if I let it pass over me? Because surely I would not be able to outrun it.

I waited a few minutes, standing in that spot I had slept for so long, watching, hoping some miracle would happen. But the storm did not abate. It was not leaving, and it was only moving closer as every second passed.

I knew this was it. I knew this would be the end, if I didn't get up and fight for my life. If I didn't go and run, then this would be all that was left for me, to die with lungs full of sand, suffocated. If I stayed here the storm would consume me, and I would have no chance of freeing Nola.

I took two steps forward, nearly toppling over from the spinning sensation in my head. My vision would not focus on one point, showing me two of everything. It was a struggle to pick up my things—to place them back over my body. I looked back towards the storm, craning my neck back at the sheer size of it, finding that it had already come much closer.

I forced my feet to move, finding it easier if I kept my eyes closed. With each step I had to fight the urge to collapse to the ground.

The storm was nearly upon me, the air becoming thicker, the sun now blocked out by it. I moved as fast as I could, even running, but it was too late. I was too slow.

A blanket of darkness consumed me as I was sucked into the storm, my feet still planted on the ground, though I could see nothing beyond my eyelids that were shut tight. I pulled my top over my nose to keep from breathing in the sand, but it did little against the storm consuming me. I fell onto my knees, covering my face with my hands, shielding myself from the storm's wrath.

But I couldn't give up yet. I need to keep moving, even through this storm. My feet began to move again, dragging slowly. I staggered back with each gust of wind, fighting against it, wincing as the sand shot into my body like a thousand sharp knives.

I couldn't tell if I was getting anywhere. I couldn't tell if this was working. I didn't know if I was wasting that little remaining energy on an act that was destined to fail anyway.

Suddenly, something happened. The ground beneath my feet cracked, which was loud enough for me to hear over the roaring of the storm. I felt like I was falling, though I could still see nothing, but the sensation was only brief, as I came crashing into something, slamming down so hard that pain shot all the way from the bottom of my feet to the crook of my neck. I seemed to have slipped away somewhere.

Chapter 9

Perhaps... this was another dream. I would have preferred that to the reality that now settled before me, so much worse than I could have imagined. Or perhaps even the darkness had come to finally take me away, and this was hell itself. That was unlikely, considering the pain now consuming my body, on top of the thirst and hunger and fatigue. I still hadn't opened my eyes. I was too afraid to. I was too afraid to see what predicament I had gotten myself into now.

But even as I did open my eyes, I only found darkness, and very, very high up, a faint trace of sunlight peeking through the opening I had fallen from. I looked around, unable to make out a thing, unsure of how big or small this space was. I wondered if I screamed, would my voice echo? Would I get an answer from something else?

I tried to sit up, to stand, but then quicker than I could react, something cold and sharp pressed into my neck, and a warm hand squeezed around my mouth from behind. I drew my arms out, trying to fight, trying to reach behind me for Fangmar, but whoever it was had pinned their chest against my back, immobilizing me. "Relax," a voice said, deep and masculine. But oddly far less unnerving than hearing Hiran's voice would have been.

I drew my head forward, attempting to slam it back into his face, but he must have predicted the move, because he released his hold on me, just before he shoved me across the cave. I slammed into a wall of rock, my hands barely stopping me before my face collided with it. I heard the clang of metal, the man's weapon being drawn again, so I quickly reached behind me and pulled my own sword free.

"Back off," I said into the dark open space. "Or I'll gut you."

A huff of a laugh. "You can't even see me, what makes you think you could get that sword anywhere near me?"

Could he see me? I didn't really care, not as I lunged forward, towards where I had just heard his voice coming from, sword poised in front of me as I attacked. I met open air, and he must have somehow gotten behind me, because seconds before I slammed into another wall of rock, his hand wrapped in my hair, pulling me back towards him, his blade again pressing into my throat. I cried out.

"Who are you?" he said, his voice deep and demanding, an authoritativeness similar to Hiran. Whoever he was, he seemed to be used to situations like this.

"Why don't you take that knife away from my throat, then I'll give you an answer," I hissed at him. But he didn't remove it. Instead, he led me further into the cave, guiding me around with his hand in my hair like it was the reigns on a horse. "Do you treat all strangers like this?"

He pushed me down onto my knees. "Sit." I obeyed, only because I had no energy to do otherwise. I heard his footsteps fade down the cave, and then return a moment later. The cave lit up, and he had his back to me, but then turned around revealing the torch in his hands. I could see now that he was tall, though I could not make out the features of his face. "Who are you?" he asked again, nothing kind in his voice. He was still keeping his distance, like he thought I would attack him again, though I had already sheathed my sword.

"I've been traveling out there for days," I told him, pointing above us. "I'm in no shape to try and fight you. I just need to rest."

He stepped closer to me, towering over me from where I sat on the ground. Then I smelled it, something tangy and metallic. Blood. I thought his clothes were dark, but perhaps it was something else covering him.

"Do you have any water?" I asked him.

He looked at me for a moment, before finally reaching into his bag, tossing me a canteen. It was full. "Drink all you want," he told me. "I have plenty."

So I did just that. I unscrewed the lid and brought the bottle up to my mouth. Then I tilted my head back and drank and drank. And drank. The water was so cold. So refreshing. I drank the entire thing in one go, not allowing myself to feel guilty over what he'd offered me.

"There's more if you need it," he said. "But I would go slow if I were you."

"Thank you," I said breathlessly. "You—That saved my life."

Silence.

He gave me a moment to recuperate, and I leaned my head back against the wall as I felt the dizziness ease, as my body stopped feeling so weak. Even the pounding in my head had started to go away.

I wondered why this strange man was out in The Wry— or, beneath The Wry—all by himself, with an unusual amount of water, hiding down here like a creep. Could he be one of the soldiers sent for me? Even if he was, that didn't explain why he was alone. In the dimness of the fire, I could see that he was wearing armor. And if I looked even closer, I could see a sigil in the center of his breastplate. The Drazos family sigil. So, he was from the capital after all.

"Tell me why you're here," I said to him. I didn't bother asking who he was, because if he was a soldier than his name didn't really matter. "What business do you have here?"

He squinted his eyes at me, assessing. "I was sent here to retrieve something."

"By the prince?" I asked him, testing the water.

"Which prince?" he replied.

"Prince Daenaron," I said, hardly even remembering that there was another, younger prince.

"Perhaps."

"And what exactly was it that you were sent to retrieve?" I asked him. "Perhaps if you told me I could help you find it."

"I know exactly where she—where *it* is," he told me. He was such a fool. He was looking for me, and he didn't know that he had already found me.

"*Do* you?" I asked, a hint of amusement in my voice.

"I don't know what game you're playing with me, but—"

"What's her name?" I asked next.

"Her—" He paused. His mouth shut. He picked up the torch, bringing it closer to my face, so I couldn't see his own face as he finally realized the truth. As he finally recognized me. "My lady," he said, bowing.

I laughed. "No need for the formality, soldier. I just found out that I was a lady only a week ago. I've lived my entire life without knowing. Nobody bowed to me before, and I don't expect them to start doing it now."

"I apologize, my lady" he told me. "It's just… tradition. It's rude not to."

"And don't call me '*my lady*' either," I snapped.

I thought he might have smiled at that.

"How did you know it was me?" I asked.

He shrugged. "You have golden hair and green eyes. You look just like your brother. And," he said, looking down at my chest, "that amulet around your neck is a dead giveaway."

I quickly tucked it beneath my shirt, not knowing that it had slid out in the first place. Was my appearance really that obvious? That someone could know who I was just by looking at me?

"You know my brother?" I asked.

"Yes," he replied coldly, telling me that he did not want to elaborate on it any further. "Why are you out here all alone? And how did you find this cave?"

"Well," I started. "It's kind of a long story." He waited, leaning back, like he had all the time in the world. So I told him. Every last detail. I told him about Nola's return to the city, how she revealed to me my true identity, how we planned to leave the city together and meet up with the soldiers. I told him how our plan failed, how I got myself banished and Nola locked up. How I ended up out here, alone, and then fell through the cave opening when I was trapped in a sandstorm.

"You've been through a lot," he said, not asking a question, but letting me know that he understood what I had gone through to get here.

"I assume you have, too," I offered him. "Tell me, where are the other soldiers?"

He hesitated, his head bowed, like he couldn't bear to talk about it. I almost told him never mind, though I really wanted to know, but then he started speaking. "They're gone. Dead. We were ambushed the other morning at our camp by a sand serpent. It came just before dawn, ripping people from their tents one-by-one. Some tried to flee, but they couldn't have made it far. I fought for as long as I could, until there was no man left for me to defend, and then I ran. I fell through that cave opening, same as you. I've been in here for about a day."

"I'm so sorry," I said to him, genuinely.

"I don't need your pity," he shot back at me before turning so his back was to me. I knew he just didn't want me to see his face, to see the sadness on it. That was okay. He didn't even know me; how could I expect him to feel comfortable enough for that?

I wanted to offer him something, if only to take his mind off of other things. "I went my entire life without knowing who I was," I said. "I came to Mortefine as a child, was taken in by Lord Rendal, and they kept the truth from me. They all did. And when I tried to flee, they did this to me."

"That's... very sad," he whispered.

"I'm guessing we can't go back to Mortefine," I said, my heart breaking. No, we couldn't go back. We couldn't free Nola, just the two of us. Which meant she would be stuck there. She would be executed unless I could retrieve the artifact. "Where will you take me?"

"Vatragon City."

"I can't leave Nola there," I said, my voice shaking a little. "I thought that I would meet up with the soldiers, and that they would go back to Mortefine, to help me free her. But now that can't happen. Not unless I retrieve the lost blade of Sazarr and return it within six months. Which is impossible."

The soldier was silent for a moment before he spoke again. "That was a foolish bargain of you to make. The blade is lost—meaning, it doesn't exist anymore. Your friend is as good as dead."

"No." I didn't have the energy to argue, or to shed tears. "I have to find it, because I refuse to let her die. It's my fault she got arrested in the first place. I know finding the blade is a long shot, but I've already been researching it for months. I've found clues."

"What does Lord Rendal want with it?" he asked me.

"Hiran thinks he can use it to keep sand serpents away from the city," I explained. "But I suspect that there's something more to it. I'll give it to him, in exchange for Nola's life, but I won't let him use it."

He inclined his head, seeming to silently agree with me, that Hiran was lying about his motives.

"I'm going to find it," I said to the soldier. "I'm not going to the capital."

"Okay," he told me. "And I'm going to help you find it."

"What?" I jerked my head back, furrowing my brows. "Why would you help me?"

"Consider it… intrigue, or… boredom." The soldier shrugged. "I came on this trip to have some fun; I think I can still manage that if we do this."

"I can't promise you fun," I said flatly. "But I can promise that helping me save Nola is the right thing to do. She's a good person. She doesn't deserve any of this."

"Karalia," the soldier said, sending a chill through me at the use of that name. "I want to help you. I know we just met, but I know Nola. I know your brother, too. And I know that your brother would choose to help her. He would want *us* to help her. If the soldiers would have… survived, any of them would have risked their lives going back to Mortefine for her as well. If you think you can find Sazarr's blade, then I want to help you. I know my orders are to take you straight back to the capital, but I think the prince would understand. We need to try, and if that fails, maybe we can go to Vatragon City and get on our knees before the king, and beg him to help free Nola. But once all of this is over, whatever outcome it has, you will take your place as Lady Havu. Can you agree to that?"

"Yes," I answered quickly, not even having to think about it. I could agree to that. I could agree to anything for Nola's sake.

I couldn't believe it—that this soldier wanted to help me. I guess having only his help was better than having none at all. But would he really disobey orders from a prince? It was odd that he was so willing, considering that he had already risked so much—had already lost so much. Perhaps he had a death wish.

"What's your name?" I asked, realizing that I didn't know it.

"Will."

"Well, Will." I smiled. "I agree to your offer. I will graciously accept your help. We will search for the lost blade—together.

"Together," he repeated, a faint smile spreading on his face. "Okay."

Will let me rest for a while, keeping the torch lit, which was reassuring because I might have gotten lost in one of my dreams of darkness if he hadn't. He offered me his coat, which I used as a blanket as I balled up in the corner, closed my eyes, and passed out.

I awoke sometime later to a pounding in my chest, having forgotten for a moment where I was and how I had gotten there. My breathing was heavy, uneven, and I watched Will from where he sat on the opposite end of the cave. He tossed me his canteen, newly refilled, which was odd. But I accepted it and drank graciously.

My senses had mostly returned since I entered the cave, after almost dying out in The Wry. While I didn't feel particularly rushed to get back out there, I knew every minute longer we spent in here was a minute wasted when it came to helping Nola.

I could tell now that my skin had burned, not from the redness that I knew was adorning it, but because every time I turned my body over, or moved at all, it hurt, as if I had rubbed against some sort of poisonous plant. I needed to do a better job of covering myself once I began traveling again.

Will sat against the wall of the cave with his head leaned back, resting against it. His eyes were open, and I wondered why he wasn't sleeping, but realized that it was probably just in his nature as a soldier, to keep watch while the others in his company rested. But he looked so peaceful, despite everything. Despite all the devastation and bloodshed he went through just yesterday. I couldn't imagine what it must have been like—to watch every one of his companions die, and be unable to do anything about it. Like me, I supposed he understood the art of hiding pain. Of making it seem like everything was okay when, in fact, nothing was.

I wanted to cry again. That seemed like all I ever wanted to do anymore. And it was welcomed, if I was in private without interruption, but not here, not around him. The last thing I wanted was for him to see me cry, to think that I was just some pathetic girl, and not a lady at all. I never shared that type of vulnerability with anybody—not even Nola.

"Are you okay?" he asked, breaking the silence. I hadn't even realized he'd been watching me.

"I'm fine," I told him, wiping my nose. "This is just… a lot."

He didn't say anything to that, which gave me no indication of what he thought. I shouldn't have cared what he thought, but I suspected that I was about to be spending a lot of time with this man, so I wanted him to at least like me. Or tolerate me, at worst.

"You should get some more rest," he whispered to me across the cave.

"What about you?" I pressed, not pushing *too* hard. "When do you get to sleep, Will?"

"I'll keep watch," was his only response.

"Nobody is coming," I insisted. "Sleep. I'm not letting you slow me down when we get back to traveling."

In the dimness, I could have sworn that I saw something almost like a smile cross his face. At the sight of it, I smiled as well, neither of us acknowledging what was happening, but both of us taking it in.

"I'll sleep," he said after a long moment of silence. "But you're going to as well."

We both dozed off without another word.

Chapter 10

"We should get going," Will said, the sound of his voice dragging me from sleep.

I answered with a muffled groan, perhaps mumbling to give me a few more minutes. But as I cracked my eyes open, and caught a glimpse of bare skin, my entire body jerked, and I was suddenly as awake as the noon sun.

Will was standing across the cave—his side, as we had determined in our short time spent there. His shirt was removed, discarded somewhere I could not see. His back was to me, his head bent, and he was looking down at himself, at something across his stomach. I was about to speak when he turned around towards me, not noticing my watchful eyes, and I saw the mass of torn flesh across his stomach.

I gasped so loud that I had no doubt he heard me. There was a gash right across his stomach, tearing through his abdomen. It looked fresh, likely from the sand serpent attack, which I could tell because the surrounding skin was red, the wound festering. I turned away quickly.

"You're hurt," I said, not meeting his gaze.

"I'll be fine."

I waited, listening, until I was sure he had put his shirt back on. He was gathering his things, putting them into his bag.

I didn't think he would be fine. Not at all. If the wound still looked this bad a few days after it had time to settle, then I didn't even want to know what it looked like when he first got it. He didn't need to tell me that a sand serpent had done it for me to know. He said he'd gotten away... but not unscathed, it would seem. If he would have died, there would have been nobody left to help me. I likely would have been dead right now.

He walked over to me. "I think we should return to my camp—to the site of the attack. We can grab a tent, some food, weapons, and anything else we might find useful. We should be able to make it there by nightfall, if we keep a decent pace."

"And what time is it?" I asked.

"Almost noon."

Noon. How long had I slept? A very long time, apparently.

"And then what?" I asked. "After we stop by the camp, where do we go next? What plan do we have for finding the blade?"

"I figured we could come up with a plan along the way," he told me. "Since we have so much walking to do."

I gathered my own things then, fastening my sword to my back, shoving what remained of my food into my bag, including my empty water canteen. Hopefully Will had more to spare.

"You can fill it up before we go," he said.

"What?"

"There's water," he said flatly. "In the cave."

"*What?*" I shouted, watching as he winced from the tone of my voice. "When exactly were you going to tell me this? Before or after I died of thirst?"

"I'm—sorry."

I sighed. "Just show me where it is."

He picked up the torch, walking farther into the cave, more than I'd dared to venture before now. I heard a faint rumbling noise, which grew louder with every step, and wondered how I hadn't noticed it before. It only took a minute or two, before I heard the rush of flowing water.

"What is it?" I asked Will, still unable to see much of anything.

"A river," he explained. "I think it's the one that runs into Mortefine."

I couldn't believe it. A river, down here? And it traveled all the way to Mortefine. I knew that an underground river flowed there, but I did not expect it to be like this.

I walked closer, all the way until I was standing on the edge, and then bent down, dipping my hand into the water, finding it delightfully cool. I debated jumping in, but that would be unwise, considering how fast the water was flowing.

I put my canteen below the surface, waiting until it was full, taking a long sip, and then dipping it below again. I returned it to my bag. I grabbed handfuls of water, splashing them onto my face, into my hair, dampening my clothes if only so it would keep me cool. Will was a few feet away, doing the same to himself, as well as trying to scrub some of the dried blood off of him.

I let Will lead us back through the cave after we finished, back towards the opening that we were going to have to find some way to get out of. We paused beneath it, the sun shining down, assessing the situation. I don't think I would have been able to reach it if I were alone, if he wasn't with me. I might very well have been trapped down there forever. But if he hoisted me up, maybe that could work.

"Do you think you can reach it by sitting on my shoulders?" he asked me. "Then you can pull yourself up from there."

"I can certainly try," I told him. "But don't let me fall on my ass if I come crashing back down."

He huffed a laugh. "I wouldn't dream of it."

Will bent down onto his knees, leaning his neck forward as if to give me a seat. This was sure to be awkward. I slid one leg over his shoulder first, and he wrapped his arm around it, securing it in place like a belt. Then we did the same with the other. Very slowly, he stood from the ground, careful to keep me from swaying. But of course, I panicked, my body rocking back and forwards slightly, my hands digging into his hair, pulling onto his scalp to keep from falling.

It had to have been painful, but he only said, "I've got you."

I closed my eyes as he lifted me higher and higher, until he was at his full height, gripping my legs so tight through my pants that there were sure to be bruises beneath. He promised not to drop me, so that's what it would take. When I opened my eyes, I didn't dare look down. I found the cave ceiling much closer, maybe even within reach. I lifted my arms, reaching as far as I could. We were too short. There was still a decently sized gap to the exit of the cave, too far for me to reach.

"I don't think—" I started to speak, but it was abruptly cut off with a scream as I was hauled out of the cave. Well, he didn't drop me, but instead threw me straight up. It felt like I was floating, for a moment, until I realized what was happening and I had to spread my hands out to hold on. I gripped the only rock I could find, the roughness of it scraping the skin on my hands. But I was holding on, barely, Will still pushing up my feet from beneath. I reached my hands up as far as they would go, hauling my body forward, up and up, out of the cave at last.

Brightness flooded me as I lifted my knees to bring my body fully above ground. As soon as I was out, I sprawled across the ground like a corpse, collapsing from how terrifying that was. That bastard *threw* me. Like a sack of potatoes. The sky was a clear blue color, not a cloud in it, the sandstorm long having passed, the only trace of it a fresh, thin layer of dirt.

I crawled back to the opening, careful not to fall through it again. "Will?" I called.

"Are you alright?" he asked me.

"I'm fine," I said. "It's… hot out here."

I might have heard laughter in response. I might have heard nothing at all. "Come on," he said. "Reach your hand down and help me up."

So I did. I put my hands back into that dreadful cave, reaching them down just as another, stronger hand gripped them, pulling on me, but not hard enough to bring me down. I planted my feet firmly on the ground, pulling back as hard I could manage, which wasn't really hard at all considering he was a rather large man. But once he got that initial grip, he was able to pull himself out the rest of the way, collapsing onto the ground same as I did.

Only when he was standing before me again did I prowl forward and shove him hard in the chest, though he didn't move at all. "You son of a bitch," I said. "I could have injured myself."

"I think you made it out just fine," he said, shrugging, casually wiping the dirt from his clothes. "We both did. So, shall we get a move on?"

I narrowed my eyes at him, assessing. Out in the open, I could clearly make out the soldier's appearance now. He was so tall that I had to crane my neck back to get a good look at his face, and he was watching me as I began to blink rapidly, overwhelmed by how handsome he was. While I hid my shock well, Will did not. He was looking at me, taking in my entire appearance, redness blossoming on his cheeks. I'd been known to have that effect on men before, though I'd never thought it was funny until now. First, he looked at my face, deep into my eyes, then at my long golden hair, which was currently resting across my shoulder in a tight braid. Then he looked lower, to my clothes, though he could have been surveying my body beneath. He turned away quickly, noticing my attention.

I didn't hide my assessing gaze from Will. He was, indeed, handsome. He had a strong, angled jaw, and a nose just the right size for his face. His eyes were brown, though if the light hit them at just the right angle, they appeared slightly… orange. Like rust. His hair was brown, though a great deal lighter than Hiran's. His skin was tan, much darker than mine, which would make sense if he was from a different part of the country. It wasn't darker in a way that meant he spent a great deal of time in the sun, but rather because he was a different race than me. I looked down further, and though his muscles were hidden beneath his armor, I could tell he was powerfully built. And the way he stood, like a soldier, yes, but almost too proper.

His leather armor, with the Drazos sigil on it, looked finely made. Expensive. A long sword hung from his hip, dangling so far that it nearly dragged through the dirt. His pack rested across his back, no doubt where he kept his food, water, and that knife he stuck across my throat when we first met.

"How old are you," I blurted, mostly just from curiosity.

"Twenty-three."

"*Twenty-three*? You're that young?" I slanted my neck at him, genuinely shocked by this. He didn't seem older, but that seemed young for a soldier who held such high ranks.

"You're nineteen," he said blandly. "I'm much older than *you*, so I would hardly consider myself young."

"Well—" I paused. "I didn't mean it like that!"

"How did you mean it, then?"

"*Never mind*," I hissed, turning away from him and crossing my arms. Yes, he knew I had been looking at him, and now he was making me pay for it. He just remained there, staring at me. "Lead the way, bastard," I said. "I think that will be my new nickname for you. It's rather suiting."

"As you wish, my lady," he said, his words laced with amusement.

"Bastard," I said again, hiding my smile from him.

Neither of us spoke for a good hour or so after leaving the cave. It's not that I particularly wanted to stay quiet, but rather I didn't want to get annoyed by another one of Will's snide remarks. I just followed him, mindlessly, trusting that he was leading us in the right direction. He had come from the camp already, but was running when he did it, so there's a chance he could have gotten confused. The silence between us didn't bother me as much as it should have. I was just relieved to have a companion—to not be alone anymore. We hadn't started coming up with the plan yet, as he had promised, but I would push him for it eventually. I knew we would have to find a town along the northern coast, and find a ship to sail us somewhere. The closest place would be Kraxoth, which was also where I'd found clues on the blade in one of the books I had read. It was the only place I could think of to start looking—our only sliver of hope.

It was sometime later, after much more silence, that I finally blurted out, "I think we should go to Kraxoth." I might have startled Will a little from the franticness in my voice, but he didn't say anything in response, or even turn back from where he was walking in front of me. "Will?"

"My lady?" he said ahead of me, still not turning around.

"We need to come up with a plan," I reminded him.

"Ah," he said, stopping abruptly, nearly causing me to plow into the back of him. "And why, exactly, do you think we should go to Kraxoth?" When he finally turned to me, there was something unreadable in his eyes, something I hadn't yet seen from him.

"I—" For some reason, words lost me. "Well, I read about a rebel leader there who once wielded the blade, and—"

"That was hundreds of years ago," he cut in. "Everyone knows about that. The man, this *rebel leader*, was killed for his crimes. It's unlikely that the blade would have remained in the city after all this time, after how badly his uprising ended."

"Well," I said, bracing my hands on my hips. "Where do *you* suggest we go?" If he had a better lead, then I was all ears, but I wouldn't allow him to lead me on a wild goose chase, when we had every reason to start with Kraxoth.

"There's a canyon," he explained. "In the northwestern portion of The Wry." I knew exactly what he was referring to, everyone that lived in Mortefine did, but I don't know how going there would help us find the blade. "It is rumored that a woman lives there, a powerful being, one that would answer any questions you may have."

"A *seer*?" I broke into a fit of laughter. "You think a magical woman, that might not even exist, is going to, just, tell us where the blade is? How do you even know she really exists? How do you know that this power she has is not just some way to trick us and steal our money?" That last part wasn't a problem for me, considering that I didn't have any money.

"Yes," he replied, condescendingly. "A seer. Laugh all you want, her existence might just be a rumor, but rumors are often based on some shred of truth."

I held his gaze, furrowing my brows. "And where does her power come from? There's no magic in these lands, except for that of the gods themselves."

"Her power is said to be even more ancient than the gods," he explained. "Her power comes from lands beyond ours, and is what created the gods in the first place."

"Whatever you say, soldier," I mocked. "I just find it very hard to believe that something like that is real. I want to make sure we're not wasting our time by going there."

"You have no idea what's real," he seethed, the sudden shift in his tone causing me to flinch. "You have no knowledge beyond what little they allowed you to know, being locked up in that city. You know nothing, so do not presume to tell me how we should go about this, lady." He might as well have spit in my face. He had turned around, facing me, anger and hatred on his face.

What I thought was a friendship starting between us faded in an instant. I took a step away from him, turned so he could not see my face, and looked far into the distance, if only to keep the tears from falling. He was right, and while his words were cruel, and hit something deep inside of me, he did know more. If he thought we should go to the canyon, then perhaps that was where we needed to go.

Still turned away from him, I spoke so softly that I wasn't even sure if he would hear. "Okay," I said "You're right. I know nothing about these lands, I wouldn't even know where to go if you weren't with me. So, I'm sorry, for being such an ignorant fool. I'm sorry that I've been lied to my entire life, by the very people that I thought cared for me. I'm sorry that I was stupid enough to fall for their tricks."

"Karalia—"

"But I'm trying to do better now," I continued. "I'm trying to learn how to trust others—how to trust myself. But you're making it very hard for me. So I suppose I could just shut my mouth and take your word on everything, but how would that be any different from what I've done my entire life? How could I learn to stand up for myself?"

"I—" I could feel him moving closer to me, standing directly behind me, but I kept my back turned to him. "I didn't mean it like that. I apologize."

"It's fine," I said, whispering, though it wasn't fine at all. I turned back to him, and he was standing there, watching me, his face expressionless. "We'll go to the canyon."

"Okay," he said. "And if that doesn't give us any straight answers, then we'll go to Kraxoth. I promise."

"I don't need promises from you," I told him. "I just need you to get me out of The Wry, and then help me find the blade." I stormed off, not bothering another glance in his direction. I heard his feet shuffle behind me, following into step as we continued on towards the camp.

The sun had nearly lowered to the horizon by the time we made it to the site of the massacre, to the ghostly abandoned encampment. As we neared it, still from a distance, you wouldn't have been able to tell that anything was amiss. From far away, you couldn't see the mass of dead bodies and the sprays of blood in the dirt, but you could surely smell it. The blistering sun had ripened the corpses, rotting them at an accelerated rate. Will looked like he was going to be sick, though the two of us still hadn't spoken since earlier.

I let him go ahead a few dozen paces, let him reach the camp first. I lost him somewhere when I finally neared, and began a search of my own. I had to carefully maneuver, past the pools of blood that had yet to fully dry, or the shredded clothes and tents and other items strewn about. I didn't pay too much attention to detail, for fear of what I might find.

I saw Will, bent down, head inside of a tent, rummaging through supplies. He grabbed a few canteens, which I saw him filling with water from a large barrel. Hopefully that would be enough to get us out of The Wry. I looked into several tents, taking as much food as I could carry, which was a lot, considering that I found another satchel I could use.

In one of the tents, I found a half-mutilated body. I clamped my hand over my nose to keep away the smell, not looking too closely at the damages to his body, to the puncture wound in his head. The sprays of blood across the tent flaps were indication enough of how brutal it must have been. Laying on the ground beside the bedroll, I found a knife small enough for me to hide in the back of my pants. I quickly plucked it up, hiding it so that Will would not know I had it.

"Hey," I heard him call from afar. There was no way he could have seen me. "Look what I found." I walked over to where he was standing, holding some sort of clothing item in his hands. He handed it to me, which I examined, finding that it was a cloak, small enough to fit me.

"Thanks," I said, stuffing it into the satchel. It would come in handy at night, to keep me from freezing to death. "What's that?" I asked, pointing to the new, rather large thing that had been strapped to his back.

"A tent," he told me. "I figure it's better to sleep in at night than just out in the open."

I didn't answer. I didn't give him any indication of what I was thinking. Eventually I walked off, towards the edge of the camp, where I waited for him until he was done looking through everything. We headed off as soon as the sun had fully set, our bags heavier, though our supplies replenished.

We only stopped for the night when the camp was long out of view—when there was nothing left of the tragedy that had unfolded. I let Will set up the tent, and then laid down on my side of it when he was finished. We had a quick bite to

111

eat, drank some water, and then I gave my best attempt at sleep.

It was only hours later, the two of us both wide awake, when Will finally spoke. "I couldn't save them," he whispered into the night. My back was turned to him, so how he guessed I was awake, I didn't know. Perhaps he was only saying the words to himself. "They didn't deserve to die." Another beat of silence. "I hoped that... that there might have been someone left. Anyone. I didn't know that such loss would make me feel this way."

I gave him three words, hoping that he understood my offering of peace that came with them. Whatever we said to each other before, it didn't matter, because we had both lost so much. We had both suffered. We shouldn't have been putting the blame on each other. "I'm so sorry," I said into the small tent that we shared, into the night beyond.

Chapter 11

The next day, we traveled as far and as fast as our bodies could manage, replenishing ourselves with the gracious supply of food and water, only stopping again once the sun had set and the night sky was full overhead. We hadn't talked much at all the entire day, and I found the silence suffering, but I wasn't going to push Will any further, not after the confession he made the night before. We were both struggling, and we both needed to figure out our own problems before we started opening up to one another.

Will again set up the tent, and I wasted no time dropping my belongings to the ground and then plopping myself down onto the dirt. My feet ached, my stomach growled, but I said nothing about it. I wouldn't complain, not to him. The quicker we made it to some sort of civilization the better.

As we sat down, I pulled the cloak around myself, the weight of it comforting over my body, even if it did belong to a dead man. I removed my boots, my socks soaked with sweat, and set them outside of the tent to air out.

Will turned to me, the first time he had acknowledged my presence in hours. Our eyes met, and it was a relief to see that he no longer looked sad, but the exhaustion on him was just as worrisome. There were bags under his eyes, and his skin, it looked much dryer than when I had first seen him. I'm sure if I had a mirror, I would find that I looked the same.

"How are you doing?" he asked me, his voice hoarse. He removed the belt that held his weapons, setting it to the side, then pulled out his canteen and took a long sip.

"I'm tired," I admitted, "but okay."

He passed me some food, an apple, which I ate so rarely in Mortefine. I wasted no time biting into it, and savoring the freshness it offered. We shared a slab of dried meat, something he got from the camp, which was the most filling thing I had eaten in days.

When we finished, Will turned over onto his side, away from me, and went to sleep. I could have slept as well, should have, but I wanted to give him his peace, if only for a little while. I stood and left the tent, sitting on the ground outside with my legs crossed in front of me. I leaned back and tilted my head up towards the night sky. It was always something to behold, especially out here where clouds were so scarce you could always make out the constellations. I didn't know any of their names, but I could recognize them by shape.

Some say that stars are lost spirits, trying to find their way to the afterlife. That when we die, our spirits go elsewhere, somewhere far from here. And the stars are just those who have gotten lost on the way. I'm not sure if I believe that at all, not any more than the claim that Drazen watches us from the sun. I suppose I'll just have to be proven wrong one day, when I die and move on.

A particularly large and bright star flickered, as it to greet me, and because I knew nobody was watching, I raised a hand to wave at it, smiling softly. If it was a spirit, then perhaps they were watching over me.

Perhaps it was the parents I never got to know.

I sat out there for a while, until Will came to join me, and we sat knee-to-knee, gazing up towards the sky. We didn't speak, we just sat there in silent understanding. Sometime later, I crawled back into the tent and fell asleep, peacefully for the first time in a while.

"I would kill for a horse right now," I told Will the following morning as we continued to travel. It was the first words we'd said to each other all day. My feet were blistered and bloody, and having to stuff them back into my boots this morning was no fun task. They could probably hear my cursing all the way back in Mortefine. Hopefully, as we continued walking throughout the day, my feet would eventually go numb.

Will grunted his agreement, which was better than ignoring me again, I suppose. He didn't seem to have any trouble with his feet, or with any other part of his body. He certainly had to be more used to physical activity than I was, but I knew there was no amount of training that could have prepared anyone for this. It was brutal, testing, and an obvious indication of why nobody survives out here. But the soldier could obviously handle it better than me.

"Are you not tired?" I asked him, stepping up to his side. "You haven't seemed out of breath this entire time."

To my surprise, he laughed softly. "I'm just… good at keeping it to myself, I guess."

"Bullshit!" I said. "I know you can hear how loud I am breathing."

He laughed again. "Your body will get used to it eventually."

I crossed my arms. "Well, I don't plan on being out here long enough for that to happen." When he didn't answer, I said, "I am in dire need of a bath. Or a fresh pair of clothes."

"I can tell," he said, his voice flat. Though if I didn't know any better, I would think that he was trying to make a joke.

I poked him in the arm. "It can't be that bad," I said, then leaned down to examine myself. "Can it?"

He fought back his smile, which might have been the most joyous thing I'd seen in days. I was breaking through some sort of surface. Seeing him like that was better than walking around with some moping, brooding man. We were warming up to one another, at last.

When we stopped for our next water break, Will seemed to be watching me more carefully, like he was searching for signs of exhaustion. I didn't know how to feel about that.

At some point, we must have veered west, no doubt thanks to Will's master navigational skills. We were headed towards the canyon, which was only a few days out of the way of traveling to Kraxoth. If everything went smoothly, we would make it to the canyon in one or two days, and then to the coast a few more days after that. That is, if something with this seer woman didn't hold us up. Or if her wise words of wisdom didn't send us on another path.

I had little doubt that we would find any valuable information at the canyon, which I would never admit to Will. I didn't think that we would even find a seer there. As far as I have ever been informed, their existence was a myth, at least in Vatragon. They are a part of history that has long been forgotten, because simply, they do not exist anymore. There have always been stories of ancient kinds of magic, of powerful unruly magic. But now, on this continent, there was only one kind of magic known to exist. That of the Drazos family. But I had yet to believe in the existence of that as well.

After further traveling, and later in the day, Will asked me, "Why did you work for Lord Rendal?"

The question caught me by surprise. "Hiran?" I laughed nervously. "I would never have done it if he hadn't begged me to. We used to be good friends, before he became lord."

"Or before you tried to kill him?"

I cocked my head to him, smile disappearing. "Would you hold that against me?"

He shook his head. "I can't lie to you and say that I wouldn't have done the same thing. He's a bad man."

"Well," I said. "We can agree on that." I offered more. "I grew up at the Rendal estate, after his father took me in when I came to the city."

"Is that when you met Nola?"

I nodded. "The three of us were close as children, up until he became lord. Nola and I moved away to live on our own, but then not long after he asked us to come work for him."

Our pace slowed, so we could better hear each other as we talked.

"Did you ever become close again?" he asked next.

"No," I said. "I never wanted to, not after I saw who he really was."

"Why did you agree to work for him, then?"

I shrugged. "I thought it would be better for the city—for the people—if they had me watching out for them."

"That's very noble," Will said, and I could tell he really meant it. "Unfortunately, they don't have you now."

"That's what I'm worried about," I admitted.

"Was he your lover?" Will asked, not like he cared whether he was or wasn't, but rather because he was just curious to know.

"At one point, yes, Hiran and I were involved. But it ended a long time ago. I had no interest in him, once he became… who he is now." I wouldn't tell him about what happened at the ball, because it wasn't any of his business, but also because I was strangely afraid of what he would think of me because of it.

"The king will be made aware of his… behavior towards you," Will promised. "And I will make sure he is punished for it." But I knew he couldn't promise that, not really. Not unless he was offering to kill Hiran himself. The king doesn't even know that I'm alive yet, and if he's so satisfied with how Hiran is ruling, like Nola claimed, then why would he care that Hiran deceived me?

"He's a waste of a human being," I said, though I knew the words were meaningless—ones I had said many times before. "He deserves to die—for what he's done to me, to Nola, and to everyone else before. He kills and tortures innocents, which the king has turned his head to all this time. Do you know, the night I was banished, a woman spoke out on my behalf, she said a prayer for me, and Hiran killed her for it. He slit her throat in the street and left her to die." I thought for a moment, then continued, Will listening intently. "He kept me locked up like a prisoner. I might have lived of my own volition, but when it came down to it, he wouldn't have let me leave the city for any other reason. And how do I know now, agreeing to go with you, that I won't be going

117

from one prison to the next? How do I know that my life won't be worse when I become Lady Havu than it was when I was nobody?"

Will stopped, so quickly that I hardly had time to notice before he turned around and put his hands on my shoulders. "I would *never* let that happen to you, Kara," he said, bending down to look straight into my eyes. "Never." And though I heard the promise there, and the sincerity in his words, I still could not bring myself to believe him.

Late into the night my mind still dwelled on the conversation from earlier. Even as we set up the tent, as we sat down to eat, I couldn't help but recall the words said, and remember Will's hatred towards Hiran. It was a relief, if anything, for somebody else to understand. For somebody else to know what I went through. I admired him for that—for agreeing with me. For accepting me.

The air had grown drastically cooler tonight, and Will warned me that the trend was likely to continue the farther north we traveled. At least it was less hot during the day as well. I didn't know—that the climate could be so different from Mortefine. I was eager to see what else changed as we made it even farther.

I could count the few times I had seen rain, on those rare occasions back in Mortefine when the clouds would swirl enough to pour a drop or two of water on us. But I had never seen snow, and Will assured me that we were likely to, considering that fall was nearing, and then it would be winter, and practically every part of the continent north of the capital would be blanketed in snow. Except for Frystal, where it snowed year-round.

But I've never even seen waters. There are no lakes in Mortefine, save for the large underground one, but nobody goes down there. I've never seen a coast along a sea or an ocean. The first river I saw was the one in that cave, though I could guess enough that most don't look like that. The only visualizations I have are from paintings and drawings, which still make it difficult to imagine.

I know little about how seasons change throughout the year, as Mortefine is just hot all of the time, but I know that it happens in other places. There are supposed to be hot parts of the year, and cold ones, and then ones in between where it's more tolerable. It seems so strange, but I suppose it's similar to how, out here, it goes from hot during the day to cold at night.

I laid down on my side of the tent and curled into a ball. I wished I had more clothes—more than just this singular cloak—but I was already wearing all that I'd brought. And Will, he seemed perfectly comfortable. My body began shaking slightly, which was a strange sensation, but I knew it was from the cold. I couldn't get comfortable, not like this.

"I'm going to freeze to death," I hissed, hoping that Will might offer me his coat or something.

"This is hardly anything." I could hear the amusement in his voice. "In Frystal, it gets so cold that your eyes could freeze shut. The pipes in your house go solid. The snow falls so thick that it buries the buildings. This is nothing compared to that. I wouldn't even consider this *cold*."

I scoffed. "Well, excuse me for not being used to this sort of thing. I've lived in a desert my entire life, you know."

The moonlight fluttered in as a gust of wind blew the tent flaps open, sending a chill over me. I curled further into myself, my knees practically pressed up against my chin.

"You would be warmer if we slept next to one another," Will said.

"No, thank you," I told him, unsure if he was being serious or not.

"I'll leave you to suffer," he said. "But please, do it silently. I need my rest."

I quickly turned over, about to add my own snide remark, when another gust of wind blew into the tent. I groaned, knowing that I had been defeated, knowing that I would have to accept his offer, if only for my own comfort. "Fine," I yelled, like I wasn't desperate for it.

My back was to him again as I waited, listening until I heard him scooting towards me. He pressed his body against mine, putting a hand on my arm to bring me closer. Instantly, warmth began to seep into me. I might have sighed out loud from the sensation of it. A few seconds later and I was dead asleep.

The days had started to blend together. I tried my best to keep track, but the exhaustion, on top of everything else going on, it made me weary. I knew it had been just over a week since I'd left Mortefine, but it felt much longer. The last day I spent in my own bed was Rebirth Day, which was also the last day I saw Nola. We didn't even get one full day together before everything happened. I didn't even get to say goodbye after she told me who I was, and after she told me about her plan to help me. But then she got arrested and I got myself banished, a result of my own stupidity. I just wished I could have seen her one more time before I left, to let her know that I wouldn't abandon her, that I was coming back. That I would stop at nothing to save her. Now, I knew she was probably just locked away in a cell somewhere, struggling to survive, wondering why I have not come for her yet.

Will was still asleep when I awoke, still right next to me. He didn't snore loudly, which was a relief all on its own, and he slept rather peacefully for a soldier, like he wasn't worried at all about the possibility of us being attacked. I didn't know if that was good or bad, but I didn't really care at the moment. I remained lying there, listening to the sounds of his breathing, until the sun arose, and he stirred at last.

We ate a few bites before packing up and heading off for the day, continuing our journey. I could tell now that my body was getting more used to the walking. My muscles weren't as sore, my feet hurt less. Even Will seemed better, the wound on his stomach having scabbed over and began to heal.

I couldn't see them last night, because of the cover of darkness, but as we walked that morning, I could see something in the distance, tall structures. The Sandsaal Mountains. They seemed to have appeared out of nowhere, towering high into the clouds, brown yet a darker shade than the flat earth of The Wry. They hardly seemed impossible to pass, and I wondered what was so dangerous about them. If we could make it out here, then surely we could make it over those. But that wasn't the way we needed to go, anyways.

Throughout the day, Will and I discussed many more things. He asked me more about my life in Mortefine, if I remembered anything from before I went there, which I didn't. Then he asked about my physical training—what weapons I could use. I assured him that the sword across my back wasn't just for decoration. Later I found myself admitting that I'd never killed anyone, to which he admitted that he wished he could have said the same. I could never hold that fact against him. He was a soldier, after all.

Will wasn't as eager to talk about himself. I asked about his family, to which he responded that they weren't close. I hoped to learn what it was like to be a part of a family, but perhaps he wasn't the person to ask.

He seemed to know a lot about my brother, Kadon. When I asked about him, Will said that Kadon was kind, brave, and utterly loyal to the Drazos family. After all, they were the ones that took him in after our parents died. He was there when they were killed, in Orothoz. He escaped, assuming that I had perished along with my parents, not knowing that I had just escaped to somewhere else. He hadn't returned to Orothoz since, which I couldn't blame him for. Kadon and I both lost our family, only he could remember it, and I couldn't. He had to live with the painful memories, which I suppose was a mercy for me.

Later I found myself babbling to Will about Nola. He had met her when she was in the capital, so he understood my fondness for her. I think just saying her name out loud relieved some of my anxiety, as if she were still here with me. As if she were already safe and free from Hiran.

Nola always had a way of influencing people—of easily getting them to like her. While me, I never had that sort of effect. I never wanted or tried to. But I suppose that it would be nice, to be friends with everyone you met, to converse so easily with strangers.

The more Will and I talked, the more relaxed we became. I hardly noticed when he had stopped walking in front of me but instead at my side. He didn't have that usual cold seriousness you would expect from a soldier. While he was broody at times, he was also lighthearted and amusing enough to make me laugh at others. I don't think anyone other than Nola had ever made me feel that way before.

The day seemed to pass more quickly, and it was the first night in a while that I didn't want to cry myself to sleep. We set the tent up and prepared for bed. Will watched me, like he knew what I was thinking about, like he knew what I was contemplating asking. But, as if to save me from the humiliation, he scooted towards me without a word, and pulled me close, keeping me warm. I leaned my head against his chest and promptly fell asleep.

I hadn't realized it before, but that usual darkness that found me as I slept, it hadn't come in a while. I wondered if it had something to do with Will, and then I wondered if it was silly of me to consider that. But out in The Wry, as I slept beside Will that night, again, no darkness came to me, and I wondered if it ever would again.

Chapter 12

We were set to make it to the canyon later that day. We awoke at dawn, packed up our things, then headed off without a word. I took bites of our dwindling supply of food along the way, with small sips of water to wash it down.

These last hours spent walking felt like nothing in comparison to the previous blur of days.

And like Will said we would, as the noon sun shone overhead, the first glimpse of the canyon came into view. While the earth remained flat, for what seemed like as far as the eye could see, there was a shift in the air, something I couldn't quite explain. The wind, which had been blowing in one direction, now blew in another. We continued forward as the canyon itself could not yet be seen, and I noticed that the dirt, which was brown everywhere else, had turned a reddish color. It wasn't as dry, either—it felt softer against my feet as we walked through it, leaving behind more noticeable footprints.

Another hour passed until we had finally made it. I was walking forward, my eyes on the horizon ahead instead of right in front of my feet, and then I heard Will yell. I turned back just in time to see him lunge for me, as he grabbed me seconds before I would have stepped off the edge of a cliff. My body slammed into the dirt—my back aching—as Will collapsed on top of me, breathing heavily.

"Kara," he whispered, genuine fear shining in his eyes. "You should be more careful."

"I know," I replied, shocked.

"You scared me."

"I'm sorry."

He climbed off of me, brushing the dirt from himself as he stood, and then bent back down, offering me a hand. I gripped it, and he pulled me up, putting his other hand around my lower back as if he were afraid to let me go. And he had every right to feel that way, as I'd almost fallen to my death.

When he released me, I walked back over to the edge, more careful this time of where I stepped. And then I saw the canyon.

My breath caught as I took in the massive opening in the ground, right before us, like the earth itself had been ripped apart, or cut into, going deep, deep to what seemed like the center of the earth. The center of the canyon seemed to be the deepest, the largest, while there were smaller tears spread about, branching off in different directions. The sight of it didn't seem real—it felt like I was dreaming.

My palms grew moist as I took in the overwhelming view, despite the little water I had consumed these past few days. There were colors I had never seen before in nature, that I never *knew* could exist in nature. Oranges and reds, even some purple, spread about in layers, going down all the way to the bottom of the canyon, forming steep vertical cliffs, like the one I had almost just fallen off of.

But even more surprisingly, there was *water*. All the way, at the very bottom of the canyon, a river snaked its way through the earth. Of course, it was thoroughly inaccessible to us, not unless we wanted to risk our lives trying to climb down to it. And though it was so far away, too faint for my eyes to see, I thought I even saw something *green*. Like plants were growing, all the way down there, out in The Wry where we thought such a thing was impossible. That must have been the same river that traveled to Mortefine, going underground somewhere at some point.

I didn't know what Will had planned or where he thought this seer was supposed to be, but I hoped it didn't involve us climbing down into the canyon.

For a while, we just stood there, side by side, standing on the edge of the world, taking in the view that you only get to see once in your lifetime. It certainly amazed me, as I think anything would have at that point, but Will was just as mesmerized. I watched him as he smiled softly, eyes lost in the distance.

"It's beautiful," I whispered, the words barely heard over the wind.

He turned to me, meeting my eyes, smile growing. "I've never seen anything like it."

"I'm glad we got to see it together," I offered, not really sure why I was saying it. I regretted the words the second they left my mouth.

But Will didn't seem to mind, not as he reached for my hand, grabbing onto it, interlacing our fingers. Not as we stood there for a long while, taking in the view, holding on to each other, not because the moment itself was intimate, but because neither of us had anybody else to share it with. In that moment, we only had each other.

Will lifted his head, and I watched as his attention settled on something in the distance. His eyes narrowed as he lifted a hand to point, but when I followed his gaze, I could see nothing out of the ordinary. I opened my mouth, to ask what it was, but then I saw it.

It was an irregularity. Something standing out against the rest of the natural formation. It looked like what could have been a long set of stairs, a walkway, or just an anomaly within the rock. It was leading towards something deeper in the canyon, something that was blocked from our view at the spot we were currently standing. Will kept my hand in his as he started to walk, practically dragging me along. We moved along the edge, though Will was careful of our footing. After a few minutes, we could see what it was.

Standing out so harshly, seeming to have been carved into the rock itself, stood eight long, carved columns. They expanded the entire side of the canyon, appearing to indicate the entrance to something. It could have been a cave or a doorway or something else, but it didn't matter, because the large opening had been blocked off with fallen rocks, keeping us out, or keeping something else in. It was obvious enough that it used to be some sort of arched doorway, but it was not that anymore. It was nothing at all. Above the archway were words, carved straight into the rock. But they were not words in any language that I knew, nor Will. They appeared to belong to some ancient, forgotten language.

Will and I turned to each other at the same time, both with weary expressions on our faces. We were both thinking the same thing, that if down there was where we needed to go, then we wasted our time coming there. But just to clarify, just to make sure that we were on the same page, I said, "We can't go down there."

Will looked disappointed, though he was already seeming to accept it. He opened his mouth to say something, but then a shuffling behind us caught our attention, and we turned around to find a woman standing there, watching us, smiling.

"Don't bother," the woman croaked, her voice raspy and ancient. From where she stood, she trapped us next to the canyon's edge, with nowhere to run. "You just found what you've come looking for."

Will reached for my hand again, gripping it hard. He took a step forward, as if to shield me from her.

She was a woman—apparently, the woman we had come looking for. The seer. But I wouldn't exactly call her a woman. She might have been at one time, if her assets were any indication, but this... this was not human. She was a mere shell of skin and bones, hidden beneath a shredded pile of rags. Wrinkles adorned every inch of her skin, even her bare, black feet that were cracked and bloody. Scarce patches of white hair grew from her pale veiny head, and her shoulders hunched forward like a wounded animal. She could only stand upright because of the staff she was using, some carved bone that had to have come from a very large creature. But the most frightening thing about her, what made me want to turn around and run right back into The Wry, was her black,

126

soulless eyes. They had no whites, no center of color, but rather blackness all around. Seer this woman may be, but something much more vile lurked beneath the surface. And I didn't want to be anywhere near her when it was unleashed.

She smiled as she took in the frantic looks on our faces, the way we were clinging on to one another like we were prepared to die together. She was certainly no stranger to people trembling from fear in her presence. And from the inhuman grin she gave us, revealing teeth that were just as black as her eyes, every one of them sharpened to a point, she wasn't just thinking about scaring us. No, she wanted to feast on us as well.

I squeezed Will's arm. *Get me out of here.* I hoped he understood my silent plea. He squeezed right back, as if to say, *I'm working on it.*

She walked towards us, her long toenails scraping against the rock, leaving bloody footprints behind.

"That's far enough, witch," Will nearly spat, angling me even further behind him.

"*Witch?*" She let out a shrill of laughter, that made my skin crawl. "I am no such thing, but you already know what I am, do you not?"

Did that confirm what we already suspected? Was she truly the person we traveled to the canyon in search of? She wasn't nearly what we hoped for, and if she wasn't a witch, then she was something much, much worse than that.

"What is that archway down there?" I asked her, if only to see if her abilities were real, if she would answer my question.

"It is not for mortals to know," she told me, though I could have sworn her lips hadn't moved at all. "It is ancient and dangerous, and any fool who has ever been brave enough to dwell down there never lived long enough to speak of it. Nor did they ever see the sun again."

"Are you the one that kills them?" I asked.

She appeared to be looking at me with those black, soulless eyes, though I could not tell for sure. "It would be a mercy for them," she started. "If I was the one to do it. But unfortunately, even I cannot enter beyond the gate."

Gate? What sort of gate was it, if it was so dangerous? Will knew the seer would be here, yet he didn't know the gate would be. Perhaps it was an entrance to the Otherealm, as rumor claimed them to be spread about the land. It didn't seem likely, but it was as good a guess as any.

"Are you really a seer?" I asked her next.

She dipped her head in confirmation. "Seer," she explained. "Sibyl. Prophetess. I am called many things by many people. I am whatever you need me to be."

"But what are you really?" Will cut in, and I was afraid of the answer she'd give.

The woman didn't answer, she only said, "I know why you are here. Ask your questions and then be on your way."

It wasn't the matter of asking questions that I was worried about—it was what came after that. She could tell us whatever we wanted to know, and then she could very well kill us before we had a chance to do anything with the information. Few people knew of her existence, which I could guess there was a good reason for. She didn't want people to know that she was here, and now, we were disrupting her peace. And if she got angry... I'd be willing to bet that her frail shell of a body was only concealing a greater power beneath—one that could snuff us out in an instant.

Will remained standing at my side, angled a bit in front of me. I didn't look too closely at him, but I could have sworn his hands were shaking. I couldn't blame him. I didn't dare reach for him. I wouldn't let the seer discover any vulnerability between the two of us, though if she already did know everything, then I supposed that it didn't really matter.

"Where does your power come from?" I blurted, mainly out of curiosity, but also to get a feel for what we were dealing with. Whatever her power was, it did not come from these lands, and it was not known to most people, if any.

"My power is beyond your comprehension," she sneered. "It comes from somewhere very far from here—unattainable to those with a mortal soul." And the way she said that, talking about mortals, it gave me the distinct impression that she was not one, nor was she a woman.

"Where?" I pressed. "Meriton?" The western continent, where magic roamed freely and was a lifestyle to many.

"Even farther than that," she explained. She gestured her hands to the sky, long nails glimmering in the sunlight. "Let's just say that it's not of this world." She paused for a moment. "You did not come here to ask about me, girl. Speak your truth."

"I thought you were supposed to be the one speaking the truth," I shot back. Her eyes narrowed on me. Yes, she knew what I was doing. Asking about the blade now seemed like damn foolery—a mockery of whatever abilities she had. But we needed to know, and we'd already come this far. I cleared my throat. "We have come to inquire on the lost blade of Sazarr, in hopes that you can lead us to its whereabouts."

The seer hissed, taking a few steps away from us, her tainted clothes blowing in the wind. "What could you possibly want with that?" She clawed at her skin. "It is lost, and with good reason. I will not lead you on a path that brings nothing but death and destruction."

"The death and destruction of what?" Will asked. When she didn't answer him, and kept her mouth closed like she was refusing to, he added, "We're going to find the blade, with or without your help."

"I cannot help you," the seer responded quickly, still retreating from us. "The blade's curses prevent me from seeing it." I suspected she didn't mean with her eyes. "There is a spell, ancient and powerful, one that not even I can rewrite. The same spell that binds these lands—that holds this continent together. I suggest you decide on something else to go in search of."

Will and I turned to one another, knowing that we were getting no straight answers, but so much more at the same time. She may not have been answering our questions directly, but she was telling us other things of importance.

"At least tell us what the blade looks like," I said, forcing myself to sound disappointed if only to lace the fear I felt within.

She turned back to me. "It is no ordinary blade. It is not forged from any metal known to man. While I have not seen it myself, I've heard whispers from beyond, that it is a dagger, forged from Sazarr's very own fang. It contains the power to not only slice into a man, but to poison them, to force an evil into their bodies. Their deaths are slow and painful, and carry on for weeks, or even years until it finally claims them."

"The blade is magic?" Will asked.

"Something of the sort." She bobbed her head, which wasn't a confirmation or a denial. "I can offer you a warning," she said. "While I hardly care what happens to the two of you as you search for the weapon, you risk unleashing a dreadful evil on the rest of the world, something that could harm even me. Many before you have tried and failed to discover the blade's location. Many have gone mad in the process, ending their own lives before they can discover the truth. If the blade knows you seek it, it may call to you, it may find you in your dreams and even in the darkness of the waking world. If it wishes to remain undiscovered, it could make you do dreadful things. You will have to find the strength to fight it—to keep it from controlling you."

"But it isn't the blade that could control me, is it?" I asked. No, it wasn't the blade, that much I could guess. It was the god that the blade came from, the mouth that the fang belonged to. Sazarr.

"That, I cannot tell you," she said calmly. "I do not interfere with the gods of these lands. We have maintained a peaceful coexistence for a thousand years, and we will for a thousand more."

Will seemed to have gone completely still. His arms slackened at his sides, sweat dripping down the side of his face. I wouldn't let myself worry about what he was feeling, not when we were getting the information we needed.

"Do you know if we will find it?" I asked, perhaps a little too desperately. "I mean, in the end, will we succeed?"

"I cannot define what you qualify as success." She flicked her hand at me, as if to wave off a fly. "And it is not for me to say, girl. I can only guide you on the path that I glimpse, but it can always change. It is up to you to determine where your fate is headed, girl."

I was prepared to keep asking questions, to keep pushing, when Will put his arm around me to pull me close. "Thank you for the information," he said to the seer, guiding me further down the canyon's edge, away from her. "We should get going. We have much traveling to do."

"Yes, I know," she said, and though I could no longer see her face, I could feel the smile she was aiming our way. I could sense those dark teeth flashing.

"Wait," I whispered to Will. I tried to pull free from him, to turn back to the seer. He might have been done, but I was not. If there was anything more she could tell us, then I needed to hear it.

"Don't get greedy," the seer cooed. "Everything has a price."

Her words scared me enough to change my mind. I allowed Will to wrap his hand around my wrist and start to drag me away. I would have even let him pick me up and carry me like a child, if that got us away faster. A gust of wind shot our way, the breeze warm and dry against my face. Everything happened so fast that I didn't even register it. I couldn't hear the footsteps approaching from behind. I couldn't hear Will shouting at me to run.

The seer lunged for me, moving faster than any human could. Her feet didn't even seem to be touching the ground, not as she glided right up to me and wrapped her hands around each of my wrists. She stared into my eyes as she said, "Who are you, girl?" the waft of her decaying breath burned my eyes from how close she was. I needed to get away. I was terrified. "Why do you seek the blade?"

I tried to pull away, but her grip was too strong. Will's hands were on her as well, trying to get between us. She was no longer that meek, frail creature, but now a powerful beast, unwilling to let go of me.

I had no idea what she meant. Who am I? I almost told her—just a girl who wanted to save her friend, who would do anything, even talk to terrifying *things* to accomplish that.

"Your blood," she started again, her nostrils flaring. "It smells like poison. Like... death." She looked into my eyes. "I can see a darkness in you, hiding beneath the surface, waiting. Waiting to be unleashed."

Again, I tried to pull free, her nails digging into my skin. It started to hurt, and I cried out, looking to Will, begging that he would help. And then above the seer's voice, the only sound I could hear was the metallic hiss of Will unsheathing his sword. From the corner of my eye, I could see the sun reflecting off of the blade as he swung it towards the woman. He had aimed for her neck, but he must have lost his footing because the sword dipped to the side at the last second, swinging down into the dirt instead. Or maybe... No, some kind of *power* had done it. The sword fell from his hands, and then he rolled onto his side, landing too far away for him to be able to reach me. He was dangerously close to the canyon's edge, one of his legs nearly dangling over it.

"Will!" I yelled. But then something wrapped around my throat, her fingers, and it kept me from speaking. I tried to use my free hand to push her off of me, but I couldn't do it. She was too strong.

"Listen to me," she said into my ear, quiet enough that I knew Will couldn't hear. "There is so much that you do not know, even about yourself. But one day you will, and when that day comes, you will take the world down with you. You will accomplish your... *quest*," she said, after having denied that she could reveal that, "but after, men will cower in fear at the sound of your name. They'll try to destroy you, like they have before, but they do not know what you keep locked

132

away. And their pathetic god won't be able to save them from your wrath."

For a moment, it felt like I was not in control of my own body, not at all as I smiled at the seer, a wicked, vicious smile, and then said, "Perhaps once I find the blade, I'll come and use it on you." I didn't recognize the person saying those words, and the seer must not have either, because one second, she was holding onto me, keeping me in place, and then the next, she was pushing me away, trying to get so far from me that I would have thought *she* was the afraid one now. She stumbled back, fell over, and then began crawling away, as if I would dare to attack her.

Then I saw Will running towards her, sword raised, as she remained completely unaware of the nearing threat. He raised it over his head just as he approached, first slamming his foot down onto her back, to keep her from moving, and then he plunged that sword straight into her heart. She did not scream. She did not make a sound at all as her body fell limp into the dirt. Will pulled his sword free, and black blood sprayed everywhere, getting onto his clothes, dripping into the dirt. To any normal person, there would be no doubt that they were dead.

I hoped that she was being sent back to whatever cold hell she crawled out of.

Her words took a moment to sink in. A darkness. I already knew that there was a darkness in me, because it haunted me every night as I slept, but I had no idea what everything else she said was about. What was waiting to be unleashed? What was wrong with me? I don't think any man would ever cower in fear from my name, not unless they thought I was a ghost when they saw me, after believing I had been dead all this time. She was probably just spewing nonsense—just trying to mess with my head.

"Let's get out of here," Will said, stepping up beside me.

I followed him as he began to walk, still too stunned to say anything. We walked for a minute or so before I dared to turn back, to where the seer's body lay sprawled, but there was nothing there. There was no body, nothing other than that black, reeking blood, scorching the earth and burning like acid.

Even hours after we had left the canyon, I could not stop thinking about the seer's words to me. Whoever she was, whatever she was, I was grateful that we got away with our lives. When she had a grip on me, she was so strong, certainly strong enough that she could have killed me if she wished. And I wouldn't have been able to get away—I wouldn't have been able to fight back at all. I didn't think that she was dead, not in the way that counted, especially because her body had magically disappeared when I turned back to peer at her.

Despite her later actions, she had actually given us valuable information. While she didn't tell us *where* precisely the blade was, she told us *what* it was—that it was forged from Sazarr's fang—which gave us a better idea of what we were looking for.

It did make me more hesitant now, knowing that the blade was magic, and that there was some curse tied to it. Perhaps that explained more why Hiran wanted it, but it also meant that there could have been a much deeper meaning for his motivation. That wouldn't stop me from finding it—from freeing Nola—but it might have made me more determined to keep it from Hiran in the end.

"What do you think she meant?" I asked Will, breaking our treacherous silence. "About my blood smelling like death."

"She's just a crazy old bitch," Will said, wiping the sweat from his face, running his hand through his hair. "Don't worry about what she said—any of it. It doesn't mean a thing."

"It seems to me like it *did* mean something," I said, though neither I nor Will knew exactly what that was, so I knew I couldn't keep pressing him about it. "Do you believe her warnings, that seeking it is dangerous?"

"I believe that we need to be more careful in how we go about this, moving forward," he said. "We knew this would be dangerous from the start. But we couldn't have guessed that the blade was... cursed. That certainly changes things." At least we agreed on that.

"But you still want to help me seek it?" I asked, because I was actually unsure, and I couldn't blame him if he said no. I hoped that he would still want to help me, but I would understand if he didn't. I was prepared to do this on my own, if I needed to.

"Of course I still want to help you," he said, shooting me a sideways grin. The sight of it forced me to smile as well. "One slimy old crone isn't going to scare me away. We can do this." He put a hand on my shoulder, shaking my body slightly.

I looked up at him. "At least now, we have a better idea of what we're looking for."

There was a long pause before Will spoke again. "I have to admit something," he said. "I didn't expect us to find any leads by going there. I thought there was a chance that the seer existed, but I didn't think the blade existed, so I thought she wouldn't be able to help us. I thought she would tell us it wasn't real and then we would be on our way. I thought once you heard that, you would realize that you'd been sent to do the impossible."

In an instant, my smile disappeared. "So," I said, not bothering to hide my disappointed, "you thought that, what, I would just decide to give up and go with you to the capital?" A flicker of rage began to surface within me. "You thought that I would abandon my friend so you could complete your mission and turn me over to the prince?"

"I—" he started, pausing, like he needed time to think of a lie. "The blade is a myth, Kara," he explained. "I just wanted to know the truth, the same as you, and now we do. We know the blade is out there and we're going to find it."

I could have argued. I could have been mad at him for lying. But I was so tired. Of everything. I knew being angry with him would exhaust me even more. "Okay," I said. "But just so you know, even if that woman would have told us it didn't exist, even if she said it was impossible to find, I would have still kept looking. I would never give up on Nola. She is my priority, and I am going to find this damned blade, even if it kills me. If you don't want to be a part of that then I suggest you be on your way."

Will shook his head, reaching for me though I quickly stepped out of his range. "I was wrong," he told me. "I'm sorry. I was wrong. We're going to find it. Together. I promise."

I should have screamed. I should have told him I was angry. But I wanted to believe him. I wanted to believe that he was there to help me. "Okay," I whispered. "To Kraxoth?"

He nodded. "We'll walk the rest of the way to one of the towns along the coast, then we can look for passage across the sea. When we get to Kraxoth, we can start by asking around for information."

"Sounds like a plan," I told him, allowing myself a small moment of relief.

We headed off, onto the next phase of our plan.

Chapter 13

Two more days' worth of traveling and I could smell the salt in the air. We had been making great progress, stopping only a few hours each night to rest, eat a bite of food, and then head off again in the morning.

Will knew of a town along the northeastern coast, Saltrenea, and claimed to be taking us in its direction. It was a small town on the edge of the Alanah Sea, mostly used as a port for traveling sailors, while they also got by on their small salt mining industry. They were only able to survive from how easy it was for them to receive imports, because, like Mortefine, they were unable to produce their own foods. But unlike Mortefine, they had no walls surrounding them, and no way to keep out sand serpents. Even that far north the beasts still dwelled, and I knew that we wouldn't be safe, not until we made it across the sea and onto greener lands.

So, probably against my best interests, I let Will guide me to this town where he was certain we could barter passage, besides the fact that neither of us carried even one gold coin on us, unless he was planning to sell my amulet, or our weapons. Would we even be able to buy food when we got to Kraxoth? Or find a place to stay? He couldn't expect that all of that would come freely, just because he was a soldier in the king's army.

Around noon that day, the two of us stopped for a break, even going as far as to set up the tent, to escape the sun for a short while. Under the cover of shade, I removed my cloak, my boots, and even rolled my pants up to my knees. Will took everything except for his pants off, using his shirt to wipe away any lingering sweat.

I could see his wound then, the one inflicted on him by the sand serpent that attacked his men. But the thing is, there was no wound there to speak of, not anymore. Only a pink scar remained, about the size of my fist, appearing to have healed long ago. Or maybe I was overreacting when I initially saw the wound. Or maybe we'd been stuck in The Wry for much longer than I thought.

But I didn't say a thing about it. I took a tiny sip of my water, forcing my mouth to pull away a few seconds later so that I would not drink the entire thing. All of the spare canteens had long been emptied, and we were down to one for each of us, each of them about half full. I wouldn't say anything about *that* either. Will handed me a small cloth, and inside of it I found a handful of nuts mixed with dried fruit. We'd run out of the good stuff long ago, and I was pretty sure that the only other food left was a loaf of something, to which neither of us could guess what it contained. It was dark, and smelled sweet, but when we broke it in half, it appeared that there was meat inside, or maybe beans. As desperate as we were, that would come as a last resort. Hopefully, if we were lucky, we would make it to Saltrenea the following day, where we could find better food to eat, and hopefully a bath to bathe in, and a bed to sleep in.

Will was lying back, his hands propped behind his head, feet resting on one another, eyes closed.

"Don't you dare go to sleep," I said, my teeth crunching as I ate another bite of nuts.

"Too late," he said, his eyes still shut, though a smile tugged at his lips.

I picked up his sweat-covered shirt, which he decided to discard on my side of the tent, and threw it straight at his face. He lurched forward, his head hitting the top of the tent, his bare feet sliding around in the dirt.

"What was that for?" he asked me.

I laughed softly. "Sorry," I said. "I didn't mean to throw it on your face. I was just trying to give it back to you." I put a hand over my lips, as if to pretend that I'd done it by mistake, but he saw right through that.

"Oh, yeah?" he said, matching my taunting demeanor. He picked up his boot, weighing it in his hand like he was debating chucking it at me. But then he pulled out the sock from within, pinching it with his thumb and forefinger as if he couldn't bear to touch it, and then tossed it towards me, landing right on the top of my head.

I shrieked, and it fell down onto my lap, the smell of it wafting up into my nostrils. I shrieked even louder then. I didn't even want to pick it up to throw it back. I managed to brush it down to my feet, and then kicked it straight outside of the tent. Will was completely unconcerned about his sock, because he was currently laughing his ass off, his face turning red from the amusement he found in torturing me.

I hissed at him, scooting over from my side of the tent and then lunging for him, grabbing him by the shoulders. It wasn't hard, and he knew I meant not to attack him, but to punish him for the embarrassment he caused me. I'd never seen him laugh so hard, and from just the sight of it alone I began to laugh as well. He tried to push me away by reaching for my stomach, and I tried to swat at him, but I was laughing way too hard. Eventually I collapsed onto my side, next to Will who was still laughing at me.

"Prick," I managed to say, but he could still hear the amusement in my voice.

"That's what you get for waking me up," he smirked.

"Don't ever put your filthy socks anywhere near me again," I demanded, looking away so I wouldn't burst into laughter yet again. "That's an order, soldier."

"Is it?" he turned onto his side to face me.

"Don't even say what you were thinking," I flicked a hand at him, pushing his shoulder which sent him back towards his side of the tent. "Put your clothes back on and pack this shit up."

He chuckled softly, scooting out of the tent and then standing to retrieve the sock I so politely got rid of. It should have only taken a second, but after I minute, I began to worry. I peeked outside of the tent, and I couldn't see him. I listened. I closed my eyes to feel.

A faint vibrating sensation began to tickle on the ground beneath me, rattling the tent and the items we had discarded around us. I would have merely dismissed it as the wind, had it not grown stronger with every passing second.

"Will?" I called.

No answer.

The vibrating grew stronger and stronger, and then I realized that it might have been an earthquake. And then I could hear it, a rumbling, similar to that of the sandstorm approaching all those days ago. I pulled myself up and out of the tent, searching, momentarily blinded by the sun. Only when I turned in the opposite direction did I see Will approaching, running straight towards me. He was saying something, but I couldn't hear it, not over whatever was stirring in the distance.

His shirt was still off, as were his shoes—his skin glistened in the sunlight as sweat dripped from his neck down to his chest. And I just stood there, watching, waiting for him to come back to me. But that's when I saw it. Behind him, far off into the distance, was a small plume of dirt, headed straight towards us. It was too small to be a sandstorm, but there had to be some other explanation.

"Will?" I called again, his eyes locking onto mine. The rumbling grew so much stronger, that my legs grew unsteady beneath me.

At last, Will had reached the tent. He put his hands on me, shaking me frantically, and while I couldn't hear him, I could read his lips. *Run.*

That sprung me into action. We both put on our clothes, slid on our boots, and fastened our weapons to our bodies. When I moved to take down the tent he batted my hands away, telling me to leave it. What sort of thing could cause so much upheave, that he would risk leaving the tent behind?

I didn't have time to ask, not as we gathered the rest of our things, what could easily be carried on our bodies without slowing us down, and broke into a sprint.

"I need you to run, Karalia," Will said, already breathless. "Whatever you do, *don't stop*."

So I ran, and I did not stop, not for a while. Even when my legs grew tired and my lungs heavy. Even when Will slowed so much that he stood a great distance behind me. I pleaded with my body, to give me one last bit of energy, just to get me out of The Wry. *I will not die like this*, I told myself. I would not die from thirst or starvation, I would not die from weakness, I would not die from being too slow, and I would certainly not die from the attack of a sand serpent. That's what was headed towards us. Without even looking, I already knew. I would not die before I had the chance to save my friend.

We weren't moving fast enough. We wouldn't be able to outrun the beast. We would need to fight.

"Will," I said, daring to look over my shoulder at him. "We can't…"

"Don't stop," he screamed to me. "Keep going." He was hunching over, limping a little with every step. If I didn't go back to help him, who knew what would happen?

The rumbling was so close that I could see the plume of dirt approaching out of the corner of my eye. It was almost upon us, about to consume Will at any second.

My body cursed at me as I slowed my running, and as I turned my feet in the opposite direction and ran to Will. He stopped before me, a million questions in his eyes, though there was a sadness as well, like he already knew what was about to happen.

"Karalia," he said, not a question or a plea, but a promise. To fight together, right here and now, with everything we had.

In unison, we each pulled our swords free, the blades hissing in the wind. I held mine upright, Will at my side, bending my knees in defensive preparation. If I was going down, then it would damn sure be with a fight.

The rumbling shook me to my very core, rattling my bones beneath my skin, taking my mind off of the fear that should have been consuming me. I turned to Will, his face reflecting my own terror. Then I turned to the beast, getting a glimpse of it for the first time.

The serpent was massive, larger even than the dead one I had wandered upon before. I'd never seen anything like it. Its skin was tan, an exact replica of the dirt in The Wry, like it had been bred to blend in with this place. Two long, sharp horns protruded from its head, right above its slitted yellow eyes. Its scales reflected the sun back at us, like it used that skill to blind its prey before it devoured them.

Will and I stood there, watching, waiting, as the serpent slithered towards us, blowing up dirt in its path. I'd never seen any other animal move so fast, curving its way closer to us, closing in.

It was almost on us, a few paces away, and then a hard body slammed into mine. Will tackled us to the ground, moving us out of the beast's path just in time, saving us from certain death. Right before the serpent's open mouth would have struck the spot we had just been standing, now meeting nothing but open air.

I whirled on Will, angry that he prevented me from having a stab at the beast, though I knew that he was only trying to protect me. But his eyes weren't on me, they were watching the serpent that had already turned around for another attack.

As soon as the two of us were standing again, Will shoved me away, my body sliding across the dirt, my knees scraping through my pants. My head was spinning, but I needed to get up. I needed to help Will fight.

"GO," Will screamed at me. "RUN."

He wanted me to run, so that I could get away. So that I could survive, while he risked his life slaying the beast. I couldn't bring myself to stand. I couldn't move at all.

For a second, just one second, I saw Will standing there, sword raised in his hands, screaming at me to flee. I stayed there and watched as the serpent approached him, and as it slithered into his path, blocking him from my view. His screaming stopped, and my heart might have as well.

I couldn't see a thing.

I didn't want to see.

Blood sprayed across the earth, splashing into the dirt, so much that I hoped it wasn't Will's, because certainly that would have meant he was dead. The serpent retreated, hissing and recoiling its body, revealing Will sprawled in the dirt, his clothes torn, though his sword was coated in blood that wasn't his own. No, he'd certainly struck his target, even though it got him injured in the process.

The serpent shook its head, blood pouring from the gash straight across its throat.

Will managed to pull himself onto his knees, his sword resting on the ground a foot away. His hand was over his chest, where the serpent's fang must have scraped across it. There was blood all over him, running down his body. But it must not have been that bad, because a moment later he was standing, again gripping his sword, again moving to fend off the serpent.

The serpent drew its head back as it approached him, readying its next attack, gaining momentum before it struck him down.

I moved like the wind.

I didn't allow myself one moment of consideration before I broke into a sprint, Fangmar raised in my hands, drawing it back in preparation to be unleashed. I reached the beast, swinging my arms down so hard that my shoulders might have snapped out of place. I had never used so much strength—I never thought I could. Yet it still was not enough. I had only managed to injure the beast further, over the back of its head this time. But it *was* enough to distract the beast long enough for Will to get away.

He headed straight towards me, but not quick enough. The serpent lashed its tail out, first for Will, and then for me, sweeping me right off of my feet and onto my ass. I tried to reach my hands out to brace the fall, not thinking at all about the weapon still in my hand. I lost my grip on it, to which it sliced into my arm. I couldn't hold in my scream of pain as a warm trail of blood dripped from my arm and into the dirt.

But the serpent hadn't resumed its attacks on either of us. No, instead it was there, watching me. Its head was propped upright, eyes narrowed, nostrils flaring, its body jerking back slightly with each drop of blood that fell from me. I might have thought the world had gone frozen, if Will wasn't walking towards me now, and if I couldn't see my chest rising and falling as I brought air into my lungs.

I held up a hand, motioning for Will to stop. And he did. I walked to the right, towards Will, and the serpent's eyes followed me. Then I walked left, its eyes following me again. And when I dared to move towards the beast, it recoiled away from me, like it was somehow *afraid*. Will met my eyes, and I knew what I saw there. He was going to attack the beast, while it was distracted watching me. I silently shook my head at him.

For some reason, I knew the beast wasn't going to attack me. I kept walking forward, closer to the serpent and Will at the same time. But it must have sensed what I was doing, because a moment later it was drawn out of its state of transfixion and back into the predatory mode from before.

It looked at Will, who was walking towards me, assessing him. Even if the thing didn't want to attack me, it hadn't given up on Will. But I got to him first, putting my body between them, like Will had done for me with the seer. I stood tall and brave, raising Fangmar to the serpent, drawing a line in the dirt to let it know that I would not be standing down, not now or ever.

Will grabbed onto the back of my arm, as if to stop me, but I nudged him out of the way.

The serpent lowered its head to the dirt, giving up on its pursuit just like that. It let out a large, angry breath, strong enough to blow the hair from my face. Again, it watched me carefully, for some odd reason.

I stood there, refusing to move an inch, even when the beast finally turned and began to slither away. Minutes later, when it was out of our proximity, I still stood there, terrified, frozen, afraid that it would come back.

I felt a strong hand on my shoulder, the weight of it comforting. He wrapped his other arm around the front of me, holding me against his body, resting his chin atop my head. Only then, did I allow myself to breathe. Only then, did I know that it was over, and that everything was going to be okay. I threw my sword into the dirt and then spun around to face him, tears in my eyes as I threw my arms around his neck and knocked him into the dirt.

He clung to me, pulling on my jacket, inspecting my body for injuries.

"I'm fine," I said to him, which was nothing more than a rasp. "Will, I'm okay."

He nodded, and then I dared to reach a hand to his own body, to the wound still seeping blood. It expanded the entirety of his chest.

"What the hell was that?" he asked, leaning his forehead against my own, refusing to let me go if only for a second.

"Will," I said, and his eyes met mine in an instant. I debated voicing my thoughts to him, asking if he saw what happened. The serpent smelled my blood, and it halted. It smelled something *in* my blood. No, I couldn't tell him that. "I thought you were going to die," I said.

"You should have kept running," he whispered.

"I know," was my only reply.

"We should both be dead right now," he told me, shaking his head in disbelief and confusion.

"I know," I said again. "I know."

Chapter 14

After all of the blood had dried and I'd scraped it away with my dirt-covered hands, the cut was nothing more than a scratch. A *scratch*. That's all I'd received after being attacked by a sand serpent. And to my immense relief, Will's own wound was less severe than I thought, having already clotted and dried as well. We were mostly okay, at least physically, but where our minds were at, that was something different entirely.

My clothes were covered in blood, both my own and Will's, and maybe even a bit of the serpent's.

It just didn't make sense—how we made it out with our lives. Nola had *twenty* guards with her, all slaughtered, and yet she was able to slay the beast, all on her own. But then with Will, fifty skilled and heavily trained soldiers, all killed but one, all at once. And us. Two people skilled with weapons, yet mostly vulnerable against the beast. It would have killed us—it *could* have killed us—but for some strange reason it retreated.

Hours later, as the afternoon turned to evening, as we walked slowly towards our destination, I was still trying to piece it all together. It was set on killing us, there's no doubt about that, but then something triggered it. Something made it back off, at least from me. It happened after I cut myself, like the smell of my blood had changed the serpent's mind. Maybe the seer was right, about my blood being strange, and maybe that scared away the serpent. But it could have left me alone and gone after Will, yet it didn't. It didn't want to be anywhere near me.

I couldn't tell if Will noticed. He hadn't said anything about it since we'd left, but he also hadn't said a word about anything else either. He must have been in shock—just coping with the fact that he'd come so close to death. I would give him his space, for now.

We had stopped for more water breaks than our supplies could handle, but we were exhausted after the fight earlier. We needed it. But everything was running dangerously low; if we didn't make it to Saltrenea within the next day, then we would start to worry.

But hopefully we would make it to the town, and then find passage aboard a ship not long after that. I didn't want to spend any more time in The Wry than I had to. I'd spent enough there already to last a lifetime. But, alas, I would have to return eventually, at least one more time.

I wondered how I had done it as a child—how I traveled all the way to Mortefine from Orothoz. The idea of that seemed impossible now, after barely being able to do it as a grown woman. I wished I could remember, not just how I'd done that, but everything about my childhood. The memories just… weren't there. I couldn't remember having a family, or having a place in the world. I couldn't remember the parents that were taken away from me, or the brother awaiting my return.

Nola told me that I had traveled over the Sandsaal Mountains, all those years ago, but I didn't understand how that could be. There had to be more to it that I just wasn't remembering. The first memory I did have was waking up, already within the walls of Mortefine, tucked into a bed at the lord's estate. I didn't remember walking up to the gate and screaming my lungs out, or anything before that. I remember Hiran leaning against my bedside, holding my hand, his father brooding in the corner, probably deciding if he should have me killed or not.

I was just a child then, as was Hiran. No hint of the person he would become later. Even though it pains me to admit it now, Hiran really helped me in those early years. He welcomed me, even if they were holding me captive. They told me that they'd saved me, and I was stupid enough to believe it. They *had* given me somewhere to live, enough food to fill my belly, a decent education. But everything went so wrong in the end, once the truth came out.

There's no way to know for certain that my life would have been better living anywhere else. Perhaps it would have been once Hiran became lord, but not in those early years.

But today, I did not need any reminding of who Hiran was. He was the manipulative, conniving bastard that imprisoned Nola—that banished me from my home. He sent me on this quest, most likely to die. He couldn't have truly believed that I would succeed in finding the blade. But he'll be in for a real surprise when I come back and slit his throat with it, just like he did to that woman the day I was banished. Nobody, not Will, not even the king, would keep me from ending Hiran.

As we continued walking, Will on my right, in the unspoken formation we'd created, I could see him watching me, like he was searching for something within me. Unlucky for him, I was searching for that exact same thing, and I was having trouble finding it.

"What's on your mind?" he asked, nudging me with his elbow.

I smiled softly, sadly, still weary with exhaustion. "Everything."

"Do you want to talk?" he asked next, and the way he said it... I already knew that if I said no, he would be perfectly okay with that. He wouldn't push me until I was ready.

I placed the canteen that I had just taken a sip from back into my satchel, then released a long breath. "Okay."

Though we kept walking, I could see him turn, angling his body as if to get a better look at me. "When did you learn to be so brave?"

I blinked. Once. Twice. Again and again as I thought of how to respond. His question caught me off guard, as it was not at all what I expected him to ask. I thought he would start accusing me of things, demanding to know how I scared the serpent off. "I guess…" I started, swallowing once, my throat dry as if I'd taken in a mouthful of sand. "I guess I've always been that way. Because I've never had anything to lose. I never thought that… the world would miss me if I'd disappeared. There's never really been anything *important* for me to live for. I don't have a death wish; I know that's what it sounds like. I just… place a higher value on others' lives than I do my own."

His eyes were the brightest I'd ever seen them as we looked at each other at that moment. They glossed over, hidden only slightly beneath his lowered lashes, even further beneath his furrowed brows. His fists clenched, and then I feared not for my sadness, but how what I said made him feel.

"Don't give me that look," I whispered, reaching for his hand, though he stepped out of the way just in time. He turned his back to me, his shoulders sagging.

"Don't try to get yourself killed and then maybe I won't," he said, his voice having grown angrier. "You don't even understand," he went on. "You don't understand how much you have to live for. You can't be reckless like that. You have a friend to save and a brother to meet. You have a whole life ahead of yourself, and you would throw it away, for what…?"

He couldn't say it. Could he even acknowledge it? "I did it for *you*," I said, my own tone having grown sharper. "I did that because the bastard was going to kill *you*, not me. I couldn't just stand there and watch while it ripped you apart."

"Careful," he snarled, finally turning back to me. "It's starting to sound like you care."

"Am I not supposed to?" I snapped right back, standing and blocking his path when he tried to get away from me.

"Am I not supposed to be afraid when I see the tether of your life to this world breaking right before me?"

"Because you'd be screwed without me?" he pressed. "Because if I wasn't here, you wouldn't be able to find your way out of The Wry, and you certainly wouldn't make it to Kraxoth to look for the blade."

He was right. He knew he was right, but that wasn't what I meant. "Don't say that," I said, hoping he would understand the desperation in my voice. "That's not what I meant."

"Then tell me what you meant, Lady Karalia."

I knew we were angry, and we were shouting, and that we didn't mean half of the words we were saying, but I was hurt. I was sad and broken and I thought that something was happening between us, and everything that he'd just said suggested otherwise. So I let him see that on my face as I told him at last.

"Because I don't want to watch you die," I said. "Because I can't do this, any of this, alone. Because I want your help and because I need it. I won't lie and say that I wouldn't be screwed without you, but you're..." I paused at that, not even sure of what I was about to say. "I need you," I told him. "Please."

I could tell then that he understood. As we looked at each other, my chest tightened, not with fear or sadness, but with something like... relief. I started to shake. I wanted to cry. I nearly let my body collapse into the dirt.

He stepped towards me, and I stayed right where I was, leaning back to look up at him as he stretched his arms out, and as he slid them over my back, moving slowly, gently, as if giving me time to push him away. My arms were still at my side as he buried his face into my neck, pulling back to whisper into my ear.

"I understand," he told me. "I'm sorry."

I closed my eyes as his breath traced over me, his lips brushing my neck as he whispered apologies onto my skin. He would have gotten onto his knees and begged for my forgiveness if that is what I'd asked him to do. I didn't hug him back, but I let him know that I was okay.

An hour or so later, after our emotions had a chance to settle, Will and I got to talking again. We needed to talk about something else—anything else—if only to take out minds off of what had occurred.

"Who taught you how to fight?" Will asked me. "Surely not Hiran."

"No." I laughed. "Not Hiran. Although we did train together. I picked it up on my own at first, and then once they realized that I had a knack for it, they gave me some training of my own. I was always better than Hiran, even though he was older and stronger than me. I paid more attention. I saw fighting more as a defensive strategy, while he saw it as a means to end people's lives."

"Well, you obviously didn't pay enough attention to keep from cutting yourself," he said, his voice full of amusement. And then more seriously, he said, "You should be more careful when handling a weapon. You could have caused a lot more damage to yourself, Kara."

"We were attacked," I retorted, waving him off. "The serpent knocked me off of my feet. It was hardly my own fault."

He shot me a sideways glance. "Just—tell me you'll be more careful next time."

"I will," I agreed. "You know, I've gone my entire life without protective assholes looking over me, I don't need you to start doing it now." He was overreacting, anyways, which I wouldn't say to his face. The serpent knocked me off of my feet, and I lost my grip on my sword.

"Thanks," he said, ignoring that last part. But somehow, I knew he wasn't just thanking me for agreeing to be more careful. He was thanking me for defending him, and for risking my life to keep the serpent from devouring him. I knew it's what had to be done. As soon as I realized that the serpent wouldn't attack me, I thought quickly, hoping that I could keep it from attacking Will as well. And I was right. My quick thinking spared us, sending the beast away.

"I think…" I started, realizing that the words would sound crazier coming out of my mouth than they did in my head. "Do you think it had something to do with the fact that we're searching for the blade? I mean, maybe it's like the seer said. Maybe the blade knows we seek it and it's… manipulating things."

He raised a brow. "Magic or no, I don't think a *dagger* could do that."

"I know," I said. "But if Sazarr has control over the blade, do you think that perhaps it could be him doing this? Sending the sand serpent for us. Maybe he's not done yet. Maybe things will keep getting worse from here."

"The gods don't interfere with our lives, Karalia," Will told me. "They only watch. And besides, Sazarr is trapped in the Otherealm."

I laughed at that, to which Will shot me a confused look. "No, the gods certainly don't interfere with our lives. But they don't watch us either. They don't give a *shit* about us. Maybe they did once, long ago, but not anymore. Why would I believe in the might of a god who, supposedly, lives on the sun and watches us from afar? Or why would I fear a god that is said to be trapped in the Otherealm, unable to get anywhere near me?"

Will whirled on me, pointing a finger in my face as he hissed between his teeth, "Just because Drazen rests does not mean that he couldn't come back one day." He might as well have shouted the words. "You should choose your words more carefully, especially when speaking of our god."

"He's not my god," I said quickly, carelessly. He was Will's god, sure. The Drazos family, definitely. But not mine—never mine. What was the point in putting my faith into someone who let me end up alone and orphaned? Long ago, I even prayed to Drazen a few times, begging for my memories back, begging to find my family. Those prayers were never answered, and even though I knew who I was now, I knew it was no thanks to the work of a god.

I'd never openly spoken my disbelief and distrust of Drazen to anyone, except for maybe Nola, only because I knew she shared my opinions. I knew there were people out there who would agree with me, and would have no problem voicing it. Some would silently shame me. But a few, those in power, could punish me for the defiance.

Even though it's forbidden, some do take Sazarr as their god. And now, as I search for his blade, I have more cause to believe that he is the real power, not Drazen. But when the ruling family of the entire country is said to be descended from Drazen, that makes it kind of hard to take another path.

I thought of the safest question I could ask to a soldier wearing the Drazos sigil. "Do most in Vatragon take Drazen as their god?"

Will's eyes narrowed on me. "I would assume so, but there are some that follow Sazarr." Perhaps more than just some, though I wouldn't correct him on that.

"What happens if they are discovered?" I asked. "These... *Sazarr* supporters." Perhaps a less-safe question, but I wanted to know.

He shrugged. "Nothing, really. Not unless they make a genuine threat against the crown. The king has had them killed before, though it's not a usual occurrence."

"Oh," I said.

"Why are you asking this?" he questioned. He didn't sound offended or cautious, or like I had overstepped some boundary. He was just curious, same as me.

"No reason." I forced boredom into my voice. "I mean, we are looking for *Sazarr's* blade, a weapon forged from his own fang. It shouldn't come as a surprise that I would have questions about him."

He only nodded in understanding.

But then a more pressing question popped into my mind. "Are there *serpent blooded*?" I blurted. "You know, like there are *dragon blooded*?"

His eyes shot to mine, almost too quickly. "No," his voice was flat. "There are no *serpent blooded*. Sazarr's last descendants died out a long time ago."

"Oh," I said. "Sorry for asking so many questions. I've just—never had anyone to ask about these things. Not without making myself seem suspicious. I'm only curious." And that was the truth, mostly. I wondered how different Will's opinions could be, since he was from the capital where Drazen support ran deepest. And, as I suspected, he seemed to have a rather high opinion of the god.

"It's fine," he told me. "Let's keep walking."

We didn't sleep that night, at least not until very late. After the sun had set, we stopped traveling for the day, though with the tent missing all we could do was sprawl ourselves down into the dirt and lay our coats down to use as blankets. I rested my head back, closing my eyes though I knew sleep would not find me. We whispered to each other, as if there was anyone out there that could hear us, as if the serpent would come back to finish what it started. Without the tent to keep out the cold wind, we had to sleep close to one another, snuggled up more than I cared to be. I kept all of my clothes on, as well as the satchel strapped to my side, for fear that we would need to get up and run at any second.

The time had come, for us to eat the mysterious loaf. Will broke me off a piece, and then one for himself, to which we bit into. Three seconds later and we were spitting it out into the dirt. It was hardly edible, the taste like poison on my tongue.

"One of the soldiers' wives must have baked it for them before the trip," he explained. "I don't know what it's made of, but there's no way in hell I'm eating it."

"Well, I'm not either," I said, tossing my piece into the dirt. "I guess water will have to do for now." But when I lifted my canteen to my mouth, the weight of it lighter though I was too tired to realize, just one small mouthful poured out, and then it was empty. I shook it, eyes wide, as if the water had somehow magically disappeared. I turned to Will, his face mirroring my own as his canteen emptied as well. We were out of food and water at last.

But rather than commenting on the realization that should have concerned us, we started to laugh. It was frantic, hysterical laughter. I didn't care that I sounded insane, or that my dry lips began to crack from how wide my mouth was open, how much I was smiling. I felt drunk. Giddy. I was losing my mind. If Will was worried, he wasn't showing it.

But I knew half a day of traveling tomorrow day would take us to our destination, to Saltrenea, to the edge of the Alanah Sea. Hopefully then there would be someone to offer us food and water, and a way for us to sail to Kraxoth. Will even said that he knew of a captain that stopped there every other week to deliver supplies. That he might just allow us aboard his ship with the promise of payment being delivered at a later date.

Sometime even later the two of us began discussing strange things, though I suspect he was only trying to scare me. He told me stories of the Alanah Sea, about the dangers and terrors in it. He claimed that it had waters as dark as the night sky with beasts that pry beneath the surface. Beasts that could take down an entire ship, or perhaps even swallow it whole. The water of the sea is so dark, that you can't even see them coming until they're already upon you, until it's already too late.

"Stop trying to scare me," I said, shoving a hand onto his chest. And I *was* scared, since we were to be traveling across that sea in the near future. But the beasts were only a rumor, not a proven threat like the sand serpents were known to be.

Sea monsters, magical weapons, seers. Those were all stories we were told as children—stories that I was terrified might come to be true.

But my excitement about traveling over the sea far outweighed my nervousness. It would be my first time on a boat, my first time seeing open water, and so much more. It would be my first time leaving The Wry in a long, long time.

"But it'll be okay," Will went on. "Whatever happens, in the end, it will all be okay."

"How can you promise that?" I asked him. "You could never guarantee such a thing."

"No," he agreed. "But I can hope."

I yawned, surprised to find that I had actually grown tired.

"Get some sleep," Will said, scooting closer to me and then draping his coat over the two of us to keep warm.

Chapter 15

I wasn't cold when I awoke the next morning. No, I was hot. Sweating, the sun bearing down on me, but also because of the body that was uncomfortably close to mine. Well, actually, I was currently resting on top of Will, half of my body covering his.

I had an arm draped over his chest, clinging to his arm on the opposite side from me. My legs were situated in between his own, our ankles intertwined as if we had gotten into some sort of fight in our sleep. But I wasn't just holding onto him, he was holding onto me as well. He had an arm resting on my lower back, keeping me pressed against his chest, and his other was propped beneath my head, as if to provide me with a pillow.

Selfishly, I remained there, still, resting. An hour might have passed since I'd initially waken up. I could have fallen asleep again, but I wouldn't have known. Because the hysteria from the night before, it was still there. I still felt like I was going mad. I willed my mind to go blank, if only temporarily, pushing away all of the other things that I should have been thinking about.

Will shifted—the risings and falls of his chests changing to alert me that he was awake, though his eyes were still closed. Perhaps he was as confused by this as I was. I closed my eyes as well, afraid that he would open his own and find me staring at him.

His arm tightened around my stomach, squeezing me, so hard that I let out a disgruntled whimpering sound, and then a second later, he started to laugh. We were both playing our own game, apparently. I cracked my eyes open to find him grinning at me, his arm still around me though his grip had lessened.

"What are you doing?" I hissed.

"Waking you," he said.

"Why are you... cuddling me."

"*What*?" He released me and then sat up, staring down at me. "You were the one that started clawing for me in your sleep," he laughed nervously. "I only held you back because I thought something was wrong with you."

I scoffed. "What would be wrong with me? Believe it or not, I'm perfectly capable of sleeping without the arms of a man wrapped around me. I know you're probably feeling lonely out here and deprived of... that sort of company, but that doesn't mean you can seek it out from *me*. We'll be into a town soon enough, since you clearly cannot restrain yourself."

"Is that what you think?" He grinned. "I am not that despicable of a man that I need to seek out the pleasure of a random woman, Kara. Your joyous company is pleasure enough."

"Do you prefer men?" I blurted, though I was sure that wasn't true.

"No," he said. "I prefer women, I am just not obsessed with them like most are."

"Have you bedded a woman before?"

"Of course I have," he said quickly. "Gods, Kara. I'm twenty-three years old."

"I don't know," I defended. "I haven't ever really been able to ask anyone about this."

"What about Hiran?"

I shot him a sideways glance. "While Hiran is the only lover I've ever taken, the same could not be said about him. He's notorious for that sort of reputation with the ladies of Mortefine." He just watched me, remaining silent. "And I was not cuddling with you."

He chuckled softly. "Okay, we weren't cuddling. But I really was worried. You were shivering, and calling out strange things in your sleep."

"It happens," I said. "Next time, just... shake me till I wake."

He stood then and brushed the dirt from his body. I got up a moment later and did the same. Without the tent and any food or water, there wasn't much for us to carry, besides our weapons. So only a few short minutes later we were heading off again towards the coast.

The wind had picked up a lot from the day before, which Will assured me was due to our proximity to the sea, from the strong winds blowing off of it towards us. The air even felt less dry, and heavier in a way that I couldn't explain, because I had never experienced anything like it before.

A few hours later and we could see faint structures in the distance. Buildings. As we got even closer, I saw that none of them were built more than one story high. They weren't brick or stone buildings like in Mortefine, but they seemed to be made from The Wry itself, plastered together like clay. And the town had no wall surrounding it, no sort of defense against the sand serpents. Should they wish, the beasts could slither right in and launch an attack.

Saltrenea was completely silent as we entered, which it shouldn't have been being that it was the middle of the day. No guards stood watch. The town seemed to be completely out of the king's jurisdiction. Or perhaps the king didn't think that a pathetic, meek little town like that deserved his protection.

Some of the buildings were broken down, the roofs having collapsed in on themselves. Some never seemed to be finished being built, the glass missing from the windows, a door missing where there should have been one. I searched the sky for smoke rising from chimneys, but I found none, at least not until we walked further into town. The houses there were livelier, like people might have actually lived there. And in the window of one house, I glimpsed someone watching me. A child. They were an unusual child, as they were not eager to run through the streets and play, but a sad and sickly one. Through the dirt-covered glass I could see the pale bony structure of their face.

We continued further into town, the sea not yet visible from our current location, though we would make our way there eventually. We started to pass more people, none of them paying much attention to us at all. Everyone walked slow, like some deadly plague had wiped through the town and left them all that way, their minds in shambles. It was very strange, even Will thought so.

A man walked right in front of us, old and skinny, wearing nothing but rags. His feet were bare, and he nearly tripped as he walked past us. Will reached out, steadying the man. "Are you alright?" he asked him. The man only nodded, offering no thanks or any other words. "Do you know where we can find food and water?" Will asked. "We're weary from travel."

The man lifted a bony arm and pointed a finger towards a building in the distance. It certainly wasn't big enough to be a tavern, but hopefully there was somebody there that could help us. We thanked the man and then walked to the building, stopping outside to examine. The windows were dark, and it was hard to tell if anyone was inside. We walked in, finding a few tables spread about, the chairs resting atop them like they haven't had any guests in a very long time. And there was a frail looking woman seated behind the bar, her feet propped up, reading a book.

Her eyes shifted to us as we entered, and she set down the book, shooting us a smile that was obviously forced. "How can I help you?" she asked.

"We were hoping to have a meal," Will said.

She watched us carefully, taking in our clothes, Will's armor. "We don't often get visitors this far into the city," she explained. "Where did you sail from?" She poured two glasses of water from behind the bar, and then walked out to hand them to us. Then she set our three chairs at a table, gesturing for us to sit, claiming one of those seats for herself.

I wasted no time drinking my water, as did Will. The woman watched us as we did it, and then wisely went back for the pitcher of water, refilling our glasses and then leaving it on the table. Only when my throat no longer felt like it was on fire did I begin to talk.

"We've come from the south," I told the woman.

"We're just passing through," Will added. "Hoping to find passage to Kraxoth."

Her eyes widened in disbelief. "You... are from *south* of here? You couldn't have been traveling through The Wry."

"We came from Mortefine," I told her.

The woman's breathing quickened, and she might have started shaking a little. "That's impossible," she told us. "Unheard of."

"You never receive people traveling from Mortefine?" I asked.

"No," she said. "I mean, we do, but... usually it's a large group of armed men, not two—"

"There were more of us to start," Will explained. "But unfortunately, they are all dead now."

"How did you do it?" she asked. "How did the two of you make it all the way from Mortefine? That must have taken weeks. You weren't attacked by sand serpents?"

"We were," Will said rather coldly. "And we narrowly escaped with our lives."

"You must be famished," she said, jumping up out of her seat. "Let me get you something to eat. A captain arrived just this morning, actually. He sold me some salted beef, which I used to make stew. I'll get you each a bowl." Then she walked behind a closed door, no doubt where the kitchen was located. Will and I just sat there, staring at each other, drinking as much water as we could manage.

The woman returned a few minutes later, a bowl of stew in each hand. My mouth began to water as she set mine before me, and as the steam swirled up into my nose. I practically had to yank the spoon from her, and then I started eating. It was divine. The best thing I had ever tasted. Will seemed to think so as well, considering that he had eaten it so fast that he then started licking the bowl.

Once he was done, while I was still eating, he asked the woman, "Why is the town so empty?"

She eyed him carefully for a moment. "Oh," she said. "I guess you would have seen that, considering that you came from the south." She ran a hand over the side of her face, as if suddenly nervous. "Nobody lives in the outer part of town," she explained. "Not for years. It's too much of a risk for people to stay there, especially the children."

"From sand serpents?" I asked.

"I didn't think they would come this far north," Will added.

She gave us a sad dip of her head. "There used to be more of us, years ago. The town was growing so rapidly that we had to build more houses, and further out into The Wry, but the sand serpents would come, and they would take people. They still come, every now and then, but we know how to hide mostly, and they don't risk getting so close to the sea. I think they're afraid of it."

"How many people live here?" Will asked.

"Maybe... two hundred?" she told us. "It's hard to say. There used to be almost a thousand, but it was hard even then to get enough food sent here. We're still recovering from the attacks, but luckily there are still some children around."

"That's terrible," I said.

"You said there was a captain," Will asked, "that brought you the beef? By any chance, is he still here?"

"He might be," she said. "I can have my husband take you to the docks. They're not that long of a walk, but it's easy to get lost, even here."

"That would be nice, thank you," Will said.

The woman stood and walked through the door again, leaving us for a moment. Will and I turned to one another.

"We can't stay here," I said.

162

"No," he agreed. "We cannot." And then he added, "I'll go to the docks, and you stay here with the woman."

I nodded and then resumed eating my stew.

The woman returned with a man trailing her, skinny yet tall, the muscles missing on his body from where they ought to have been. There was nothing pleasant about the expression on his face, and he didn't greet us at all as he stalked through the front door and headed outside. Will followed after him, glancing back at me once before he left.

I wanted to go and get a look at the sea, but I supposed that I would soon enough, if we were to be sailing over it. It would be quite convenient if this captain was the one Will mentioned before. And if he was, hopefully that would mean we would be leaving as soon as possible.

The woman sat down next to me at the table. "You guys can stay here," she said. "For as long as you need. I know we don't have much to offer, but there is a spare bed, and we have enough food to feed you."

"We don't have any money," I told her.

There was something like pity in her eyes. "I wouldn't ask you to pay."

"That's very kind of you," I said.

"I can tell the two of you have been through a lot," she said. "It's good that you have each other."

"Yes," I agreed. "It is."

"Why did you leave Mortefine?" she asked, and then the look on my face probably told her she shouldn't have asked. "I know it's not my place, I just can't understand why you would travel all this way."

"My friend's life is at stake," I told her, which was all she needed to know. "I'm doing this to save her."

"Oh," she said, and then was silent for a moment. "Well, then I envy you for that. For being brave enough to do so."

We didn't talk much after that, mostly because I didn't want to. It got me thinking about Nola, which was never a good thing. I didn't need to be reminded of why I was here or what would happen should I fail in finding the blade.

163

Maybe thirty minutes later, the front door again opened and Will walked in, the woman's husband right behind. Actually, he more like barged in, like there was something urgent he needed to say.

"What happened?" I asked.

"Well," he said breathlessly. "I found the captain, but we need to hurry, because he's leaving in three hours."

"*Three hours*?"

"We won't be staying here, after all," he said to the woman. "Let me pay you for the food." He reached into a pocket of his cloak, pulling out two gold coins and handing them to the woman.

"Where did you get that?" I asked.

"The captain was generous," he told me. "I asked for a few coins in the king's name, though he made me promise to pay it back ten times over."

"We can't afford that," I told him, which I wasn't certain of, but I could guess enough about the salary of a soldier.

"The king will pay it back," he said. "Eventually."

"You thief," I said. "What lie did you have to tell him to get him to agree to this?" I lowered my voice to barely a whisper. "You better not have told him who I was."

Will laughed, waving a hand at me dismissively. "No, nothing like that. He likely wouldn't have even believed me even if I did."

"Did you steal it?" I asked, letting him see my frown.

"No," he said. "Would you relax already?"

The woman still had not taken the money, so Will grabbed her hand, slapping the coins into it. She only shook her head, reaching out to give them back to us. "You need it more than I do," she muttered, clearly having heard every part of our conversation. Will didn't take it, so I did instead, pocketing the money for my own use.

"Come on," Will said, bending down to where I was seated and grabbing me by the hand.

I stood, turning back to the woman and her husband. "Thank you," I told them. "For everything. I will not forget the kindness you have shown us."

The woman smiled and waved goodbye, and then we strode through the door, towards the docks where we would be sailing to Kraxoth in only three hours. I couldn't believe it.

Chapter 16

I wondered why Will was in such a rush, since we did have three hours left until we would be departing. But he wasn't leading me to the ship. No, he was instead taking me away from town, to the sea, further down the coast.

I let him lead the way, guiding us to where he seemingly already knew we were headed, just like he knew everything else about navigating. Though I could see nothing, not yet, I could hear the crashing of waves nearby and the shouting of sailors. The town must have been busier than I'd seen, yet only contained to the edges of the coast, in case a sand serpent came, and they needed to flee. It was smart, if anything.

There was a sort of dirt road that sat between the edge of the city and the sea, which we walked along, and on the side of us closer to the sea there were large sand dunes, towering high, blocking out any view of the waters beyond. There were no people this far out, as there were also warning signs planted in the sand, alerting people not to venture too far. But I didn't think anyone would willingly go out there, not unless it was necessary.

We walked for a while, Will assuring me that we would have time to make it back to the ship before it set sail. We kept mostly to ourselves, I think still in disbelief from how soon we would be leaving this land, and how soon until we would be free.

Will stopped in place where he had been walking in front of me and abruptly turned towards the sea. "This should do," he announced, bending down and running his fingers through the sand. Then he turned to me. "Are you ready?"

I shook my head. "I'll never be."

He laughed as he reached his hand out for me, an offer of his support as we walked over the sand. I graciously took it, squeezing his hand a little too hard, as if to tell him he would be punished if he let me fall. He stepped into the sand first, and I watched as his boots sank beneath it, some of it even pouring through the top of them. He walked backward, keeping an eye on me, making sure that I was okay.

The smile on my face lingered, filled with such excitement, eagerness, raw joy, and pure determination. And I didn't hide it from Will, I let him see just how much this meant to me.

He let go of my hand, only for a second, as he climbed to the top of the sand mound. It wasn't very tall, maybe a little taller than me, and he reached down for me, ready to haul me up. I thought about the cave, how it was me helping him up then, and now, he was the one helping me.

I stepped further into the sand. It wasn't hard and dusty like further into The Wry, but soft, almost liquid. My feet sank into it, my toes warming inside of my boots. Sand went everywhere, shooting out with every step. I laughed a little, even when I tripped, but Will was right there to catch me. He latched onto my hand, then pulled me up the rest of the way.

As soon as we were standing atop the sand dune, my knees buckled beneath me, and my body began to shake—not from fear, but from *awe*. The sight of it was unlike anything I had ever seen before. Like something out of a dream, though I don't think even my dreams would have been able to conjure something so splendid.

Black waves, as dark as obsidian, crept up to the shore before they slammed themselves down into the tan sand. And beyond those waves, going as far out as my eyes could see, the dark waters continued, eventually fading into nothing, the same as the desert ground in The Wry.

Will shot his hands out, holding me upright beneath my arms. "I've got you," he said. "I know, it's a lot."

I couldn't believe that just the sight of it alone was enough to make me fall to my knees. I felt like there had been a hole punched through my chest, or that maybe even my heart had been ripped out. I'd never seen such a thing, nor could I have ever imagined that it would be this splendid, this beautiful. I began to cry then, from the sheer beauty of what lie before me, but also from the realization that hurt more than any physical wound ever could

I could have experienced such things, if only I'd been given a different childhood. I could have lived in Orothoz and spent my days swimming in the Southern Bay. I could have lived anywhere else, even. Somewhere with lakes and rivers and streams, a land full of life and joy. But I wound up in the worst place of all, with the worst people. I was forced to live in the city of death, when the entire rest of the world was made of such life.

I wasn't overwhelmed or terrified by it, not like I should have been. At that moment, I felt more powerful than I ever had before. I felt brave. I felt... happy. Could life be such a way? Could I live somewhere else without having to fear the wrath of sand serpents, or without having to import my food from lands beyond? Could I live where it grew cold for half of the year and then warm the other? Could I live, even, deep in a forest where I would learn to fear nothing, not even the emptiness in my own life?

"What do you think?" Will asked, releasing me once I was steady.

"I think..." I started. "I think that you've ruined this for me. The world, I mean. How could it possibly get better than this?"

"It will," he said, smiling back at me.

I began to laugh then, at the same time that I cried. And these were the first tears that I had released in a while that did not come from a place of sadness, but instead a place of joy. Could this be happiness? Not in a way that I was satisfied with my life, and content with how it was going, but in a way that despite everything that I had going on, I could still learn to be happy during it. I wouldn't let my guilt over Nola's imprisonment keep me from living. She wouldn't want it to be that way, either. She would want me to be happy.

"I've never dreamed of anything like this," I said.

"It's even better up close," he said, grabbing my hand again and leading me nearer to the shore.

The air was different, what I now realized to be salt. A faint mist coated my face, even far off from the shore, growing stronger as we neared. A cool, comforting breeze blew the hair back from my face. I imagined that the waves would crash violently, scary, even, but this was almost subtle, as if the waves themselves were hands, reaching towards dry land, retreating and then coming back again and again. The reflection of the sun on the water was so bright, appearing almost white though the waters were black. I had to squint my eyes as we at last approached.

We started to walk down the shore in silence, further away from town. I kept quiet, silently observing, Will giving me the space that he probably realized I needed. I wanted to memorize every detail of this place—and then I would never allow myself to forget it.

White birds with grey wings squawked as they flew overhead. They were skinnier than chickens, and didn't seem like ones you could get much meat from. Obnoxious, is what they were. As the waves washed ashore, they left behind pale colored shells, some pink, some yellow, some even violet. A small white creature skidded past, and I retreated a step, terrified of how strange it looked. Will told me that it was called a *crab*. And even as I looked towards the sea, I could see things jumping in the water, fish.

I bent down to take off my shoes, just needing to *feel* the sand on my feet, in between my toes.

"What are you doing?" Will asked, curiosity lacing his voice.

"I feel like running," I said, rolling up my pants and bearing my pale legs to the sun. "I need to feel free."

He smiled, but made no further comment, not as he crouched down to remove his shoes as well. "Well, you'd better wait for me."

But I was already off—already lost in my own fantasy. It was harder to run through the sand than I expected, and the meal I had just consumed was sloshing around in my stomach, but I wouldn't let that stop me. For the first time, I wasn't running away from something. No, I was running towards the future—towards whatever possibilities were in store for me next. I had my whole life ahead of me, and this was only the beginning.

"Karalia!" Will yelled from behind me as he laughed, and for the first time it didn't feel weird to hear that name spoken—the name that had never belonged to me up until very recently. Perhaps it was something I could get used to.

I only stopped running when my chest began to burn, and my legs simply would not take me any farther. I slowed down, eventually stopping, and Will was already at my side, putting his hands on me. I yelped in excitement. We were both bent over with our hands on our knees, panting like dogs.

When he steadied himself again, he leaned towards me and said, "Damn, you're really fast."

"Am I?" I shot back, raising my brow. "I thought *you* were just really slow."

We laughed again, and then he plopped down into the sand, patting the spot beside him for me to sit as well. I joined him, nearly collapsing from exhaustion. He was silent for a while, which was okay with me. I watched as every wave neared us, never quite reaching us, and then retreated back to the sea. It wasn't as hot here, not with the sea breeze.

"Thank you for this," I said to him, breaking the silence. "I will cherish this memory forever."

"Will you?" he asked, though there was almost something sad in his voice.

"Yes," I said, and then again, the silence lingered between us. I watched him as he looked out to sea, and there was something there that he wasn't telling me, something bothering him. "What's on your mind?" I asked.

He turned to me, blinking away whatever I had just seen in his eyes. "Well, I was just thinking about the first time *I* went to the beach."

"Oh?"

He sighed. "The memory wasn't nearly as pleasant."

I didn't say anything, just waited for him to decide if he wanted to say more. Whatever this memory was, it must have been bad.

"I was young," he said. "Maybe… six or seven. My parents wanted to take a break—to take a trip as a family. You know I'm from the capital, so we headed to a house along the western coast. The five of us crammed into a carriage and rode for three days, only stopping at night for sleep. When we got there, I felt exactly as you do now. I was so amazed, so overwhelmed by the beauty of nature. The water there was as clear as a diamond, and it was safe enough to swim in. We had a fun couple of days."

The smile that had been beginning to form on his face quickly melted away. I saw the brightness leave his eyes, and the very sky itself seemed to dim, like the sun had gone behind a cloud. This time, I was the one reaching for his hand, though it was tense under my grip.

"I was supposed to be watching my younger sister while she swam in the water," he continued. "My parents and brother had gone off somewhere, I can't remember. She was only three, and didn't yet know how to swim, but I left her there because I wanted to go look at something further down the shore. I wandered off, far enough that I couldn't even see her anymore if I looked back, and I explored. I thought it was only for a few minutes, and I thought that she would be okay, but… When I came back, she was face-down in the sand, the oncoming waves crashing over her limp body."

My heart sank in my chest.

"She was dead," he told me. "She drowned, because I hadn't been watching her like I was supposed to. As soon as I

171

saw her, I ran. I pulled her body from the water. She was so cold, her lips dark, her face lifeless. I began to scream, and my parents and brother came running from the other direction. My mother screamed in terror, and pulled her from my arms, cradling her cold body. I tried to reach for her again. I thought… I thought I could still save her. But it was too late. My father dragged me away. He pulled on my wrist so hard that it snapped, and then he beat me with his own fists until I could no longer walk. My brother had to carry me back to the house, and they refused to call for a healer. It took me thirteen months to recover."

Tears fell from my eyes, against my own volition. I released Will's hand, only to press my own against my mouth, to keep from crying out. I didn't expect this. I didn't know. When he told me before, that he didn't have a good relationship with his family, I could never have thought it was because of something like this.

"My mother never looked at me the same again," he continued, "for killing her daughter. My brother tried to care for me, but he didn't want to have to take sides, so I never begged for his help. And my father…" His voice broke, and I could feel the pain in his words. "They have every reason to resent me. I deserved far worse for what I had done. And now, I spend as much time as I can away from then, to escape… the pain." He lowered his eyes to the ground, and I thought for a second that he might cry.

I guess that would explain why he became a soldier, why he went on this mission to rescue me. What happened to him… that was worse than my situation. I think that having no family would be better than having one that resented your very existence.

I reached a hand up to his cheek, turning his head so that his eyes faced me. Surely enough, a tear fell, and I wiped it away with my thumb. "Will," I said.

"I know what it's like not to have a family," he explained. "I understand, Kara."

Then we were hugging, and I was pressing my face into his chest.

"I'm so sorry," I said to him. "I didn't know. I'm sorry."

He shook his head, forcing a smile. "Why are you apologizing?" he said. "I didn't mean to… dump my trauma on you like this."

It was becoming an odd trend between us, I thought. How vulnerable we could be with each other. The strange sort of understanding that had come about after only having known each other for a few weeks. I was thankful for his honesty—that he thought he could confide in me. But the weight of that truth… it must have been tearing him apart from the inside. It was terrible.

The sun had begun to lower in the sky at some point, casting an orange glow over the seawater.

Will stood, wiping the sand from his pants, and then reached down for me. "We should go," he said, flashing only a glimpse of a smile. "We don't want to miss our boat."

Chapter 17

The sun had faded entirely by the time we reached the docks. I could hear the water, but I could no longer see it anymore, not with the moon hidden behind the clouds. The dock, made mostly of rotted wood, was illuminated with its own lantern, hanging at every corner, lighting the way so you wouldn't walk straight into the water. Most of the boats were smaller, run-down, even, but at the end of the dock was one very large ship, which I assumed would be the vessel to take us across the sea.

Since it was already night, I'm sure activity at the docks had slowed down immensely, but not on that ship. As we approached, I could see workers scrambling, hauling cargo on and off of the ship, moving things around, raising and lowering sails. Some were barking commands, others electing to remain quiet. I let Will walk in front of me, afraid that I would get in somebody's way.

I nervously glanced back towards the water, regretting it almost immediately. It looked even more terrifying now, like if I fell in, I would just keep falling and falling, on and on forever until I reached complete nothingness. It would be like one of my dreams of darkness, yet this time there would be nothing to pull me out.

A middle-aged man approached us, walking over the thin piece of wood off of the ship and joining us on the dock. He had a scruffy, unkempt grey beard, though his clothes looked finely made and were colorful, adorned with strange sorts of jewelry. He flashed us a smile, revealing a set of golden teeth.

"Hello again," the man said to Will, his voice deep and oddly authoritative. "This here your lady friend?"

I shot the man a glance, and not a pleasant one, but he only smiled when he saw my uneasy expression. He continued walking up to Will and then patted him on the back, like they were the best of friends and hadn't met just a few short hours ago.

"Yes she is," Will told the man.

He again turned to me, smiling, and then without asking, took my hand and placed a kiss atop it. His lips were dry, and I almost caught myself cringing when I realized that he was likely the man allowing us to stay on his ship. So instead, I flashed him a smile, one that I was accustomed to giving Hiran in public settings.

"My lady," he bowed at the waist. "My name is Captain Samuels, and it is an honor to have you aboard my vessel. I hope you will enjoy your time on *The Wandered*, as short as it will be."

My eyes flashed to the side of the ship, where those exact words were carved onto it.

Had Will told him who I was? That didn't seem particularly wise. But, I suppose I couldn't be mad about that it if it got us passage aboard the ship.

"How long, exactly, will the trip take?" I asked the captain.

"Less than a week," he told us. "Four or five days at most, depending on the wind."

I didn't reply to that, and Will must have noticed that I was uneasy, because he slid an arm around my back, tugging me close. I remained standing there like a statue.

"Let me escort you to your room," Captain Samuels said, and then he winked at Will. It made my blood boil, and the next thing I knew I was shoving out of Will's grip, leading the way onto the ship with him behind me.

My feet were unsteady as we walked over the wooden board which served as a ramp onto the ship. It seemed that it would snap at any second. And even though the dock was raised far from the sea, the deck of the ship was even higher. I had to climb up to it, like some large floating building. Men were still running around as we stepped onto the deck, and I had to walk carefully so as not to slip over the slick surface. I took in the sight of it, which some things I could recognize from paintings, but mostly I had no idea what anything was. The sails I knew were what propelled us, relying on the wind. The most strange thing was how it felt to walk, like my body was floating, rocking side to side, my knees uneasy.

The captain led us down a short set of stairs, below deck, to a dimly lit hallway that must have stretched the entire length of the ship. There were a few doors on either side, no way to tell them apart, but the captain stopped in front of one, unlocking it and then handing Will the key.

"I hope this room is to your liking," he told us as he opened the door. "I know it's not the most comfortable accommodations, but I'm sure it's better than what you've had recently." How much had Will told this man? "I'll give you some time to settle in before I have your dinner sent. We set sail within the hour."

"Thank you," I told the captain, then stepped into the room, Will behind me.

The captain left without another word, shutting the door behind himself.

The was an oil lamp lit in the corner, which allowed me to see the room clearly, finding that it was much larger than I expected. It wasn't *large* by any means, but it wasn't tiny. It was certainly more than we needed, after living in that shabby tent. And the captain was having *food* sent, wasn't that something? He was housing *and* feeding us.

"How did you pay for this?" I whirled on Will, slightly suspicious.

He shrugged. "The captain is a generous man."

"You told him who I was, didn't you," I said, the annoyance rising in my voice.

"No," he said. "I did not. Don't worry, I didn't have to say that, though I didn't think he would believe that you were

176

back from the dead, anyways. I only said that you were a very high-class lady from Mortefine, privy to the Lord Rendal, and that it was extremely important we sail to Kraxoth."

I frowned, then told Will bluntly, "I think it's obvious to the captain that I'm not a high-class lady."

"Well, it isn't technically a lie, Kara."

"I know, I know." I waved a dismissive hand at him. "I'm just trying not to think about that, okay?"

"Why?"

Why? That was a heavy question, though it was only one word. I didn't want to explain it to him, that I honestly couldn't care less that I was the Lady of Orothoz. That the only thing I *did* care about at the moment was freeing Nola. He must have already understood that.

"Never mind," Will said after a minute. "I'll leave you to settle in, okay? I'm going to speak with the captain, but I'll come get you before we set sail."

"Okay," I said, but he was already out of the room, shutting the door and clicking the lock behind himself.

Then I was standing there alone, in the dim room. There was a rather large bed set in the center, with two nightstands on either side. It was certainly big enough for the both of us, not that I was particularly swooning over that idea. Across from the bed was a small table with two chairs, and on the wall behind it, a small porthole. I could see nothing through it with how dark it was outside. There was a bookshelf in the far corner, and a cushioned chair beside it. The walls weren't really walls, but rather wooden panels, splintering and ready to break at any second. I did not think I would be particularly cozy staying in this room.

The only thing I had time to do was run my hands over the sheets of the bed, finding them soft and cool, before a knock sounded at the door. I walked over and opened it just a crack to peer through. There was a girl standing there, much younger than me, holding a tray of food in her hands. I opened the door wider, letting her in.

"Your food, miss," she said, standing uneasily as if she was nervous.

"Thank you," I said. "Can you set it here?" I pointed to the table, and she seemed to hesitate before walking further into the room and then setting it down. She was young, maybe ten or eleven, and she certainly did not want to be here. After she set the food down, she just stood there, waiting for me to say something.

"Are you alright?" I asked her.

She nodded.

"Are you a servant?" I asked next.

She shook her head.

"What is your... purpose on the ship?"

She looked at me with wide, pleading eyes. "Um—" she started. "Well, my grandfather is the captain, and my parents are dead, so I stay here with him, mostly, helping out around the ship, serving guests from time to time."

"That's nice," I said. "I would love to live on a ship." She didn't answer. "You know," I said. "My parents are dead, too."

"They are?" she asked, her eyes still not meeting mine.

"Yes," I told her. "And I never got the chance to know them. But you know what?" She looked up. "When you're older, everything will be okay. You can make your own way in life, decide where you want to go and who to go with. If you want to stay here on this ship, then you can do just that. If you want to sail across the Great Ocean to lands beyond, you can do that, too."

"Is that what you're doing?" she asked me, her eyes lightening just a bit.

"It sure is," I said, smiling. "I left my home and now I'm going on an adventure of my own." I couldn't tell her the truth, I just couldn't. "As bad as things may seem now, I promise it will get better."

She smiled then, for the first time.

"Why don't you stay to eat?" I asked her. She looked hesitant, but then I added, "I'll tell the captain myself that I asked you to stay, that way he can't get mad."

She nodded, and then we both sat at the table. I uncovered the tray of food, finding a simple meal of cheese and bread, as well as a pitcher of wine. I poured some for myself, but none for the girl. We each took half of the roll of bread, and half of the block of cheese.

"Thank you," the girl said. "You don't have to tell my grandfather. I mean, you can, but he wouldn't get mad. He's not that kind of man. He's good to me."

We ate and talked for half of an hour, the girl telling me about her life, which I was more than interested in hearing. She'd traveled far and wide, all around the continent, but now they primarily sail around the Alanah Sea, shipping supplies and food. She had even been to Orothoz, years ago, so she couldn't remember much about it though she said it was a beautiful place. I told her about living in Mortefine, about serpents and sandstorms. I didn't tell her about the seer, as I think that might have scared her too much, but all the other parts she enjoyed.

We were in the middle of talking when the door swung open, Will barging in. "Why is the door unlocked?" he asked, but then he saw the girl sitting there, the food between us, and he put two and two together. "You've met Sammi, I see," Will said. "Your grandfather is looking for you," he told the girl.

To that, Sammi stood from the chair, running past Will and out of the room. Will and I looked at one another and started to laugh a bit.

"Are you alright?" he asked me.

"I'm good," I said, though it didn't sound convincing. "I'll be fine." He studied my face and then walked further into the room. "I'm sorry we ate all the food," I told him.

"It's okay," he said. "I'll eat with the crew later." He stepped up directly before me at the table, extending a hand.

"We're about to set sail. I mean, you can come… if you want to watch."

I gave him a soft smile, taking his hand. "I would love to."

He led me down the hall, up the stairs, and back onto the deck, where men were again shouting commands and preparing for our departure. The captain was at the front of the ship, Sammi standing beside him.

Tan, weathered sails fell from tall wooden beams, catching in the wind and stiffening. Some men were pulling on long ropes, others were trying them up in various places. Large wheels cranked, bringing up the heavy metal anchors.

Along each side of the ship were long slender weapons of some sort, pointed out towards the water. Hopefully we would not be needing those for anything.

Shouts continued, commands, confirmations, men cheering as if they were excited for the voyage.

"We're all set," Captain Samuels yelled from the helm.

"Aye," the crew said in unison, even Sammy.

A moment later, the ship began to move. It was even more strange than before, drifting out and yet rocking side to side at the same time. My feet were on solid ground, but not really, not at all. The wind caught in the sails and pulled us out to sea, away from land, away from The Wry at last.

I ran over to the edge of the ship, leaning against the railing, looking out into the beyond. I could see nothing past the stars in the sky, and the lands behind us growing smaller in the distance. I stayed there and watched until all I could see was darkness surrounding the ship, and could feel Will at my side.

"Kraxoth, here we come," he whispered.

Chapter 18

Will walked me back to our room a short while later, and then left me alone again to presumably spend his time with the crew members. I couldn't blame him, not really. He'd been stuck in The Wry for so long, with only me around to entertain him, so any time he could spend with them was probably more preferable. It was fine by me if he chose to eat with them, and maybe even play cards and drink a little, but I didn't want to be shut inside of that room by myself for the duration of the trip. Or I should say, I couldn't bear to.

I asked for some more food to be brought, which little Sammi delivered again, this time a glass of rum with some dried fruit, as close to a desert as they could get on the ship, I suppose. She helped herself into the room after that, sprawling her body across the bed, already in her nightclothes. I didn't mind, her company was better than none at all.

She sat on her stomach, facing me, feet in the air behind her. "Is this really your first time on a ship?" she asked.

"Yes," I said, taking a sip of the rum. It was my third or fourth sip, I might have lost count, but the glass was much emptier than it had been initially. "It's my first time seeing anything beyond the dirt of The Wry."

She crinkled her nose. "That sounds boring."

"It was," I sighed, leaning back in my chair and propping my feet up on the table. "Tell me all you have seen," I said to her. "I mean, tell me how the world is so different from Mortefine."

"Well," she started, "I've never been to Mortefine, but I've heard that it's nothing more than a desert, surrounded by even more desert as far as the eye can see." I nodded, waiting, and then she continued. "Most other places have grass," she explained, "and trees. Green things, at least in summer. Summer is the warmest part of the year, but everything grows the most then, the trees spreading out wide, flowers growing in fields. And then there's fall, when the leaves change from green to orange and red, and then in winter they fall off entirely. Winter is when the snows come, too. You spend most time indoors then, as it's often too cold to do anything else. But it's not like that everywhere. The farther north you go, like in Frystal, the winters are far colder, and the summers are less warm. If you go south, to Orothoz, the winters and summers are warmer."

"What is snow like?" I asked her.

She gave me a funny look. "Well, it's not really all that pleasant. I hate the cold, so anytime there's snow, I'm already in a bad mood. It falls from the sky, similar to how rain does it, though I suppose you wouldn't understand that either. Sometimes it falls gracefully, melting as it touches the ground, and other times it is violent, piling up so high that you can't even open the door to your house. It's worse out here on sea, because there's nowhere for you to run to if there's a storm."

I took another sip of rum. "Have you ever been to the southern continent? Faulton. What about Meriton?"

She shook her head. "It's forbidden to sail there," she said, her voice having turned meek and small. "The king would punish us if we went there."

"Of course," I said. "I know that. I didn't mean to make you uncomfortable."

"It's okay," she said, and then a moment later she jumped out of bed and strode over to the bookshelf, looking through the titles before finally pulling one free. "Will you read to me?" she asked.

I looked at her wearily, never having done such a thing before for anyone. "I suppose I could," I told her. "Why not?"

She picked a story about some ancient adventure, a princess sent on a noble quest with her prince, to dangerous lands where they had to complete impossible tasks. It didn't take long for her to grow sleepy, and then I watched as she fell asleep a few minutes later. The sight of it was almost a relief, that there were still children in the world that could sleep peacefully through the night, that could trust someone they'd only just met, without living in fear that they could be attacked at any moment.

I debated pulling the covers over her and fluffing a pillow beneath her head, but a short while later a knock sounded at the door, and Captain Samuels had come to take her to her bedroom. He thanked me for keeping her company. For giving her a source of entertainment, at least for the next few days.

I bid them each goodnight, locked the door, and then climbed into bed myself. I hadn't realized how exhausted I was, for being awake most of the day, for sleeping uncomfortably these past weeks. If I could have sunk through the bed, all the way into the sea, I surely would have. I pulled the blankets up and over myself, curled onto my side, and closed my eyes.

The sound of a door closing awoke me, pulling me straight out of that momentary stupor. The sky was still dark, as far as I could see through the porthole, and if I were to guess it was somewhere near midnight. Will had been out for a while, and he was finally coming back, waking me up as he did.

He stumbled straight through that doorway, somehow still managing to lock the door as he entered. He had to put his hands on the walls to steady himself against the rocking of the ship, and it took a while, but he made it over to the bed, leaning down on it. As my back was turned to him, and my eyes closed, I couldn't see exactly what he was doing, but I could guess that after removing his shoes and whatever outer layers of clothes, he jumped onto the bed. Feet fully off the floor, flying through the air, practically landing on top of me from how small the bed was. He groaned, and I thought that if he hurt himself with that little maneuver, then he rightly deserved it.

I didn't say one word to him. I didn't pretend that I was asleep, nor did I reveal that I was awake. I was simply there, lying in bed next to a drunken idiot.

It took him a while to settle down—to get comfortable, I guess. He tossed and turned, and a few seconds before I would have turned around and started shouting at him, he finally settled. His head hit the pillow beside mine, his breaths loud and heavy beside my ear, caressing the bare skin of my neck. I could tell he was facing towards me, not away, as one of his knees dug into my lower back, and his toes brushed against mine. That should have been enough of a sign for me then, to shove him onto the floor, but I didn't.

And then without any warning, before I had the chance to object, one of his hands was on me, sliding over my hip, from my back and towards my stomach. He released a soft sighing noise as he pulled me towards him, pressing our bodies together, landing that hand over my stomach and resting it there. His other arm reached towards my face, brushing the hair from my cheek as if he were trying to get a better look at me. I didn't dare move or say anything. His leg wrapped over mine and there was no getting away then.

Despite the smell of booze reeking from him and the loud breathing, which had already turned to snoring, I felt rather comfortable there in his arms. Tomorrow, I knew he would deny it as cuddling, or pretend that it hadn't happened at all, but right now, I would allow myself one selfish moment. It didn't matter that it was him, I think I could have been in any man's arms, but it felt good to be held that way. So I found myself leaning further towards him, nestling our bodies together, savoring whatever momentary comfort this would bring me.

But, alas, he was not asleep yet. He must have hit the back of his elbow along the wall, or the nightstand, but a moment later he let out a string of violent curses. And then a moment after that he began to mumble some sort of tune, no doubt what he and the sailors had been up to. Singing. He was so close to me that I could hear every word, even though he was whispering.

He hadn't taken his weapons off before he climbed into bed, but they weren't on him at the moment, either, which meant that he must have taken them off sometime earlier. And if they weren't in this room, then where the hell were they? Fangmar was currently resting on the far table, my knife tucked into the back of my pants where it usually stayed. At least I would be able to protect us, should something happen.

He continued to sing, and I finally turned my head towards him. "Would you be quiet," I hissed. His eyes were closed like he was asleep, though his mouth was moving.

"Oh, sorry." He let out a laugh, hiccupping at the same time. Despite my current annoyance, it made me want to laugh, too. How did he even find his way back to the room this drunk?

"Goodnight, Karalia," he whispered into my ear, and then I felt something wet across my cheek, like he was trying to kiss it, though it ended up being more like a slobbery smooch. But his voice, something about it sounded sad, almost hopeless.

I wondered if him getting drunk had something to do with what he told me earlier, about his family. Or if it was just such a usual thing that he hadn't been able to do out in The Wry. I wondered if he thought telling me was a mistake—if he regretted it. If he thought even that I would judge him for it. He needed to know that I never would. Even though he was drunk, even if he wouldn't remember it, I still needed to tell him.

"Will," I said into the silence, the only other sound our hushed breathing. "I want to thank you," I continued, "for helping me. You don't have to be doing this. You could have taken me straight back to the capital, but you chose to help.

You're a good person, and I fear that it is a kindness I will never be able to repay."

He didn't answer for a moment, to which I thought he hadn't heard me. I don't know if I would have been more relieved or disappointed if he hadn't heard me. But then he said, "You're a good person, too."

And perhaps I would have believed him if he wasn't so drunk.

I awoke to the sun shining onto my face through the small porthole, finding me even when I was hidden away, always drawing me out of the darkness.

Will remained asleep beside me, but I sat up, stretched, and realized I hadn't gotten sleep that good in a long time. I felt refreshed, which could have perhaps been due to the fact that we were at sea, but I'd never felt such a way in my entire life.

I scooted out of bed, leaving Will beneath the covers, his hands still outstretched towards my side of the bed. If his behavior last night was any indication of how drunk he was, he was going to be sleeping in very late. So as I stood to replace my sword across my back, and tighten my boots on my feet, I was sure to make as much noise as possible, not that he heard it anyways. He was out cold.

I left the room, and though I debated slamming the door, I made sure to shut it lightly, afraid that I might wake anyone else still slumbering nearby. I walked down the hall, up the stairs, and onto the deck, less crowded than it had been yesterday, but men were already up and about, hard at work. None of them paid any attention to me, except for Sammi who ran right up to my side and wrapped her arms around my waist. I hugged her back and we walked to the edge of the ship.

The sea looked different in the morning. There was a faint layer of mist covering the surface, appearing more white instead of black, hiding the churning darkness beneath. There was no life out there besides us, not even a bird in the sky. But there were clouds in the sky, so many of them that the blue above it couldn't even be seen, such a strange sight compared to what I was used to.

Sammi dragged me to the front of the ship, where the waters churned below as the wind propelled us forward. She giggled and pointed into the water, like there was something so fascinating, though I could see nothing at all.

"What is it?" I asked, but she just continued to point and laugh.

I was about to ask her again when a male voice shouted nearby, "Sammi, get your ass over here and mop the deck. The captain said you were supposed to have it done before breakfast."

Her face turned red, and she smiled at me nervously. "Whoops."

"I'd be happy to help," I said to her, to the man.

And so Sammi and I each took a mop, along with a bucket of water smelling strongly of cleaning chemicals, and got to work. It was quite a tedious task, as the deck was rather large, but Sammi seemed to enjoy it. Watching her laugh and toss around the mop as if it were a weapon made me enjoy it as well. It seemed to take a while, though she said with my help it went by quickly, and then a voice called for breakfast.

I debated returning to the room then, but Sammi again grabbed onto my hand and led me to the set of stairs that led up instead of down, towards a large open room with a table in the center, and seated around it a few dozen sailors. The captain was seated at the head of the table, and when he spotted Sammi he motioned for her to come over, to which she dragged me along as well. She sat beside him, and then shoed away another man to make room for me, which I then had to apologize for, though the man said it was okay.

An older man walked in from an adjoining room, who must have been the cook, and set down stacks of wooden bowls on the table, then all of the sailors took one and passed the rest down. The spoons came next, metal clanking along

187

the table. And then the cook brought out a large steaming pot, and the smell of something delicious filled the air. He spooned a glob of something into everyone's bowl, including mine, and poured one for himself before joining us at the table.

"Eat," the cook commanded. And everyone did. They dug in, rather savagely, some of them electing to not use the spoons at all, but rather pour it straight into their mouths. It was porridge, seasoned with garlic and onion, and a lot of salt. Though it wasn't the most tasteful food, it was nice to have a hot meal for a change.

And it was even more nice to be invited to this table, to dine with these people that didn't even know me. Though Sammi could have been my sister, with her short golden hair, tied back in a bun the way a boy would wear it. Except her eyes were blue instead of green, and her face was plastered in freckles. She talked to me as she ate, like we too had been acquainted for more than just one day.

After the meal everyone cleared out, including Sammi who wandered off somewhere like she had forgotten I was even there. I smiled to myself as I exited and walked down below deck, back to our room. I would have to tell Will that he missed breakfast.

I reached our door, at least, what I thought was our door, and was about to open it when the next door over swung open instead. "What are you doing?" Will asked me as he walked out of that door. "Where were you?"

"I was bored," I shrugged. "I went for a walk, and then Sammi invited me to dine with the crew."

His eyes flashed to the door I was about to enter, and then back to me. "You shouldn't go around by yourself."

"Oh, please," I said. "I met a very nice sailor. He invited me to his room, I was actually just about to go in…"

His eyes were huge, like he actually believed me. I couldn't hold in my laughter as I took in his disgruntled expression.

"That's not funny," he said, and he wasn't laughing.

"Oh, relax," I said. "I know how to take care of myself." I pushed past him and strutted back into our room. "It's not my fault you drank too much last night and missed breakfast. Don't get all cranky with me."

"What—"

"You know, you woke me up last night when you stumbled in here like a drunken idiot," I snapped at him. "You could have at least invited me to drink instead of keeping me locked up in here." I sat on the bed, crossed my arms, waited as he walked back into the room and closed the door.

"I wasn't that drunk," he retorted.

I raised my brow, suggesting otherwise.

"The captain was practically shoving drinks in my face," he said. "I couldn't really refuse."

"Whatever," I waved a hand. "I forgive you."

And then Will started to laugh, as did I a moment later. He jumped back into bed, pulling me down as well, tickling my stomach so much that I had to kick him in the shin.

"What are we going to do for the next three days," he sighed.

"Get drunk?" I laughed.

He shook his head as he continued to smile, and we sprawled ourselves across the bed, taking in our long-deserved rest. I would be content to sleep for the next three days, though it would have been nice to at least have a bath. There wasn't one on the ship, except for maybe in the captain's quarters, so we had to use a sponge and a bucket of soapy water.

Will and I didn't leave the room for the rest of the day. We mostly slept, sometimes talked, or I sat in the chair and read while he did exercises on the floor next to the bed. Sammi brought us dinner later in the evening, and I invited her to stay, but she declined, like she wasn't comfortable with Will being there. But she made me promise that we could play together tomorrow.

We went to sleep early, bellies full of dinner, which consisted of boiled potatoes with onion. And of course, we drank some more rum, which didn't really matter in the end because we both fell asleep not long after.

Will kept to his side of the bed that night, which I didn't know if it was a relief or a disappointment, but I didn't have time to think about it, not as I fell asleep soon after.

The evening after that, after a long day spent with Sammi above deck, Will returned to the room bearing a tray of food, dinner, and a glass bottle of some amber colored liquid, which I could only hope was more rum. I didn't get out of bed as he approached.

"What's wrong?" he asked.

I sighed. "Does something always have to be wrong with me?"

"No," he said, setting down the food. "But something obviously is now. You look terrible." And to add to that, he cringed as he looked at me, at my messy hair and sweaty clothes.

"I'm sick," I said. "I simply cannot get out of bed."

"What's the matter?" he asked, walking over to me now with an expression of such worry on his face that it almost made me angry. He had no reason to be that concerned for me.

"Nothing," I snapped, maybe a bit too harshly.

He ignored me and placed his hand over my forehead, checking for signs of fever, but I knew there were none, because it was not that type of sickness.

"My stomach hurts," I explained. "I think I'm seasick." That wasn't exactly the truth. My cycle had come, as it was bound to at some point, but I think being at sea made the symptoms even worse. Usually I could handle what came my way, but now... I thought I was going to be sick.

"Oh." He walked back over to the table. "Well, then perhaps you should eat something. That might help."

"I don't think so," I said, sitting up in bed. "But I suppose I could try. What is it they've made tonight?" He hesitated for a moment, like he didn't want to tell me. "What is it?" I demanded.

"Fish stew."

The sound of my gag filled the entire room, and I had to squeeze a hand over my mouth to keep from retching. I knew there was no way I could eat that. Luckily, the stew came with some bread, so Will handed it to me along with his portion and I ate it even though it felt dry in my mouth.

"I need a drink," I said. "Right now." He reached for the pitcher of water. "Not that," I said. "I need a *drink*."

He shook his head a little, like he knew this would lead to nothing good, but he couldn't deny me. He handed me the entire bottle, and I plucked the cork from the top and tossed it to the floor, then took a long swig. I held my breath for a moment after, and then wiped the back of my hand across my mouth.

I knew the rum wouldn't make me feel better. In fact, it would probably make me even more sick. But it could take my mind off of things for a while, at least. I knew enough about going to Hiran's many gatherings over the years about the consequences that came with drinking, though I was usually smart when it came to that. Right now, I didn't want to be.

Will finished his food and then immediately left to take the empty bowls away, knowing that I couldn't bear to smell them. While he was gone, I might have taken a few more sips of the rum. When he returned and saw how empty the bottle had gotten, his eyes grew so wide I thought they would fall from his skull.

"Give me that," he said, yanking the bottle from my hands. "I need to get some before you drink it all." And then he took a long sip of his own. And another. And another. Until, I would say, we were on even ground.

My head had already started to feel lighter, my eyes heavy. I saw Will in the room though his figure was nothing more than a spinning blur. I was tired of lying in bed, so I crawled out and attempted to stand, though I just ended up on the floor on my knees, hair hanging over the front of my face like I was a rabid animal. Will grabbed me by my stomach to help me up, to which I yelped loudly from the pain that it caused. He threw me across the bed, and then I might have barked a few curses at him.

He didn't care. He just laughed as he slumped in the chair in the corner of the room, his legs spread in front of him like an arrogant man would do. I rolled my eyes at the sight of him.

"My stomach still hurts!" I pouted. "Do something."

"What do you want me to do?" he asked.

"I don't know!" I shouted back.

Then we both started laughing again.

He ran his hands over the bookcase, knocking some books from the shelves where they sprawled across the floor. "Oh my god!" Will said, scaring me a little from how abruptly he started speaking. "I have an idea. Why don't I read to you?" A smile tugged at his lips as he began sorting through the titles.

"How is that going to help me?" I asked.

"What do you feel like?" he asked. "An adventure story. A love story. A scary story."

"*Not* a scary story," I said quickly. "How about a poem?"

He continued looking through the books, squinting his eyes like he couldn't even make out the titles. Then he pulled one out, flipped through it, landing on a page about halfway through, and turned to me. "This will take your mind off of your stomachache. It gives you something to listen to, something else to think about."

I recognized the book he selected. It was a collection of children's poems, common in every household back in Mortefine, and in the entire country, I supposed. I rested my head back across the pillow and closed my eyes, waiting for him to start. Listening to him read to me was better than nothing.

"I used to love this one," he said, and then began:

Come alone to the Eastern Sea
For he who dwells is bound to be
Locked away in a land so bland
You would have thought it made of sand
Most would fear him, most would flee
But a lucky few have gotten free
And lived a life near that of grand
Unlike that of the beast turned man

I sat up in bed so quickly that I had to fight back the pain in my lower gut. My eyes were wide, full of shock. "That's a children's poem?" I asked. "It's so… morbid."

I'd heard the poem before, like most people had, but I'd never thought about what it meant. I never considered *who* the poem could be about. But hearing it now, it just seemed so obvious.

"What is it?" Will asked.

"The poem is about… Sazarr," I told him, gasping even as I admitted it out loud. "It has to be. The Eastern Sea of sand is The Wry. The beast turned man—Sazarr was turned into a serpent."

"What?" He laughed nervously, like he thought I was joking.

"It makes sense," I went on. "I always thought that the sand serpents in The Wry had something to do with Sazarr, that perhaps he placed them there, and this mostly confirms that. Do you think he dwells in The Wry? Or, perhaps, the Otherealm lies beneath it?"

Will lowered his brows. "It's just a poem, Kara."

He didn't believe me, and I was too drunk to explain it anyway. Perhaps my mind was not my own, and the poem only sounded odd because of that. Maybe it wasn't about Sazarr. But something did feel strange, and I couldn't quite explain it.

"Whatever," I said, shaking my head. "I'm going to bed. Don't wake me."

"Does your stomach feel better?" he asked.

"No." I turned onto my side, away from him so I didn't have to look at his face. I didn't feel like talking anymore. Not to him, or anybody.

I stayed that way for a while, unable to sleep despite how exhausted I felt. Perhaps I was waiting for Will to go to sleep, or just wondering what he was doing. I vaguely heard one of the chairs scrape across the floor and the chair creak from Will sitting down in it again. I lifted my head, though he couldn't see me, and found him leaning back, his feet propped up on the chair like he was planning to sleep there.

"What are you doing?" I said loudly across the room.

Will jumped, startled from hearing my voice. "Oh," he whispered. "Well, I figured you would want some space, since you're not feeling well. I don't want to crowd you, or anything."

"You don't have to do that," I said, lying back down again. "Just get into bed, I know it's not comfortable over there."

"Are you sure?" he asked, sounding almost sober though I knew there was no way he could be.

"*Come here*," I practically growled.

I heard him laugh softly, and then I heard quiet footsteps against the floor. I felt the bed shift as he put his weight upon it, and the heat of him as he neared me. There was still a good distance between us, but his presence then felt closer than ever, yet not crowded by any means.

"Still not feeling better?" he whispered, the nearness of his voice startling me. I shook my head, though I couldn't tell if he saw from how dark it was in the room. "I have an idea," he said, a rough edge in his voice that I'd never heard before. And I knew he was grinning—even with my back to him, I knew. "I think I can soothe you, enough to sleep."

"No," I said quickly.

"I promise, it will help," he said, scooting so that his chest was pressed against my back. Then he reached a hand and settled it on my hip, waiting for me to give my answer.

194

"No," I said again. "I can't."

"You can't what?" he asked, with a hint of amusement. Then he brushed the hair from my cheek and leaned in close, "All I'm offering is a simple belly rub."

His hand trailed lower, onto my stomach, brushing softly as if to show me what he would do if I said yes. And I could have said yes, I could have agreed to more than that, but I simply didn't want to. Obviously I craved the touch of another man, but I didn't want that from Will. I cherished his companionship, and nothing more. We were friends and allies in the most basic sense.

I grabbed onto his hand that was sprawled across my stomach, squeezing it harder than I probably should have, and then threw it back towards him, listening to it slap the wall. He yelped, muttering curses under his breath, but he didn't touch me again. I turned around to face him, unable to see his eyes, and reached to shove him hard in the chest, back to his side of the bed.

"Don't get any ideas, wise guy," I said to him.

"I apologize," he said, though the amusement was still in his voice. "I just find myself so... entranced by you. And I fear that you'll hate me forever once you learn the truth. I couldn't bear it if you hated me, Karalia."

"What are you talking about?" I asked, still turned onto my side so we were facing one another. The only part of our bodies that were touching was our knees, though the fabric of our pants kept the skin from touching directly.

"Nothing," he said. "Never mind. It's not important."

"Okay," I said, still not really believing him.

Our heads rested across the pillows, the blankets pulled over our bodies as we looked into each other's eyes. The moonlight illuminated Will's face every once in a while, giving me a brief glimpse of his tan skin and dark eyes.

"Karalia," he said quietly.

"Hmh?"

"I have to ask you something, and I want you to promise not to get angry." There was something almost... desperate in his voice. I began to dread what he was about to say.

"Okay," I told him.

"Can I kiss you?" he asked.

I almost laughed. "No."

"Why?"

"Because I don't want to be kissed," I told him simply. There was no other explanation I could offer than that.

He was quiet for a moment. Thinking. "By me, or by anybody?"

"Will, you know it's not like that." I almost caught myself reaching for him, squeezing his arm reassuringly, but I knew that wouldn't be wise. I kept my hands tucked into my chest, underneath the blankets.

"What is it like?" he asked.

I looked into his eyes as I spoke. "I can't allow myself to feel that way for anyone, not after what Hiran did to me. But if I did want someone to kiss me, it would be you."

"How romantic," he said, laughing a bit more. "A profession of your feelings and yet I cannot even kiss you in return."

"I'm sorry."

"Don't be."

"Hiran ruined me," I offered, hoping that this would make him understand. "I wouldn't say that I'd never take a lover again, but I couldn't do that with someone... when there are so many feelings involved."

"You don't have to explain yourself," he said, averting his eyes from me and shifting as if to turn away. That was the last thing I wanted, for him to be upset.

"Will," I said, and then he turned back. "I don't want you to think that I do not care about you. I do, and you have done more for me in these past weeks than anyone has before in my entire life. I'm grateful for that, and long after we have gone our separate ways I will continue to be."

He smiled sadly. "I hope that one day, after all of this, after you have finally found a way to move on, that you will find someone worthy of you."

"Are you not worthy of me?" I asked.

"No," he said. "I am not."

My face heated, and I was suddenly mortified. I knew he wasn't upset with me for turning down his advances, but rather that the reasoning for doing it wasn't what he'd hoped. I didn't know what to say to him to make him feel better, so I just hoped that in the morning I would know, once my mind was my own again.

"We should get some rest," Will said, pulling the blanket further over his body.

I didn't have the chance to respond, not as something very powerful jolted the entire ship, throwing me out of bed and sending Will tumbling on top of me. I screamed, unable to help it. He reached for me instantly, as if to assess for damage, but I brushed him off, telling him that I was fine. We both sat still for a second, listening, and then it happened again, sending us flying into the closed door.

Then loud and terrifying screams broke from somewhere above. The crew. Something was happening. But there was one other scream, heard above all others, and that scream did not belong to a human. No, that scream was purely monster, the voice of evil itself.

Chapter 19

Will was already standing and leaping across the room before I had the chance to think. He ran for his weapons, strapping his sword at his side, his dagger behind it. He put his boots on, so quickly that they were bound to be loose, which wasn't good if there really was danger up above. He didn't glance my way, not once, as he strode for the door and commanded, "Stay here." No hint of that vulnerable, drunken man I had just been in bed with. Only a soldier, poised to protect and defend the people on this ship. He slammed the door behind himself as he left, yet I could not hear his footsteps fade down the hall over the screaming up above.

"Stay here!" I said into the empty room. If there was trouble, I wanted to help in any way I could.

There was one thing, that had been in the back of my mind this entire time, ever since Will initially brought it up. That perhaps it could be a sea monster.

I stood upright, my mind sobering up in an instant, long having forgotten that strange occurrence with Will only minutes ago. Right now, there was something much more important to deal with.

I grabbed Fangmar from where it was discarded on the table, reaching behind me to fasten it across my back. I fastened my boots, taking more time than Will had to tie them tight over my feet.

When I reached for the door, another jar jolted the ship, from the other side this time, sending me stumbling back and falling onto the bed. I stood as fast as I could, even though my legs still felt unsteady as the ship righted itself. All this tumbling around, I was sure to have bruises, if not worse from whatever transpired.

I reached the door and swung it open, at the same time more screams sounded from above, as well as that piercing one that sent a chill down my spine. It had to be some sort of sea monster, because what else was out here? What else had the strength to move the entire ship? Very carefully, I weighed each of my options. If this creature took down the ship, which was a very good possibility, I could either run, or I could fight. Considering that I do not know how to swim, I could take my chances trying not to drown after the ship has been destroyed, or I could try and fend off the monster now before it has the chance to do that. Which was what I assumed Will was currently up to. What I knew I was *not* going to do was stay locked inside of the room like some helpless child.

As I walked through the door, I was instantly sprayed in the face with sea water, from an opening just above that hadn't been there before. The moonlight shone through, and I could see the mass of damage to the ship. Pieces of splintered wood had been blasted everywhere, planks ripped apart, protruding where they ought not to be.

I looked down the hall, towards the stairs, and I saw a man running towards me, blood covering him from head to toe. As he reached me, he grabbed onto my shoulders, shaking me. "Run," he breathed. "Run, or you'll die." He started screaming. "We have to flee."

I pulled out of his grip, and he continued on into a room further down the hall. I ran towards the stairs, was almost to them when my feet skidded to a halt. Where the floor had once been, there was now only a large gaping hole, blocking me from the stairs. Seawater poured up from it, though it wasn't bad enough to sink the ship. If I hadn't seen it, I would have fallen right through, down into the sea below.

I reached for the thin wooden railing along the wall, still intact, hoping that it would support my weight as I held onto it and hauled myself over the hole. I practically dragged myself onto the stairs. And once I was on solid floor again, I broke into a sprint, taking the stairs up two at a time. The screams grew louder as I ascended, and louder still as I made it to the deck above.

People were running, in every direction possible, yet I still could not see from what. There was blood everywhere, so much blood, covering the deck, turning everything red. And there were even... bodies. They had been mutilated—teeth marks in their torsos, decapitated heads. I felt sick at the sight of it. And it all seemed so familiar, too familiar. Because there were beasts in The Wry that could do something similar, that did not attack us for sustenance, but rather to obliterate.

Though I couldn't see the monster, I pulled Fangmar free, holding it up just in case. I couldn't see Will, either. He wasn't at the front of the ship.

There were men at the sides of the ship, loading those massive weapons with cannonballs. But what were they aiming at? They didn't get a chance to set them off, not as out of nowhere, something struck them. Their bodies were pulled straight overboard by something, down into the water below, their screams echoing until they sank beneath the surface.

I caught of glimpse of what had done it, though I couldn't see that clearly. There were dark scales, with a bluish tint, as if this thing could blend right in with the water. It dipped beneath the surface, before lunging yet again, catching another man with its teeth. It continued to screech, but also hiss, and I realized then that it must have been some sort of serpent, adapted to live beneath the sea. Where nose slits would have been was only smooth skin, but across its scaled neck, there were slits down the sides. Gills.

I kept my sword gripped in my hands as I ran to the edge of the ship, to look into the water below and search for the beast. I saw something launch itself beneath the ship, reflecting vaguely from the moonlight, and then I heard screaming from the other side. I looked over, and sure enough, the sea serpent had launched itself from the water to pull another man overboard. It grabbed him by the head, ripping it from his body and discarding it in the water.

But then something strange happened. The serpent almost seemed to *look* at me. Its body was sprawled over the edge of the ship, barely holding on, and I could see it more clearly now. Like the sand serpents, it had large horns protruding from the top of its head, glowing slitted eyes, and a large mouth full of very sharp teeth. But where sand serpent's bodies are smooth past its head, this was not. It had a large ridged structure running down the expanse of its body, almost like a large fin, to help it propel itself through the water.

It watched me as I watched it, eyeing me carefully as if I would be its next target. I wouldn't let it get that close for something like that to happen, not without a fight. Unless, this beast, too, did not mean to attack me. But this was certainly no sand serpent, so I couldn't be sure.

A crew member ran across the deck to where the beast rested, a hatchet raised in his hands. But the serpent twisted itself and lunged back into the water, tail slashing in its wake, nearly knocking that man into the water as well.

I needed to find Will. I turned away from the front of the ship and instead headed towards the back. He had to be there, if he hadn't already been taken. I made my way down the narrow walkway, the handrail having been destroyed, leaving nothing but open air to the side, that I could fall through at any moment. Crew members ran past me, shouting to get inside, but I ignored them.

And that's when I saw little Sammi. My heart ached from just knowing that she was out here, witnessing such bloodshed. She had her back pressed towards the inner wall of the boat, facing the water, eyes full of terror. I could tell she was crying from the way the moon reflected off of the trails running down her cheeks.

I yelled her name, and it must have startled her because she let out a loud yelp. But she needed to be quiet—she didn't want to risk alerting the beast of her presence.

I continued running towards her, closing the distance between us, and she watched on in horror, like she knew exactly what was about to happen. My sword was in my right hand, pointed towards the sea, and my left hand was reaching for her, almost having her in my grasp—

The serpent lunged from the water, straight towards her. I yelled for her to duck, but she couldn't hear me, not over her own screaming. The serpent's mouth was wide open as it approached, a second away from devouring her. But I was already there. I did the only thing I could think to do, and shoved Sammi to the side. She went flying, but the serpent's mouth instead crashed hard into the wood. It attempted to recoil, but I was still there, weapon in hand. I drew my sword back and brought it down upon the serpent's neck, as hard as I could.

The serpent let out a pained shriek and dropped back into the water. I had barely harmed the thing. I looked over the edge of the ship to see if it had swum off, but at the same moment it again lunged from the water, not for me, but for Sammi who was a few feet away, dangerously close to the edge of the ship because I had shoved her there.

"No," I said, though the word wasn't heard by a soul.

The serpent's mouth closed around Sammi's arm, but her other arm was wrapped around a nearby railing, the only thing keeping her from being pulled into the water. My feet moved. I couldn't think of anything else to do, so I again struck the serpent with my sword, this time across the top of its head. It turned a little, attempting to impale me with one of its horns, but I was quick, I dodged it just in time. It released Sammi's arm, but hadn't yet retreated into the water, so I planned to attack some more, until this bastard left us alone for good. It must have sensed what I was doing, because a moment later it was throwing its head back and then I heard its body splash into the water.

I would have again looked over the edge, to see if it was there, but the sound of Sammi crying overtook every other sense. She was clutching her arm to her chest, kneeling on the deck, blood running down her body. I could see the wounds— teeth marks across her upper arm. It was by no means a pleasant sight, but she could survive a wound like that. She could. So I slid one hand around her back, the other under her knees, and carried her over to a cluster of barrels, setting her down behind them.

"I need you to say here," I said to her, turning back over my shoulder to make sure the serpent wasn't approaching.

"Don't leave me," she cried. "Don't go."

I ran a hand across her cheek, wiping the tears away. "Sammi," I said, using a voice that was both soft and reassuring, no hint of fear in it at all. I would fake such a voice, if only to keep her calm. "I need you to hide here, so the serpent doesn't see you and come back. I'm going to fight it off. We're going to make it go away. And once that's done, I promise I'll come back for you. Then we'll get your arm all better, okay?"

Though her face was still filled with terror, she gave me a shallow nod. "Okay," she whispered, her lip trembling simultaneously.

And then I bent down and placed a kiss on the top of her head. It was both a promise and a goodbye, for whatever was about to happen. I set her down gently, even moving the barrels around a bit to make sure she could not be seen at all, and then I headed off. I ignored the spray of blood across the deck. Her blood.

I ran again, as fast as I could, towards the back of the ship. I couldn't see anybody else around, and I hoped desperately that they weren't all dead. The screaming had mostly stopped, but there were still splashes in the water nearby.

My feet halted in place as I at last reached the back of the ship. I couldn't see anyone at first, but then I saw him. Will. Leaning over the back of the ship, peering into the waters below, his weapon not even drawn. Was he trying to get himself killed? He was completely alone, standing there like an idiot, like he was using himself as bait.

I opened my mouth to shout for him, but the sound died in my throat, because I heard a splash of water and then saw Will stumbling back a few feet. The serpent came straight for him, and he quickly stepped out of the way, drawing his sword and aiming it at the serpent in a matter of seconds. He looked at the other wounds across the serpent's body, likely wondering who had done that, and then he added to the mess, cutting the beast over the side of its face, just beneath its eye.

There was so much open deck at the back of the ship that the serpent had managed to bring its entire body aboard, slithering up into a tight coil, only using its neck and head to attack. Neither of them knew I was there, which meant that I might be able to sneak up, attack the serpent as well. But Will was holding up surprisingly well, dodging the beast's attacks, getting in a few blows of his own.

But then something odd happened. The serpent struck for Will's hand, as if to remove the weapon from it, and succeeded. His sword clattered to the ground, sliding away as the ship rocked from side to side. Will walked back a few more feet, out of the immediate vicinity of the serpent. And then he began to rub his hands together, in a way one would do if they were cold. I had no idea what he was doing, but the serpent must have, because a moment later it had uncoiled its body and was *retreating* back towards the water.

It was too slow. It didn't get away in time to miss the thick stream of flames that shot out and flew straight towards its body. I clamped a hand over my mouth as I saw what was happening. Brightness flooded my vision, but not enough to keep me from seeing where those flames were coming from. *Who* they were coming from. The flames were released from Will, shooting straight out of his upraised hand.

Somehow, Will had the ability. He had the power of fire. Magic. It was unbelievable, yet here he was, saving us.

A screech of pain bellowed from the serpent, its open mouth reaching for Will, but then he aimed that flame right into it. He lifted his other hand, flames shooting from it as well, and I could see now that the serpent's skin had begun to burn, to melt away. And then I could smell it.

The serpent's head slumped to the deck, but Will continued to shoot those flames at it, until its body fell from the back of the ship and splashed into the sea. The ship steadied itself, as if an immense weight had been lifted. Will's hands extinguished, steam rising from them in the wake, and he kept them away from his body as if afraid to burn himself.

He killed the serpent. He *burnt* it, with whatever ability he possessed. It was silent then except for my own heavy breathing, and I watched as Will fell onto his knees, head bowed, like doing that had taken everything from him. I should have run to him, I should have seen if he was okay, but nothing about this was okay, because Will had lied to me, about a lot, apparently.

I moved quickly, hiding myself around the corner of the walkway in case he decided to turn his head around, but he didn't. I stood and started to run, back to where I had left Sammi, finding her still crouched there, alright except for her injured arm. Her hands were covering her ears, her eyes shut tight. I scooped her into my arms, and she didn't try to fight me, not at all as I ran straight for the captain's quarters.

He wasn't there, but then again, I hadn't expected him to be, so we sat there and waited until he returned. The room wasn't much larger than the one I was staying in, but there was a large bed on one side of the room, and a smaller one on the other, where I assumed Sammi stayed. I set her on the bed, holding her hand tightly as she continued to cry.

The door burst open, and the captain ran in, completely out of breath, his own body covered in blood. "Sammi!" he yelled, pausing when he saw the two of us. "Oh, gods," he called. "Sammi. What happened?" At the sight of the blood covering her, and the wound on her arm, he fell to his knees, tears filling his eyes.

"She's okay," I told the captain. "It bit her arm, but she'll survive it. She just needs some stitches and then she'll be okay."

He nearly crawled towards us, taking her from my arms, cradling her in his own. He examined the wound, his expression softening only a bit when he realized that I was right. She would be okay.

He didn't look at me as he spoke. "I assume that you have something to do with her being safe, and I thank you for that, lady. Half of my crew is gone, but the ship is mostly intact. You should go get some rest; we'll discuss more tomorrow."

I stood, nodding, not really wanting to say anything else. Half of the crew was killed. What did that mean for the rest of us? Would we make it to Kraxoth? With the ship in one piece, we could survive at least a while longer, and wait for someone to come find us. The serpent certainly would not be coming back, not after Will turned it to ash.

Will. I didn't want to think about him right now. I didn't want to even look at him, but I knew I would need to. When I left the captain's quarters, he was standing right outside, like he had been waiting for me. I met his burning eyes, let him see the pain in my own, and he returned that same exact pain. He extended a hand for me, apparently not wanting to talk, either, but I refused it, stepping past him and walking back towards the stairs, down them, and then into our room.

I waited for him to approach, and then slammed the door shut right in his face, locked it, and then climbed into bed.

Chapter 20

Will had the key, of course. He unlocked the door a minute later and walked right in, though I knew I would do my best to ignore him. I didn't know what to feel or even what to think. He lied to me.

I had the covers pulled all the way up to my neck, my eyes shut tight, though he had to know I wasn't sleeping. How could I sleep after what had happened? Whatever I just witnessed, it felt like one crazy dream, and I don't mean the part about the sea serpent. Although that was probably the most terrifying thing I had ever experienced. The beast had to be twice the size of the sand serpent we encountered, if not bigger. It killed so many people—so many of the captain's crew.

I recalled something then, that I had hardly noticed before as I carried Sammi to the captain's quarters. There was a man, covered in blood, his legs torn straight off beneath the knees. He was screaming at me for help, and I just ran right past him. I left him there, and perhaps maybe now he was dead. What could I have done, anyway? He likely would have bled out whether I stopped for him or not.

The ship was alright, as the captain had claimed. Since he was still alive, I thought that it gave us a pretty good chance of making it to Kraxoth. I might have seen him above deck, fighting alongside his men, but again, my memories of everything were a little foggy. He certainly seemed to have put up a fight when he showed up looking for Sammi, more blood covering him than me and her combined.

Will stepped into the room, his breathing heavy. I wondered how much of a toll that took on him, to use his powers—and how long it would take him to recover. I listened to the clink of metal as he removed his sword belt and set it on the table, then a heavy thud as he removed his boots. His footsteps neared the bed, and then he hesitated.

"Are you alright?" he asked me, barely more than a whisper.

"No," I said.

"What happened to you?"

I debated keeping my mouth shut, and seeing if he would leave it alone, and then I debated confronting him about everything, but that conversation could wait, and right now I just needed to rest. "I went looking for you," I admitted. "I found Sammi first, and the beast had her arm in its mouth. I tried to fight it off, enough for it to let go of Sammi, and then it fled. Then I picked her up and ran to the captain's quarters."

Will would never pick up on the lie. He hadn't seen where I really was, or what I saw. "I'm sorry," he said, sitting on the edge of the bed right beside my legs. He rested a hand on me through the blanket, like he just needed to feel that I was there.

"What happened to you?" I asked next, though I didn't expect the truth.

"It's gone." He leaned in towards me. "We're safe now." He brushed his hand over my shoulder, squeezed softly.

I wouldn't ask more questions, not tonight. I was too angry and confused to think of anything else to say. I didn't have the energy to pretend like everything was fine. "I want to sleep alone," I said to Will, and his hand vanished from my arm immediately. He sat back up, scooting further away from me.

"Okay," he responded, and it didn't sound angry or unpleased. It sounded like he understood. "Get some rest, Kara." I could sense him questioning himself as he stood from the bed and walked back towards the door. He didn't say anything else as he exited the room.

Our words hung in the air for a long while. As betrayed as I felt at the moment, I didn't want to hurt Will. I just wanted him to be honest with me—to tell me why he lied. I would need answers, soon, but more importantly, right now I just needed space.

I had already known the truth. I knew since I saw him there, shooting flames out of his hands, fighting off the serpent, like it was the easiest task ever. I hadn't allowed the thought to enter my mind, not until I was alone in the room, where I could react to it by myself.

Will had magic, or some other sort of ability. He had *fire* magic. And there was only one reasonable explanation for why someone would have that ability—because they were descended from Drazen.

Will was *Dragon Blooded.*

And while him being *Dragon Blooded* was a shock all on its own, it also confirmed something else. The only remaining descendants of Drazen are the Drazos family. The ruling family of Vatragon. Will is young, twenty-three years old to be exact. He has said before that he has an older brother. King Daemien has two sons—Prince Daenaron, and… the other one. What was his name?

Shit.

I couldn't believe it. Was I that foolish not to have realized the truth? I was so angry at myself for being so sheltered, so unknowledgeable about the basic gods damned facts of my country.

Will was really Prince William Drazos, second in line to the throne, Prince of Vatragon. I was traveling with a *prince*, not a soldier. Not even close to that. I had shared a bed with a prince, I had cuddled with a prince, I had gotten drunk with him, let him run his hands over me.

My breathing began to quicken as I lay there in the dark room, listening to the waves as they collided with the side of the ship. Why did he lie to me? Why did he let me think that he was nobody? Lying about his power was more understandable, as most people would run away with their tail between their legs if they witnessed that. I didn't think anybody knew that truth about him. But why would he lie about his identity? All the trust that had been built between us faded very quickly.

I dreamt of darkness that night. A terrible, consuming darkness. It was alright, nothing I couldn't handle, but I had to wonder if what happened had something to do with the sudden reappearance. I had to wonder if it was because of the betrayal I felt from Will. Before, I had been mostly content, but now, there was nobody in my life that I could trust, except for Nola, but that didn't matter because she was locked away back in Mortefine.

It was likely the lingering fear and rush of adrenaline from the attack, causing my mind to wander all over the place as I slept. It was a wonder that I managed to sleep at all, after everything I'd been through. Part of me wanted to stay awake, just to make sure that everyone was okay, that Sammi was fine, but another part of me was too exhausted to even care about those things.

Like usual, this darkness consumed my being, taking away who I was and making me into something new, something temporary. It pulled me from the surface, from reality, from that bed on *The Wandered* in the Alanah Sea, deep down into nothingness. Mist swirled around my presence as I floated around in the unknown, and I tried to reach for it, but I simply did not have arms to do so. And it was cold, at least, I imagined it to be. I had no body that could have been affected by such things, but in my soul, I could feel a sheet of ice blanketing everything.

I seemed to be headed towards something, not on flat ground, but rather in a plain of constant space, with no end and no beginning. I was rising from somewhere far below, though there was no way to know what below truly was, or if there was a top to reach. And then I glimpsed movement, a sea of darkness that reflected back to me the dim beams of moonlight. I recognized the sea first, and then I saw what was in it—the massive scaled beast, lurking beneath the surface. It was the sea monster that had attacked the ship, rising from the depths of the sea, shooting towards the surface. It was above me, somehow, so I must have been below. It launched itself at something far away, a faint round shape, what must have been the ship.

I continued to ascend through the space that was the sea and yet so different. I didn't need to breathe here. I didn't need to do anything except watch. I stopped finally when I had an eye-level view of the attack. The serpent tore at the ship, pulling off pieces or wood and bodies at the same time, discarding them into the water and then going in for more. It shrieked, loud and painful, retreating back into the water where blood had started to pour from its neck, turning the water red. That must have been what I had done to it.

I moved closer, trying my hardest to get a look, and then I saw. It was me, standing there, sword in hand, fighting off the beast as it again launched itself at me and Sammi, taking her arm into its mouth. The beast could have easily pulled her from the boat, or torn that arm off, but for some reason it didn't. The serpent again retreated, and I watched as it swam beneath the water towards the back of the ship. I watched myself run, my golden hair shining in the moonlight.

This was starting to feel less and less like a dream, and more like... I was reliving the events, only I was not myself this time. Had someone really been out in the water, watching us? Or was my mind creating this all on its own? It was horrific to remember what had happened when all I wanted to do was erase the memories.

My past-self halted when she reached the back of the ship and spotted Will. He was looking over the edge of the ship, into the water, and I could have sworn that he looked straight at me. But his attention snapped away when the serpent emerged from the water and climbed onto the ship. They fought, Will trying hard to fend off the monster, preparing to unleash his flame.

But then something strange happened—something that hadn't happened before. The body that was once Will transformed, into something entirely inhuman. Massive wings sprawled from his back, his hands and feet extended, sharp claws growing from them. His neck lengthened, revealing a massive head filled with rows of sharp teeth. And then he flapped his wings, launching himself into the night sky.

What the hell kind of dream *was* this? I hardly even knew what a dragon looked like, so there's no way my mind would have been able to conjure such an image. But this felt so real—so believable.

The dragon opened its mouth and then flame erupted, consuming not just the serpent, but the entire ship as well. People screamed as their flesh melted from their bones. Some jumped into the water in an attempt to flee. Some crouched down to the ground as if that would protect them. And the serpent, it was certainly dead this time. First it melted into a pile of gore and then it turned to ash, blowing away in the wind.

The beast that remained there, the dragon, its eyes shot right towards me, locking on where I was crouching in the water. I wanted to see what would happen next—to find out what this all meant, but something pulled me away.

Darkness again swarmed my vision, and I remained that way for a while. What I could only guess was until the sun arose and pulled me from the dream. Whatever my suspicions were before, about who Will was, this only seemed to confirm that they were true.

I was still alone the next morning, though a part of me wished that it were otherwise. I knew it was selfish to think such a thing, especially after practically commanding Will to leave, though he should have been the one giving *me* commands, being a prince and all that. But on nights that I dream of darkness, and especially when it's as terrifying as it was last night, I long for the companionship of someone else, to remind me that I haven't been taken away entirely. Usually, it would be Nola that I sought out, because she mostly knew what I was going through, though she didn't understand it. Not even I understood.

But now, Will remained elsewhere, and I thought that perhaps I should seek him out, and apologize for what I had done last night, but how could I apologize knowing that there were still secrets between us? Maybe I would give him the chance to speak the truth, to admit it to at least me if nobody else.

I could see the light of day through the small porthole, and the waves sloshing against the side of the ship. Last night, I thought for sure that the ship was going down, and me with it. It was amazing that we had survived, and though I knew who to thank for that, the rest of the crew did not. What would Will tell them about what happened? I guess I would find out soon enough.

I sat up in bed and stretched my arms wide, nearly hitting the roof of our small cabin. My clothes were still damp from the night before, and not just with seawater. I looked back down at the bed, finding smears of blood clinging to the sheets. When I finally managed to stand out of bed, I dressed and readied myself for the day, taking one deep breath before I opened the door and walked out—

I tripped on something blocking the doorway. *Someone.* Because sure enough, Will was sitting there, his back resting against the nearby wall, his feet spread out, blocking the walkway. My foot hooked under his legs, which I then fell on top of, and I cursed more viciously than I'm sure even those other sailors were accustomed to. Will was awake and lunging for me in an instant, his hands on me, making sure that I was alright.

"What in the bloody hell are you doing out here?" I hissed, and then asked, "You weren't out here all night?" But judging from his current state, I already knew that he was. He didn't answer those questions, he just grabbed me by the arms and helped me stand, pulling the two of us back into the room.

213

I wasn't going to tell him to leave this time, but I could see it on his face that he thought I might.

But his eyes are what really got me. As they locked with mine, my breath caught at the sight of them. They were no longer their usual light brown color, but now slightly orange. A shade of fire. I tried to hide my surprise but I'm sure he saw it all the same.

"What is it?" he asked me.

"Your eyes," I explained. "They look strange." And then he turned away from me quickly, realizing his mistake. I waited for him to offer some sort of explanation, but he didn't, so I figured I would just continue to play dumb. "They're just a little bloodshot. I'm sure it's the exhaustion from last night."

He nodded, as if to agree with me, though he still wasn't meeting my eyes. "There was nowhere else to go," he whispered, and I realized that he was answering my question from before. "Every other bed is filled with the injured. They told me not to offer ours up because a lady was sleeping in it. I went and helped as much as I could, and then I came back to sleep."

His words took a moment to register. Yet again, I had been a selfish idiot. There were people—injured people—that could have used our bed, that probably needed the space, and there I was sleeping soundly in it at night, while Will was up above helping as any good prince would. Will must have read what was on my face.

"Don't beat yourself up over that," he said. "Nobody blames you for staying in here. We all went through the same thing, and now we'll get over it together. The captain is already indebted to you for saving his granddaughter."

"Is she alright?" I asked quickly, having forgotten about Sammi.

"She's fine," he said. "They gave her some stitches, but she's recovering now."

I nodded. "That's good."

I could see the pain on Will's face—the exhaustion and weariness. But I would not allow myself to feel sorry for him. He was still lying to me, and I would confront him about it soon.

"Are we going to talk about what happened?" I asked.

He didn't understand that I meant between just the two of us, because he answered, "The captain wants us all to have a meeting at midday, to talk about the attack and plan for what comes next. We've been anchored since last night so the trip should take at least a day longer now."

"Will," I said, and his attention focused in on me. "That's good and all, but I'm asking *you*. What happened with you, and are you alright? You look like you've just fought in a war." And it was true, he was covered with blood and bruises, dark circles under his eyes like he hadn't slept in days.

"I'm fine," he said. It was the only explanation he would offer. I hid my annoyance and the fact that I could see right through his lies.

At midday, we went above deck for this meeting with the captain. The damage to the ship was much more visible in daylight. The damage to the hallway was temporarily repaired—the hole in the floor being loosely covered with planks, enough to make a narrow walkway to reach the stairs.

Above deck, I had to wonder how we had survived at all. There were men already at work, getting the sails back into place, re-tying ropes that had come loose, hammering and nailing all around. I told myself that after the meeting I would offer my assistance with repairs. The captain was yet to be seen, likely still in his quarters with Sammi.

I listened to the sailors' quiet conversations as we passed. They, too, were wondering why they were alive. They questioned what had happened, where the beast had gone, and why it left them alone eventually. So, nobody had seen what really happened except for me.

And as the noon sun was directly overhead, Captain Samuels limped over from across the ship. He looked worse than he had last night, even though he had cleaned up a bit, like he had been up the entire night with Sammi. She wasn't with him, though I hadn't expected her to be. She needed rest. His expression was grave, his face solemn. The crew members lined up, pausing whatever work they had been doing and gathering around the captain.

"I'm glad to see you are all alright," he told them. "Last night was... dreadful. As you know, we were attacked by some sort of sea serpent. It pulled sailors straight from the ship and devoured them. We couldn't fight it off. We were helpless against it. But eventually, it retreated on its own, leaving us in shambles."

"Aye, captain," one of the men said. "What are we to do now?"

"We'll spend the rest of the day repairing the ship," he explained. "And then as soon as we are ready, we will again set sail for Kraxoth. We lost seventeen men total. That's seventeen members of my trusted crew. I will not forget them. I will not forget that they died trying to protect the rest of us. There shall be a memorial this evening to amend them, and to say our final goodbyes."

"And what of your granddaughter?" another sailor asked.

The captain's face again turned sad, but his voice was strong as he spoke, "Little Sammi suffered an injury to her arm. She received stitches and will spend the next week at least recovering in my quarters. I must say that her life is owed to our guest, the lady from the desert." He gestured to me, and I did my best to stay hidden, even though everyone's eyes now stared in my direction. "She fought bravely against the beast. If it were not for her, Sammi would not be alive right now. For that, I am forever indebted to you, lady."

I gave him a curt nod, though I could feel the tears burning my eyes as they welled. "Anyone would have done the same," I said. "And all I could ever ask of you, captain, is to get us safely to our destination. You have been more than generous this entire time."

I could sense Will at my side, and then he was resting a hand on my shoulder as if to comfort me. It was an effort not to shrug him off.

"Know that you will always have a place on my ship, should you need it," the captain said to me, bowing at the waist, his own eyes lined with tears now. "Now," he clapped his hands together, "let's get this show on the road. Repairs are going smoothly. The injured are resting. Save your mourning for tonight. We'll be sailing in no time, men."

I spent the rest of the day above deck, helping in any way I could—mostly with small repairs, while Will helped with the heavier lifting. The sailors thanked me for everything I had done, which was odd, but I didn't refuse them. I wasn't used to this, to any of it.

By night fall the ship was in one piece again, and we ate together in the dining room, sailors saying words for the friends they lost, though no tears were shed. And then everyone got drunk, and went back on deck to celebrate. There was music, courtesy of a sailor who knew how to play the flute, and there was dancing. It was a happy celebration of life, rather than a sad memorialization of death.

I mostly kept my distance from Will, though I didn't go out of my way to be rude to him. He was completely unaware that I knew the truth. He had no idea that a reckoning was coming.

Everyone was still drunk and celebrating by the time we set sail, cheering as we left behind the site of that dreadful attack. The captain had disappeared at some point, likely attending to Sammi, and though I was thoroughly drunk, I also knew when it was time to call it quits. I stumbled below deck, unaware of where Will was or the last time I had seen him. But I halted as I entered the room, finding that he was already in bed.

He turned to me, though I couldn't see his face in the darkness. His eyes had returned to normal at some point throughout the day, though I don't think anyone else noticed that they had changed in the first place. He scooted further onto his side of the bed, pulling the covers back so that I could climb in next to him.

And I did climb in next to him, but I made a show to shove him hard in the chest to keep him away from me, letting him know that I did not want to be near him. I didn't wait to hear if he had anything to say before I fell asleep.

The following day was more somber. I stayed in the room, mostly, and asked Will to bring me my meals, explaining that I couldn't bear to get out of bed because I was simply in a bad state. He asked no questions.

In the afternoon I left in search of Sammi, finding her exactly where I had left her the other night, sleeping in bed, her arm bandaged so I couldn't see the extent of the wound. I kissed the top of her head and left her there to rest, saying a silent prayer for a speedy recovery, though I knew there were no gods listening.

When the time for dinner came, I refused to join the others, again asking Will to bring me back some food. I ate it in silence at the small table in our room, Will sitting across from me, watching me. I knew he could tell there was something wrong with me, but he didn't ask about it. Perhaps he was also waiting until we were ashore for a confrontation.

Later I curled up in bed, my back turned from Will, pretending like he wasn't there at all. I fell asleep as I cried silently to myself, wondering how my life had become such. I thought being banished from Mortefine was enough. I thought leaving Nola behind to suffer was the worst it would get, but then this happened, and it was hard to keep hope that things would eventually get better in the end.

Chapter 21

We were docked in Kraxoth when I awoke the next morning. Will wasn't next to me in bed, nor was he anywhere else in the room, and I had to wonder if he'd abandoned me. I wouldn't blame him, if he silently slipped ashore, leaving me there to deal with the rest of this on my own. My life was a lot, and I was certainly undeserving when it came to the help of a prince.

I started to gather my things, figuring that it would be better to have it all ready now so when Will did return, we could just head ashore. Though I didn't have much left, neither of us did. After being attacked by the sand serpent, we left most of our things in the tent, which got left behind when we had to flee. But I still had my satchel and the water canteens, and my weapons and the clothes on my back. Hopefully, we would be able to find fresh clothes in Kraxoth, as well as some other necessities.

I was replacing the books on the bookshelf, whether from me reading them or from them falling during the attack, when Will reentered the room. He was covered in sweat and smelled horrible, his hand on the pommel of his sword, but he was still there. He hadn't abandoned me. My relief must have been evident, because he walked right up to me and grabbed me by the shoulders, shaking me slightly.

"We made it," he said. "We're safe now."

My face was neutral, holding no indication of what I truly felt. Of course, I was happy that we had finally made it to Kraxoth, where we could no longer be attacked by serpents, whether in The Wry or in the sea. At least, I hoped we would not be attacked again. I just wanted to continue with the mission, but in order to do so I first needed to clear things up with me and Will. Hopefully, we would find an inn in the city where I could confront him in privacy, without other sailors listening through the thin walls of the ship.

When I didn't say anything, Will added, "Are you ready to go ashore?"

"Yes," I said. "If I never have to set foot on a ship again in my entire life, it still would still not be enough to erase this dreadful voyage from my mind."

He laughed softly, because he thought I was joking, but I wasn't. After a moment his face changed back to neutral. "I'm sorry," he said. "That you had to go through this. I know it's hard, I know you've been through a lot, but I promise things will get better now."

"Can you promise such a thing?" I asked.

He narrowed his eyes on me. "I suppose I cannot, but is it wrong of me to have hope?"

"Yes," I said, and then I gathered all of my things and walked out of the room, leaving him there, not really caring whether he followed me or not. But alas, a moment later I could hear his footsteps echoing down the hall. We ascended the stairs, and the ship was emptier than I expected.

"Hello," the captain called to us, beckoning us over. "How are you, lady? Soldier?" We nodded, though kept our mouths shut. "Most of the sailors went to shore the second we docked. They wanted to see their families after everything that happened."

"As they rightfully should," Will said.

It's a pity I have no family to go see, not here nor anywhere else, I thought, and almost said out loud before catching myself. I suppose I was wrong though, because I did have a brother out there, waiting for me. Will's eyes remained narrowed on me, like he knew exactly what I was thinking. I turned away from him and back to the captain.

"How is Sammi doing?" I asked him.

He shrugged. "She's fine, though she refuses to get out of bed. I'd give her a week or two before she feels well enough to come see everyone again." He shut his mouth into a flat line, like he didn't want to talk about the subject any further.

"Would you tell her I said goodbye?" I asked the captain. "And let her know that I'll never forget her."

He smiled sadly. "She would like to hear that, I think." He paused. "But she would like it even more if you promised to come visit in the future."

I smiled as well then. "Oh, I don't think I can make that sort of promise," I told the captain, clapping him on the shoulder. "You know I'm a lady, right? Who would I be to go parading around with pirates?"

He laughed then, a full-bodied laugh, which was a joyous sight all on its own. "Of course, my lady. Would you forgive an old man for hoping to see a beautiful face one last time before he parts?"

I smirked. "Captain, that's very brash of you. What sort of example would that set for Sammi?"

"A very good one, I think," he replied, and then we both broke into another fit of laughter.

I knew Will was still standing beside me, but he had grown so very quiet. I turned to him, finding his attention elsewhere, towards the city beyond. So I wrapped my arm through his.

"Goodbye, Captain Samuels," I said one last time.

And then Will added, "I will have your payment sent as soon as I can get in contact with my associates in the capital. I assume this is the port we would be able to find you at?"

"The sea is my home," the captain said. "Though, yes, Kraxoth is my city of choice when I am forced to go inland."

"Very well, then," Will said.

He gave me and Will a final wave as we turned and headed towards land. I kept his arm linked through mine as we made it down the walkway, all the way off the docks, and then into the city at last. And then I practically shoved him away from me, though he made no comment on the gesture.

And my attention was not on Will anymore at all, it was on the wondrous city beyond. It was bustling with excitement of all sorts, like nothing I had ever seen before. Certainly not in Mortefine.

The streets were made of stone, and they were packed with people and carriages and horses. The buildings were cramped together, though not crowded, and doors and windows were open, businesses up and running. There were street vendors with carts, though they weren't harassing the people who walked by them. It was early in the morning, so some people were heading out to work, some towards the sea where they would go and fish for the day. Others were out shopping, buying food and other necessities. And there were even children playing in the streets, unsupervised as if this were the safest place in the world.

And sure enough, passing right beside us was a group of city guards, who I assumed to be the Lord of Kraxoth's men. They had swords at their hips, though they had no inclination to use them. They didn't even seem to be on alert, like they too knew the city was safe.

The people in Kraxoth seemed so different. So much livelier than those in Mortefine. The people in Mortefine were mostly content, they just felt trapped. How happy could you really be if you were forced to live in a city like that? But here, there was so much freedom. You could go wherever you wanted. You could do whatever you wanted. When you got bored with this city, you could just pack up and move on to the next one. There were no sand serpents or food insecurity. It was an oasis.

But why would anyone ever want to leave this city? It wasn't dominated by the wealthy upper class, like Mortefine was, and from what I could tell, there were no beggars on the sides of the streets. Kraxoth was notorious for its high criminal activity, but I could see no evidence of that. It wasn't dangerous activity, mostly just theft and smuggling, and people coming into money illegally. Things that those in power could get away with turning a blind eye to, which is how I supposed the Lord of Kraxoth operated. Everyone knew Kraxoth was the place to go if you needed to come into money, quickly and quietly.

The headquarters for the Kraxoth Assassin's Associated were even hidden within the city, though their activity is a secret that not even their lord has been able to discover. Their operations are completely hidden from the public. The assassins employed with them are so skilled that they'd even managed to come and go from Mortefine multiple times without being detected. Though they are based in Kraxoth, they operate all around Vatragon, and have even been known to travel through the Great Ocean to Meriton, and even Faulton.

Nobody knows much about the other continents at all, except for maybe the assassins who have ventured there. In Vatragon, we are forbidden from traveling to them, and most wouldn't dare to because the sailing takes months, if not longer depending on the winds. Those who have tried to sail there have not returned to tell of it.

Will and I continued walking through Kraxoth, further into the city, away from all the restaurants and shops and more towards the residential areas. We needed to find an inn, but I continued to take in the amazing sights. Some buildings stood three stories high, some even higher. I turned back, still able to see the sea behind us, taking up most of the view.

It felt safe here, and I thought I might have even liked Kraxoth.

Will led the way, and most people didn't pay us any attention. Though our clothes were worn and our skin dirty, they likely assumed that we had just gotten back from sailing.

He stopped in front of a building, and from their door hung a painted vacancies sign, the words worn though still legible. He turned to glance at me, as if to ask if that place was alright, and I just shrugged, not really caring where we stayed as long as I could bathe and sleep in a bed. He walked up to the door and held it open, gesturing for me to follow.

We stepped inside, finding the place packed with people even though it was so early in the day. The downstairs area was a tavern, serving hot meals and cold drinks. Will led us to a table in the corner, mostly hidden from view, and we sat down, setting our things on the floor beside us.

I knew he was looking at me, though I refused to look at him or show any hint of emotion. He had no idea the anger that would be released as soon as we entered our room.

A server woman walked up to greet us, setting down two glasses of water. "How can I help you folks?" she asked.

Will sat up, cleared his throat. "We need a room," he told her. "We don't know how long we'll be staying, but I can give you a day's notice at least. We're weary from travel, and would appreciate a hot meal before we go to our room."

The woman nodded and then walked away, to talk to more customers at another table. She returned a few minutes later with two bowls of stew and two pints of ale. I started eating without another word. Will finished first, so he took our things upstairs while I finished, promising to return in a few minutes at most. I merely shrugged and continued eating.

Only two minutes had passed before a stranger approached me. He was older, though still obviously handsome. He had on the clothes of a sailor and smelled somewhat like the sea. Without asking, he took up Will's empty seat.

"Hello, miss," he said to me, smiling.

"Hello," I said back, smiling as well.

"Are you alone?" he asked, a rough edge to his voice. He was either dumb or he was playing me, because obviously I was not alone since there were two bowls and two cups at the table.

"My companion has wandered off somewhere," I said, leaning back in my chair, taking a sip of ale. The man watched my every movement. I knew I shouldn't have been talking to this man, but why not have a little fun? I of all people deserved that.

"They left you here all by yourself?" he asked, leaning in. "How rude of them. They must not be a very wise person at all if they left such a beautiful woman sitting all alone. Someone might just come along and snatch you up."

I gave him a wicked smile. "I'm perfectly capable of taking care of myself. And it almost sounds as if you're the one threatening to do the snatching."

"I don't snatch," the man said, his eyes hungry with desire. "I could show you exactly what I do. What's your rate?" His hand reached for me under the table, grabbing softly onto my knee.

I let out a loud cackle. "My rate? Oh, you foolish man." He obviously thought I was some sort of working woman—a harlot. How wrong he was. "Unfortunately, I am not in that sort of business. Though if I was not already in the companionship of another man, I'd have to say I think you and I could have had some fun."

"My apologies," he said, though he was still smiling, with his hand still on my knee. "How long until he returns? I think that—"

"You think what?" a deep, familiar voice cut in. "She will not be doing anything with you, nor will she be talking to you ever again. Now, I'm going to have to ask you to leave my seat before I have to force you to." Will's hand rested on the pommel of his sword, and his face was laced with pure rage.

The man merely looked back at Will, like he was aching for a fight. But before anything could happen, I brushed the man's hand off of my knee, slid out of my chair, and again linked my arm through Will's. I turned back to the man. "Unfortunately, I'm busy. Maybe another time." I gave him a wink, knowing that Will was watching.

Will tugged on my arm, leading me across the room and over to the stairs. I let him do it, because I knew exactly what would happen as soon as we were in that room. But it was hard not to laugh, at Will's obvious jealousy. He was a fool for that.

We walked up to a dim hall, dozens and dozens of doors running down either side, all marked with a number. Ours was number nine, not that far down the hall at all. Will pulled out the key, unlocked it, and then opened the door for me to enter.

As soon as I heard the door click shut, I knew it was time to strike. I pulled the knife free from the back of my pants, the one that I had hidden away all that time ago. I lunged for Will, sticking that knife against his throat, shoving him into the wall.

Chapter 22

"What are you doing, Karalia?" Will said too calmly, though his eyes were panicked, filled with such betrayal. I didn't care about that—he was the one that betrayed me first by lying. I had to remind myself of that. I couldn't let him deceive me any longer.

"Shut your damn mouth," I hissed at him, getting in his face close enough to share breath. I had him backed up against the wall, the knife against his throat, my knee digging into his groin, either of those methods of attack ready at any moment. "You don't get to ask questions."

"Karalia," he whispered, his hand coming up in between our bodies and wrapping around my wrist, not forcefully, not to move it, but rather to beg me to rethink what I was doing. "Whatever this is about, I will tell you anything you want to know. But if you want me to fight you, that's not going to happen."

I pushed the blade harder into his neck, perhaps too hard, because he flinched away from me, letting out a painful groan.

"Please," he begged, closing his eyes. He sounded genuinely frightened. Good. I watched as a trickle of blood ran down his neck. "Please," he said again, his breath quickening.

At the sight of the blood on his neck, his closed eyes, and the fear on his face, it made me pull away. I might have been angry as hell, but I was no monster. I shoved him by the shoulders, again knocking him into the wall before turning away. I wanted to scream—at him, at myself. But I didn't. I kept my voice unbelievably quiet as I said, "You lied to me."

"I'm sorry," he said, and I turned back to him quickly. Did he already know what he was being accused of? Or was he such a filthy liar that it could have been a number of things he was apologizing for? "Can we talk about this?" he asked, bringing a hand up to his neck and wiping the blood away. "Calmly," he added.

"I don't want to hurt you, Will," I said, though my actions suggested otherwise. "I just want you to be honest with me." That was the truth, and although I was sure I'd already figured out *his* truth, I wanted him to tell it to me himself.

"Okay." He put his hands up defensively, one of them smeared with blood. "I'm going to sit down," he said, gesturing to the table and then walking over to it when I didn't refuse. I hadn't even noticed there was a table there. I hadn't noticed anything about the room since we'd entered because I was so focused on attacking Will.

I watched as he sat down, and though I still held my knife poised to strike, I walked and joined him at the table. I took a deep breath before I started. "I saw you on the ship," I said. His eyes turned to me quickly, like he had already started to calculate his excuse. "I saw what you did to the serpent. I saw how you killed it."

He continued to think for a moment before speaking. "How?"

I rolled my eyes, amazed that of all the things he could have said, this was it. "What do you mean, *how*? I left the room to go and fight off the beast. I went to find you to see if you needed help. And I found you, alright. Shooting flames out of your hands like a damned wizard. I ran away afterward because it terrified the wits out of me, and then I couldn't speak to you for the next three days because I didn't know what to say. Or think. Or feel. You lied to me."

"I didn't lie," he said. "I just didn't reveal to you that I had the ability."

"Oh, *bull shit*," I said. "Don't pretend like that's the only lie you've told. I know that you think I'm this ignorant foolish girl that you had to come and rescue from Mortefine, but I know things, Will. More than you think."

"What do you mean?" he asked.

I ignored him, shaking my head and moving on to my next point. "What really got me was that you used it then, when there was nobody watching, but you wouldn't use it the other times you were attacked. Like in The Wry when your men were being slaughtered, or when we almost were. Or even when the seer had me locked in her grasp. Are you too proud to let anyone see you use it? Is that it?"

"You think it is a matter of pride?" he said, his voice growing angrier. He was grabbing onto the edge of the table, his knuckles turning white, as if to keep from lunging for me. A part of me wished he would.

"If it is not, then explain it to me," I said. "That's the only way you're going to get out of this, is if you tell me the truth. All of it."

He eyed me carefully for a moment, and then turned away, towards a nearby wall, as if he couldn't bear to look me in the eyes as he said the words. "I can't use it when I'm weak. Believe me, I have tried. Every other time I was deprived of food and water, closer to death than I ever wished to be. If there's anything I could have done then, I would have. So do not presume to blame it on *pride*, lady."

"You have magic," I said, which wasn't really a question.

He nodded anyway. "Yes, I have magic, if you want to call it that. My family has been known to have the power of fire."

"I'm not an idiot," I snarled, raising my hand from the table and again pointing the knife in his face. "I know where that type of power comes from. You're *dragon blooded*, aren't you?"

"I never said you were an idiot," he shot back, still not meeting my eyes. He was beginning to sound more and more frustrated. "Yes, I have the dragon god's blood within me, or so the legends claim. I'm a descendant of Drazen."

He was still leaving out the most important part. "And you're a goddamn *prince*?" I said. "Prince William, right?"

"Yes." He finally turned back to me. "I am Prince William, okay?" He tried to reach for me, but I recoiled away from him. "I didn't want to lie to you. I didn't want it to be this way—"

I abruptly held up a hand, silencing him. "I don't give a shit," I said to him. "I don't care why you lied, or how much you regret doing it, but the fact remains that you chose to lie to me in the first place." Before he could say something else, I cut him off again. "I just want you to tell me one more thing. Just this, and then I will decide what happens from here." Like if I wanted to continue traveling with him, or if I wanted to end his life right then. The second option seemed to become more and more justifiable with every word that came out of his mouth.

I asked, "Why are you really bringing me to the capital? Why do I get a prince as my own personal escort? And what are you planning to do with me when we get there?" It was the only thing that really mattered, at least at the moment. From the beginning I suspected that there was more to it, that both he and Nola were not telling me about, and now that I know he's a prince, I suspect even more.

He hesitated for a moment before bringing his hands up and running them over his face, like he was hiding from me, hiding from the truth. "I'm so sorry," he said. "I didn't want it to happen like this."

"*Tell me*," I hissed.

He shook his head slowly, not like he was refusing to answer but more like he knew the truth was going to hurt. "Please don't be angry with me," he said. "Maybe—put down the knife before I tell you?"

Angry? I wanted to laugh. I was already angry. Beyond that. When I kept the knife in my grip, Will finally went on.

"Okay, then," he started. "It's true that I traveled to The Wry to come rescue you, and then to bring you back to the capital. After Nola revealed the truth to us, my brother and your brother were determined to help. Daen dispatched a group of soldiers behind our father's back, and I volunteered to come with them. I lied to you about who I was, I did, but the truth is still that I came to free you, Karalia."

"But?"

He took a calming breath before telling me. "But you weren't meant to become Lady Havu. Your brother is expected to become the Lord of Orothoz eventually." He paused. "You were meant to become queen, or at least, that's what my brother intends."

"What?" I said. "*Queen*? You're joking, right?"

He shook his head. "When you were a child, before you... lost your memories, our parents arranged a betrothal between you and Daen. The two of you were to marry when you came of age. And we thought you were dead, but when he learned that you weren't... he wants the betrothal to be upheld."

I didn't have words. I held a hand over my mouth, hiding my shock, hiding my horror. They wanted me to not only marry a stranger, but to become queen? What the hell? I knew I would never allow that to happen. I would do *anything* to make sure that didn't happen. They find out I'm alive and their first decision is to force me into a marriage?

"Daen wanted to retrieve you so he could have you as his bride," he continued. "He kept it from our parents because I expect he wants you securely in the capital when he tells them, so you have no chance of escaping."

A wave of anger flared through me, burning my face, nails digging into my thighs from where I clutched them beneath the table. I didn't allow myself to think as I lifted that hand that was holding the knife, as I drew my arm back, and then launched that knife straight across the table, towards Will. It skidded right past his head, as I intended, but nicked

231

the tip of his ear, landing in the wall behind him. He didn't flinch one bit.

"You kept this from me?" I said.

"I didn't want to," he said, ignoring the trickle of blood sliding from his ear, as well as the forgotten cut across his throat. "Please believe me, I did not want to. But I won't allow it to happen. I won't allow him to force you into a marriage and keep you locked up there like a prized mare. I agreed to help you find the blade so we could delay me taking you there."

"But after, you still plan to take me to him, right?" I said. "Regardless of how the search for the blade goes, one way or another, I will end up in his clutch eventually?" I knew I was a fool. It's what I had agreed to, unknowingly. He helps me search for the blade, and in return I go with him to Vatragon City.

But I was surprised when he said, "No." I looked at him, brows furrowed, confusion on my face. He continued, "I won't let that happen. We'll search for the blade, and then we'll find some other way to make things right in the end."

My head began to ache as I took in all of this information. It seemed like recently, my entire life had been taking turns for the worse. One bad thing coming my way after another. Would it ever stop? Would there ever be a time when I could live in peace? There was one other thing on my mind, though. One other question that still needed answering.

"Will," I said calmly. "Why did you ask to kiss me in the room on the ship?" I knew he remembered, and I wouldn't allow him to dismiss it on the rum. "Because it seems to me like you and your brother loathe each other, and that was your way at attempting to get at him, by trying to sleep with the woman he thinks he's going to marry."

"No," he said, his voice raised slightly. He waved his hands frantically in front of him, likely stressed that things weren't going the way he wanted. That's what happens when you lie, I wanted to tell him. "That's not it at all. That had nothing to do with my brother. It would have been easier if you had no attachment to him at all."

I lunged. I reached across the table and grabbed the hem of his shirt, pointing my finger in his face. "*I have no attachment to him*. None. And I never will. It would have been easier, for what? For you to want to kiss me without feeling guilty?" I released him and slumped back into my chair, laughing slightly at how ridiculous this all was.

"No—"

"That's all you men think, isn't it?" I continued. "That you can just kiss anyone you want? Why don't you try listening to your goddamn head instead of your dick, Will? Or actually, why don't I just tell this to you instead: I want nothing to do with you. I want nothing to do with your brother. I'm not a lady and I certainly have no interest in becoming queen. I have no interest in being associated in any way with the Drazos family, and I will not be going to the capital."

Will again shook his head. "I only meant that it would be easier for me to admit that I have feelings for you. So forgive me for caring about you, Kara."

I again laughed. "Well, I don't forgive you, *William*. And I'm afraid I don't return those feelings, either. So there's nothing for you to get so damned worked up about. Why don't you just head back home to your family, Will? Why don't you leave me to do this alone?"

"None of that even matters," he said. "I'm here to help you search for the blade, and I'm here to help you free Nola. I know you probably don't want my help now, but you're getting it." He stood from his seat and walked over to me, getting onto his knees before me. "I plan to uphold my end of the deal, but I will not take you to the capital. I won't tell my parents, or anyone else, that you're alive. I will keep you hidden from my brother, if I need to. You should be the one to decide how that happens, or if it ever will." He rested a hand on my knee. "I'm sorry," he said, "for everything."

As much as I wanted to refuse him, and to send him away, he was right about one thing. I needed his help, and I wasn't going to find the blade without it. I still didn't believe him, that he wouldn't take me to the capital, but when it came to that point, I would just have to find some way to get away. To escape.

I crossed my arms, shoving his hand off of my knee. "Yes," I said. "I will be the one to decide what happened with *my own life*." I knew I shouldn't have said this next part, but I was hurting, and I wanted to hurt him. "You know, you're no better than Hiran, with all your lies and you trying to control me."

He quickly stood from where he had been kneeling, pointing a finger in my own face now. "I am *nothing* like him." Oh, yes, he was certainly angry. "So do not compare me to that pathetic excuse for a man. I would never do to you what he did. *Never*."

"Well, that's not very obvious from how you've treated me so far," I told him. "I would rather have spent my entire life trapped in Mortefine with Hiran than be forced to marry someone I don't even know—than be forced to become the queen of a country that I have no interest in ruling. You think you're better than Hiran? At least he never did *that*."

His eyes saddened. "Karalia—"

"*Do not call me that*," I shouted.

"I'm sorry," he said, his voice lower. He backed away, towards the other side of the room. "I know there's nothing I can say that will make you hate me less, but I never wanted it to be this way. I never wanted to be your enemy."

"My *enemy*?" I laughed. I couldn't tell anymore, who my enemies were and who my friends were. It seemed like everybody was my enemy—that nowhere was safe. But I think I knew, deep down, that Will was not my enemy. I think I knew that he did honestly want to help me, whether from guilt or for his own reasons that he still had not revealed. He wanted to help me, and here I was, hurting him like this.

"I know you're not my enemy," I said, refusing to meet his eyes. "But it *hurt* me when you lied. After everything that I told you about my life, and all of the lies that I've been told by others, you still chose to lie to me. I want to trust you again, I really do, but I don't know if I can. But I can at least admit that your help with finding the blade is necessary, and that I need you here for this."

"I will be," he said. "I will be by your side."

And then he walked back over to me, softly grabbed onto my hand, pulling me out of my chair. I stood before him and watched as he opened his arms, an invitation for me to go into them. And damn me, but I accepted the invitation. I kept my arms still at my side but rested my face against his chest, and his arms curled around my back.

"I'm sorry," he whispered into my hair.

"I know," I whispered back, standing there like a fool. I leaned my head back and peered up at him, meeting his eyes. "Will," I said, and I could see something glimmer within him, and I knew that he thought he was forgiven. "If you ever betray me again, I will kill you. I will not hesitate to slit your throat, even if you are a prince. Do you understand that?"

His arms froze around me, and his breathing might have stopped entirely. "Yes," he said. "I understand."

I turned my head away, then brought my hands up and hugged him at last.

Chapter 23

Will left shortly after our little conversation, probably because of how much I'd terrified him. Obviously I would never actually harm him, but it was good to let him believe that I had some control. I assumed that he just needed some space, or time to cool down, but his excuse for leaving was to start gathering intel on the blade, asking around, and seeing if anyone had any leads.

"You can't just announce to everyone that we're looking for it," I had told him. "These people are religious freaks; they might just report you for speaking of the serpent god's weapon."

"Relax," he said. "I know how to remain inconspicuous."

And then he left, leaving me alone in the room, asking me not to leave, though I knew it was more like a demand. I didn't mind, not really. But Will seemed to hesitate as he stepped through the door, like he wanted me to argue, like he wanted me to ask him not to go. I would never give him that sort of satisfaction. I merely waved him off and sat back down at the table.

But mostly I wanted to be alone because of everything that I had just discovered. The shock still rang through me, even over an hour later. It all started when I found out who I was, when Nola told me the truth, and that I had a brother who was alive. And then I found out I'd been traveling with a prince—a prince with magical abilities. And then I found out that I was expected to marry another prince, and eventually become queen. A part of me wished I was still dead to the world. I didn't get a warm welcome; I got a bitterly cold one.

I wasn't given a moment's consideration for what *I* wanted. They just planned to pick me up and deliver me like a chest full of treasure—like something that doesn't have their own wants and dreams.

I didn't think my impression of the royal family could get any worse from here, unless maybe until I actually met them in person. Will seemed like an alright person, until I found out that he'd been lying to me. And his brother is the one that asked him to lie. Daen seems like a despicable bastard, and if I ever do meet him, well, he would surely be in for it. He's the man that's planning to force me to marry him. I still had this small sliver of hope that the king himself would be more considerate, but it didn't seem likely considering the rumors I'd heard about him.

Hopefully Will was at least right about me never having to encounter them unless I wanted to, and I knew I would never want to, but unfortunately, I would have to eventually. I had a brother who was waiting for me, living with those very people. I didn't know what to think about him, and what his involvement was in everything, but I knew that he was eager to meet me. Or I guess he would be seeing me again, if we're telling it from his perspective. It's been a long time for him.

That meeting would not come for a while, though. Not until I found the blade and freed Nola, and figured out everything with Hiran. For now, that was my priority. I wanted to believe that Will would not betray me—that he wouldn't end up taking me to the capital instead—but it was very hard to.

I remained seated at that damned table long after Will left, staring at the knife I'd lodged in the wall.

I finally had a chance to look around the room, to see where it was we'd be staying for the next unknown amount of days. The bed was huge, big enough to fit at last half a dozen people, and the sheets were of the finest silk. There were paintings hung along the walls, depicting various random things, nothing really standing out that much. But on the wall behind the bed was a massive woven tapestry depicting a serpent slithering through a dreary field. Why did it always have to be serpents? Everywhere I went they seemed to follow me. The tapestry made me feel slightly uneasy, knowing that it was likely a depiction of Sazarr, and also knowing that a *dragon blooded* would be sleeping in the room. I debated taking it down, but Will had to have already noticed it.

Could the rebellion that happened here all those years ago still have some sort of presence within the people? Did they still worship Sazarr like they once had?

Across from the bed was the table we sat at before, and next to that a couch with two side tables. On the wall to the right of the bed were long auburn curtains, the sun peeking beneath them. I drew them open, lightening the dusty room and giving it life, especially after the argument that had just occurred in it. There were windows on either side of the wall, and in the center a wooden door that seemed to lead outside. I opened it, finding a small balcony with a seating area.

I sat outside, catching a glimpse of the sea in the distance, which didn't look nearly as terrifying now as it had when we sailed through it. My attention shifted to the city below, finding it loud and bustling with excitement. I watched for a while, catching glimpses of couples smiling as they walked hand-in-hand, or children laughing as they played. It was truly a joyous sight, and I could have stayed there to watch forever, if there wasn't something more important that needed taking care of.

It had been more than two weeks since I'd bathed, after traveling through The Wry and building up a layer of grime on my skin. It must have been the longest I'd ever gone without cleaning myself.

I was relieved to find that our room had a small adjoining bathing chamber, and even a toilet. I had to crank the water from the pump myself, but I didn't mind. The water came out clear enough, though it vaguely smelled of the sea. There was even a bathrobe sitting on the counter, which was good because I wouldn't have to get back into my filthy clothes.

I poured some soap into the tub as I filled it, stopping when the bubbles had risen about halfway. Then I peeled away my clothes, wincing from where the blood and dirt and sweat had molded the fabric to my skin. I was about to step into the tub when the sight of myself in the mirror caught me by surprise.

It was truly horrid—the first look I'd gotten of myself in a while. The life seemed to be drained right out of me, as dark circles had formed beneath my eyes, my lips had become thin and pale, and the very bones on my face seemed to protrude more than they had before. Even the rest of my body had changed. I had gotten thinner, the muscles of my arms and legs having grown weaker. It would take more than one wash to get all of the dirt out of my hair, from under my nails, and all the other places that I couldn't yet see.

Another thing that seemed to have changed was the shade of my skin. What usually was pale and gaunt was now tanned to a light golden color. Freckles had spread about my nose and cheeks, which were not there before. Even through everything else, I thought this made me prettier. Not that I particularly cared about impressing anyone at the moment. The green of my eyes stood out more with these changes.

After examining myself I got into the tub and bathed, relieved that the water was not unbearably cold. In Mortefine, our water came from the underground well which was usually much colder than what you would expect it to be. I spent over an hour scrubbing and washing, and then doing it again and again. I looked like myself again. I looked feminine, even.

As I stepped out of the tub and let it drain, I wrapped the bathrobe around myself and sat at the small vanity. I ran my fingers through my hair to untangle it and then twisted it into a long golden braid. I rubbed my skin with lotion and sprayed some perfume. I left my amulet tucked beneath the robe, wondering how it was even still on me after everything I'd been through.

When I went back into the main room, I didn't bother fastening either of my weapons to my body, hoping rather than knowing that I would be safe there.

I waited a while for Will to return, sitting on the balcony as day turned to evening and evening turned to night. The city grew quiet and eventually silent, and yet he had still not returned.

I went back into the room when the air outside grew too cold for comfort. I was tired of waiting and I was hungry and if he didn't come back soon...

I strode for the door into the hall and grabbed onto the handle, but then I felt it twist from the other side. I knew it wasn't locked, but was somebody trying to get in? I quickly pulled my hand away and then backed up a few steps. I watched as the handle continued to turn, and as the door opened and Will walked in. I was standing there staring at him, like I had been waiting, like a damned fool.

I tilted my head back to meet his eyes as he halted coming any farther into the room. He stared at me, hard, in a way that made me start to feel uncomfortable.

"What is it?" I asked, worried that something had gone amiss.

"You bathed," he said, and he wasn't asking a question. I realized then what all the staring was about. I was wearing a thin bathrobe, the top of it opened slightly, the bottom of it barely covering my thighs.

"You pig!" I said, averting my eyes from him. It *was* his first time seeing me presentable and cleaned up. I tended to have this effect on men, so I knew his reaction was nothing personal. But you would have thought he'd never seen a beautiful woman before in his life. "Don't get too worked up about it."

"I'm not getting worked up about anything," he said in defense. "I only noticed that you were no longer covered in dirt, and that your stench had disappeared."

I rolled my eyes, and then realized that he had also bathed. "I see you've cleaned up, too," I said. His clothes had even been washed. Why couldn't he have done that for me?

I walked further into the room, and he finally shut the door, following me over to the couch. I sat down; he remained standing. "I would ask you where you were about to go," he said, "and I would tell you that it was likely a bad idea, but I know you would just yap at me that you can take care of yourself, then get mad at me for caring."

I raised my brows, unsure if I should laugh or be offended. "You must be getting to know me better, prince."

His eyes turned away from me, towards the wall, where the knife I'd thrown at him was still currently lodged. He had to know that I wasn't actually aiming at him, but the look of distrust on his face suggested otherwise.

"So?" I finally said. "What happened? Why were you away for so long?"

"I met up with some soldiers here from the capital," he said. "They've been stationed here since the Rebirth Day festival, saying that the king ordered them to look into some supposed rebel activity. I told them who I was before swearing them to secrecy, and then I demanded money on the king's behalf, and promised that when they return to the capital they will be paid back in full."

"Rebel activity?" I questioned. "Is that common?"

He shrugged. "Not really, but I'm sure it's nothing. The soldiers said they've found nothing much of interest. Just religious Sazarr fanatics preaching nonsense to the public."

"Are they punished for that?" I asked.

"It depends," Will said. "Usually they go on trial, but very rarely are they punished at all. They might spend some time in a cell, but it wouldn't be much worse than that."

"Hiran punished a woman once, for speaking out about Sazarr," I told him. "He slit her throat in the middle of a crowded street."

He was quiet for a moment. "I hate that man."

"Don't we all," I murmured. "So what of the blade? Did you find any leads?"

"We've got a meeting tomorrow," he said casually. "She's an elder woman that lives further in town." It seemed like good news, but his cold tone suggested otherwise. "She's a known Sazarr supporter, so she'll probably tell us nothing but lies."

"Why do you think that?" I asked him.

"Why do I think that?" he repeated. "Maybe because Sazarr is the sworn enemy of the god that I am literally descended from."

"And that gives you the right to talk down to those that don't share your beliefs?" I said. "You know, they might think the exact same thing about you. What would you say then?"

"It doesn't matter," he told me.

"Now you're getting it," I said. "It doesn't matter that this woman is a known Sazarr supporter. It wouldn't make a difference if she supported Drazen instead. Can't you put away your pride for one day and just listen to what the woman has to say? It has to be better than nothing."

He stared at me for a moment. "I don't want to argue with you anymore." And then he turned and walked into the bathing room, shutting the door behind himself, leaving me alone again. Obviously he wasn't taking a bath, as he had done that earlier, but rather he just wanted to get away before we broke into another screaming match.

While he was in there, a woman came to the door to deliver us some things, which I assumed again was courtesy of Will. It was mostly just clothes and food, and some other random things. I took them and thanked her, examining them thoroughly. But as soon as I saw the clothes that had been brought for me, I left everything else forgotten. There were pants, just my size, long and thick, the inside lined with some sort of soft material, no doubt designed to keep me warm. There was also a dark blue tunic and a black cloak with matching black gloves. It wasn't my usual style, but it would do.

Will returned from the bathing room. There was something different about him—something that made him appear more youthful. And I realized that he had been shaving his face. The layer of stumble that had been there before was now nowhere to be seen. It made him appear more handsome—more regal.

He assessed the items that had been delivered, seeming satisfied enough, and then started rummaging through the food. It was nothing hot or cooked, but rather food that we could eat while we traveled. He separated out a portion of dried meat for each of us. It wasn't any meat I could recognize, having a dark reddish color and tasting slightly tangy, but I ate it because I was hungry.

Sometime later I climbed into our enormous bed. Will walked over and handed me a glass of water, for which I thanked him, and then I pulled the covers over myself and prepared to sleep.

I felt so conflicted. I knew I should have still been mad at him—furious—but I didn't want to be. He was being kind to me, which was likely just a scheme to beg for my forgiveness, but he was always kind to me before, wasn't he? I didn't know what to think or say or do. I just wanted to fall asleep and think about it tomorrow.

Will walked to the other side of the bed, hesitating, like he didn't know if he was allowed to sleep in it or not. It would have been justified for me to say no, but what kind of monster would that make me?

"It's okay," I whispered, though my back was still turned to him. "It's fine, Will. Get in the damn bed."

I heard his boots clink as he removed them and tossed them to the floor, then the curtains hiss as he slid them closed, and then the mattress creak as he slipped under the covers and collapsed into bed. The warmth from his body seeped over to me, even though there was so much space separating us.

I turned to face him and watched as he rested his head against the pillow, his eyes closed, though I knew he wasn't asleep yet. His chest rose and fell unevenly with every breath.

"Kara?" he said, and I thought it was odd to hear him use that name.

"Hmh?" I replied.

"Why aren't you angry with me?" he asked. His voice was so quiet, so vulnerable. "You should hate me for what I have done."

"Do you want me to hate you?" I replied, just as quietly.

"No."

I watched him remain there with his eyes closed, like he couldn't bear to have this conversation, like it was paining him to ask me these things.

I replied, "I think... that enough people hate you already." His eyes shot open, and his head turned to me in an instant, like that was the opposite of what he expected me to say. "What good would it do if I hated you as well? I don't think that would be fair."

He let out a long sigh, and might have even shuddered. "Thank you."

Another long moment of silence passed. "Will?"

"Yeah?"

"I didn't mean what I said before," I told him. "You're nothing like Hiran. It was wrong of me to compare you to him like that." I waited for him to say something, but he didn't, he only stared at me intently. "I'm sorry," I said, tears starting to fill my eyes.

"It's okay," he said, still holding my gaze. But beneath the covers, his hand carefully traveled over the mattress to find mine. He squeezed onto it gently. "You don't have to apologize for what I deserved to hear. You had every right to say it. I only lied because..." His throat bobbed. "Because I wanted to make all of this easier for you. But I know now that it was wrong of me."

Something inside of my mind shouted, *this is wrong* and *don't trust him*, but then something else begged me to forgive him. I didn't know what to think and I didn't know how to respond to whatever declaration he'd just made.

"I just want to be here for you," he said. "As a friend, if that is what you need, and as a protector."

I pulled my hand from his, maybe somewhat aggressively. "I need time," I said. "I need time to learn how to trust you again."

He only nodded and then turned back away from me, onto his side, so I did the same. I *did* need time, but not for me to learn how to trust him, rather for me to understand why I already did trust him, and why I had never stopped trusting him in the first place.

Chapter 24

I awoke the following morning to Will carrying a tray of food in from downstairs, or rather, I awoke to the smell of it. It had me practically leaping out of bed and running over to the table like a wild animal. How could I ever refuse a meal again, after nearly starving in The Wry? But Will didn't smile as he saw me—he didn't say anything at all—he only set the tray down and a plate for each of us.

If he didn't want to talk, then perhaps I didn't either. Instead I began helping myself to the food. There was a dish of scrambled eggs, another of fried potatoes, as well as sausages and toast with jam. There was some juice to drink, which I didn't recognize, but it tasted sweet and a little tart. This food felt like a blessing, and I wondered just how much Will had paid for it, or if perhaps it was due to the generosity of the innkeeper. Wherever it came from, I would appreciate it all the same. I might as well have licked my plate clean from the way I tore into that meal. I didn't think I'd ever had such a nice meal, even eating at the Rendal estate.

When we finished I climbed right back into bed and beneath the covers. It was still early in the day, so surely Will didn't want to get going so soon. The meeting with the elder woman wasn't until later in the afternoon.

I had expected strange dreams last night, considering how worked up I had gotten, but they never came. Was it ridiculous of me to think that it was because Will and I had mostly resolved our dispute before I fell asleep? All that time we spent together in The Wry, the dreams never came, and the darkness never found me. But the night that we were attacked by the sea serpent, the night that I found out Will had been lying to me, I had a terrifying nightmare. Perhaps it was only a coincidence, but it sure felt odd. It's like—when I'm feeling afraid or alone, it lets the darkness in, and the dreams return.

Will went to sit on the couch, me on the bed, and I was prepared to fall back to sleep if he hadn't started speaking.

"Can we talk?" he said to me across the room.

"Yes," I replied, though it was more of a muffled mumble because my face was shoved into a pillow. When he didn't respond, I realized that he was probably asking so I would turn to face him. I sat up. "What is it?" I asked.

"When we head out into the city later," he said, "I think we should try and keep a low profile. Wherever we go, I don't want us getting recognized. I mean, I know nobody knows who you are, but they might know me."

"I agree," I said. Of course, nobody could have known who I was, as I had grown up in Mortefine away from prying eyes, and if anyone did recognize me, it wouldn't be as Karalia Havu, but as Lord Rendal's advisor. "But what happens?" I asked, "If you do get recognized? What happens if we get caught?"

"I'm not sure," he said. "It might come off as suspicious if the Lord of Kraxoth were to discover me in his city unannounced. His guards could technically bring us in if they were to capture us. But I'm not that worried because we aren't doing anything explicitly *illegal*, so unless my father were to command our arrests himself, then I should hold authority over anyone else who would try to. But again, I'm trying to keep my presence here a secret, so let's hope it doesn't come to that."

"You would play the prince card to free us?" I asked, with a hint of amusement that Will did not return. "I should like to see that, I think."

He huffed a laugh, though he didn't seem to think it was funny at all. "As I said, only if it were necessary. I wouldn't let us end up in a dark cell when we're on such an important mission."

"Yes, I agree," I told him. "We stay hidden."

He ran a hand across his face. "It should be enough just to keep our hoods on, and our faces shadowed beneath. I don't think we should bring our swords, as they would stand out to any guards keeping an eye out."

"No," I told him quickly. "My sword comes with me. It goes wherever I go."

"And what do you plan to do if a guard stops you to ask about it?" he said. "What story will you tell them?"

"That I'm employed by the Lord of Mortefine, and that he has sent me on a mission that may require the use of a sword," I replied nonchalantly.

The side of his mouth quirked into a smile, though he turned his head quickly away from me as if to hide it. "You're a smart ass, you know?" he said. "Fine, you can bring your sword. I don't think anyone would see you and think you're a threat, anyways."

"Bastard," I mumbled, then sat up further in bed. "I suppose you're one to talk, since you could just use your power rather than carrying a sword around. That must make things very convenient."

Something flashed in his eyes, but it was gone a moment later. "My power is not a joke to me," he said quietly. "I use it sparingly, and I would never use it on an innocent guard who is just doing what his lord ordered him to. I'm not a monster, Kara."

"I wasn't implying that," I told him. "I only meant that you do not need to worry about carrying a sword because you know that there's another way for you to protect yourself. It's not the same for me. Without any weapons I'm just a small, weak girl."

But he wasn't listening anymore. He had already stood and walked out onto the balcony, and when I thought he would slam the door behind himself, it only clicked shut, ever so quietly. I felt like shouting.

We left our room an hour past noon. When we prepared to leave, I strapped Fangmar across my back, waiting for Will to argue, but he never did. He left his sword behind, of course, but I saw the few knives he tucked beneath his clothes. It was funny, thinking that a prince would need to defend himself so much. I always thought that they were guarded by dozens of men, untouchable to anyone, but this proved otherwise.

I tried not to think about the fact that it was likely because of his family's resentment towards him, that they just didn't care enough to warrant him that level of protection. But Will also claimed that he hadn't told his parents he was leaving, and there was clearly no report of the prince having gone missing, so did they care at all? Were they wondering where he had gone off to? And were they awaiting his return? I guess I would never know, because when Will finally returned to his family, I did not plan on being with him.

I almost laughed at the sight of me and Will with our hoods pulled over our heads, my long braid tucked behind me. Surely this would make us stand out more than if we were not wearing our hoods. But as we walked onto the street from the tavern, people did not turn our way, and I thought that perhaps it was because they were afraid of the sight of us, two mysterious people with their faces covered. We could have been anyone. Thieves, assassins, rebels. Too bad we were only a prince and a lady.

It was quieter out today than it had been yesterday, like more people were working now than shopping. And though it was in the afternoon, the sun was not out, but hidden behind a mass of grey clouds. The air was cool, maybe even a little cold. At this time of day in Mortefine you would hardly even be able to step outside. But there the air was dry, and here it was different—moist and heavy, dampening my skin as we walked. Though the temperature was cooler, it made me sweat more.

The woman we were to meet lived on the opposite side of the city, as far as you could get from the sea. I wasn't sure how big the city was, but I hoped it wouldn't take too long.

Will kept a few feet in front of me, his eyes scanning like he was ready for battle at any moment. But I didn't feel such a necessity. I felt like I could have left Fangmar behind and have been perfectly safe. I didn't see any of this infamous criminal activity. Perhaps they were somewhere nearby, lurking in the shadows. But even the guards we passed paid us no heed, some of them glancing us over but them dismissing us a moment later. They seemed to have been looking for a specific set of people, that we were not a part of.

It took us no more than an hour to reach the woman's house. Will had her address written down, so we knew we were at the right place. It was a one-story cottage, tightly packed in with the houses on either side of it. The front yard was well maintained, containing flower bushes that appeared freshly trimmed.

I followed Will as he walked the stone path to the door and knocked gently. A few seconds passed and then the door opened, and I could see a child. He was skinny, and behind him was another skinny boy. They were definitely siblings, maybe even twins with their matching black hair and same-colored eyes. The sight of them sadly reminded me of little Sammi, and I wondered if she was doing okay.

Will was about to speak when one of the boys yelled, "Gran!" They walked away and left the door wide open, but we stayed outside. A minute or so later a woman walked up, a very old woman.

She was tiny, and just as skinny as the boys. Her back had slightly hunched over from age, and her long silver hair flowed all the way down to her knees, thin and stringy. Her face was wrinkled, and her eyes sagged so much that I could hardly tell if they were open or not. But she seemed to be looking at us.

She turned back to the boys, "You two go play outside." They immediately ran past us and out into the street. "Can I help you two?" she asked us at last.

"Jacol sent us," Will said. I had no idea who this *Jacol* was, but the woman apparently did as she nodded with recognition. "He said you could help us with something we're searching for."

"Perhaps," the woman said, stepping aside and letting us into her home. "Come in, let me make some tea and then we'll get talking."

So we walked in. It was small, yet clean and cozy. The decorations seemed outdated, but perhaps I just didn't understand them. She led us into a small living area and pointed to a couch, which I assumed meant she wanted us to sit there. So I did, yet Will remained standing close to me.

The woman disappeared behind a door, what I assumed was the kitchen where she would prepare the tea. She walked out a few minutes later with a tray in hand and set it on a small table along the wall. She made herself a cup, and then one for me, and then offered one to Will, but he refused. She walked over to the couch and sat beside me.

"Who were those boys?" I asked her.

"They're my grandchildren," she smiled sadly.

"Where are their parents?" I dared to ask.

"Oh, they died years ago," the woman told me. "Drowned at sea." And her vacant expression suggested that she didn't still mourn the loss.

"I'm very sorry," I offered.

She waved off the apology. "My name is Trona. I understand that you have come to me for information?"

"Yes, we—" I paused. The woman, Trona, had scooted closer to me, taking my hands in her own, leaning in to get a good look at me. I could see her eyes then, and they were green, the same as mine. And then her eyes lowered down to my neck, to the amulet that must have come untucked. Her breath caught, though I was sure there was no way she could know what it was.

She released me and leaned back onto the couch. I suspected then that she saw me for who I really was. "My lady," she said, bowing her head. "You're a long way from home. And a long way from the grave."

My eyes darted to Will, and he looked just as surprised. But he didn't say anything, like he was waiting to see how this played out.

"Please," I said to the woman. "You do not know what you speak of." And for good measure, I grabbed onto my amulet and quickly tucked it beneath the cloak, hiding it like I tried to hide every other part of me.

But I did nothing to stop the woman as she reached out and pulled the hood back from my head, revealing my golden hair, un-shading my emerald eyes. "You are Karalia Havu," the woman said, her eyes sparkling with something that must have been admiration. "The Lost Daughter of Orothoz. The Queen of the Otherealm."

"What?" Will cut in, speaking for the first time. "She is no such thing."

"It's fine," I said to Will, even though I had no idea why the woman would refer to me as such a thing.

"I apologize, lady," she said. "I only meant that you were said to be dead, and now, you are clearly not."

But I didn't think she believed that. She said it like it was a common title, like people had said it often. But didn't everyone believe that I was dead? How could such a thing be?

"I must ask you to keep my life a secret," I said to her. "For just a little longer. There is something important that I need to do before I reveal myself to the world."

"It would be an honor," she said. "And I assume that is why you are here, lady, because of this secret?"

"Please, do not call me that," I said, trying my best to sound polite.

"We have come for information," Will cut in. "What do you know about the lost blade of Sazarr?"

Whatever joy had been on the woman's face vanished entirely. "What do you want with that?" she hissed.

"That's irrelevant," Will told her. And I knew that if he kept talking to her like that, she wouldn't give us any valuable information. He was being rude. I shot him a warning glance that told him to keep his mouth shut.

I spoke instead. "I know the history surrounding the blade is not a pleasant one," I started. "But we have no intention to use it in any way. I know it is evil and contains dark magic within it, but it is very important that we locate it." That seemed to have assured her enough to regain her interest. "There was a failed rebellion here five hundred years ago. The man who led that rebellion was said to wield the blade. Do you know if it remains in the city?"

Trona leaned in closer to me, like she didn't want Will to hear. "Before I tell you anything, I need you to make me a promise." I nodded intently. She continued, "I want you to promise that should you locate the blade, it will not be used for evil."

"I promise," I told her quickly. "I have no intention to use the blade at all." That wasn't entirely the truth. *I* had no intention of using the blade, but I didn't know what Hiran planned to do with it. However, I would try and uphold my end of this promise as best as I could. Hiran wanted the blade for a reason that I'm sure he hadn't revealed to anybody, so I just needed to make sure that I killed him before he had the chance to use it.

"Okay, then," the woman said, seeming to relax slightly. "What you said is true. Five hundred years ago, a man led a rebellion here in Kraxoth against the reign of the Drazos family. I have no idea how the blade came into his possession, but many suspect that he was *serpent blooded*."

Will scoffed, and I turned to find him shaking his head like he didn't believe a word of what the woman had said. I shot him another glance, one promising fury if he continued whatever tantrum he was throwing.

The woman ignored him. "But of course, the rebellion failed. The man was killed, and the blade disappeared along with him. I do not know where it is, but I have heard rumors of it being seen in Frystal within the last fifty years. However, I cannot guarantee this to be true as there is no definitive proof. The blade is still believed a myth to many."

"But you do not think it is a myth," I said to the woman.

"No," she said. "I know the blade is real, the same way I know that it is not dangerous in the right hands. I believe in your good intentions for finding it, and I think that more can come from all of this, for Sazarr's sake."

"What the hell does that mean?" Will nearly spat, shooting up from his spot along the wall and stalking towards us.

The woman merely laughed. "Boy, you know nothing of hell. You go to the Otherealm where Sazarr dwells, and you make it back alive, then you try using that word so lightly."

"I only meant," Will lowered his voice, "that it almost sounds as if you sympathize with Sazarr."

"And what if I did?" The woman laughed more. "Are you going to report me for it, boy? Are you going to execute me yourself?"

I could sense Will tensing from where he had come to stand beside me, but he didn't say anything else to the woman.

"This isn't the capital," she went on. "Support for the Drazos family doesn't extend very far here. Most don't believe the lies of Drazen—for he is not our god."

If she knew Will was the prince, surely she wouldn't be saying this. But before he could do or even say anything, I asked the woman, "What lies? What do you mean by that?" I wanted to know. I didn't take Drazen as my god, so nothing she said could really offend me. I heard Will scoff again so I turned to him and said, "If you don't want to hear it then you can wait outside." He remained silent, but also remained standing beside me.

"I will tell you the story of the gods," Trona began. "The truth of Drazen and Sazarr. This is the truth that we teach our children in secret, and we're good at hiding it."

So don't go running your mouth about it, is what she didn't say, but what I knew she meant. I almost felt like I should have forced Will to leave, because he's exactly the type of person that Trona hid her beliefs from, and she was about to reveal everything.

"A very long time ago," she began, "two young mortal men traveled Vatragon together, when the land was known by a different name and ruled by ancient families that no longer exist. Together they went on quests and adventures. They were the best of friends, brothers even, and would have gladly sacrificed their lives for the other.

"During one of their travels," she went on, "Drazen and Sazarr came upon the keep of a strange female. She was a foreign, ancient, and powerful enchantress, and she thrummed with power. As any young man would, Drazen and Sazarr wanted a taste of that power for themselves, so they acted, attacking the woman. As punishment for their selfish and greedy impulse, the enchantress cursed the friends and wrote a spell so cruel it destroyed them for all eternity. It was an undoing—a damnation.

"She transformed the men into dragons, great and powerful immortal beasts, and set them to live out eternally as terrifying and vicious creatures. But like any spell, there was a way for it to be broken. If one friend betrayed the other, they would come to find themselves in the body of a mortal once more, only with eternal youth and the power like that of a god. It was what they were after in the first place.

"It was a testament of their faith to one another—in one another. For hundreds of years they led separate lives, deciding that it was better to keep their distance, promising to never betray one another. But it did not last, as one friend would come to turn on the other.

"It was Drazen who broke," Trona said. "It was he who sought out Sazarr, with every intention to kill him. And when Drazen found him, Sazarr did not fight his friend, because he had promised long ago not to. Drazen ripped Sazarr's wings from his body, tore off limb by limb, leaving him to bleed out and die, and to claim his reward.

"As the enchantress had written into the spell, Drazen regained his once mortal form. His power to transform into a dragon remained, as did many new powers. He would never die. He could never be killed. So he did what any man would,

255

and he turned himself into a god. He taught the people of Vatragon to believe in his might—to fear him. He has been manipulating us for the past thousand years.

"But that was not the end of the story for Sazarr. He was ready to die at last, to break free of the curse, but the spell had something in store for him as well. His wounds healed, his blood turned to poison, and what remained was something else entirely."

"A serpent," I said, and Trona nodded.

"A serpent," she confirmed. "But a god as well, in his own rite. A god of death and darkness. He was sent to the Otherealm, confined to the caves of hell. And now Drazen supporters use his name to incite fear and evil, when they do not even know the truth of it. Sazarr remains in the Otherealm, ready to be unleashed, ready to get revenge on his friend from long ago. And funny enough, you seek his blade, forged from his own fang."

Will and I looked at one another in question.

"Neither of them are a god," Trona went on. "Not real gods, anyways. But we choose to believe in them because that's what the people need. Hope. Only, those who follow Sazarr are supporting the true hero of the story, and those for Drazen, the villain."

She finished, giving us a moment to take in everything. Will's face was angry, so full of rage that I was afraid he would burst into flames at any moment. But he just stood there with his arms crossed, not saying a word to anyone.

Finally, I decided to speak. "Isn't Drazen on the sun? Surely Sazarr can be freed with him gone?"

"Drazen remains hidden," Trona confirmed. "But whether that is here or elsewhere, we do not know. Sazarr can only be freed if the curse is broken once and for all, meaning he and Drazen would no longer be immortal beasts."

"And how can the curse be broken?" I asked.

"That's enough," Will cut in, resting a hand on my shoulder and glaring at the woman. "You've told us enough lies already."

But to her credit, Trona turned to face him fully, not a hint of fear on her face at all, only displeasure. "You may believe whatever you wish, but I have spoken only the truth to you here today. I am an old woman, what would I have to gain from lying to you?"

Will again scoffed. "That's the thing—you're so brainwashed that you don't even realize that you're wrong."

Trona let out a soft, amused laugh. "And perhaps I would say the same about you, boy. Maybe we can't prove the verity to each other right now, but we will eventually. More people are learning the truth. There's an uprising coming, and you best make it known that you are on the right side when it happens. Lady Havu here seems to have more sense than you."

I kept my face void of emotion, even when I knew they were both staring at me. But Trona was right, if I had to pick a side, it would be Sazarr's. "Do the people plan to rebel?" I asked her.

"I do not know what they plan," she said. "I am old and have no interest in participating, and I don't want my grandchildren anywhere near that mess, either. I can only tell you of the whispers I hear in the streets."

"What does any of this have to do with the blade?" Will asked.

Trona smiled, and it sent a shudder down my spine. "The blade is said to be the way to end Drazen once and for all. If you find it—"

"I'm not going to use it for that," I said quickly. "I mean... I couldn't." She made me promise that I wouldn't use it for evil, but I didn't want to use it at all. If Hiran wanting it was somehow connected to this...

Trona stood and walked to the front door, clearly her indication of our dismissal. Will and I stood as well, both of us ready to get out of there. But as I walked past Trona on the way out, she whispered, "There are much greater things at work here than you could ever understand. You need to be wise in the decisions you make from here on out, Lady Karalia."

Will grabbed onto my wrist and pulled me away, out into the street, and I couldn't really blame him. But those final words that she spoke to me, that omen, would stick with me for a very long time.

"Are you alright?" I asked Will as we made our way through the city, back towards the inn. He hadn't spoken a word to me since we'd left Trona's home, and I wanted more than anything to know what he was thinking. His walk was gait and his arms hung limply at his side. His eyes were pointed to the ground, like he couldn't even bear to face the world. I noticed that his hood was still down. "Will, somebody may recognize you," I said. He merely pulled his hood up without a word.

The woman, Trona, had terrified me, despite the fact that she gave us valuable information. She might have scared me even more than the seer in The Wry had. I believed what she said, even if Will did not, and I believed that she wanted to help me. She wouldn't have risked exposing herself as a Sazarr supporter, and possibly even as a rebel, if she wasn't planning on helping me.

I didn't want to push Will to talk, not yet, and especially not out in the open street where anyone could overhear us. He had been greatly affected by what we just heard, by the story that Trona told. I was too, though I knew he had it worse. What Trona told us went against basically everything he had been taught growing up, and everything that he believed in.

Most people believed that Sazarr was the one who betrayed Drazen, though it was the other way around. This story makes much more sense than the one I was told as a child. The entire history of Vatragon is based on a betrayal— of greed and lust for power. Of evil and misfortune. Sazarr had been trapped in the Otherealm for all this time, banished there because his friend betrayed him.

The day we celebrate, Rebirth Day, is nothing more than a joke. It's not the day a god was born—it's the day that Drazen betrayed his friend, stole his title, and forged his identity from misery, pain, blood, and deception.

I didn't care whether Will believed this or not, because *I* did. But not just me—there were so many others in Vatragon that knew the truth as well. I feared that Trona might have been right about an uprising coming, and that we could do nothing to stop it. Will would be right in the center of that conflict, because of who his family was, unless… there was some way for me to keep him out of it.

"Let's hear it," Will said, pulling me out of my thoughts. He was still walking ahead of me, rather fast, but had turned his head to the side so I knew he was speaking.

"What's that?" I asked him, even though I'd heard perfectly clear.

"Let's hear what you have to say to me," he said. "Don't you want to convince me that the woman was right, and that everything I've ever believed in is a lie?"

"Will," I said, in a rather scolding tone. "I would never say such a thing to you. But I just want you to hear me out." He continued walking, but nodded his head so that I knew he was listening. I chose my words carefully, for both Will and knowing that fellow city dwellers might be listening. "I understand that you don't believe what she told us, but can't you just consider for one second that there might be some factuality to what she was saying? I mean, we can't prove that she's wrong, so how would you even know if *you* were wrong?"

He kept walking, faster, not answering.

"Will?"

He whirled on me, turning so fast that I had to stumble back to keep from running into him. He reached his hands out and gripped me by the shoulders, pulling me slightly out of the center of the street. "You don't understand," he said. "I…" He was breathing heavy, like it actually pained him to say the words. "I *did* believe her," he finally said, rather shouting it at

259

me. "I believed her that Drazen is a false god—my own ancestor—my own blood. How could I not? But believing that also makes me a traitor. I'm not supposed to question those kinds of things. I'm not supposed to doubt my faith."

People turned in our direction, some of their faces blank, others slightly puzzled. I grabbed Will by the arm and pulled him further out of the street, down an alley of a building.

"You believed her?" I asked him, the surprise in my voice completely genuine.

He ran a hand through his hair. "I don't know, Kara. I don't know what to think. I don't know what to feel. I wish I could find that bastard Drazen himself and ask him the truth. You weren't raised like I was. It's not so easy for me to abandon the beliefs I've held my entire life."

"I understand," I told him. "I really do."

"I think I might believe her," he said. "I've always had doubts, I've just never been able to voice them before. So many people support Sazarr in secret, I mean, they're plotting an entire rebellion in his name."

I looked back towards the street, to make sure there was nobody nearby, but also because I needed to think without seeing Will's trembling face right in front of me. I finally took a long breath and said quietly, "They're not gods." It was as much defiance as I had ever admitted. "I know I go against everyone's beliefs when I say that. People are putting their faith into beings that were created with what is essentially dark magic, that does not belong in these lands. They should not exist here. If there are gods, Drazen and Sazarr are just pawns in a much, much larger game. They are born from magic, they are unnatural, but that doesn't mean that Sazarr is undeserving of our sympathy. It wasn't his fault, what happened to him. Don't you think that his curse deserves to be broken?"

Will's brows lowered, with something that must have been disappointment, as he said, "You want to use the blade, don't you? To free Sazarr. To destroy Drazen."

"I don't know," I told him. "That isn't really my decision to make. I wouldn't be the one to do it, but at the least we could make sure that the blade ends up with the person who should make the decision. After we free Nola, of course."

He continued shaking his head, but then a smile began to form on his lips, and then he let out a soft laugh. "This is madness," he said. "We could be executed for this."

I smiled back. "Betrayal *is* in your nature."

"That's cold of you," he laughed. And then a moment later, "I can't believe we're actually doing this."

"Me neither," I said. "So what's next? Where do we go from here?"

"To Frystal?" Will suggested. "Trona claimed that it was last seen there, and fifty years ago is much more recent compared to how long ago it was seen in Kraxoth. I think we'll have a pretty good shot if we go there."

"I agree," I said.

We headed back onto the street, back towards the inn where we would plan for our departure. Things were coming along, and though we hadn't found any definite leads yet, at least we weren't finding dead ends.

Chapter 25

The following day we headed out into the city to purchase some supplies for our next trip. We would have gone the day before, but it was already so late in the evening by the time we made it back from Trona's. So today, after breakfast, we headed out, in hopes that by this afternoon we would be on our way.

First we stopped at a clothing store. I got a pair of thick leggings that Will explained I was to wear beneath my pants, like undergarments. The temperatures would be much colder as we made our way to Frystal, so I also got a pair of gloves, long socks, and a thicker cloak.

After that we found an armorer. Will purchased a large knife, which the merchant explained to us was for hunting. We each also got our swords sharpened, and Will bought me a sheath for the *little knife*, as he'd called it, that I always carried around in the back of my pants.

"I wouldn't want you to stab yourself in the ass," he explained, to which I punched him in the arm. The armorer chuckled.

We bought another tent, this time a much smaller one that could be rolled up tight to fit inside of a satchel rather than carried across Will's back. We also purchased some sort of mat that went beneath us in the tent, which was supposed to keep us from getting wet when we slept on snow.

Then we headed to the market for food, and I thought I knew what to expect, but I was very wrong. There were fruits and vegetables like I had never seen before. *Fresh* ones. The colors were bright, like a rainbow. I'd seen some of them before, but only in their preserved forms. Apples were red like blood. Oranges were… orange. Berries were mostly violet or blue. I thought vegetables were all green, but there were orange, and yellow, and red, and even purple ones. It was amazing. I wanted to try everything, but Will said that most of it would go bad within a few days. For the trip we bought rolls of bread, dried oat bars, dried meat, and skins of wine that probably wouldn't last long. It seemed like a lot, or just more than I particularly wanted to carry. I also wondered how Will could possibly have paid for all of this, but when I really started to pay attention, the prices were much, much lower than I thought. Nearly half of what they would have been in Mortefine.

The last thing we did was meet with a stable head and arrange to pick up two horses later in the day. This, I had not expected. Riding on a horse would save us so much time and it wouldn't be nearly as exhausting. On horses, we could make it to Frystal within a fortnight.

When we returned to the inn with all of our new belongings, I took most of it upstairs to set down while Will acquired us a table and a hot meal for lunch. I had to lug it all up the stairs, and then down the hall, finally reaching out room, reaching a hand out to open the door—

I halted. The door was open, slightly ajar, not at all locked like I knew we had left it. I toed it with my foot, listening as the door creaked and slowly opened. From where I stood in the hall, nothing seemed amiss, so I unwisely decided to enter. Everything seemed fine, so I walked in all the way, set everything down, and then turned to shut the door.

I heard a hiss of something in the air, and felt something sweep right past my face. It was barely noticeable, but from the light pouring in through the windows, I could see the sun reflecting off of the knife that had just been thrown right at me, which had lodged itself into the door, not an inch away from my head.

I quickly turned around, searching for the source of the knife, already reaching for my sword. Again, I saw nothing, not until I looked into the far corner of the room and could see something lurking in the shadows. My pulse quickened, as I was reminded of the darkness that searched for me in my dreams. I wondered if it had finally made its way into my life, into the real world.

But then the shadow moved towards me, and I saw that it was not a shadow, but a person. They were dressed in all black, with a hood over their head, and a mask over the lower half of their face. Their skin was dark, and I couldn't make out much of their face, but I could vaguely tell that they were female. She must have been an assassin.

I took a step backward, towards the door so I could make a quick escape. The assassin's eyes narrowed on me. "Move," she said, her voice piercingly cold, "and the next one I thrown won't miss." That was the last voice you heard before death swept you away, I thought. I could see then that there was another knife in her hand, poised to come my way at any moment.

Why was there an assassin here in our room? Even if someone had discovered us being in the city, what cause would they have to want us dead?

I stood still and watched as the assassin moved towards the table and then sat down, propping her feet up, leaning back casually. Everything about her terrified me. She pulled her hood off and her mask down, revealing her entire face to me. She looked about my age, but felt so much older. Her very presence seemed to invite trouble. She watched me with her dark eyes, almost feline-like, and I could see her dark hair, twisted into a long braid that fell down her back. She watched me like she was sizing up prey.

She set a short sword down on the table, the clang of it causing me to flinch, but left the twin daggers hanging from each of her hips. I had no doubt that she carried more weapons, hidden beneath her clothes. Even the pins in her hair looked sharp enough to pierce through someone's skull.

264

"Can I help you?" I said, surprised that I didn't sound scared at all, but rather annoyed that I had to deal with this.

She did not speak. I heard footsteps shuffle from the hall, and then the door opened again, and Will walked in. "Hey," he said. "You forgot this—" I wasn't even looking at him to know whatever it was I had forgotten or if he could see the assassin. But then I heard his feet halt, and he came to my side, not touching me, but protecting me all the same. "Who are you?" he demanded, bravely yet foolishly.

The assassin looked at Will, almost with recognition. And then a large grin spread across her face, revealing teeth that looked too sharp to be natural, yet straight and pearly white. She began to laugh softly. "How rude of me," she teased, like she was playing with her dinner. "I haven't introduced myself." We waited. "My name is Aerez Yrongul, and I have come to kill you."

Fear crept over my skin as the assassin's eyes locked on me, marking me as her target.

"Wait," Will said, already pushing me behind him, shielding me from the deadly woman. I stayed where I was, though I didn't feel unsafe at all. She could have killed me the second I walked into the room, and yet she hadn't.

"Relax," she said. "I *was* going to kill her, but now I'm more interested to know who she is, and why she travels undercover with *Prince William Drazos*."

Will went still, as did I. He glanced over at me, clearly more concerned than I was. Rather than cowering behind him, I walked past him, towards the assassin. He reached out, as if to stop me, but I stepped out of the way. I approached the assassin and slowly pulled Fangmar from my back, then set it on the table next to her own sword. I even pulled the knife from my pants and set that down as well.

"Smart girl," the assassin said, smiling at me. Then her eyes flashed to Will, filled with unpleasantness. "Prince," she called, "why don't you wait outside." She held out her knife as she gestured towards the door.

"Do you think I'm a fool?" Will said.

"Yes," the assassin responded. Then she turned to me. "We talk, without him, or I'll just kill you right here and now, and then go collect my payment."

"You'll just kill her whether I go or not," Will seethed.

"I will not," the assassin said calmly. "I give my word that we will talk, and that I will give her a proposition. What she decides then will determine whether I kill her or not."

I turned to Will, foolishly putting my back to the assassin. "It's fine," I told him. "If she wanted me dead, she would have done it already."

The assassin let out a low, dangerous chuckle.

"I can't," Will said.

"Oh, put away your male arrogance for five minutes, would you?" she shot at him. "Just stand in the hall, I don't give a shit. We'll even leave the door unlocked if it's getting your balls in that big of a knot."

If this woman were not there to kill me, I thought perhaps I would have liked her.

Will was still reluctant, so I practically had to force him out of the room, leaving him in the hall, promising that I would scream if I needed help. Though I couldn't really scream if I was dead. I knew I wouldn't be safe with the assassin, but at the least I could try and talk to her. When he was out of the room I sat and joined the assassin at the table.

Her smirks and swagger had disappeared, and what appeared before me then was merely an ordinary woman. "I need you to listen to me," she said, her voice having grown softer. "I'm not going to hurt you. I am employed by the Kraxoth Assassin's Association, and it is true that I was hired to kill you, but under contract I am legally able to back out of any job I deem unjust."

"And why is this unjust?" I asked her.

"Well, for one I don't even know who you are," she explained. "And you don't seem like the usual grunts I'm hired to kill. You're just a girl."

"Who hired you?" I asked.

"I have no idea," she admitted. "I received an envelope with the contract the other morning. It told me exactly where you were staying, and left specific instructions to kill you but to spare the male who was accompanying you."

"How did you know he was the prince?"

She smirked slightly. "It's my job to know what important people look like."

"And yet you do not know who I am," I said. The person who hired her obviously did, but I just didn't understand why someone would want me dead.

"So, you *are* important?" she asked. "I figured you had to be, since you were traveling with the prince. And since someone had placed such a high value on your head. This would have been my highest paid job *ever*. Pity."

"Then why didn't you kill me," I said coldly.

"Because I want to help you," she said. "I'm offering a proposition. I spare you, and you allow me to come with you. You're leaving, right? I've been following you around all day—you're buying supplies for a trip."

I frowned. "Why would I want someone who's threatened to kill me to come with me?"

"I'm an assassin," she said. "Killing for me is casual. I have nothing personally against you, so I would find killing you just as easy as I would find being your companion. Only, you get to decide which it will be."

"Again, why would I want you to come with me?"

"I will be your protection," she told me. "I'm good at killing. I will promise to get you to wherever it is you're going safely."

"How long would I be granted this *protection*? And how much money would you require for it?"

"Well, I wouldn't get paid until after the job is finished, so how about, we figure it out in the end? And as for the timeframe, as long as you need me for. I couldn't really abandon you and run off, because then I wouldn't get paid." She smirked. "I couldn't let you die, either, because then I still wouldn't get paid."

"I don't have any money," I told her.

"I don't believe that for a second," she said. "You're traveling with the prince. You must be someone of importance, which means you have a lot of money, but there's always the prince to pay me too."

"Okay," I said. "You're right. I do have money, only I cannot access this money. Not yet."

"Why not?"

"Because the world believes me to be dead," I said.

"Who are you?" she asked wearily.

"Karalia Havu," I said. "The Lost Lady of Orothoz. And the future Queen of Vatragon, apparently."

And then I told her everything. I didn't do it because I felt that I owed it to her, or that I thought telling her would spare me my life, but because I wanted her to know. I hadn't been able to tell many people my truth yet, and for some reason I believed her about wanting to help me, I just didn't know what *her* motives were.

"What the hell," she said, mouth agape. I told her everything about my life, about losing my memory, about living with Hiran. I told her about being banished from the city, and then running into Will. The only thing I left out was Will's magical ability, as I knew that was not my secret to tell. I told her that I was looking for the forbidden blade, and that doing so could land us in a lot of trouble.

"You'd be getting yourself into quite a mess," I told her, hoping that would somehow deter her from wanting to come and yet spare me at the same time.

It only seemed to make her more eager. "This is perfect," she said. "This could be a lot of fun."

"It's not supposed to be fun," I snapped at her. "Why do you even want to come? Why are you so eager to do this?"

"I want to help you," she said. "I need to. I know you can't trust me, and I know the prince definitely won't, but... please," she begged. "Just let me come with you."

"Are you in some kind of trouble?" I asked her wearily.

And then the first hint of fear shone on the assassin's face, just a flicker in her eyes, and then it disappeared. That told me enough about what I needed to know, and that I didn't need to keep asking questions, not until she was ready to share the answers. Although, we would have to come up with something to tell Will.

"You can come with us," I said. "I agree to your… proposition. You will not kill me—not now, and not ever. You will be my protector, and you will fight by my side if need be."

"I will," she said.

"I don't know what lies in store for the future," I admitted. "It could be dangerous, we might fail, we might die, or worse, I could end up in the hands of my enemies. But I think I would be glad to have you there, Aerez Yrongul, and I hope that eventually I can come to trust you."

"That's very good to hear," she said, and I watched as she nearly sagged with relief. She smiled then, and it was a warm and joyous smile. She was obviously hiding from something, which wasn't really my business, but I could tell that she needed help, and that this was the way to give that help.

We let Will back into the room, and he walked over to Aerez like he was about to pounce on her, but I held a hand out to halt him. "You will not touch her," I said. "Aerez will be joining us on our journey. We will need to hire her, and she will eventually be paid for the protection that she provides me."

Aerez stood from her seat at the table and stalked over to Will, standing about a head shorter than him, though still just as fearsome. Her body was slim, and she moved almost ghost-like. She put her hands on her hips and said, "The lady is finally going to have some real protection, not you, a pathetic excuse for a prince. I heard you were parading around as a soldier—I don't know how anyone could have believed that."

"So she's a bitch?" Will said, talking over Aerez to me.

"I'm a bitch that knows how to kill," Aerez replied, turning back to me and smirking. I smirked right back. Yes, this was going to be fun.

Aerez could make all the threats she wanted, but she didn't know who Will really was. She didn't know what ability he possessed, which he could use at any moment to turn her to ash. She might have been more skilled with weapons than he, but it would amount to nothing against the wrath of flames.

Will ignored her and walked back over to my side. He put a hand on my shoulder, leaning in to ask me, "Do you trust her?" I neither nodded nor shook my head. "If you do, then that's fine, but if she's holding something against you—"

"She is not," I cut him off. "She will, under contract, be required to protect me. How could I not trust that?"

He only watched me carefully. "Did you tell her the truth?"

I nodded. "Most of it." And he knew what I meant. I told her *my* truth, not his. His secret was safe, and something to possibly use against her in the future if the situation came to that.

"Okay," he said, seeming to relax a little. "She comes with us. We still need to leave as soon as possible. If somebody already knows we're here, they might just send someone else after you next. It's only a matter of time before something else happens."

"You can come to the headquarters tomorrow to sign my contract," Aerez said. "I'll tell them I wasn't able to kill her today, so they don't know that I've decided against it yet."

"We leave tomorrow, then," Will said.

"And where exactly are we going?" Aerez asked him.

"To Frystal," I told her.

"Oh," she said excitedly. "I've never been to Frystal."

"Me neither," I added.

"Well," Will said, "It's a cold, miserable shit hole."

Aerez smirked. "Sounds delightful."

Chapter 26

Aerez promptly left after we struck our little bargain, disappearing as if she had never even been there to start with. She claimed that there were many loose ends for her to tie up before leaving the city, since she seemingly planned on never coming back to Kraxoth, at least not for a very long time. It wasn't really my business, nor did I particularly care as long as she did what we planned to pay her for. But I did hope that eventually a time would come when the three of us could trust each other.

I worried about going to the assassin's headquarters the following day. It was delaying our departure yet another day, just so we could go and sign a contract, something that I think could have taken only a few minutes. I also worried about the price that would be requested of us—not that it really mattered now, as we wouldn't be paying it for a while, but Will already did not seem too keen on the idea of bringing an assassin with us, and now the cost of it was going to be dumped on him as well.

Will and I went downstairs to eat, as originally planned, just at a much later time. The downstairs tavern was packed with people, some of them enjoying a meal, others drunk out of their minds. I thought that would be a very good idea at the moment, but Will was completely against it. So we shared a meal of roasted pork and vegetables, smothered in some sort of brown gravy. It was delicious, and I savored every bit of my last cooked meal for a while.

Afterward, we went back upstairs, back into our room, and got ready for bed. I was exhausted; it had been a long few days. First with our visit to Trona, and that entire unpleasant conversation. And then coming back to the room and finding an assassin in it, poised to kill me. I needed sleep; I just wasn't entirely certain it would be restful.

Will slid into bed beside to me, and we both savored what would be our last night in a bed for a while. He was closer to me than he had been the night before, and after our argument. Was I forgiving him too soon? I tried not to think about it, and instead focused on what was to come.

"How are you feeling?" Will whispered to me.

"I don't know," I replied. "Hopeful, scared, concerned."

"It will be okay," he told me. He reached beneath the covers of the bed, finding my hand, and then squeezed onto it gently, as if to reassure me of the words he'd just spoken. I squeezed it back, and then we eventually drifted off to sleep.

No.

It would not be okay. In fact, nothing would be okay at all. The darkness had found me. So much darkness. Pulling. Consuming. *Wake up,* something shouted. *Wake up.* I could not. Not in the way that I wanted.

The sun shone high in the sky wherever it was I had drifted off to tonight. The sky was clear, not a cloud to be seen, and a pale shade of blue. Beneath the sky were a set of mountains, the tops of them brown and dull, dead, even.

I was walking—walking on solid earth, moving my feet along, step by step. I was weak and exhausted, my throat parched and in need of water. But somehow, I felt... different. It took more effort to lift my legs, like they were heavier, and I could see more around me because I was taller. This was very strange indeed.

There was someone beside me—a man. "I think we're almost there," this man told me, his hazel eyes and light brown hair glimmering in the sun. He looked so familiar, somehow, or perhaps it was just because of how handsome he was. His hair fell to his waist, one side of it braided back in a strange way. He was so different, and even the clothes he wore were odd.

"Good," I said after a moment, but it wasn't my own voice that left my mouth. It was the voice of another man, deep, strange coming out of my mouth. I looked down to examine my body, which was also that of a man, powerfully built, and also wearing those odd clothes. My hair was dark, perhaps even black, and it too fell to my waist. At least there was one thing in this body that I was familiar with. I tried not to think about the strange thing I could feel between my legs. There was also an odd-looking weapon hanging from my side, some sort of curved sword.

"There's nothing to worry about, Sazarr," the other man said, resting a hand on my shoulder, smiling softly, with a friendly gleam in his eyes.

Sazarr? If the body I occupied was Sazarr, then the other man must have been... Drazen. How odd this was, indeed. This could have only been a dream, but it felt different somehow, like a memory. It felt like I was really there, and really in another man's body.

Suddenly everything grew fuzzy. My surroundings blurred, like the world was changing, but it only lasted for a moment until a new setting appeared in front of me.

Drazen and I were in some sort of hut, with strange looking objects spread about the room that I did not recognize. On the walls, painted in what I hoped was not blood, were even stranger looking symbols. My attention turned to a woman on the other side of the room. She was beautiful, like nobody I had ever seen before, and she was tracing shapes in the air with her fingers. She moved towards us, faster than what ought to have been normal, and began to speak in a language that I did not recognize.

I realized it then—that she was the enchantress, and she was setting her curse onto Drazen and Sazarr.

Again, my surroundings blurred, and the world was changing once more. We were outside again. I was on my knees, tears falling from my eyes. I looked over to Drazen, to my friend, and watched as his body began to transform. He screamed out as his limbs elongated, and as wings splayed from his back. His neck lengthened, bones cracking and popping as it happened, and his mouth adjusted to fit the mass of teeth that were growing. He continued to scream out in pain, until it turned into a roar, into a sound that was not human at all.

I reached for him, as if I could stop what was already done, and then I fell over, pain consuming me now as well. I was overwhelmed with the sensation of my body changing, becoming something terrible. I could feel things moving beneath my skin, the magic taking hold, as my body and mind transformed into that of a beast. Pure, vicious hunger filled me, as did a desire to kill, and the urge to kill my own friend that was right next to me.

He watched me, through slitted orange eyes, as if thinking that same exact thing. But then he turned towards the sky, flapping his wings and jutting away.

I was pulled away again, unable to do anything as my surroundings changed. It felt like I was traveling a long way, through much time and space. It took a while to steady myself again, but when I did, I could feel the wind against my skin, and the beat of my heart as I flapped my mighty wings and soared through the clouds. I was still in Sazarr's body, when he was a dragon.

But then suddenly flame erupted, not from my own throat, but from something behind me. It obstructed my view, and I banked left, turning around to see another dragon coming straight for me.

It was my friend, Drazen, or what used to be my friend. Now, it was only a beast.

He again shot his flame at me, and while it didn't burn, it distracted me from my flying, sending me tumbling down back towards the earth. As I fell, I heard a roar, and then I felt teeth around my throat, biting onto me, tearing me open. Blood sprayed through the air, and I knew then that I was going to die.

I continued to fall, doing everything I could to flap my wings and carry me away, but then Drazen returned, grabbing onto me with his claws, biting down onto my right wing and tearing it straight from my body. I cried out, unable to do anything as he did the same to my left wing, and then to my legs.

I could see the earth growing nearer beneath me, but all I could think about was the pain, and the fact that there was nothing I could do to save myself.

My body collided with the earth, and I was dead.

My friend.

How could you?

I was revived, saved by that very magic that turned me into a beast all those years ago. A warm and tingly sensation rippled through my body. At first, I thought it was death taking my pain away as I faded from existence, but then I realized that it was the magic, doing exactly as the curse had intended. My wounds healed, but my blood... it was changing. It turned cold, burning like ice as it thrummed through my veins.

Drazen was there, in the body of the mortal that he has once been long ago. There was sadness on his face for what he had done to me, for the regret he felt. And the worst pain of all wasn't the physical wounds he had inflicted on me, but my broken heart—and the betrayal that I felt within it.

The darkness took me. I was in a cave, filled with mist and screams in the distance. It was the Otherealm, and I had been banished there for all eternity. My body was serpent, slithering its way through the nothingness as I would continue to do for a thousand years.

I could never tell how much time had passed. My mind was hardly my own, and while I was granted the ability to transform back into my body that was once a man, I preferred the body of the serpent.

I heard footsteps echo nearby. They were so quiet, so dainty, but I went towards them, slithering, staying silent. I hid in the shadows of the cave as I came upon her. No, *me*.

It was *me* there in the darkness of the Otherealm, watching myself through Sazarr's eyes. I stared at myself staring at him, the green in each of our eyes reflecting back at one another. I wanted to move toward her, but I knew that I should not frighten her. It had been so long since I'd had a visitor, and she was someone unique, indeed.

Complete darkness exploded around me yet again, and I knew my time was up.

I shot up in bed, the blankets tangled around me, burning like I was encased in flame. I screamed in terror, clawing at my body, making sure that every part of me was still intact. The bed was drenched in sweat, likely mixed with my tears. My arms and legs were there—human limbs. No wings, and no cold serpent skin. I was back in my own body, back in my own mind.

I was crying, not for myself, but for what I had just witnessed as I slept. Was it a dream? That would be the most plausible explanation, but yet it felt more like I was reliving the events, that they were being shown to me. It felt so real, and my heart stung, like I was truly the one who had been betrayed.

Will was awake, terror and concern on his face, already right at my side with his arms around me. "It's okay," he said. "It was a dream. You're okay."

I flung myself at him, wrapping my arms around his neck, burying my face into his chest. I sobbed as I never had before—as I had never allowed anyone to ever see before. I screamed out in pain and sadness, wailing into the night.

"I can't," I said in between sobs. "I can't do this. He's looking for me. He knows."

"It's okay," Will said again, and I knew that he had no idea what I was talking about, but he would comfort me all the same. His arms remained a tight force around me.

For a very long while, hours, I remained trembling in fear. The crying ceased, but I was far too frightened to go back to sleep. The dream, it was the most vivid and terrifying one I had ever had, and it made me never want to sleep again. It made me want to force myself to stay awake even if it killed me.

Finally, when I thought that I could again form words, I whispered to Will, unsure if he was awake or not, but still needing to just say it. "I dreamt about what Trona told us. I *saw* it. I saw it happen, from Sazarr's eyes. I could feel everything."

"It was a dream," Will said, running a soothing hand down my arm.

"I don't think it was," I told him. "It felt like I was reliving his memories. Do you think something like that is possible?" I waited, but he did not answer. "I... I saw myself. From another time I thought I was dreaming. I saw myself from Sazarr's eyes, as if I had really been there then, too."

"We can figure it out later," he told me, turning us so that he was laying down, though he was still holding onto me. "Get some rest."

And I wanted to, I really did, but I knew I wouldn't be resting any time soon. Never again, it seemed.

I was still awake when morning came. From the bed I watched the sky turn from black, to pink and orange, and then to blue. The sound of Will's soft snoring was the only thing that kept me from going completely insane, as did his body pressed against mine. Even when he slept, he held onto my hand. My eyes burned from both exhaustion and from all of the tears that had fallen from them in the past hours.

Will stirred beside me, so I closed my eyes as if to pretend I was asleep, only because I did not want to concern him any more than I already had—not after what he had done for me last night. If he hadn't been there to help me, I didn't know what I would have done.

I stretched out my limps, listening as Will yawned, and then I did as well. He rubbed a hand over my back, in a way that I would not have allowed if the situation were otherwise. I'd already shared enough with him last night to start being embarrassed now. So I opened my eyes to find him watching me, and I slid a hand around his neck and pulled him in for a hug.

"Thank you, Will," I said. "For everything."

We were still hugging as he said, "I was terrified. I thought you were dying. I thought... I was losing you."

My eyes again watered. "I'm sorry. It felt like I *was* dying. But I'm glad that you were here to help me."

"You don't need to apologize," he said, his voice more sincere than I had ever heard it.

"Will," I said, leaning back and looking up at his face.

His mouth opened to reply, but then the door to our room burst open, and in walked Aerez, clad in black clothing, weapons at her sides, and a huge grin on her face. "Wake up time, lovebirds," she crooned.

Will and I casually scooted away from each other. "I know I locked that door," Will told her grumpily.

Aerez scoffed, like it was such an insult to suggest that a locked door could keep her out. Will stood from the bed, his chest bare, his bottom covered in nothing but undershorts. Aerez sized him up and down, smiling as she did it. He walked over to her and put his hands on her shoulders, turning her towards the door and then shoving her out of it.

"Wait outside," he growled, and then slammed the door shut so hard that the paintings on the walls rattled.

I sat up in bed. "You two need to learn how to start getting along," I told him. "I don't want to hear you bickering the entire was to Frystal."

He gave me a sad smile, like he was relieved I was already making jokes again so soon.

"I'll be fine," I told him, though I wasn't exactly sure it was the truth.

We met Aerez downstairs a short while later, finding her seated at the bar nursing a glass of brown liquid. It was quite early in the day to be drinking, but I wasn't one to judge. I thought I could use a drink myself.

I looked mostly presentable again, after cleaning up some in the bathing room. Though there would be no hiding the red puffiness of my eyes, or the faint scratches on my arms beneath my clothes from where I had clawed at myself. I didn't want Will to see that.

Aerez was picking under her fingernails with a dagger, looking bored and carefree. "Ah!" she said. "About time." Then she sheathed her dagger, picked up her drink, and finished it in one swallow.

"In a rush?" Will asked her.

"Oh, you know," she said, waving a hand dismissively. "I'm always eager to start a new job. Something new and exciting." She looked at me, like she would comment on my appearance, but wisely kept her mouth shut. I liked that there was already this strange understanding between us, even though we had only met yesterday.

"So, here is the plan," Will said, clearing his throat. "We go and sign this contract, and then we leave the city as soon as we can. I can get the horses and meet you guys at the western gate. From there we can take the capital road most of the way, but we'll still have to stay hidden, as we have been here. It should take a couple of weeks to get there, and even though it's summer, fall is nearing, and the closer we get to Frystal, the colder it will become. When we get to Frystal, we can come up with another plan, or start by searching for information on the blade."

Aerez and I nodded in understanding, eagerly ready to get on with the next phase of our plan. We left the inn and headed out into the city, allowing Aerez to lead the way.

Chapter 27

As it would turn out, the headquarters of the Kraxoth Assassin's Association were not as hidden as one might have expected. We entered an ordinary building, one packed in tightly with other shops, and what could have been a shop itself. From the street there was no sign indicating any sort of business, and the windows were too dark to see into, and as you stepped inside you realized that it was no ordinary shop.

There was only one small room, occupied with a desk, and a woman sitting behind it. Behind her was a set of double doors, bolted shut. The woman looked up from the book she was reading as we approached.

"Hello, Aerez," she said in a bored tone. "Who are your friends?"

"Oh, them?" Aerez asked, amusement lacing her tone, though I didn't know what was funny. "They're here to sign a contract."

"For you?" the woman asked.

"Yes," Aerez said. "They seek to hire me."

The woman shook her head and let out a long sigh. "You know he won't like that, Aerez. I don't know why you insist on challenging him with your every action."

"I'm not challenging him," Aerez protested, but the woman was already up and out of her seat, raising a key to unlock the doors. I had no idea who this man was they were talking about, and I was a bit afraid to find out.

Aerez motioned us towards the door, and Will rested a hand against my lower back, not to push me forward but rather to let me know that he was there with me.

That little set up they have, the woman at the desk, was simple enough, but I wondered what exactly they did if somebody unexpected walked in. What would they say to deter them—to send them on their way? As we walked further inside of the building, I got the sense that this was not the true assassin's headquarters, that this was just the place they conducted business with outsiders. It was a front for the real headquarters that were hidden somewhere else in the city.

We walked down a long dimly lit hall with doors on either side, which I would have thought was an inn if it weren't for the eeriness. One of the doors that we passed was open, revealing a decently sized room, only there was nothing in it except for one singular chair. The walls were lined with mirrors, and I caught my reflection as we passed. My face was pale and ghostly.

The building wasn't empty, either. We passed many people, some of them dressed in all black and clearly recognizable as an assassin, others wearing normal clothes, but everyone keeping to themselves. Some people's faces were covered entirely by masks, while Aerez only wore a hood to conceal hers.

We stopped in front of a nondescript room, and Aerez opened the door to let us in. The only thing in there was a rectangular table, what could have been a dining table if it were any other place, surrounded by about a dozen chairs.

"Wait here," Aerez told us as soon as we entered. "I need to fetch my master." Then she walked back into the hall, shutting and locking the door behind herself, leaving me and Will alone.

"Master?" Will whispered to me, and I was wondering the exact same thing. Could that be the man she was talking about before? That word gave me a very bad feeling. She couldn't have been a slave, because slavery was outlawed in Vatragon, but her having a *master* did not seem like a particularly good thing.

Will and I sat next to each other at the near end of the table, closest to the door. We didn't say a word, for fear that someone might be listening in on us.

Only a few minutes passed before Aerez returned with this *master* in tow. He was older, maybe in his late thirties, and I would have thought him handsome if it weren't for the unbelievable number of scars covering his face. Most of them were small, but one extended from his temple diagonally to the opposite cheek, going through his eye which he clearly had lost the ability to use. His other eye, however, was a reddish-brown color, as was his hair.

He did not smile or speak as he approached. He did not acknowledge us at all. Aerez shot us an apologetic glance, as if to warn us that things were about to get very unpleasant. She sat down on my right, with Will on my left, and her master sat at the head of the table.

The man frowned as he took me in. "Isn't this the bitch you were supposed to kill?" he asked Aerez.

Will shifted a little in his seat, but I reached a hand beneath the table and placed it atop his knee, begging him to relax. I had been through far worse before, so certainly I could handle the vicious words of this vile man.

"I decided not to kill her," Aerez said, with something softer in the way she spoke. "I invoked clause forty-seven, so you can tell whoever hired me that they can find someone else to take care of their problem. That is, if they can find her." She smirked, turning to me and winking, like she was so sure nobody ever would.

"Perhaps I should just kill her here," the man said. "You've brought her to me, and I would get paid handsomely for what you've failed to accomplish."

"You cannot kill her," Aerez said. "I invoked—"

"Yes, I know," the man said. "You deemed her life unworthy of being taken. I know the damned clause because I'm the one who wrote it, Aerez. You're going to cost me a lot of money for this."

Aerez turned to me and Will. "Well, this gentleman here is going to hire me instead, and he's promised to pay three times of what your other client has offered."

Will didn't say anything, but I knew he was angry because I could feel the muscles of his leg tense beneath my hand. He certainly had not promised anything of the sort.

"Who does *he* want dead?" the man asked Aerez, looking at Will as if he loathed him. Did he know who Will was? I didn't think so, because he wouldn't have allowed him to enter the building if that were so.

"Nobody," Aerez told him, her voice having grown quieter. "They want to hire me as… as protection."

Fury lit the man's face. "You're not a gods damned bodyguard, Aerez," he yelled at her, causing me to jump in my seat. "You're an assassin. I didn't train you to protect people, I trained you to *kill them*."

"Well," Aerez said wearily. "I suppose that their protection may require me to kill a few people, maybe even more. I think that should satisfy you, correct? We already know that somebody wants her dead, so it's not foolish to expect that others will be coming after her."

I didn't dare speak. I was terrified, so I couldn't even fathom how Aerez could stand to argue with the man. I had to applaud her on her bravery, but she did also know the man better than I, so perhaps he was not as cruel as I thought.

She further coaxed him, telling him lies and promising that she would prove that this was the right choice. It was convincing enough, though I knew it didn't matter because she never planned to return to this city. Which also meant that the payment Aerez promised him didn't matter either. Her master finally agreed, though he did not seem happy about it. He went to write up the contract, leaving the three of us alone.

Aerez seemed to have such a strange relationship with the man. It seemed like he cared for her, in an odd way, and that her skill was something he prided, but he treated her like a pet. Like she was a dog ordered to obey every command given. I had to wonder how she came into the employment of this man. It reminded me all too much about how I was treated in Mortefine, and filled me with a sense of pity.

The man returned, asking for each of our signatures. Aerez went first, her signature sloppy and nearly illegible. Will went next, using an alias that I did not recognize. He surely couldn't put his real name, and neither could I. I tried not to make it too obvious that I was thinking of what to put, so I pretended to read the document over as I came up with the name: Kara Westchase. I carefully and clearly signed it, and then the man signed his own name and rolled up the piece of parchment, sealing it with wax where he would likely keep it tucked away in his records.

"Why did they want you dead?" the man asked, speaking to me directly for the first time.

Goosebumps prickled my skin as his gaze assessed me. "I don't know," I said. "I was hoping you could tell me."

"I don't even know who it was that ordered it," he said. "They left a sealed envelope at the door in the middle of the night."

"Well," I said. "I'm sorry that my life has cost you so much money."

He waved me off. "Don't get Aerez killed and perhaps I'll forgive you." And he wasn't being stern then, he sounded almost… sincere.

Aerez stood from her chair and strode over to the man, placing her hands on his shoulders from behind. "I'll be fine," she said to him. "You shouldn't worry so much, it's bad in your old age."

And to his credit, the man let out a soft chuckle. "Goodbye, Aerez," he told her, almost as if he knew it would be the last time they saw one another.

The three of us left the man alone in the room and quickly left the building. I had seen enough of that place to last a lifetime. The woman at the front desk said goodbye as we exited and walked back into the city.

"Well," Aerez said, leaning against a nearby wall, "that went better than I expected."

I wanted to ask her more about it. About that man, about her life as an assassin, but I didn't want to press. She was running away, whether she admitted that or not, and for her own reasons.

"Okay," Will said. "Here's the plan. I'll go to the stable head and pick up the horses. You two can go back to the inn and gather all of our belongings, then meet me at the western gate."

Aerez and I nodded, and then headed south back towards the inn, while Will headed north to the stables. We walked quickly, but not fast enough to seem suspicious to the guard's eyes.

Once we were back in the room at the inn, I began shoving our things into satchels, filling our water canteens, and bringing only what was absolutely necessary. I left behind the clothes I had worn in The Wry, as they would be useless now against the cold we would be going into. Aerez had her own bag, though it was lightly packed, and contained no food at all. I wouldn't question her on it. I even took the bar of soap from the bathing room and shoved it into my bag, for when we found somewhere to wash up as we traveled.

I fastened my sword across my back, and my knife at my hip, and strapped the satchels along my body. I pulled my hood over my head, and turned to Aerez, who was also ready. But as we went for the door, heavy footsteps sounded from the other side, and then the door shot open, and Will ran in.

He was panting and covered in sweat, his sword gripped in his hand as if he had just been in a fight. I was about to ask what had happened when he shut the door behind himself and pushed a chair up against it, and then walked over to the windows and drew the curtains shut. Aerez and I watched on in confusion.

"We will not be leaving today, after all," he told us.

"What?" I said. "What happened?"

He ignored me and instead set down his things, removing his boots and then shucking his coat. Then he went into the bathing room and shut the door.

"What the hell was that about?" Aerez whispered to me.

I shrugged, as I was just in the dark as she was. We walked over to the windows, pulling back the curtains just an inch to peer outside. There were men in the street below, guards, but they were not Kraxoth guards. Instead they bore the Drazos sigil, the same one that Will had when I first met him.

I set down all of our things and then went to sit on the couch to wait for Will. Aerez sat down beside me. When he finally did emerge, he had clearly bathed and was running a towel through his hair, looking as casual as ever, like he hadn't just burst in here like a maniac.

"Sorry about that," he said. "I just needed to cool down for a minute."

"What happened?" I asked again.

He sat down beside us. "There were guards patrolling the gate, checking everyone who entered and exited the city. Capital guards. I don't know if they're looking for me or for somebody else, but they would certainly have recognized me."

"Why would they be here for you?" Aerez asked.

"Well," Will said. "My father is likely unhappy about me leaving without saying a word to him, and taking a bunch of his soldiers with me, so if he somehow heard that I'm in Kraxoth, he probably wants me captured and brought back to the capital."

"This is not good," I said. "How are we going to leave?"

"Leave that to me," Aerez smirked. "I could distract the guards so you guys can slip out of the city unseen."

"But how will *you* get out?" I asked.

"Oh, don't worry about that," she told me.

"There are a lot of guards," Will said to Aerez. "I don't know if you would be able to distract them all."

"Well, if anything you two can get the horses and make a run for it," Aerez said. "If you make it into the forest, you can hide and wait for me to catch up, or you could keep going and I would still catch up eventually."

"But what if you get caught?" I asked her.

She shot me a sideways glance. "I will not get caught."

"We can leave tomorrow," Will said. "Get our rest tonight and then leave first thing in the morning."

And so we had our plan, which was again changed, and our departure from Kraxoth was again delayed, but it was the best we could do at the moment. If those guards were looking for Will, I had no idea how they knew he was here. We tried to remain mostly hidden, but I suppose it would have been easy for him to get recognized, out of all the places we'd been to.

I had a very bad feeling about what was to come

Chapter 28

We ate dinner downstairs that night. Will insisted on eating in the room, as did I since I knew it would keep him hidden, but Aerez refused to be shut up with the two of us in a room all night. So we went to the downstairs tavern and sat in the corner, Will with his hood pulled up and his back to the rest of the room. After all, he was the only one of us that was likely to be recognized, and the only one that the guards were after.

The meal was like many I'd had before, but it was good to eat something hot and fresh, so I savored every bite of it. We shared a pitcher of ale, which I only drank about one mug of, but Aerez insisted that it wasn't enough, that we needed to have a proper drink for our last night in the city.

I knew it was not a good idea.

She took us to a bar just next door, and from the street I could hear music blasting and people cheering and clapping. When we walked in, I saw people dancing, wide smiles on their faces. They did not dance to the elegant waltzes that I had come to know living at the Rendal estate, but rather they danced to fun and upbeat tunes. Some people were clapping their hands, others were stomping their feet. Couples spun each other around in circles, skipping and jumping. Nobody wore fine gowns or tailored suits. They wore ordinary clothes, as the room was filled with ordinary people.

I'd never experienced such a thing.

We sat at a table farthest from the dancing, where we were least likely to be recognized. But I didn't think anybody would dare to approach the table with Aerez sitting at it, not with the two gleaming daggers hanging from her sides.

She held up a hand and then snapped her fingers, gesturing for the barkeeper to come over. It was a kind of rude gesture, if I might add. But the man behind the bar walked over, a wary expression on his face.

"We'll start with three mugs of ale," Aerez told the man. "And not the horse piss you usually serve, I want the good stuff, what you import from the southern breweries." The man opened his mouth to protest, but Aerez quickly cut him off. "I know you keep it hidden in the back, do not lie to me." The man wisely shut his mouth. "The in a little while we'll take three shots of whiskey." The barman nodded in understanding, and then Aerez added, "Each."

His eyes widened a little, and he looked nervously between the three of us, but then walked back to the bar, like he was putting as much distance between Aerez and himself as he could get.

He returned with the three mugs of ale, which we all sipped at. It certainly tasted better than the ale we had with our dinner, but it wasn't the best thing I'd ever tasted. We never really much got our hands on stuff like that in Mortefine. I only ever drank wine, as that was what Hiran preferred.

But later, when he brought the whiskey over, that was when the real trouble started. I liked the toasty flavor of it, sweet and yet hot as it went down your throat. It certainly could work wonders when you wanted to have a good time.

"Another round!" Aerez yelled across the loud and crowded room, and somehow, over the loud music, the barman heard her. Moments later he approached with three more small glasses of whiskey, cleaning away the empty classes that we had already consumed.

Will watched me nervously, hesitating with the drink in his hand. I merely shrugged and then drank my own, slamming the empty glass down onto the table. He smiled as he shrugged as well, and then drank his.

Aerez climbed out of her seat then, very clearly drunk, and stalked over to Will. She put her arms around his neck from behind, rubbing her hands over his chest. She moved clumsily, nearly pulling him from his chair. She ran her hands over him, which Will seemed to like, but while she did it, he watched me the entire time. My face heated, and I truly felt drunk then as I turned away from him, and then began laughing, confused as to why I had blushed.

"I want to see if the prince can have some fun," Aerez said to him, a bit too loudly, though we were all too drunk to care.

I thought maybe that Will would get mad, but instead he leaned back, further into Aerez's touch, then tilted his head up and laughed. "I can have fun when I want to." He turned his face and pressed it against her neck, quite sensually, and I again forced myself to look away.

She pulled away from him and stalked over to me, keeping her hands on my chair for balance. "What about you, lady?" she asked. "Do you want to have some fun?"

I grinned, probably looking like a drunken idiot. "Maybe," I said, and then I raised my brows, as if to ask her what she had in mind.

"I want to watch the two of you dance," she said, giggling softly. "You do know how to dance, right?"

I nodded mindlessly, and it didn't even occur to me that I in fact did *not* know how to dance. Will nodded as well, and then said to Aerez, "You won't join us?" There was a rough edge to his voice.

Aerez just pointed across the room towards the mass of dancing people, and then Will stood from his chair, pulling me towards them. When I stood my head began to spin and I thought that I might fall, but Will had his hands on my waist, keeping me upright as we stumbled our way across the room.

I wasn't sure either of us would be able to dance at the moment, but at least we could try. He extended a hand to me, bowing unsteadily. I let out a childish giggle and then placed my hand in his, and then he was pulling me into the circle of people who were spinning around and around and around. Why were they dancing in a circle? I couldn't possibly understand it, but I joined in anyway, Will's hand holding mine the entire time.

I had no idea what I was doing, but I just watched and followed along with everyone else, not caring if I looked like a fool or if anyone was judging me. I had not a care in the world at the moment. I could have stayed there and danced like that forever.

I glanced back at the table at some point, finding Aerez standing on her chair and smiling at us. "Dance!" she called.

So we did, with whatever shred of willpower that I had left within me. My feet moved beyond my own volition. I was lost within the crowd of people, some of them old, some my age, and some even younger. But they all had smiles on their faces, and I thought that it was the most joyous thing I'd ever seen.

Everyone laughed and cheered. There were no specific movements to the dancing, you just moved with rhythm to the music. At one point Will took me by my hand again and spun me around until I stumbled and nearly fell over, but then he caught me, holding me upright as he smiled down at me, and as I smiled right back.

At some point we'd managed to walk back to the table, where the three of us engaged in amusing conversation long into the night. When the barkeeper announced that it was closing time, people slowly began to make their way out of the bar and back to their homes in the city. I didn't want to leave. I didn't want the night to be over at all.

But Will took both me and Aerez by the hands, pulling us out onto the street even when we protested. I would not have been able to make it back into the room on my own, even though it was only the next building over. I don't think I'd ever gotten so drunk before. And though my mind was starting to clear, it would still be a while until I felt like myself again.

Aerez walked between the two of us, her arms draped around both of our shoulders. "This was fun," she slurred. "I'm glad you guys are letting me come with you. I'm glad I'll finally be free."

"Well, I'm glad you're coming with us," I smiled back at her.

We paused outside the door to the inn, and through the windows we could see that the downstairs was mostly empty, save for a woman cleaning off the tables for the night.

Aerez poked a finger into my chest. "You guys can meet me upstairs in a little while," she said, and then she winked at Will, though I was far too drunk to understand what that meant.

Then she walked inside, and we watched through the window as she made her way to the stairs. I almost wanted to go and make sure that she made it safely, but she moved with surprising ease.

"She is... interesting," Will whispered into my ear, and the nearness of his voice frightened me a bit. He ran a hand down my arm, then said, "Come on." I allowed him to pull me down an empty side street.

"What are you doing?" I asked with genuine curiosity.

He turned to me, his expression unreadable, and then before I could give it another thought, he was moving towards me, wrapping one hand around my waist and the other over my neck. He softly pushed me into the wall of the building, the warmth of his body quite inviting compared to the coolness of the night.

Without even realizing what I was doing, I pulled him closer to me, pressing our chests together as I tilted my head back and looked into his eyes. They were hazel, filled with a different kind of warmth. I was so lost in the moment that I didn't even realize what was happening.

He leaned down and pressed his mouth to mine, his soft lips pushing against me, his tongue sliding its way in expertly.

He certainly knew what he was doing. His hands ran over my body as his mouth performed a dance so different from the one we had done earlier.

For a moment, just one moment, I was lost in him. I felt happy and free, but it wasn't for the reasons that I knew Will hoped for. I think I could have been kissing anyone at that moment and I would have felt the same way. It was only when he spoke that I was pulled out of my lucid transfixion. "I have wanted to do that for so long," he said to me. "Karalia, you've been driving me insane."

And when he bent down to kiss me again, I pulled away from him. What he'd just said to me… I couldn't do that to him. I couldn't kiss him and let him think that it meant something to me—because it didn't.

"What is it?" he said to me, his expression turning nervous.

"You shouldn't have done that," I told him, and I tried to say it as softly as I could, but it might have come out a bit harshly.

"Karalia," he said pleadingly. "Please." I shook my head and made to move away from him, but he ran after me. "Why?" he demanded. "All night, you have been looking at me like you… like you cared about me. You danced with me. You smiled at me as I'd never seen you smile before. Why?"

I knew he was right. I had done all of those things, but not with the intention to… seduce him. I had just gotten lost in the moment, and now I regretted it all. I continued to shake my head, not really sure what to say or do.

"Please just tell me how you feel," he said to me. "Honestly."

I put some distance between us, but then turned back and said, "I don't know, Will. I don't know what I'm supposed to feel about anything. You lied to me, not that long ago, if you don't remember. I'm still trying to learn how to be your friend, so I certainly could not be something more than that. And besides, your brother…"

"What does my brother have to do with this?" he said angrily.

And I was getting angry now, too. "I don't know what he has to do with this, other than the fact that he wants to steal me away to be his bride. What happens if he gets his hands on me? Would you betray him to stop that from happening?" I hardly knew what I was saying, but I continued anyway. "I can't betray him before I've even met him."

"What is that supposed to mean?" Will seethed.

I moved away a couple more feet. "I just don't want to make a bad impression, when he thinks that I'm *with* his brother."

"What?" Will said, on the verge of shouting. "I thought you didn't care what he thought—I thought you wanted nothing to do with him."

"I don't want to *marry* him," I said. "That doesn't mean that I don't want to have a good relationship with the future King of Vatragon."

He pondered my word for a moment before he spoke again. "I don't understand anything about you," A pause. "I feel like this isn't even about saving Nola anymore. Do you even care?"

Such pure, undiluted rage filled me. I stalked over to Will and wrapped my hand in his hair, pulling his face down so I could scream directly at it. "You're right," I hissed. "You don't know anything about me, and you never will. But understand this, I will stop at nothing to save Nola. I will not let anybody get in my way, and I would marry your brother in an instant if it guaranteed her safety, because I would do *anything* for her."

I released his hair and then shoved him away from me. He just stood there, stunned into silence.

"I want nothing from you beyond the help you are providing me in searching for the blade, and if you ever kiss me again, I will stab you in the gut. Is that clear?"

It was better for him to think the worst of me. With everything else going on, I didn't want to have to worry about him, too. I didn't want him worrying about me, either. I cared about him, I did, but if he got in my way that care would go out of the door in an instant.

He didn't say another word as he turned around and stormed off somewhere, away from the inn. I didn't care where he was going. I didn't think I would even care if he never came back, because I had Aerez now, and I knew she would prove helpful. I knew he was more hurt than angry, but that wasn't my problem.

When I walked back inside and up to our room, Aerez was already asleep in the bed. I immediately crawled in next to her, my head spinning and a headache already forming. I tried to stay awake, to see if Will would return, but I quickly drifted off to sleep. The drinking, the dancing, and everything else, it made me so exhausted. But the one thing that I selfishly found myself worrying about the most was the fact that I might have a nightmare, and that Will wouldn't be there to help me.

But luckily, I slept peacefully through the night. And when I woke up a few hours before dawn to relieve myself, I found that Will had returned, and that he was sleeping on the floor next to my side of the bed, a hand outstretched in my direction, like he had been reaching for me. A sad pain welled up in my chest, but I forced any thoughts out of my mind as I fell back to sleep.

I felt like I had died the next morning. I felt like I was a corpse rising from a grave. The sun was peeking through the curtains, shining directly onto my face, and it hurt just to see the light. It felt like a weight was holding me down, pounding on my head. But I knew this would be the result when I so willingly drank enough last night to sate an entire army.

I smelled something odd, like fresh cut roses, and I realized that it was a smell I hadn't yet familiarized myself with. Aerez. She had somehow made it to my side of the bed, and had an arm draped over my stomach, her face resting against my arm. She looked so peaceful as she slept, not at all like the fearsome killer she actually was.

I heard footsteps approach from the hall, like someone was running, and in an instant Aerez was awake and out of bed, stalking towards the door with a knife in her hand. It was impressive, how trained her senses were.

The door burst open, but it was only Will that walked in, no longer at his place beside the bed. He hunched over, out of breath, his sword again in his hand, only this time it was covered in blood.

"We have to leave," he told us. "Right now."

Chapter 29

Only a few short minutes later and we were making our way through the city. We were running, though that did nothing to help us remain inconspicuous. Will wanted us to make it to the gate as quickly as possible, so that's what we were doing.

After he barged into the room before, he informed us that those guards we were trying to stay hidden from, they were seen breaking into private businesses and searching the city, no doubt looking for Will. If we would have stayed at the inn, they would have found us eventually.

So Aerez and I again gathered all of our things, and Will went downstairs to pay our bill. We left the inn, Will heading in the opposite direction as us so he could go and get the horses. Aerez and I ran for the gate. She grabbed onto my hand and dragged me along, and I did not protest.

I wouldn't allow myself to think about what happened the night before. I couldn't tell if Will was angry, mostly because he was so shaken up about something else. I regretted the drinking immensely, because I had a terrible pounding in my head and nausea working its way up my body.

The morning was cold, and the men heading to work for the day stepped out of our way as they saw us approaching. It was an odd courtesy, but one I was grateful for. That's something I've noticed about the city—everyone turns a blind eye to anything that doesn't affect them directly. It can be helpful, in this situation, but harmful in others. They wouldn't alert those guards if they saw people that seemed to be hiding from them, but they also wouldn't alert us if there were guards stationed just around the corner.

And as soon as we turned down a busier street, a handful of guards were making their way straight toward us. Their attention was elsewhere, but as soon as they saw us running, they went on high alert. In a matter of seconds, the guards had their swords drawn and were working their way through the mass of people towards us.

Aerez took me by the wrist in an attempt to pull me down a side street, but as soon as we turned, we could see the guards coming from that way as well, and the direction we had just come from. They were surrounding us. We needed to be clever if we were going to get away safely, that is, without Aerez having to kill anybody.

There was only one way left for us to go—behind the street vendors and along the walkway out from of the shops, where we would mostly be hidden from the guards, if only we could get over there.

"Run," Aerez told me, like she already knew what I was thinking. "I'll hold them off for now, but you have to run to the gate."

And so I did. I broke off into a sprint, slipping behind the street vendors and blending myself in with the crowd of people. I dared to turn my head back, finding that Aerez had also gotten away, somehow, and was walking behind me at a casual pace, like she was only a woman shopping at the market. I thought I had a good eye on her, but a moment later I could not see her anymore, and when I turned back around, there were two guards at my back, one of them pointing their sword straight at my side.

It wasn't hard enough to cut me, not with how much clothes I had on, but it was enough to let me know that he could hurt me if he wanted to, if I tried to escape. The second guard moved in front of me so that I had nowhere to run, and then the same one with the sword wrapped his hand around my arm and started to drag me away, towards an empty side street. I struggled to break free, but with every move I made, I was reminded of the sword poised to slice into my gut.

They shoved me onto my knees, cornering me against the wall of a building. "She's the one they want," the man sneered. "Go tell the others to come back," he said. "We have what we need."

It was only then that I realized it—that these were not the guards after Will. They were not guards from the capital at all, but rather the Lord of Kraxoth's men. What would the Lord of Kraxoth want with me? How would they even know to look for me? Was he the one that hired Aerez?

I couldn't believe that I'd let myself get cornered like this, alone without either of my companions, both of whom were supposed to be protecting me. I hadn't been fast enough, and I was too busy looking back to make sure that Aerez was okay to even notice the guards on my own trail. It was foolish. But perhaps I didn't need them—perhaps I wasn't completely helpless. I had a few good weapons and enough training to show these men what I was capable of.

There were three of them now, the first one standing over me with his arm propped against the wall, sneering down at me as if he'd just caught his dinner. Before the man could even realize what I was doing, I slid my body to the side, my knees scraping through my pants against the hard ground, but I had to ignore that for now. I turned around and reached for the guard's sword, balling my fists together and slamming them down onto the flat side of the blade. It fell from his hands and clanked to the ground.

Another guard lunged for me, but I was already on my feet, and I quickly jumped out of his reach. The fools hadn't even restrained me. If I wanted to, I could have drawn my sword and used it to cut every one of them down, but I knew I could get away from these men without using it. Or I hoped that I could.

A crowd had gathered from the street, people coming over to see what was happening, to get a look at the fight that was about to go down.

The first guard moved to pick up his sword, and I ran for him, slamming my foot down onto his wrist, and then kicking him in the face with my other foot. The second guard reached for me, only to meet the elbow that I jabbed backward into his face. I heard something crunch, like bones were breaking, and it could have either been a wrist or a nose. I didn't particularly care.

With the two guards immobilized, I turned and started to run for the street again, but then something grabbed onto me, pulling me backward. The third guard had wrapped his hand around my hair, and used it to sweep me off of my feet and drag me further down the alley. I thought my skull was coming apart. I was trying to reorient myself after falling to the ground, so I didn't even notice the fist coming straight for my face. Hard knuckles slammed into me, just beneath my eye. My vision went black, but then returned just in time to see that fist coming back, meeting my jaw that time.

I was sprawled across the ground, a sharp pain welling across my entire head and face, bruises already taking hold.

"Bitch!" I heard one of them spit at me. I could hardly even open my eyes as I felt a hand again grab onto my arm and begin to drag me, like they would lug me across the city to wherever it was they needed to take me.

But then I heard something odd, and then the men began to scream. I heard a body thud to the ground, and the man who was holding onto me dropped me to the ground and started backing away, like he was afraid.

"Don't leave now," I heard Aerez croon. "The fun is just starting."

I opened my eyes to find that one of the guards had been killed, by Aerez. I felt dizzy as I saw the cut across his neck, and the blood pouring from it. His mouth was open like he had been screaming when it happened, and I could see a dark spot across his pants, like he was so afraid, he'd soiled himself.

Aerez prowled over to me, all the terrifying assassin. Her black cloak blew in the wind, red blood splattered across it. She smiled down at me, before reaching and helping me up.

"You're alright," she said. "You put up one hell of a fight."

She had a hand under my arm to keep me upright, but then we heard footsteps near, and the other guard was running towards us. She released me and I leaned against the wall, watching as she took down the man without any weapons. First she lifted her leg and kicked straight into the man's gut, and then she kicked his hand, sending his weapon flying straight from it. He stumbled backward a bit, but Aerez was already coming for him again. She punched him straight in the face, blood trailing from his nose, and when he bent over in pain, she brought her foot down on the crook of his neck. The man collapsed to the ground.

I didn't know if I should have felt relieved or terrified, or a bit of both. Aerez walked over to me with a smile on her face, like what she had just done was so satisfactory. She picked up her knife, the one she had used to cut the first guard's throat, and wiped it on her clothes, cleaning it before concealing it down the sleeve of her cloak.

She walked back over to me and wrapped an arm around my shoulder, gently, like she knew I was in pain. "You almost had them," she told me. "Come on, there's more coming."

We managed to make it to the western gate without any other guards spotting us. There were capital guards standing patrol at the gate, but they paid us no attention, as we were not the ones they were looking for. As long as the Lord of Kraxoth's men didn't come back this way, we would be safe.

But Will was still nowhere to be seen. One minute passed, and then five, and then twenty, and he was still not there. It shouldn't have taken him long, and with us being delayed I would have expected him to have already been there, but he was not. It made me nervous, like perhaps we should have gone and looked for him, in case he needed help, but Aerez assured me that he would be fine.

"Would you stop worrying," Aerez snapped at me, after I had been pacing back and forth for the past five minutes. "What's the deal with the two of you, anyway?"

"Deal?" I said. "With who?"

She rolled her eyes and let out a long sigh. "With the prince," she said matter-of-factly. "I see the way you two are with each other. Aren't you supposed to be marrying his brother?"

I turned to her and frowned. "I don't think it's any of your business." But I felt like she saw straight through my lie. I couldn't tell her what the *deal* was, because I didn't even know myself. I certainly couldn't explain it to her.

"So it's complicated, then?" she asked, smiling slightly. "It's that kind of shit that makes me glad everyone's too scared to even talk to me most of the time."

I knew she was joking, but what she said made me feel... sad. I wouldn't pity her, but I knew she must have been lonely. But for some odd reason, I found myself wanting to confide in her, and to tell her about everything with Will. Maybe I hoped that she could give me some advice.

"How do I tell him that... that I don't care for him the way he wants me to?" I asked her.

She raised a brow, and continued smirking. "Well, for starters I would suggest that you stop leading him on. I don't know what happened last night after I left the two of you outside, and I won't make assumptions, but it doesn't seem like it ended very well." My silence told her everything she needed to know. "And if you really don't feel that way for him, then you should just tell him that."

"I have told him," I said. "I don't... I don't know." I didn't know what to think. I knew I liked Will as a friend, and he was a kind person, even if he did lie to me before, and I knew that he cared about me as well. But I didn't want feelings to complicate the situation. I just wanted him to help me find the blade, and to help me free Nola, and then after, we could figure everything else out. "You know," I said to Aerez. "I think you and I are going to be good friends."

302

She gave me a nervous smile. "I guess we'll see about that. I've never been friends with a lady before."

I laughed then, and opened my mouth to say more, but then something else captured my attention. The largest raven I had ever seen flew straight past our heads, the sun reflecting off of its feathers, casting a blueish sheen. It landed atop a nearby building and let out a loud caw, causing both me and Aerez to startle.

"Are you okay?" I asked her, finding that her expression had turned rather sour at the approach of the bird.

She didn't answer me. Instead, she pulled a small knife free from under her shirt, then launched it straight at the raven. The bird hopped out of the way before it could get hit, and Aerez let out a hiss. "Stupid bird," she scowled. "Where the hell is the prince?"

That was odd. I turned towards the city, looking for any sign of him, but instead I saw something else. Guards. There were a lot more of them, and they were running straight in our direction. I tugged on Aerez, who still seemed out of sorts from the bird, and we quickly hid down the side of a building.

They were the Lord of Kraxoth's men, but they stopped before the capital guards, like they were working together.

"What is all this about?" one of the capital guards asked.

"We're looking for a young woman with golden hair, she carries a sword across her back, with a black jewel welded to the bottom." Aerez and I went completely still. "She's traveling with a man, and a woman that we suspect she hired from the assassin's association."

"What is it she's wanted for?" the guard asked.

"She is a suspected rebel sympathizer, and we think they are plotting something big," he said. "We brought in a woman, she's old as hell but we managed to get her to confess before she gave out."

My heart stopped. He couldn't have been talking about Trona, right?

"We know nothing of this," the capital guard said. "And we will not help you. We are here on order of the king to retrieve the prince, nothing more."

"And what if I told you this same girl was spotted with the prince? What would you say then?"

"Do not lie."

"It is the truth. They arrived here together on a ship from Saltrenea. We do not know the identity of this girl, but if you find one you will find the other. The prince might very well be plotting rebel activity alongside her."

"I shall keep an eye out," the capital guard said, rather unkindly. "Now, you all should be on your way."

Aerez and I stood there in complete silence, barely breathing, and waited for the guards to disperse. I reached for my hood, to make sure that it was covering my head thoroughly.

Aerez turned to me and whispered, "What kind of mess have you gotten yourselves into?"

"I have no idea," I told her.

Even after the guards passed, we remained hidden on the side of the building. These guards were after me, not because they knew who I was, but because they suspected that I was a rebel sympathizer. And they know that I am with Will, they know that the prince is mixed up with the rebels too. Even though, we're not really. If they captured me, what would they do? Have me executed? If they captured Will, what would they do with him? They would likely drag him back to the capital where he would be forced to confess the truth. Perhaps going with him would be better than being captured by the lord of this city.

"Who is the Lord of Kraxoth?" I asked Aerez.

"Lord Vonhal," she told me. "He has been the lord for thirty years. His family moved here from the capital after the uprisings all those years ago, after the former ruling family allied with the rebels. He's got blood on his hands, just like everyone else in the city. I've been hired by him a couple of times to do his dirty work. He's more of a crime lord than an actual lord, if you ask me."

"Do you think he could have been the one that hired you to kill me?" I asked her.

She shook her head. "I would have known if it was him. He never takes such lengths to conceal his identity. The guards looking for you now don't want you dead, so it can't be him." She seemed so certain of that, which made me relax only slightly. If Lord Vonhal doesn't want me dead, someone else certainly does.

We heard a commotion coming from nearby, and I was quickly pulled from my thoughts. We walked back out into the street, to find that the guards had abandoned their posts at the gate, and were instead running towards something.

Sure enough, Will was atop a horse, another one at his side, running straight towards those guards, towards us. I could barely hear his shouting over the clank of horse hooves, but I could understand enough that he wanted us to run, through the gate of the city.

Aerez urged me through the gate, and then she herself ran towards Will, towards the guards. I couldn't see what was happening, but I assumed that it was not friendly. I hear screaming and the horses bellowing, swords clashing.

And then Will blew through the gate of the city on the back of his horse. Aerez appeared behind him, on the back of the other horse, and they galloped over to me quickly, the guards still chasing behind. Aerez reached her arm down and lifted me atop the horse, and I wrapped my arms around her and clung to her with everything I had.

We sped away, leaving the guards behind us forgotten, as they could not catch us on foot. We headed for the forest, towards the wide dirt path within, and left Kraxoth once and for all, ignoring the shouting in the distance.

Chapter 30

Aerez, luckily, knew more about navigating a horse than I did. Their presence was scarce enough in Mortefine, and I'd only ever ridden one maybe two or three times. I wouldn't have known what to do if I'd been on one by myself, so I guess it was a good thing that Aerez came along with us. I felt that there were a great many reasons that would come to remind me of how bringing her along was the right decision.

I sat behind her with my arms wrapped around her stomach as she held the reins, Will leading the way up ahead of us. The road—the *capital road*, as they called it—was packed with people. Some of them were heading towards the city, some of them away. Some of them on horseback like us, others in carriages, others on foot. I assumed that they were the people that lived on the outskirts of Kraxoth, venturing to the city for food or work—merchants and farmers selling goods, fishers heading to the ports for a day at sea.

The capital road would take us a straight shot west to The Crossing, and from there we could head north to Frystal. It would go quicker, with us having horses, but Will wasn't exactly sure of the timeframe, and he worried that the cold weather we headed into would slow us down even more.

When we were a couple of miles out of the city, we stopped for the first time to settle ourselves. We strapped our satchels and bags across the sides of the horses, which was even more of a relief. Not only would my feet get a break, but the rest of my body would as well.

We walked into the woods a bit to catch our breath for a moment. Will leaned against a tree, while Aerez drank some water. But I wasn't worried about either of those things, not as I began to take in the scenery.

It was amazing—like nothing I had ever seen before. I was enveloped in a world of green. A forest. There were trees back in Mortefine, but nothing like this. Here, the trees huddled together closely, creating a blanket over the earth, keeping us cool even when the sun was high in the sky. There seemed to be no end to it, like once we entered there would be no getting out. And it was so *alive*, with things other than just trees, everywhere I looked. Birds of all sizes flew overhead, squirrels jumped from tree to tree, and loud bugs hummed higher up in the canopy.

After our short break, and no sign of guards or anyone else chasing after us, we continued down the road, the silence growing louder with every minute that passed, until eventually there was no sound at all. Or rather, no sound from people. They grew sparse, only passing by occasionally, instead of being surrounded by them as we had in the beginning. Hours passed, and it filled me with a sense of peace that I didn't think I had experienced even one time since leaving Mortefine. We all got the silence that we desired, after everything that had happened before. Our departure from Kraxoth hadn't exactly gone to plan. If we were captured, what would we have done then?

We continued riding until long after the sun had set, and my thighs ached and burned, as did my back. If either of my other companions were suffering as well, they didn't say a word about it. I hoped we would be stopping soon, not just because I was in pain but because I was starting to feel scared, being out in the woods at night.

The darkness unnerved me, and the shadows of the trees stood out like monstrous figures. They swayed side to side, remaining mostly in place as if they were watching my every move. I kept my head forward, not wanting to spook myself too badly. But to my luck, a short while later, Will halted his riding and pulled off the main road. "We'll stop here for the night," he said, and then he led us a few minutes into the woods, so that anybody passing by would not be able to spot us.

He began to dismount and unload his things, Aerez and I following suit. We tied the horses to a tree and then got to work on the tent. Once that was done, Will built a fire, and then the three of us ate our dinner in silence. Our situation was better than nothing, I supposed. We had a tent, a warm fire, and food to keep us from going hungry. But for some reason, I still felt incredibly uneasy.

As we sat around the fire, Will spoke to us again, barely above a whisper. "Are you going to tell me what happened today?"

I looked up, but not to Will. My eyes met with Aerez's, and she appeared to be shooting me the same weary expression that I currently wore on my own face.

"What?" I said to Will.

"What the hell happened to you two?" he said, slightly sharper this time. "You were both covered in blood," he turned to me, "and your face looked like you took one hell of a beating."

I reached a hand up to my face, touching the spot just beneath my eye, remembering that the guard's fist had collided there. I tried not to wince from the pain, but I knew it was bad because I could feel warm and swollen skin beneath my touch.

"She's fine," Aerez said coldly. "I slit the throat of the man that did that to her." There was no hint of regret, or remorse, or even sorrow in her words. She did not care. And I didn't hold that against her, because I knew it was a tactic likely learned in her years of being a lethal killer. But *I* couldn't imagine taking someone's life and then speaking so casually about it afterward.

"You killed them," Will said, and it wasn't really a question.

"Yes," Aerez told him. "They were going to take Kara— they worked for the Lord of Kraxoth. What was I supposed to do?"

Will ran a hand over his forehead and let out a long sigh. "I don't know," he said. "Maybe you could have *not* killed them. Would that have been so hard? You could have injured them, knocked them out, broken their legs, removed their weapons, *allowed them to surrender*. But you did not give them that option, did you?"

I watched silently as the two of them went back and forth.

Through the fire I could see Aerez smile, and that scared me far more than any of those guards could have. "What would the fun in that be?" she crooned.

I saw Will clench his fists atop his thighs, anger almost simmering from him. "It's not supposed to be *fun*," he spat. "Anything even remotely related to killing should not be used in the same context as *fun*. And if you think otherwise, then I'm sorry, but I think there's something seriously wrong with you."

"What are you trying to say," she shot back at him, though she didn't sound nearly as angry, more like she was trying to get a reaction out of him.

"I'm just saying," Will went on, "that it was wrong for you to have killed them. They were only doing as they were ordered. Would you kill an entire army because of the crimes of one king?"

"I'm not going to apologize for it," Aerez said. "So if that's what you're after, then you should just give up now. I'm an assassin—I kill people. That's my job, the last time I checked, and you are the one who hired me—*to do my job*." I saw her reach beneath her clothes, but I didn't realize what she was doing until she had already moved from her spot and reached Will's side. The fire reflected off the blade as she held it across Will's neck. "Maybe I'll cut your throat, just like I did to that guard," she whispered into his ear. "Would you try and stop me, prince?"

I moved from my spot as quickly as I could manage and crawled over to them. I didn't know what I could do—there was no way I could have gotten between them. I wondered what Will would do—if he would use his power on her. While

309

that would be interesting to see, Aerez might be too quick for him to even try that.

But Will only sat there, not even seeming to breathe. I watched them nervously. A very, very long moment passed before Aerez pulled the knife away and shoved it into the earth beside them. She allowed herself to fall backward, and then she began to *laugh*.

I did not think anything about this was funny.

Will stood and walked away from her, away from the both of us. "Crazy bitch," he spat, kicking up dirt as he turned his back to us.

That only caused Aerez to laugh harder. "*Crazy?*" she said. "That was not crazy. Crazy is what I do to those who get on my bad side. And *bitch*? You are not the first, nor will you be the last man to call me that. I have lived my entire life around disgusting men, so I've had plenty of time to learn to deal with them. If you think I won't hesitate to kill them, then you are wrong. You don't know what they would have done to Kara. They tried to drag her away by her *hair*."

Will turned to me, something like worry crossing his face, but it was gone a moment later. He didn't know how bad it was. He didn't see what they were doing to me, and he couldn't have known that they would have surrendered if given the chance. I opened my mouth to say something, then realized that I had nothing to say, not when he was already so angry.

"Maybe I didn't have to kill them," Aerez continued, acknowledging at least that much. "But that *does not* give you the right to question me. Do not tell me how to do my job. I agreed to protect her, not to be ordered around by a pompous arrogant prince."

Suddenly, the dying flames of the fire came to life. It forced me to crawl back a bit, to get away from the rising heat. The flames grew as if something had ignited them— some*one*. I cocked my head to Will, finding his anger all too apparent. And then I turned to Aerez, who hadn't seemed to notice anything at all.

"Are we clear on that?" she asked him.

Will released a long breath, closing his eyes and stepping away a few more steps. "Yes," he said. "We are." The flames subdued, retreating their dancing until it was nothing more than a small ember.

"We should get some rest," I said to them, hoping to reduce the tension.

Will's face was cold and utterly unreadable, but Aerez seemed to have relaxed a bit. She smiled at me, like that entire conversation had meant nothing to her at all. "Good idea," she said.

Aerez and I climbed into the tent, and I waited for Will to join us, but he did not. I only knew he was still with us at all because of the soft snoring I heard after a while, and I knew that he was sleeping outside. I drifted off to sleep then.

Unfortunately, things had not improved the next morning. Though we managed to remain mostly silent as we rode, Will and Aerez would not stop shooting each other glances. She would flash him a wicked grin, and he would return a disgusted frown. It was quite funny, but annoying for me because I had nobody to talk to. I knew they hated each other; I just wished they weren't making it my problem as well. If they didn't learn to start tolerating each other soon, then I would just have to do something to change that.

But for now, I supposed that silence was better than arguing.

The further we got from Kraxoth, the fewer people we saw. Hours into the day, we'd still only passed one man, who was a farmer hauling a wagon of wheat, headed in the opposite direction as us. And other than him, there has been nothing but silence.

I much preferred being in the forest to being in The Wry. Here, you didn't have to worry about dying of thirst, because there were streams and ponds all over the place. There were no sand serpents roaming the woods, and nothing else that would want to kill us, other than maybe any people we ran into. Luckily, I had two glorified bodyguards always watching my back.

Nothing much of note happened as we traveled throughout the day, other than the tension between my two companions creating a stiffness in the air, and the silence filling my head with mostly dreadful thoughts. The hours passed in a blur—only stopping a few times to eat, refill our water, or relieve ourselves. And before I knew it, the sun was setting, and the night was luring us in.

We stopped to make camp, the same as the night before, staying a short distance from the main road to go unnoticed. We built a fire, ate some food, set up the tent, and then prepared ourselves for sleep.

Unfortunately, the others had something else in mind.

"What are you doing?" I heard Aerez yell from inside the tent, after Will had just walked into it. She sounded angry, but I hardly cared what they were arguing about now. I just hoped it would end soon so I could join them and then go to bed.

"What?" Will replied, in a tone that suggested he wanted to know what he was being accused of now.

"Go sleep somewhere else," she said to him. "I'm not sleeping next to you."

It was silent for a moment, and I was afraid that something might have happened. I knew Aerez was being unreasonable, as she could not expect him to sleep outside of the tent just because she didn't want to be near him. I waited, hoping that they would settle it themselves.

Finally, Will said, "You're a stuck-up bitch." His words surprised me so much that I turned to the tent, expecting to hear or see them fighting, but it was too dark, and the wind was too loud. Those were cruel words, but I knew Aerez could never be deterred by them.

"Me?" Aerez laughed. "Stuck-up? Don't act as if you know me, princeling."

"I know that you're annoying, arrogant, cruel, and selfish," he shot back at her. "I would say that I know you well enough."

"You don't know the first thing about me."

"How can I?" Will said somewhat hysterically. "How can I know anything about you when you're always so quick to attack me when I speak or when I come near you? I don't think we've had *one* civil conversation together since we met. I don't think you can even stand to be civil, or talk about yourself, or care for others. Not for one second."

"Oh, really?"

"Yes," Will said bluntly. "And I know why, *Aerez*." He went silent after that, like he was giving her time to answer. "Because you *hate* yourself. You can't stand to be in your own company, so much that you have to take it out on everyone else. And you know what? I can't stand to be around you either, because you are a bad person, Aerez. You are an evil person, and I never should have let Karalia bring you with us."

I waited for the shouting to resume and the fighting to start, but it never did. Perhaps Will had taken it too far.

"Is that what you think?" Aerez said quietly, and with terrifying calmness. "That's good to know. But you should also know something about me, since you are so eager to." The wind blew through the trees, sending a chill down my spine. "When I was a child, I watched my father beat my mother. Then I watched my mother kill my father. And then I watched another man kill my mother." She waited, like she wanted Will to say something, though he didn't. "Then I killed the man that killed my mother, and I haven't stopped killing since. I became an assassin, because I thought that was the only thing I'd ever be good at. So yes, Will, I hate myself for being a killer—for being a coward. But now I finally have the chance to do something else with my life—to get away from all the terrible things I have done—and you are ruining it for me. You are making me want to crawl back to my master, to let him tell me what to do and who to kill. *You* are

313

reminding me of why I find killing so easy. I could end your life in a second, but does that mean I would feel no remorse? Am I the monster that you have made me out to be?"

Again, I waited for the shouting and fighting, but none came. Tears began to well in my eyes, though I quickly wiped them away. What Aerez had said... I hoped it wasn't the truth, but a part of me already knew that it was.

"Your parents died?" Will said. "Well, I killed my own sister. How's that for hating yourself? You think you're the only one with issues, Aerez, and you're wrong about that. Karalia's only friend is being held hostage and she's doing everything she can to help her, and you're sitting here fighting with me when we should be doing everything we can to help as well."

I couldn't believe that Will admitted that, nor could I believe what he said after that. I needed to end this, now. I stood from my spot around the fire and stalked to the tent, pulling the front flaps open and leaning in. They were on opposite sides of each other, like snakes that had recoiled and were about to again strike. They paid me no attention, like they hadn't even seen me there.

"The noble prince has secrets under his tiara?" Aerez laughed evilly to herself. "So, you're a cold-blooded killer too? I suppose we have more in common than I thought."

"I'm not noble," Will told her. "What is it you called me? A pompous arrogant prince?"

"You're an embarrassment to the crown."

"You sound exactly like my father."

"That's a disturbing thought."

"I imagine all the thoughts you have are disturbing."

"Fine," Aerez finally said, and from the tone of her voice I grew nervous for what she was about to say. "You may be a prince, and you may think that what you are doing is noble and good, but the result will never be pleasant for you. She will never choose you." She pointed to where I was standing, and I watched on in horror as Will's attention shifted to me. "Why would she choose you when she could instead have a king? Why would anyone choose a sister-murdering bastard? Once she gets your help with saving her friend, she will want nothing to do with you. And good riddance when that day comes."

I backed away from the tent, thinking that Will would finally lash out, that he would unleash his anger and perhaps something else. But he emerged from the tent, his face solemn, and he looked straight at me and halted, like he really believed what Aerez had told him. I outstretched an arm, taking a few steps in his direction, but he only shook his head and began to walk further into the woods.

"Will!" I called.

He turned around. "You know, I should just leave the two of you here to deal with this on your own. I didn't sign up for this, Kara. I didn't sign up for any of this, and I'm sorry, but I can hardly do this anymore. I should have taken you back to the capital like I was supposed to."

"Will!" I yelled again, but he was already walking off into the woods. "If you leave me, I will never forgive you. I will never go to the capital, not even to meet my brother. If you run away like a coward, I will resent you for the rest of my life!"

"Let him leave," Aerez yelled from the tent.

"Please," I said into the night, but Will was not there to hear me.

I sat next to the dying fire for most of the night, waiting for Will to return, allowing my tears to fall because I knew nobody could see them. After hours had passed, I wasn't sure that he would return, and I began to worry. I thought about doing the rest of this on my own, without Will, and I honestly didn't think I could.

I heard Aerez tossing and turning from within the tent, which probably meant that she was still angry, so I had no intention of joining her, for fear of my own safety.

315

I must have fallen asleep at some point, crouched beside the fire, but I awoke to arms wrapping around me, scooping me up, and I knew then that Will had returned. He smelled like smoke, but different, like something had burned, but I was far too tired to question it.

He brought me into the tent and set me down beside Aerez, and then he laid down himself on the opposite side of me. If Aerez was aware of it, she didn't say a word. Perhaps she had finally come to her senses.

I turned to face Will, though I could make out none of his features in the darkness, I could tell that he was watching me, so I reached out my hand and ran it down his arm until I found his hand, and then I pulled that hand towards me and cupped it to my chest.

I could feel him shudder, and his breathing quicken. And even though I knew it was selfish and wrong, I scooted towards him and buried my face into his chest. It only took him a moment to wrap his arms around me and hug me back.

"I'm so sorry," I whispered to him, and I hoped that he understood what my apology was for—all the many things it was for.

"You don't have to apologize," he said.

And then I fell asleep, more peacefully than I deserved.

I awoke to a sound in the middle of the night, what I thought at first was a dream of darkness, but then I realized that it was just outside of the tent. There was a sort of rustling, what I thought I might have imagined, until it happened a second time, and then a third. Aerez remained asleep beside me, as did Will who I pulled myself from to go and find the source of the sound.

I assumed that it would be some sort of forest animal, curious about us, so I wasn't very afraid. After seeing first-hand what dwelled in The Wry and in the Alanah Sea, I didn't think this would be of much interest.

I scooted toward the front of the tent, poking my head out to get a look at whatever it was, but all I found was darkness. The wind blew through the trees. I knew something was there, but I could not make it out. I would have thought that perhaps the noise came from the horses, but they were on the other side of the tent, and long asleep.

The rustling sounded again, almost like a rhythmic flapping of sorts. It was above me, within the trees, and I tried to follow the sound with my eyes, but it was nearly impossible.

Then a cloud must have drifted and uncovered the moon, because my surroundings illuminated slightly enough for me to see a small pair of beady glowing eyes. They were too small to be anything of danger, but it still scared me all the same. The eyes moved down, like the creature had fallen out of the tree, or like it was jumping down at me, but then it glided away, and I realized what it was.

That damned raven from Kraxoth, the one that seemed to spook Aerez. Was it following us? I couldn't be certain that it was the same one, but it was surely big enough to be, and the moonlight reflected a blue sheen from its feathers.

It flew to another tree and perched atop a branch, like it knew I had spotted it and was trying to get away. If I had a bow, I would shoot that thing straight out of the canopy. But it merely sat there and watched, and I knew enough to know that ravens were mostly harmless. So I crawled back into the tent, back to Will's side, and when silence again filled the forest, I drifted back to sleep.

Chapter 31

A resolution had not yet been reached after last night's debate. I was traveling with children—two deadly people, arguing, bickering, acting like utter fools. I didn't know how much more of it I could take. They remained silent as we packed up and headed back towards the road, pretending as if nothing had happened at all.

Not ten minutes down the road, we ran across something suspicious. I had a hunch about what it was, but I wouldn't dare bring it up.

There was a sweet smell to the air, like toasted pine, but also smoky and woody, like something had burned. I would have dismissed it as a campfire, if it wasn't the exact scent that I smelled on Will last night after he returned from the woods. I was too taken by sleep then to know, but now I was sure.

Through the tall trees and within the beams of sunlight, I could just make out the grey smoke of dying flames. It was close, just off the road. Too close to the road, even. I was prepared to ignore it, to keep moving, but Aerez took notice, and seemed interested in the smoke. She pulled the reins of our horse, stopping us in place, while Will rode ahead, like he could not wait to get away from there.

"We should check it out," she said to me, and before I could protest, she was already dismounting and walking into the woods. I remained atop the horse, as did Will who was a few dozen feet ahead of us. "Fine," Aerez said when we didn't move. "Stay here. I'll be right back."

I did stay right where I was, mostly because I was unsure of myself atop a horse. Will didn't utter one word, and he wouldn't even meet my eyes, but I knew the truth. He looked disinterested, as if he were trying to hide from it, but he couldn't.

I managed to guide the horse over to Will, stopping directly beside him. Aerez had been gone for a few minutes, so I knew that she could be returning at any moment.

"Will," I said softly, and then he turned and met my eyes. There was something like sorrow within them, and I wondered what exactly it was for. I opened my mouth to say more, but then Aerez emerged from the brush, bringing an even stronger scent of the burnt forest with her.

"Something caught the forest on fire," she told us, looking slightly unsettled. "Nearly two dozen trees, completely turned to ash." Will and I remained silent. "It could have come to us in our sleep," she said. "What on earth could have caused this?"

She turned to us for answers, and Will merely shrugged. "Someone probably left their campfire burning," he explained, and I remembered then how skilled he was at lying. His eyes met mine, like he knew exactly what I was thinking, and I held his gaze for a long moment, letting him see my unamused recognition.

I know what you did, I tried to tell him.

Not that I would tell Aerez, nor would I want to make him feel guilty for using his power like that. But he was angry last night, and he wandered off to burn the forest down. A part of me was terrified by that, but another part of me was grateful for it.

"We should get going," I announced. "I'm sure it's nothing."

Throughout the rest of the day, Will remained his usual broody self, while Aerez and I struck up an interesting conversation. She had a strangely advanced knowledge of the forest and the organisms within it. She pointed out some of the different trees and other plants to me as we passed.

The pine trees were obvious, as they were the most abundant, but the birch trees were what really caught my attention. They had a different sort of bark—a stark white color that stood out harshly against the rest of the forest. In a strange way, those trees reminded me of Nola. She was never afraid to stand out, and not just with the bright red color of her hair. She was never afraid to let her true self show, and never afraid to speak her mind even when she knew there would be consequences.

It made me sad, thinking about her, and eventually we grew silent again, as Aerez likely picked up on my shift in demeanor. Nola was the reason that I was there, searching for the blade. And that wasn't a burden to me, because she was the reason that I would do anything at all, she was the person I would do anything for.

I knew Nola would do all the same for me—she'd already done more than I could ever repay. The life that I lived now had nothing to do with me being Karalia Havu. The only thing that mattered was that I found Sazarr's blade, and that I brought it back to Mortefine in time to exchange it for Nola's freedom.

The promise that I made to myself, to kill Hiran, seemed so inconsequential now compared to everything else I'd been through. Maybe all I needed was a bit of time for my vengeance to ease. He did deserve a terrible end for everything that he'd done, but maybe I didn't need to be the one to deliver that to him. It would catch up with him eventually. Once Nola was free, we could both leave Mortefine and forget about Hiran once and for all, and then I could ask someone else for help with getting my revenge. I could ask the king himself, perhaps.

Will was a prince, after all. Surely he could be the one to help me. I worried that I forgave him too easily, for lying to me about who he was, and what his reasons were for helping

320

me. I didn't think that he would betray me again, but I couldn't be certain.

And Aerez. I desperately wanted to trust her, but I was finding it hard to do so. I knew nothing about her, other than what she'd revealed last night in her shouting fit with Will. But I knew that there was this odd sense of understanding between the two of us, and that we were not as different as we thought. I could sense a friendship growing between us, and when it came time, I hoped she would help me, too.

My thoughts were cut into by the sound of Aerez's voice. "Bloodberries!" she shouted, directing our horse into the woods, towards a small bush covered in small red fruits. "We must already be farther from Kraxoth than I thought. These only grow in the northwestern part of Vatragon."

She dismounted and then walked over to the bush, bending down and plucking some off, and then throwing them into her mouth. I nearly laughed at the sight of it—the fearsome assassin foraging for sweet little fruits. I was beginning to think that she had a hidden soft side to her.

"Aren't those poisonous?" Will asked as Aerez tossed a few more berries into her mouth.

She shrugged. "As long as you spit out the seeds, then it's fine," she explained. "One of the cooks back at the headquarters used to make the best bloodberry pie. I scarred a boy's face once when he tried to take my slice." She spat out the seeds, large brown pits, onto the ground.

I flashed her a nervous smile, but Will merely scoffed.

"What do they taste like?" I asked.

Her eyes lit up in delight. "Like sugar and magic and candy in winter."

She tossed one to me, and I hesitated before plopping it into my mouth. At first, it was sour, but then the sweetness rushed in like a sandstorm. It was delicious, but there was also a strange iciness to it, leaving my mouth feeling as if I had just eaten something frozen. I spat the seed onto the ground.

"Aren't they just delicious!" she said, and I nodded in answer. "Would the prince like any bloodberries?" She didn't

321

ask Will directly, but rather just announced it with her back turned towards him.

"The prince would appreciate some, *thank you*," Will said, though he did not sound the least bit thankful, but rather more annoyed.

And instead of giving them to him herself, Aerez handed *me* the berries. I brought them over to Will, letting them see my annoyance.

"Thank you, Kara," Will said, and it sounded more genuine that time, as he flashed me a small apologetic smile.

I ate probably far too many bloodberries, and the fact that the seeds were toxic didn't scare me nearly as much as it should have, but Aerez assured me that she'd been eating them her entire life.

We filled our stomachs and then stuffed our bags with as many berries as they could carry, riding west late into the afternoon. The sun shone through the trees, surrounding us in an almost magical veil, glistening like starlight.

But up ahead, I saw something odd. It looked brighter, and the trees... there were fewer of them. I watched cautiously as we neared, anticipating what we would find, though neither of my companions seemed concerned.

"There's a clearing up ahead," Will announced, and I realized then that he'd been watching me from where he rode beside us. I relaxed a little, slouching back down and feeling my breathing slow.

When we made it to the clearing, it was again like nothing I had ever seen before. This strange and unfamiliar world continued to delight me still.

It was a field of flat, grass-covered earth. It was mostly green, except for the splotches of color spread about. They were colors that I didn't know could exist in nature, bright and vibrant, beautiful. Nothing could ever grow such a way in Mortefine.

"I've never seen anything like this," I whispered, mostly to myself.

Aerez craned her neck to look back at me. "The flowers?"

"I've never seen so many in one place. They just grow here like this, all by themselves?"

Aerez quietly laughed to herself, while Will said, "Yes, all by themselves." Neither of us fought back our smiles. "I think we should stop here for the night," he said, and I couldn't help but feel like he was doing it as a favor to me.

We dismounted, allowing the horses to graze the grass and drink from the nearby stream, while I too began to graze for flowers. I sorted through them all, plucking the ones I liked best and bundling them into a bouquet.

Aerez stayed near the edge of the forest, sitting against a tree as she practiced with her knives, tossing some into the air and balancing others on the tips of her fingers.

After a while, I wandered off further into the clearing, collecting the prettiest flowers I could find. There was one, a deep orange color, like the sky at dawn, or like…

"Are you having fun?"

I gasped, dropping the flowers and leaving them forgotten on the ground as Will approached me from behind. His eyes. That was what the flower reminded me of, like swirling flames. They turned that way after he used his power, for whatever reason.

"I didn't mean to scare you," he said, smiling softly. "Will you walk with me?" Then he held out a hand, waiting for me to take it.

I swallowed back the uneasiness I felt, though I connected my hands behind my back and only walked to Will's side. He eventually dropped his hand when he realized I wasn't going to take it.

We started to walk, and I looked up to the sky, finding that it had dimmed a little, turning into a pale pink color, the first hints of sundown. I thought that I could sleep more peacefully out in the open than we did in the forest, that is, if that creepy raven didn't come back.

"Are you alright?" Will asked me, though he sounded like he was already convinced I wasn't.

"Of course," I told him, forcing a smile. "What would be wrong?"

"I don't know," he said, and then he changed the subject. "We're making good progress. We should make it to The Crossing in just over a week, if everything goes to plan."

I nodded, remaining silent.

"Is something wrong?" he asked again, shifting his entire body so that we were facing one another, and so he was blocking the direction I had been walking in.

I stopped in place and crossed my arms, dropping the fake smile. "You mean, other than you and Aerez annoying me with your constant bickering and threatening? No, nothing is wrong."

He sighed, then told me, "She's irritating."

"I'm sure she would say the same thing about you," I said flatly. "You nearly burnt the forest down, Will. Were you that out of control?"

"I was in control," he told me, a bit sharply. "I just needed to... release my anger, and I didn't want to be anywhere near you when I did."

"Better on the forest than us."

He turned away from me, clearly hurt by my words. "You think I'm a monster."

"I don't think you're a monster. I think you're dangerous, and sometimes I think you're the biggest fool I've ever met, but you're not a monster, Will."

"Then what is it? Why are you acting like this?"

I didn't answer, because there was nothing for me to tell him. I didn't really know why I was being cold with him. I was more angry with myself than I could have been with him or Aerez. I just needed time to myself, so I could think, and breathe.

Eventually Will walked away, leaving me alone with the flowers. I listened to the hum of nearby insects and watched the birds fly back to their homes for the night. I could no longer even see the edge of the forest that we had come out of, only an open field as far as the eye could see.

Eventually my path was blocked by a very large pool of water, a lake, and while the water was dark, it rested calmly and flat unlike that of the sea we sailed over to get to Kraxoth. And it was completely silent, other than the quiet splashing of fish.

I walked back in the direction I had come from, only so I could find Will and Aerez to tell them that there was somewhere for them to bathe. The fading traces of sunlight allowed me to easily find my way back. Aerez was exactly where I'd left her, and Will was just getting started on setting up the tent.

"I found a lake," I told them. "Care for a swim?"

Aerez shot up quickly, clearly very interested in my offer. Will looked reluctant to join us, though he knew he couldn't refuse. I led them back to the lake, finding it more easily than I'd expected.

Aerez was already removing her clothes before Will and I had even made it there completely, and I was thankful then for the cover of darkness, because she clearly felt no shame in undressing before us. "Aren't you coming in?" she said as she was already halfway into the water, covered only by her undergarments. She swam out a bit, until only her head was sticking above the surface.

Will stood beside me, like he was waiting to know if I was going in as well. "I can't swim," I reminded them. "I'll wash up from the shore."

Aerez laughed. "I guess you wouldn't know how to swim, being from Mortefine. I hear they don't even take baths there."

"We take baths," I said. "Well, only those who can afford it. I suppose I was more fortunate than most."

Will walked further down the shore of the lake, removing his boots, coat, and then his shirt, revealing his muscled chest beneath. He couldn't see me staring, so I allowed myself another few selfish seconds, until he began removing his pants. *That*, I certainly did not need to see.

Aerez had gone for a swim, apparently, because I could no longer see her near the shore, so I began to remove my own clothes. I balled my shirt up and used it to wash my skin, only getting into the lake deep enough to cover my ankles. When I felt mostly clean, I got out and sat for a second, allowing my skin to dry. Nobody was around to see me.

After I dressed, I laid down on the grass, staring up at the sky, watching as the stars began to appear. I heard faint splashing nearby, but only assumed it to be one of the others washing up. But minutes passed and the splashing continued, and then I began to grow suspicious.

I looked out over the lake, finding that an eerie mist had covered most of it, and I could make out nothing in the darkness. The splashing continued, and I walked to where I thought it was coming from. I reached the spot where Will had discarded his clothes, unable to see him either.

I removed my shoes and rolled up my pants as high as they would go, and then I climbed into the water, knowing that I couldn't swim, but needing to find the source of the splashing. If one of them were in trouble, then they might need my help.

I was only about waist deep when I found the source of the splashing. Will and Aerez were in the water, together, throwing punches at one another. They were fighting, pulling each other's hair, blood trickling from unseen wounds into the water. Somebody's head was being forced beneath the surface, and from the look of it, it was Will's. And then I heard what seemed to be a blade piercing flesh. Hadn't they left all their things on shore? No, of course Aerez had a knife hidden on her somewhere.

"Stop it!" I yelled, though they were still a great distance from me, and were too deep out for me to walk to them. The sound of my voice echoed across the water, along with their muffled grunts and pants. "What the hell is wrong with you two?"

I got no answer. I watched, unable to do anything, as Will tried to push Aerez away from him, failing, as she flailed her knife out and it slid across his chest.

"Stop!" I shouted again. "Right now!"

Will managed to shove Aerez off him, though she was lunging for him again in an instant. He tried to swim towards me, blood dribbling from both his chest and nose, and also his wrist. When he reached my side, he wrapped an arm around my waist and pulled me to shore, but I turned around, looking for Aerez. She was slowly following behind us, but no longer attacking.

When we were all out of the lake, I turned to them both and said, "What was that about? Are you two insane?"

"She attacked me," Will said.

"He annoyed me," Aerez retorted.

"I don't care who attacked who," I said. "I don't care who started it, but I saw both of you fighting back." I was talking to them like a pair of children. "Either you cut this out, or I will leave here with neither of you at my side. We will never accomplish anything if you guys keep trying to kill each other. Now, go put your clothes on."

Surprisingly, they both obeyed without another word. Aerez walked further down the shore while Will dressed beside me. I replaced my boots as well, annoyed that my clothes were now wet. Will kept his shirt off, what I assumed was so he could address the wound on his chest, just beneath his collarbone. It was still dripping blood. Aerez walked back and rejoined us a few minutes later.

I released a long, annoyed breath. "I don't know if the two of you truly intend to kill one another, or if there is just some odd competition between you, but for my sake, and for Nola's freedom, can you *please* stop fighting. I don't care how much you dislike each other—you need to learn some tolerance. After we find the blade, I don't give a damn if you kill each other, but right now, you both are here to help me. Aerez, I'm pretty sure you can't kill the man who signed your contract. And Will, it would be very beneath you to kill a woman. You two need to learn to take your anger out some other way, instead of trying to drown each other, because I am not putting up with this shit anymore."

They glanced at each other, like they still wanted to rip each other's throats out. Aerez might have even growled a bit.

"Gods," I said, shaking my head. "Okay, here's what we're going to do." They shifted their attention to me. "First, you two are going to apologize to each other, and then you will promise not to harm one another until after the blade has been found."

"What is a promise worth to her?" Will raised a bloody finger towards Aerez.

"A *blood* promise," I told them, "is worth your lives if broken. So I would suggest choosing your words, and later your actions, wisely."

"I will not share blood with that *killer*," Will said, taking a few steps back.

"And I will not be soiled by the blood of the dragon," Aerez said, though there was still humor lacing her tone. She meant to taunt him. She wouldn't say such a thing if she knew he truly did have the blood of the dragon.

"You two will do this," I said. "Or I leave here right now by myself."

Will turned to me, and the look he gave me suggested that he would do anything to keep that from happening. "Fine," he said.

"Okay," Aerez grinned, taking a few predatory steps towards him.

"I can't believe we're really doing this," Will said.

"I can't believe it either," I told them. "I never thought you would have such hatred for each other that I would need to make you swear a blood oath, so I don't have to watch anyone die. This is clearly necessary, so say the words, both of you. Now."

Will stepped up first. "I, William Drazos, swear on my blood, on the blood of the dragon, that I will not harm Aerez Yrongul during our search for the lost blade of Sazarr." He pressed his finger to his chest, coating it in the blood from his wound, and then held it up before him.

"And I, Aerez Yrongul, swear on my blood, the blood of my slave mother, that I will harm Prince William Drazos only after the lost blade of Sazarr has been retrieved." She flashed a wicked grin as she took a knife to her palm and made a small incision across it. She ignored Will's outstretched hand and pressed her palm flat against his chest, causing him to stumble back and groan from the pain.

Afterward, they turned to me, and I glanced between them nervously. "Okay…" I said. "I guess that will do."

Aerez sheathed the blade to the inside of her thigh before bringing her palm to her mouth and licking the blood from it. My stomach went queasy at the sight. She began to walk away before turning back over her shoulder and whispering, "I'm sorry."

We didn't say a word as she walked off into the night.

Chapter 32

"Sorry for what?" Will said aloud to nobody in particular.

Aerez had walked away—to where I wasn't exactly sure. Was it too much, to make them do that? I could only hope that she returned, and soon.

Only time would tell if the blood promise would actually keep them from fighting again. They wouldn't actually die if they broke their promises, as it was a superstitious practice meant to incite fear—to threaten people with the wrath of Drazen if they stepped out of line and broke the promise they had so willingly drawn blood over.

Other than the power of the promise being fictitious, it was almost intimate to perform such a thing. Sharing blood is nothing idle, and should mean a lot to the two or more parties involved. Husbands and wives sometimes do it when they marry, as a way to ensure they remain faithful to one another. It can also mean more than just a promise. It can mean that a debt is owed, or it can be as simple as an agreement, but it can even be an oath for vengeance. Slavers from Faulton have been known to share blood with their slaves to amend their debt. Kings have been known to share blood with their lords, to ensure that they remain loyal.

The thought sent a chill over me from where I remained standing beside the edge of the lake. The air had grown noticeably cooler within what seemed like the span of a few minutes, or perhaps it was just because my clothes were now wet. And all of this thinking about blood promises, I hoped I would never have to agree to one, because the thought of sharing my blood with somebody made me uneasy.

I turned away from the lake, finding Will beside me dabbing the cut across his chest with a cloth. The sight of his blood, and the thought of it being mixed with Aerez's, made me very queasy.

I left Will there and headed back in the direction of where we'd set up the tent. I could barely see anything in the darkness, as the moon was mostly covered with clouds, but I listened carefully and followed the faint sounds of the horses nickering. They were tied up next to a tree along the edge of the forest, not far off from the tent. I had hoped that Aerez would have come back here, but she was nowhere to be seen.

I climbed into the tent and sat down, not really prepared to sleep just yet, but much in need of some rest. There were flowers sticking up from the ground on the inside of the tent, and the color of them reminded me of a warm summer day back in Mortefine. Or a warm winter day as well, because they weren't much different. Maybe the gardens of Hiran's estate had the same flowers.

That thought strangely made me miss being in Mortefine. I didn't miss Hiran or the work I did as his advisor, but I missed the rest of the city. It was familiar there. It was my home. I knew it would never be the same again, but I *was* very fond of the city, just not the person who ruled it.

I tried and failed to fall asleep. My mind simply would not allow it, as thoughts were bubbling up one after the other. Eventually Will returned and situated himself beside me, though he left some space between us. He must have known I was awake, and yet he said nothing.

I hated how awkward everything had become.

An hour or so later, I continued to evade sleep. I scooted towards the opening of the tent, sitting there and peering up at the sky, hoping to find the stars twinkling back at me, but they were covered with clouds. I closed my eyes and listened to the sounds of nature, hearing an owl hoot from somewhere in the forest, and bugs hum from the grass beyond.

Will had started to snore softly from where he lay, and I stayed that way and listened for a while, until I realized that his snoring was the *only* thing I could hear. Everything else had gone silent, and even the wind had seemed to stop blowing. I sat up straighter and looked around, unable to see a thing in the darkness. But the silence, it was unnatural.

"Will," I whispered rather loudly, but he didn't move a muscle. "Aerez?" I called, hoping that she had somehow returned.

I crawled completely out of the tent and stood to look around, then thought to myself that I would have preferred seeing that damned raven again instead of all the other things my mind was conjuring. But way off across the field, in the direction that the lake had been, something caught my eye. There was movement, and though I could not see what it was, it remained utterly silent, inching its way closer, moving like…

That was impossible.

There's no way it could have been a… a…

The sand serpent slithered towards me. Even under the cover of night, its tan sand-colored skin stood out harshly against the green of the meadow. It wasn't the same one we'd escaped from before, as this one was much smaller, but how could it possibly have gotten here? Sand serpents lived in The Wry, and nowhere else.

It stayed low to the ground and moved much slower than I knew it could have, but it would reach us in no time, and we needed to start running.

"Will!" I screamed now, shaking the outside of the tent. "Wake up!"

I heard a rustle and then a low groan. "What?" he asked.

"We need to run," I said to him. "Right now. Get out of the tent and bring your weapons with you."

In a matter of seconds, he was up and out of the tent, joining my side, his sword unsheathed and raised towards the darkness. I took a few steps back from the serpent, though Will could not see it approaching us. I didn't bother to free my weapon as I grabbed onto Will's wrist and pulled him in the opposite direction. We ran to the right, along the edge of the forest, but not going into it.

We ran. And I knew the serpent could have reached us by now if it wanted to. I knew it could have killed us and moved on. But for some reason, it hadn't. I turned back to find it still following us slowly, almost like it was matching our pace.

Will saw me looking behind us and then looked himself, his face turning bone white as he realized what it was. "Shit," he said, grabbing me by the wrist now and running even faster. "How in the hell did that get here?"

"I don't know," I said in between breaths. "Will. Wait."

He looked back at me, clearly confused, but did not stop running even when I'd slowed my pace. I knew it was foolish of me, but I had an idea. I slowed down even more until I was no longer even walking.

"What are you doing?" Will yelled, but he was already far ahead of me, wisely putting as much distance between himself and the serpent as he could. I wouldn't have done this if he decided to join me.

"Keep going," I called to him as I stayed right where I was. His eyes widened in horror, and his hand raised to cover his mouth, like he was watching something gruesome unfold. I turned to see what he was looking at, but then I stumbled when I saw it, falling backward as the beast loomed over me.

The serpent had already reached me, but instead of attacking and devouring, it had stopped. It was no more than a few feet away. When I tried to crawl backward, the beast hissed at me, revealing a mouth full of sharp teeth.

"What do you want from me?" I said rather quietly, so that Will would not hear. The serpent's eyes took me in, blinking twice, before lowering its head closer to where I was sprawled across the ground. "You don't want to kill me," I told it. "I can tell that much, but I just wish you would leave me alone. You're scaring me."

It pulled its head back a bit, like it could understand me, though I knew that was impossible. I had no idea why I was suddenly talking to the thing, thinking that we could come to some sort of understanding, and it would spare my life.

I could hear Will screaming from nearby, but I couldn't make out his words over the sound of my own heart beating within my ears.

"Why do you keep finding me?" I asked the serpent. I pushed my arms onto the ground and forced myself to stand, straightening out directly in front of the serpent. I outstretched my hand towards it. "Why—" It immediately recoiled back a few feet. "This is insane," I muttered, and then turned around to Will to signal that everything was okay.

"Do you work for Sazarr?" I asked it, not really expecting an answer. "Is that it? He knows I'm looking for his blade and he wants to scare me off? Well, you can tell him that it's not going to work. He might as well kill me instead."

A moment later the serpent's head cocked to the side, like it had spotted something hidden in the darkness of the forest. It wasn't scared, because surely nothing could ever scare such a beast, but it seemed to go on alert. It slithered away from me and towards the trees, putting its body between me and whatever it was that was hunting us. The serpent couldn't have been... protecting me.

I tried to peer around the serpent's body, but I could see nothing. Running seemed like a very good idea at the moment, just in case the thing decided to change its mind about wanting to kill me. Why had I even stopped in the first place?

I started to back away, refusing to take my eyes off of the invisible standoff. But then I saw movement within the trees, something smaller.

Dressed like the night, Aerez launched herself towards the serpent and out of the trees, knives in both hands, a vicious smile on her face. She ran straight towards it, like it was nothing more than a garden snake that she would crush beneath her boot.

The serpent struck, but Aerez ducked and rolled to the side just in time. Seconds passed before she regained her footing and again ran for the serpent, somehow managing to climb onto its back, just behind its head and out of striking distance.

The beast attempted to shake her off, lashing its head back and forth like a whip, but she held strong. When it stopped thrashing, Aerez dragged herself higher up towards the serpent's head and then plunged those two knives deep into the serpent's head, straight through its eyes.

"No!" I tried to yell, but it was too late.

The serpent continued to hiss and thrash as blood coated its tan skin. Some of it splattered across my face, on my clothes, and in my hair. I screamed out in horror. Eventually its body fell limp to the ground, just as Aerez jumped out of the way.

"What…" I said, looking over at her and wiping blood from my face. "What have you done?"

"I saved your life," she snapped at me. "Don't give me that shit."

"You killed it," I stated.

"Yes," she said. "You wanted trust, right? I killed the beast before it could kill you."

"It wasn't going to kill me," I said, shaking my head and then turning to find that Will was walking toward us. I met him halfway and we grabbed onto each other as if to check one another for wounds.

"You don't know that," Aerez seethed. "That thing was a monster. It could have killed all of us. *I save you.*"

"She's right," Will said to me, a hint of disappointment lacing his tone. "Why did you stop running, Kara? What were you thinking?"

They both watched me as if I was insane. And maybe I was, but I didn't feel like explaining myself to them at the moment. "It doesn't matter," I said, pulling away from Will. "It's dead now."

None of us particularly felt like sleeping after that. Will built a fire, which we sat around and then ate whatever remaining food we'd brought from Kraxoth. The next night, we would need to hunt or forage for our food.

We sat there in complete silence, and, ironically, I thought that I would have preferred Will and Aerez's bickering over whatever was happening now. They seemed like they were too afraid to even speak to me, like they thought I was crazy.

I knew Aerez must have seen what happened right before she intervened. She must have *heard*. So it didn't surprise me at all when she blurted, "Why were you *talking* to it?" I didn't answer, nor did I even acknowledge that I'd heard her ask me a question. "It didn't attack you. It was listening to you, like it could understand you."

"I don't know," I whispered after a moment. "I realized that it wasn't trying to kill us, so I stopped running. I don't know why I talked to it, I guess I just wanted to understand why it wasn't attacking me."

"It should have killed you," Aerez said flatly. "I've never heard of something like that. Never."

"I've never heard of a sand serpent being seen outside of The Wry," Will said, shaking his head almost absently. "It couldn't have traveled all this way, could it?"

"I don't know," I said again. "Maybe it's been following us." They both frowned at me. "I have a strange feeling about this," I admitted. "I want to get out of here as soon as possible." And then I looked across the meadow, to where I could still see the faint outline of the serpent's body through the darkness.

"Yeah," Aerez agreed.

"We'll leave at first light," Will said. "Get some rest."

As promised, we left at dawn the next morning. The sound of Will readying the horses awoke me, as did the sound of Aerez cleaning her knives, bloodied from the night before. I didn't

336

want to think about the sand serpent, so I made sure not to look back at it as we packed up our things and headed off across the meadow.

The sky was gloomy, and I expected it to brighten as the day went on, but it never did. When we reached about midday, the clouds began to swirl violently overhead, and the sun was nowhere to be seen, hidden somewhere far away. Even living in Mortefine, I knew what this meant. A storm was coming, and from the looks of it, a nasty one.

The air was noticeably much cooler than it had been any other day, and I wondered if it was only from the approaching storm, or if it could mean that summer had begun to turn to fall. But there was something else, too. It made the hairs on my arms raise and left behind a strange sinking feeling within my gut.

Neither Will nor Aerez seemed all that concerned, so I didn't say anything, hoping that they were adept to these sorts of situations. But a part of me was terrified. After what happened the night before, could things get any worse?

We continued riding, stopping once at a shallow stream to allow the horses water. There was no arguing today between Will and Aerez—not even their usual deadly glares that they thought I couldn't see. At least one good thing had happened.

In the early afternoon, we reentered the forest, leaving the meadow behind. Our surroundings became even darker, with both the grey clouds and thick trees overhead. I could hardly make out what was ahead, as the trees looked to be covered in mist. And there was a loud sound, a rumbling, growing closer every second.

Suddenly, something like a heavy wet blanket fell over us. Rain. My nervousness eased just a bit, as my curiosity began to take over. I had never seen such rain. It poured down so thoroughly that it quickly puddled on the road, covering the bottom of the horses' feet.

And the raindrops were freezing, stinging my skin as they fell. I thought that it was an amazing sight to see, and that I couldn't simply just sit there and watch it happen. I needed to be in it.

"Stop the horses!" I shouted over the rain, and then Will led us just off of the road. I dismounted in an instant, landing ankle-deep in thick mud. But I hardly cared, not as I looked up and watched the heavy droplets fall from the sky. I smiled, for the first time in a while.

"Have you never seen rain before?" Aerez shouted down at me.

"I have," I yelled back. "Just... never like this!"

"Give her a moment," I could vaguely hear Will say as I began to delve deeper into the forest, smiling widely as I did.

After a moment I began to run, like I did that day on the beach. I welcomed the raindrops as they pelted me, amazed by how much water was just wasted to the earth. If this ever happened in Mortefine, everyone would set out buckets and barrels to collect as much of it as they could for free. We would have the occasional rain shower, maybe once or twice a year, but it was never more than a sprinkle and it never lasted for more than a few minutes.

I wondered what snow looked like, and was suddenly very eager to see it. We *were* headed to Frystal, which was basically a city of ice. And from what I'd heard, it snowed there all year long.

The rain lightened a bit, and I slowed my run down to a walk, making sure that I would be able to find my way back to the road. I bent over and panted with my hands on my knees, but then something caught my attention in a nearby tree.

It was the raven, perched on a low-hanging branch, watching me creepily. I immediately froze and began to walk backward, wishing that I wasn't so tired so I could have run back instead.

The bird cawed once, to which I shuddered, and then it jumped and flew onto another branch, even closer to me that time.

"What do you want?" I shouted to the bird. Of course, I got no answer. I turned around and started walking. "Why does this shit keep happening to me?" I muttered and stomped away.

I heard a cracking sound, like perhaps a branch had snapped, and I quickly turned back to the last place I'd seen the bird, only it was not there anymore. It was nowhere at all. I hadn't heard it flapping its wings away, but where had it gone? I picked up my pace, not really caring whether I found out or not.

When I made it back, my companions were exactly where I'd left them, waiting patiently for me. But Will must have seen the look on my face, because he asked, "What happened?" He was already dismounting and walking towards me before I'd even fully reached them.

"There was a bird," I said, and Aerez's head shot to me, though she said nothing. "A raven. I think it's following us. I saw it first in Kraxoth, and two more times since then. Do you remember, Aerez?"

She slowly shook her head, indicating that she did not remember that first incident. I knew she was lying, because I knew she could not have forgotten throwing the knife at it.

"It's starting to scare me," I admitted. "Neither of you have seen anything?" They both shook their heads. "Well, I'm sure it's nothing. There's a lot of birds out here, perhaps I'm mistaken."

I held Aerez's gaze as I walked back up to the horse, but she said nothing. The assassin was hiding something, and I was going to figure out what it was.

Chapter 33

We were starving. Not literally, of course, but it has been almost a day since we'd eaten our last meal, and we were starting to feel the effects of it. We stopped for the night to set up camp just off of the road, beside a narrow stream. Will tied the horses up and then asked that Aerez and I gather firewood while he went and hunted something for dinner.

By the time I finished setting up the tent, Aerez had returned with her hands full of twigs and branches. I sat against the trunk of a tree while she built the fire, feeling somewhat helpless. She said she didn't mind, but she probably knew I'd be a burden if I attempted it myself.

The coldness every night prior had been nothing in comparison to what it was now. The closer to Frystal we got, the colder it would continue to become. I suddenly missed those warm sunny days back in Mortefine. I would have much more preferred feeling the sun against my bare skin to hardly seeing it at all throughout the day because of the dreary clouds. Unfortunately, the fire would have to do to keep me warm.

"How did you learn to build a fire?" I asked Aerez.

She shrugged, snapping a branch over the top of her knee and tossing it into the flames. "I kinda just *learned*. I mean, I didn't have a choice. Taking on certain jobs, sometimes I spent weeks without being near a town or even indoors. And sometimes in winter. So I had to learn to build a fire, or I would freeze to death."

"You'll show one day?" I asked.

She nodded. "It's really not all that hard. You just—"

One second, Aerez was lowering another branch into the fire, and then the next she was throwing that branch as hard as she could into the darkness. I thought she was throwing it at Will, but he was not there when I looked, and the branch went too far for me to see where it landed. When I turned back to Aerez she was reaching for something on the side of her pants, freeing a weapon of some sort.

"What are you doing?" I asked her, starting to worry a bit.

"You didn't hear that?" she whispered to me.

"No," I said back. "Maybe Will has returned. Put the knife away."

She quickly shook her head. "That's not it." Then she motioned a hand for me, beckoning me over to where she was standing. "Get up. Stay behind me."

I could feel my heart begin to race in my chest. I hadn't heard or seen anything, but Aerez did, and I trusted her instincts because they'd saved me more than once before. I hoped it wasn't another sand serpent, because I didn't want Aerez to have to kill it. But then I thought that perhaps it was something worse.

Aerez pulled her arm back, in preparation to launch that knife through the trees, but then a moment later she was lowering it, her body sagging as if the threat had disappeared. "It's nothing," she said, shaking her head and then turning away, walking back towards the fire to attend it.

"What?" I said, somewhat urgently. It couldn't possibly have been nothing if she was on such high alert only a moment ago. I remained staring out into the darkness, failing to find anything out of the ordinary. But then I heard a twig snap, and it scared me so much that I stumbled backward, slamming into Aerez and knocking us both to the ground. I screamed when I saw something move towards us.

"Relax," Aerez said, shoving me off of her.

I landed on my side, but could turn my neck enough to see Will emerge from the brush and walk towards us.

"What is wrong with you two?" Will asked when he saw us both sprawled across the ground.

"We thought you were something else," I explained. "There was an odd noise, and we got spooked."

"It was probably just me," he said.

"No," Aerez cut in. "There was… it was something else."

Will looked at us with a hint of concern. "Well," he said, "whatever it was, it's gone now. I caught us some rabbit." He held up two small dead animals.

I slept rather unpleasantly that night, mostly because Aerez had scared the wits out of me with that nonsense before dinner. I kept finding myself peering out of the open tent flap, thinking that I would see something staring back at me. I thought I might have heard wings flapping at some point, but it might have been my imagination. There was nothing out there, I had to remind myself more than once. And when I eventually did fall asleep, my dreams were filled with unusual things. But not darkness. It was a relief to remain hidden from it.

The next morning, like every other day, we awoke at dawn and continued riding. I wanted to try something different today, though I wasn't really sure why. I was tired of the blunt casualness between me and Aerez, and I wanted that to change. She was there because she wanted to help me, and yet I knew nothing about her. As we rode through silence, I figured it was as good enough of a time to ask her as any.

"So," I said behind her on our horse, my arm wrapped around her stomach like it usually was. "Am I allowed to finally ask you about yourself? Or is that too much of an invasion?"

"I'd rather not," she said quietly, keeping her head forward.

"We've known each other for a while now," I went on. "I think after saving each other's lives, I'm entitled to know at least one thing about who you are."

"Just one thing?"

I sighed. I had said that, I supposed, and one thing would be better than nothing. "We can start there," I told her.

Will trotted ahead a bit, wisely keeping out of our conversation. I didn't mind if he was around, but I didn't think I could get Aerez to open up with him lurking.

She thought for a long moment about what she would say, and I started to think she wouldn't answer at all, until her head turned slightly to the side, and she began to speak. "My mother was a slave from Faulton. And my father... I was never close with him. We only met a couple of times before he died."

A slave. That was truly morbid, and messed up, knowing that her mother was in chains, the same way she was shackled to the assassin's association.

"How did you come to Vatragon? Or Kraxoth?"

"My mother fled with me when I was very young. We sailed up the Forbidden Sea and settled in Kraxoth. She was killed not long after that, and then the assassins took me in, and I became a trained killer."

"How did your mother die?" I asked. She flinched slightly, and she turned her head back to look at me, but halted before I could see her face. "I'm sorry. You don't have to answer that if—"

"It's okay," she said quickly but quietly. "I'm an assassin, remember? I can handle far worse than a few personal questions."

Will was even further ahead of us, barely even in sight anymore.

"I know you can handle it," I said, smiling to myself. "But that doesn't mean that you have to. You make your own choices, Aerez."

"I make my own choices." She repeated my words, and I couldn't tell if she was asking me a question or making a statement. I didn't think she knew either. "Never at any point in my life have I been the person to make my own choices. There has always been someone controlling me, using me, telling me what to do or who to kill."

She sat so still atop the horse that I wasn't even sure she was breathing. I wasn't sure what to say to that, or if I should have said anything at all.

She finally whispered, barely loud enough for me to hear, "Not anymore."

"What?"

"Not anymore," she said, louder that time. And then she turned around and met my eyes. "I lied to you. I didn't come here to help you; I came so I could escape the assassins. I needed a way out. My life was never my own, and it was time for that to change."

"Aerez—"

"I used you," she continued. "And I'm sorry for that, but I truly do want to help you, Kara. At first, I planned to just leave you when we got to the next town, but I couldn't do that now. I couldn't do that after what we've been through."

I wasn't surprised by this, I mean, I had already assumed enough before without her having to tell me. I knew she had no plans to go back to the assassins, and I couldn't really blame her if she just decided to up and abandon me, but...

"Well, it's a good thing I could really use your help," I told her. "It's okay if I don't know everything about you, because I trust you, and I think we're even becoming friends. One day I hope you will be ready to tell me everything, but for now... I'm glad you are here, Aerez."

She gave me a smile filled with such sadness, like nobody has ever said anything so kind to her before. That thought made me want to cry.

I leaned in closer and whispered, "Will feels the same, even if he'll never admit to it."

She laughed, a genuine laugh, and when we looked towards Will, he was staring back at us with a puzzled expression on his face, which caused us to laugh even harder.

A few minutes later I said, "Tell me about your mother?"

She inclined her head. "I don't remember much about her. I don't even remember what she looked like, but I know she was beautiful. Her skin was darker than mine, but we had the

344

same hair and eyes. She was a fighter, too. She died fighting for me—protecting me. I didn't know it at the time, but the man who killed her, she worked for him. I don't know why he wanted her dead, and I don't really care, but I knew he needed to die for what he'd done."

I remained quiet as she spoke, because I knew it made her uncomfortable to speak of such things.

"The day I killed that man," she said. "That was the first day the raven showed up." She waited for me to react, to call her out on her lying, but I didn't. "I know I told you before that it was nothing, but that bird has been following me around for most of my life, and I have no idea why. It only watches me from a distance, but it's terrifying. No matter how hard I try to make it go away, or to even kill it, I never can. Even when I can't hear or see it, somehow, I always know that it's around."

I rested a hand on her shoulder from behind and she actually shuddered from my touch, like she was afraid. I couldn't blame her—if I had a creepy raven following me around, I would feel the same way.

"It's here now," she said, and I looked up to the trees, but she only shook her head. "It hides, but I can feel it watching us. Always."

"Is that what it was last night?"

"Yes," she answered quickly. "When I realized what it was, I knew there was nothing to fear. I didn't want you to call me out on my lies, so I pretended like there was nothing there."

"Okay," I said, and then another long moment of silence passed. "I wish I remembered my mother," I admitted. "Or. My father or brother. Or the city they once ruled. Have you been to Orothoz?"

"I have, actually," she said. "It's beautiful there. Clear skies, palm trees, and white-sand beaches. The Alanah Sea is nothing compared to the beauty of The Southern Bay."

I smiled, and tried to imagine what it would look like. But I couldn't. The memories—and I knew there were memories—had long been locked away somewhere, somehow. Everything about who I was had been erased. I recently began to wonder if it was just me blocking out the trauma of my parents being murdered—if it was better that I did not remember it. But it would have been nice to know—to remember the parents and the family I once had.

"You've had a hard life," Aerez said, like she knew exactly what I was thinking. "You deserve freedom more than anyone."

I smiled again, and we sped up a bit to catch up with Will. A minute or so later, I said to Aerez, "You know, you're a very likable person, despite what you might think about yourself."

She huffed a laugh, though something about it felt strained. "You just don't know me well enough yet to think otherwise."

But even though she said that, it didn't seem true.

Chapter 34

It took another week for us to make it to The Crossing—or at least to the outskirts of the surrounding town. We started to pass more and more people over the past few days, though luckily no guards had been in the mix. I was eager to make it to town and find somewhere to eat and bathe, to be again surrounded by civilization.

In the past week, the three of us had been getting on surprisingly well. There was no more arguing between Aerez and Will, not since the night that sand serpent appeared. And ever since I got Aerez to open up with me, she seemed more comfortable within the group as well. I never pried further into her life, as I would wait for her to decide when she was ready, and I could tell talking about it made her very uncomfortable.

The raven—the one that creepily followed Aerez around—made a few appearances over the last week, but as she said, it mainly kept to itself and out of our way. Mostly, we chose to ignore it—to pretend that it wasn't there. Aerez certainly preferred that, and I'd grown quite used to its presence by then. But I couldn't help but think that Aerez had some strange curse placed on her, one that meant a raven would follow her around for the rest of her life.

It had been twenty-six days since I'd left Mortefine, almost a month. While we were making good progress, that thought made me sick. Nola had been waiting for me to return for twenty-six days. I desperately wanted to believe that she was okay, and that Hiran hadn't locked her up somewhere awful, but knowing him, that wasn't likely. And knowing that Nola was in this situation because of me made it even worse.

Time was literally counting down until I either freed her, or her life was ended. Five more months seemed like a long time, but if things didn't go well in Frystal, then we would have to carefully plan our next steps. Five months to find the blade and bring it back to Hiran.

I didn't want to dwell on what-ifs, but how could I not? I didn't want to think about what would happen if Frystal turned out to be a dead end, or if every place was a dead end, or if I did find the blade but I was too late in traveling back to Mortefine. I wouldn't think about that—only time and patience would get us where we needed to be.

It would be a few more hours until we reached The Crossing, so Will wanted to stop for a quick break before we continued on. We pulled off of the main road until we found a shallow creek. We dismounted. Will led the horses to the creek so they could drink some water, and munch on the nearby grass. Aerez took on filling each of our own water canteens, and I walked off just a bit, hoping to find some privacy for a short while.

The creek was narrow, but still too wide to cross comfortably. The current wasn't as strong as some of the other ones I'd seen, and the water was a dark brown color, so I could not see how deep it was. It was cold enough out that wisps of steam arose from the surface and danced like a magical mist. I could see small fish swimming beneath the surface, and turtles on the opposite shore perched with their heads to the sun.

I walked farther than I probably should have, knowing that I could stay along the edge of the creek to find my way back. But I realized that I was too far for either of them to hear me yell if anything should happen, so I turned around to walk back—

First, the sound of a twig snapping caught my attention, and then I could hear footsteps, a few pairs of them, moving closer to me, as well as the murmur of hushed whispers.

There were people nearing me, and they were not my companions. I turned back towards the creek, unsure if I should try to run or just try to play dumb when they finally reached me. I did have Fangmar with me, after all. I listened as their steps crunched fallen leaves, and I kept my back to them, allowing them to believe their presence anonymous, so I had time to come up with a plan of escape.

They continued towards me, and I knew they were about twenty feet away when they finally stopped. I surveyed the area, looking around without turning directly towards them. My only reasonable path of escape would take me through the creek, which was fine, except I couldn't tell how deep it was and I didn't know how to swim.

"Is it her?" I heard a deep raspy voice whisper from behind me. I could tell from his slight accent that he wasn't from a city, but rather the countryside. He was likely a farmer.

Another man spoke, "I thought she was supposed to have others guarding her?"

"She's only a peasant's daughter," another one spoke, a woman this time. "That can't be her."

"Then why does she carry weapons?" the first man asked.

I knew there were at least three of them. They were trying to keep quiet, but I could very obviously note their presence. If they were here to kill me, then they weren't being very smart about it. I turned around, very slowly, finding half a dozen men, and one woman, lurking towards me. They weren't guards or even soldiers. They wore no official uniforms or crests to signify any allegiances. They were merely peasants.

I stood to face them fully. "If you wish to know who I am, then I would suggest asking politely rather than lurking behind the trees like common criminals."

One man smiled at me, revealing a mouth of yellowed teeth. He had a knife in his hand, but as he walked, I could see his slight limp, and his swollen ankle. They appeared to have already been in a fight. Either that, or they were just in such poor health.

349

I reached over my back for my sword, but another man held up his hand and said, "I wouldn't do that, girl. We've got an archer hidden in the trees, ready to shoot you at any moment."

"Who are you?" I asked, hoping to buy as much time as possible. I looked in the distance for Aerez and Will, but they were nowhere to be seen. I shouldn't have wandered off so far.

"We are nobody," the woman said. "We do not know who you are, but we are here to kill you so that we can get paid."

I narrowed my eyes at them. "If you really had an archer in the trees, then you would have killed me already. How do you even know that I'm the one you're after?"

"Your eyes," one man said. "We were told you have green eyes like nobody's ever seen before, and hair like liquid gold."

"Well," I said. "Green eyes are very common, and mine are no different from anyone else's." I said that, though I wasn't sure that it was the truth. If my family was known for their unusual eye color, then perhaps mine were different, and more recognizable.

"I've never heard of eyes like that," one man said. "Except for those royals that used to rule Orothoz. They all died long ago, but it's said their eyes were greener than the Southern Bay."

"Well," I said to them. "I'm not sure who it is you speak of, but I'm from Mortefine. I'm nobody."

I supposed I never had seen eyes as vibrant as mine on anyone else. And if my brother had the same eyes, then it must have been a family trait. These men were sent here to kill me, and they knew exactly what to look for, but they didn't know who I really was. They were only going off of my appearance.

"We don't care who you are," the woman said. "We've come to get paid. Now, we can kill you here and bring back your head, or you can come with us alive so he can kill you himself. Either way, we're getting paid."

"And why would I choose either of those options?" I asked them.

"We already told you, stupid girl," a man said. "Somebody wants you dead, and they're paying a lot of money to make it so." All of the men snickered at that.

"I suppose you will have to kill me," I told them, reaching behind me again for my sword. "Because I am not going anywhere with the likes of you." I slid Fangmar free and held it up in front of them, the sun glistening off of the black diamond on the hilt.

I knew I wouldn't be able to fend them off, but maybe I could get away and run back to Will and Aerez. I couldn't think of a much better option at the moment.

I took a few backward steps away from them with my sword raised in front of me. They watched me with amused anticipation, prowling towards me like they were hunting their dinner—like they were waiting for me to act so they could pounce.

Maybe I could make it past them, down the bank of the creek, and then break into a sprint. I started to run, and I saw only two of the seven of them follow me.

I didn't make it far. One of the men jumped in front of me and stuck his foot in between my ankles, tripping me, sending me falling into the dirt. I braced the fall with my hands, but a sharp pain rang through my wrists, and I had to hold in a scream.

I stayed on the ground for a moment, knowing that the men were right beside me. I closed my eyes and curled up into a ball, bringing my hands over my neck so they could not hurt me there. I heard footsteps and then a foot connected with my side, a boot shooting straight into my gut. I bit my tongue to stay quiet, but it was extremely painful.

A hand grabbed onto my hair, pulling on my braid like a rope. They lifted me from the ground by my skull, and then wrapped their hand around my throat, squeezing. I tried to kick my legs at the man, but he had a knife poised to enter my stomach at any moment. He dragged me closer to the creek, and then lifted me enough for him to throw me straight into the water. I landed close enough to the shore that I could grab onto a bundle of tree roots, because the water was surprisingly deep. I hardly noticed how freezing the water was with the adrenalin boiling through my veins.

The man on the shore was holding something, and it took me a moment to realize that it was my sword. He examined it, like he was deciding if he should keep it for himself, before finally chucking it into the creek, far away from me where I would surely have to swim to retrieve it. It sank beneath the murkiness and disappeared.

I stayed in the water, because I didn't know what else to do, and when I turned back to the shore, I saw one of the men bending down and reaching for me. He grabbed me by the hair and pushed me down into the water, shoving my head roughly beneath the surface. I knew enough to suck in a deep breath before he did it, but I needed to get away or else I might drown.

He could only reach me from where I was holding onto the tree roots, so I let go of them and tried to back away from the shore. I reached in the back of my pants and pulled my knife free, and then I brought it up to the man's arm and sliced right through it, right in the crook of his elbow. Blood sprayed into the water, and the man pulled away, releasing me at last.

I turned to the other shore, assessing if I could make it over there or not, and then climb out and run free, but then I heard shouting from the men behind me. The man whose arm I cut, he was still standing there watching me, but his face was vacant. He fell to his knees, and then his face collided with the ground, and I could see the knife protruding from the back of his skull.

Aerez ran over from out of nowhere, pulling the blade free from the man's skull and then quickly moving towards the other man who had beaten me. She kicked him in the groin, to which he huddled over in pain, and then she stabbed the knife through his back and into his heart. She did not pull the knife free that time.

The other men were running over to us now, so Aerez quickly moved to hide from their sight. "Stay there," she hissed at me, and then hid herself behind the trunk of a tree.

I stayed in the creek, but managed to drag myself towards where my sword had been thrown, in hopes to retrieve it. And to my luck, I could feel it with my feet, so I dunked beneath the surface and picked it up, and then I pulled myself back towards the shore.

When I climbed out of the water, the five men were standing before me, watching me, ready to kill me.

Aerez's voice sounded from not far off, though I could not see where she was hidden. "If any of you lay one more finger on her, I will end your lives in the most brutal ways imaginable. It won't be quick, and it won't be painless. I might even take pleasure in torturing you. I always enjoy having a bit of fun in the process. Actually," she paused for a moment, like she'd come up with a brilliant idea, "take one more *step* towards her and I'll force you to kill *each other*. Maybe I'll let the last one standing live, so you can run back to whatever burrow you crawled out of. Or," she continued, clearly becoming amused by this, "back away from her now and I'll make your deaths quick."

"Why don't you show us your face and we'll make *your* death quick," one of the men spat. "You can't stop us. You're both little girls and you're far too outnumbered."

That same man took a step towards me, just one step, and then a blade found itself in his face. Actually, two blades. One had been thrown through his right eye, and the other into his left temple. All I did was blink, and they were there. The man collapsed and I had to crawl out of the way so that he didn't fall on me. He slipped into the creek, red pouring into the water.

Aerez emerged from the brush then, a terrifying smile on her face. Her hood was up, concealing her face in shadows beneath. You could hardly tell that she was a woman, or that she was young, but she looked terrifying all the same.

A man charged at her, and she pulled a dagger free, spread her legs, and held out her arms in anticipation as if she would embrace the man. He didn't even have a finger on her before her blade slid across his throat. That certainly seemed to be her specialty—cutting people's throats—and it was something I could have gone forever without witnessing.

She casually walked to the edge of the creek, towards me, then bent down to the water to rinse her blade off. I wasn't sure if the others had finally gotten wise, or if they were just too terrified to attack, but they all backed up a bit and watched us, waiting.

Then one of the men made his move. He had a rather large sword, but Aerez pulled her twin short swords free just in time to meet the man's blow. She crossed them in front of her, creating a barrier from any further attack. The man swung again, and Aerez threw her arms outwards, slicing into his arms in more than one place. He let out a howl of pain before falling to his knees. Aerez kicked him, sending him also into the creek, where he would likely drown.

I was so busy watching her that I had left myself completely unguarded. My sword was clutched in my hands, but it was not raised in defense. A man charged for me, a dagger in his hands. I held Fangmar up, knowing that I would have to use it if I wanted to live. It felt surprisingly light, and easy, like I was doing the right thing.

I knew it was necessary. I stood before the man and held a defensive stance, as I had been trained to do my entire life. All I needed to do was immobilize him, so I could keep him from harming me. But as he ran at me screaming, I began to panic.

Or perhaps I knew exactly what I was doing.

I swung my sword down upon his wrist, cutting into the skin, forcing him to drop his dagger. He clutched it immediately to stop the bleeding, but continued moving towards me, holding up his fists like he would kill me that way. He swung for me, and I again stopped it with my sword, cutting into him. He kicked a leg out, making to sweep me off of my ankles, but I jumped backward, leaving him kicking nothing but air. He swung another fist, and another, and another. He wouldn't stop. Even as I continued to cut him, he would not stop trying to kill me.

I pointed Fangmar straight at him, straight for his chest, and as he lunged forward to punch me, it slid straight into his heart. It made agonizing sounds—gurgling and gushing as blood spilled free. I twisted the blade, releasing a scream from the man that morbidly satisfied me.

"You bitch," he said, blood spilling from his mouth.

He collapsed onto the ground, and as he did my sword pulled free, and I watched as his dying body sprawled limply before me. I watched the man die, from my own doing.

Did he deserve what I'd given him? Could I have stopped him another way? I didn't hesitate when I had decided to do it. I could have made it easier, perhaps. I could have made him suffer less. But what terrified me the most was how easy it had been. I did it to save my own life, but I would have done it to save the life of anyone else I cared about. I would have done it to save Aerez, the same way she had done for me so many times before. And I think I would even do it again.

They came with the intention to kill me, so what other option did I have? I could spend my time regretting what I had done, doubting myself and my goodness, or I could move on. There was nothing that would come from me dwelling on it.

I turned back to Aerez, and Will was now at her side. They were watching me, like they had seen everything I'd just done. I sank to my knees. Out of exhaustion, or terror, or disbelief—I wasn't sure. I was relieved that my friends were at my side, as bloodied and bruised as they were as well.

"We killed them all," I said quietly.

"It was necessary," Will said. "They would have done the same to us."

"Were there others?" I asked.

Will nodded. "There were three that came for me, and two more that came for Aerez before she got to you. The only one left is the woman. She fled when she saw both of us, and I don't think she'll be coming back."

I nodded absently.

"It was necessary," Will repeated.

"Yes," I said. "Thank you. They would have..." I didn't allow myself to finish the thought. "They were here for me. They knew exactly who to look for, but they didn't know who I was. Someone was paying them to kill me."

"I know," Will said. "They didn't know who I was, either. They weren't told anything other than to kill you. I don't know who would even know you were here, or why they would want you dead, but I'm willing to bet it's something related to the person who hired Aerez to kill you."

"This is insane," I said. "I can't even properly look for the blade, because there are people out there trying to kill me. How is this fair?"

"It's not," Will said. "Come on." He reached down to me and offered a hand. "We need to hide ourselves as quickly as possible, before anything else happens."

Chapter 35

"How do you do it?" I asked Aerez an hour later, when we'd finally calmed down enough to stop for a break. I didn't want to be anywhere near the bodies of those men, so we'd left right away, but after an hour I asked to stop for a break because I needed a moment to collect myself. I walked into the woods, and Aerez had decided on joining me, refusing to leave my side after the attack. We stood across from each other, each of us leaning against a different tree.

She immediately understood what I was asking. "I know it's hard," she told me. "It may seem like I have no remorse—that I live carelessly when it comes to the lives that I take—but none of it comes without burden." She turned her head to the side, as if she didn't want me to read what was on her face. "I remember the first time I killed a man. I was seven years old, my mother had just died, and I was living on my own in Kraxoth. He broke into our house, stole from us, and then beat my mother to death for trying to stop him. He got away—he let me live because he wasn't above killing a mother, but killing a child, apparently, took things too far. I lived for months on my own, begging for scraps from people on the streets. And one day, I saw that man again, walking down the street, holding the hand of his wife, and his daughter in the other. That didn't stop me from killing him. I followed him to his house, waited until he was alone, and then I took a knife from his own kitchen and plunged it into his gut. I would have gone for the heart, but I wasn't yet tall enough to reach it."

I blinked at her, unsure of what to even say to that. But I was completely surprised when she began to smile slightly, like the memory was amusing. It terrified me.

"I watched him piss himself," she went on. "And then I watched his innards fall to the ground as I drew the knife across his stomach, in every direction, carving until there was nothing left to recognize. And when it was over, I turned to find that his daughter had seen the entire thing. She was standing at the base of the stairs, watching, but she did not cry out or run screaming, she simply walked back into her room and closed the door, like she was too stunned to react."

"Did you feel remorse then?" I asked.

She gave me a shallow nod. "I did," she said. "Even though my actions were fueled by vengeance, I felt guilty for what I had done—for leaving a child without a father. But you know what? It's those kinds of thought and feelings that remind us that we're human—that we have souls, and we can feel pain and regret."

"Would you do it again?" I asked her. "If you had to?"

"Yes," she told me without any hesitation. "That bastard killed my mother in cold blood. I would have always regretted not killing him more than I actually regret killing him."

I wasn't sure if I should offer her my condolences or run away scared, or even take her words to heart. I wasn't really sure what to think of that at all, but I was slightly relieved that she had told me more about herself. "Thank you, Aerez," I said quietly. "Thank you for sharing that with me."

"It gets easier," she told me. "When it's your job—you stop thinking of them as people but rather as targets or missions. But that shouldn't stop you from feeling. Never stop feeling, Kara."

I wasn't sure why I asked her this, but the words seemed to have slipped from my mouth. "Would it have been easy for you to kill me?"

Her eyes turned sad, narrowing on me like she genuinely disturbed by my question. "No," she told me.

"Why?"

"Because you have done nothing to deserve death. Anything that you have done in the past, it does not equate to the crimes that most other people have committed. Those men that came after you, they were only doing it for the money, and *you* would never have done something like that. It doesn't matter that they had no personal vendettas against you, it's the fact that they would agree to kill you in the first place, without knowing or understanding who you were."

Again, I wasn't sure how to respond to that, so I asked another question. "Will you keep killing after you are done helping me?"

She smiled faintly, and hopefully. "I hope..." she started. "I hope that one day I never need to kill again. I hope that I find peace in my life. I want to do something that matters—something that involves enriching life rather than ending it."

"That was very well spoken," I told her, offering a sad smile in return. "You are so much more than an assassin, Aerez. I see the good in you, even when you hide from it. Don't let anybody treat you like less than who you really are."

Her eyes formed thin silver lines, tears swelling as her bottom lip began to quiver. I pushed off of my tree and walked over to her, pulling her in for an embrace. It took her a moment to hug me back, but she did. We were both crying then, and neither of us tried to hide it. We wouldn't hide something like that from one another.

"Nobody has ever said such kind things to me before," Aerez whispered into the crook of my neck.

I pulled her closer to me, two friends embracing one another after just confessing probably the most personal and vulnerable things about our lives. "Aerez," I said to her. "I don't know what life has in store for me, but I wouldn't mind having you at my side through it all. I would love to have you at my side, actually."

She pulled back, quickly wiping her tears away. "I think I would like that."

"Yeah?" I smiled.

"Ready to keep going?" Will's voice cut in from where he stood a short distance away.

Aerez released me immediately, turning away like she was afraid Will had seen her. It hurt me, that she was afraid he would judge her, even after everything we'd been through.

"Would you kindly *piss off*," I yelled to Will. "I told you I needed a minute of privacy, now *leave me alone.* Go find somewhere else to be." He just stared back at me, his face full of concern. He didn't move, and while I wasn't that unnerved by his presence, I knew Aerez did not want him around. I picked up a rock from the dirt beside me and chucked it in his direction. "Go."

He put his hands up—defensively and sarcastically at the same time. "Sorry," he muttered, and then began to walk away. "Take all the time you need, lady." I wished I would have aimed the rock at his head.

When I turned back to Aerez, she was gone. She had slipped off between the trees somewhere, wandering through the forest. It was fine. We both needed time to ourselves, and I was just glad she had decided to open up with me again.

"Great," I muttered to myself, sighing loudly.

I sped up to catch up with Will, and he seemed even more confused then, when he saw me beside him.

"I wasn't trying to intrude," he explained to me. "I was just concerned for you. Both of you."

"It's fine," I said, though it sounded like anything but. "Aerez needs some time to herself. Sorry if were delaying the trip."

"Karalia," Will said, turning and halting me in place. He put his hands on my shoulders and frowned down at me. "You don't have to pretend with me. You killed someone. I know the toll that has on a person. If you don't want to talk about it, I understand, but just don't pretend like everything's okay when I know it isn't."

"I took his life," I said, my voice a raspy whisper. "I took a man's life. I hadn't planned on doing that. I wanted to avoid it. But the things he said and did…"

"I know," he said, looking at me with both understanding and pity. But I didn't want him to look at me that way. I didn't want him to feel bad for me. What I did… he shouldn't forgive it so easily.

I hesitantly looked back into his eyes, knowing that I would find the usual warm kindness that was always there.

"I'm fine," I said again.

"Stop," Will said, gripping me even harder by the shoulders. "Stop pretending like there's some barrier between us. I know you don't care for me like… like I do for you, but that doesn't mean you have to shut me out. I understand. I do. So please, just stop, and let me hug you."

The tears began to fall again, and Will watched me as if he thought he'd said the wrong thing. I didn't want him to be upset. I didn't want him to feel bothered by me. I flung myself towards him and wrapped my arms around him, nearly sending the both of us flying to the ground. He hugged me back like he never had before, and I knew then that it was different, that something had changed.

It was what I needed. Not just then, but forever. I needed my friendship with him to be permanent. I needed to know that he would be there for me even when I wasn't there for myself.

Will brushed the tears from my cheeks, and then I closed my eyes and leaned my head against his chest. "I'm so tired," I told him. "I'm tired of feeling sad all the time, and hating myself for what's happened to Nola. I'm tired of searching for the blade, even though I know I'll never stop until I find it. I just wish… I wish things were easier."

When I looked back up at him, he was smiling. A sad sort of smile, but one of understanding. He placed a kiss on the top of my head and continued to hold me, for a long while. For as long as I needed.

"Will," I said, breaking the silence after an unknown amount of time. "You are a good person. Don't let anyone ever tell you differently."

He huffed a laugh. "I think *you* have told me something different before."

"Well, I was a fool."

Another moment of silence passed between us. "Karalia," he said. "I will always be here for you. You know that, right? I will be here as your friend, as your protector, or as whatever else you need me to be. You could never be alone for as long as I live."

What should have given me relief, only filled me with dread. Promises are complicated things, though I didn't feel like explaining that to him at the moment.

"I know," was all I said in return.

Will and I returned to where he'd left the horses alongside the road, and then Aerez joined us a short while later. It was obvious that she had been crying, but it was certainly none of my business. I had cried, too.

We mounted and continued riding, the first hints of the setting sun appearing as the town at last came into view. It was much smaller than Kraxoth had been, and yet still larger than Saltrenea. As we neared, we could see guards posted at the town entrance, and I thought Will would hesitate and want to come up with a plan, but he didn't. As we passed into the city, the guards gave us curious glances, but averted their attention a moment later to the next traveler entering.

They were capital guards, but they had not been sent in search of the prince. They didn't seem to think the prince could have been there at all. But they were standing post and clearly looking for a specific person, or many people, just not any of us.

The stables were a few minutes down the road, and we dismounted and left the horses there, taking all of our belongings into the city where we would search for an inn.

The town was nearly empty, as night was approaching, but as we found a passing man, Will asked him where we could locate the nearest inn.

He gave us all a wary glance. "Just a few more minutes that way," he said, pointing in the direction that we were already headed. "Or," he continued, "if you're looking for somewhere more private—somewhere others won't look your way..." He pointed in a different direction, down a different street.

"Thank you," Will said to the man, and before he could walk away, Will added, "Sir, if you would be so kind, could you tell me why there are capital guards posted at the town entrance?"

The man turned back to us, appearing even more uncomfortable that time. "Er, there's been some... *criminal* activity lately. Rumors of rebellion and such. The king seems to want to keep everyone on a tight leash, though I don't see what all the fuss is about."

"What manner of rebellion?" Will asked the man rather urgently.

The man didn't speak for a long moment, like he was unsure if he should or not. "Sazarr supporters," he whispered to us, and my heart sped. "They're planning something—something big. If you know anything, you shouldn't stay here." Then the man turned away from us and broke into a run, nearly tripping because he couldn't get away quick enough.

None of us spoke a word. We would wait until we were in private.

We continued in the direction we had already been walking in, and like the man said, in a few minutes we were at the doors of a small inn. It was like all of the others I'd stayed in before: cozy yet still somehow uncomfortable. The lobby smelled faintly of roasted meat, which made my stomach growl, but we quickly retrieved a key and walked down the hall to our room.

The room was small. Only one bed, a nightstand, and a cushioned chair in the corner. There was a small connected restroom with two buckets, one to wash ourselves with and the other to use as a chamber pot. I might have preferred the forest to that.

Aerez wasted no time with removing her shoes and then situating herself on the bed. It squeaked beneath her weight, and I began to worry that it wouldn't be able to support three people.

"I'm exhausted," she said, letting out a long yawn.

"Me too," I said quietly, mostly to myself, as I began removing my own boots, then my weapons and cloak. I collapsed onto the bed beside her and rolled onto my side, leaving room for Will, though he never joined us.

I knew I had fallen asleep when I awoke to Will reentering the room with two trays piled with food. My stomach again grumbled, and then Aerez was jumping out of bed and running for the food like a wild animal.

Before we ate, we each took turns tidying ourselves up in the washroom. I did my best to wipe my skin down with the rags they had left for us, but it didn't much help with the stench. I would need a proper bath to get the blood out of my hair and from under my nails.

We all sat atop the bed as we ate our meal. There was cheese and bread, beef stew, fresh vegetables. For dessert we even had some little chocolates, and red wine to drink. It all looked absolutely divine. And it tasted divine, too. I would know because I ate it in a matter of minutes.

We ate everything, and a short while later the only thing remaining was a bottle and a half of wine. We were each taking turns sipping from it when Aerez cut in.

"I have an idea," she told us excitedly. "I think we should play a game."

"A game?" I said flatly. "Seriously?"

She let out a somewhat childish giggle. "Yes," she said. "A drinking game. We each take a guess about one another. It can be guessing a secret or guessing something about each other's lives. If we guess correctly, then you have to take a drink."

"I don't see this ending well," I told her hesitantly.

"It won't," Will said, sitting up and leaning against the headboard. "But we're going to do it anyway, aren't we?"

Aerez's grin was answer enough. She poured each of our glasses full to the brim, and I knew someone would end up spilling it on the bed. "I can start." She turned to me, with an evil sort of look on her face as she said to me, "Will was your first kiss."

I almost burst into laughter, until I realized that it might have been humiliating for Will. Heat flooded my cheeks. "Um," I said wearily. I hadn't expected her to start out with such a question. They both watched the glass in my hands, waiting.

"No?" Aerez asked.

"Obviously not," I said. "Not that it's any of your business, but no, Will was not my first kiss. I'm a nineteen-year-old woman, not some prudish maiden."

Aerez was still smiling, but Will just looked flat-out uncomfortable.

"Was it Hiran?" she asked me.

I raised my glass in salute, taking a sip, though I didn't even think her question was part of the game. Maybe I should have been angry, or even embarrassed, but I wasn't. I began to laugh instead, clearly having become a little drunk.

Aerez turned to Will next. "Prince," she said, flashing her teeth. "You hate being a prince. You played soldier when you met Kara because you didn't want her to hate you, just like everyone else does. But you failed, didn't you?"

"Aerez," I said in warning, but then I saw Will smiling, as if he thought the question was amusing.

"Why would you ask me that?" he said, the side of his mouth quirking up. He wasn't angry like I expected him to be. Perhaps he was drunk as well.

"We're all friends here," Aerez said, leaning over and sliding a hand up his arm. I noted the way his eyes shot to it, watching her carefully. "I think we established that enough earlier. You can be honest with us."

He pulled his glass up to his mouth and then took a drink. "My turn," he said, his voice having grown colder, and his attention shifting to me. "You liked me when we met, before you knew who I really was."

"Yes," I said. "And I still like you, Will." I started to raise my glass to my mouth, but he shook his head.

"That's not what I mean. You had a different set of feelings for me. And when you realized who I was, and who my brother was to you, you locked those feelings away."

I set my glass on the nightstand. "I'm not sure what has led you to believe such a thing, but I never felt that way for you, Will, and I've never lied about it either. If I somehow led you on, then I apologize for that, but you know the truth now, so can we please move past it?"

He didn't answer, he just continued to stare at me with sad droopy eyes. Aerez, however, was watching us with a face lit up with joy, like this is exactly what she wanted to happen. She drank from her cup though it wasn't even her turn.

"My turn," I said to her. "You would have killed me, for the money. If I was anyone else, if I was anyone of little importance, and if the prince wasn't with me, you would have ended my life."

She drank, though I wasn't surprised. "You can't hold that against me, Kara. You know that's my job."

"I don't hold it against you," I said, taking a drink.

I wasn't exactly sure what direction the game had turned in. If it was supposed to be fun, then we certainly weren't playing it right. Making us admit these things to one another just seemed... cruel.

Will turned to Aerez now. "Aerez," he said. "You act like you hate me, but that's all it is—an act. Because really, deep down, you actually *like* me."

She continued to smile, though it had changed to something pained. And she did not raise her glass. "You could never expect me to admit such a thing, could you? Even if it were true."

"I don't know," Will said. "That's why I'm asking."

Again, she did not raise her glass. Instead, she set it on the nightstand before standing and moving for the door. "I think we've played enough for the night," she told us without turning back. "If you'll excuse me." And just like that, she left the room, leaving me and Will alone.

"What was that all about?" Will asked, but I was already turning onto my side in bed and falling asleep.

Chapter 36

I awoke sometime in the middle of the night with a pounding headache, knowing that the drinking had caught up with me. I heard the door open and close, and listened to the near silent footfall as Aerez walked across the room and towards the bed. The mattress creaked quietly as she crawled and situated herself in between me and Will. She had returned at last from wherever it was she'd gone off to, and yet I was still too tired and drunk to give it a thought.

I hoped it would be a dreamless night, and I was sleeping rather peacefully, until...

I knew what was happening before I'd even been pulled away, like I could sense it coming. Like I was getting so used to it now that it had become second nature—this second reality.

There was that usual darkness, at first, but then it changed. It changed into something much less preferable. I found myself again reliving some sort of memory, only this time it did not belong to Sazarr, but to a small child. It didn't last nearly long enough for me to fully understand it, and I only caught glimpses before the sight disappeared entirely.

The body was not my own. It was smaller, almost clumsy, their limbs not having fully grown yet. They were a child. Tears fell from their eyes, blurring my surroundings, as they attempted to crawl towards something on the other side of what I could only guess was a courtyard. It was nighttime, and the moon was high up above, the stars glistening.

I cowered close to the ground and shifted my hands to cover my ears as a loud screeching sound began to rumble the earth. The sound was impossibly human, coming from something that could only be described as a monster.

The keeper of the memory looked up to the sky through blurry eyes, just as massive scaled wings appeared and blocked out the moon—blocked out everything. Its eyes were a deep orange color, like rust, while its body was covered in red scales, like the color of blood. It dove towards me, jaw open, smoke seeping from its mouth, preparing to unleash its flames upon me.

I curled up into myself and closed my eyes, terrified yet prepared to die. I knew this beast had come to kill me. But then I felt something strange within me, like some sort of tether had been pulled. It was pulling me—urging me to run and to not stop until I'd gotten very far away. It could have been intuition, yet a child as young as her wouldn't have understood such a thing. It was almost like a voice, shouting at me to get up and run.

And so we ran, and we never stopped. Even now, we run.

The memory was my own—some fragment of my past that had been given back to me. I suspected it was the day my parents were killed, the day that I left Orothoz. And though I was shown nothing else of this memory, it was enough for me to learn the truth.

Drazen killed my parents.

I didn't understand why. I didn't know why he wanted me dead as well. I knew it was him, because he looked the same as he had in the memory from Sazarr. Had Sazarr somehow known, and shown me so I would realize? No, that couldn't be it. But it was undeniably Drazen.

Even though I was within a dream, I could feel my heartbeat quicken. If Drazen wanted me dead then, and he thought he succeeded, then perhaps he was the one that wanted me dead now. If he somehow found out that I was alive, then that would explain things. This only furthered my suspicion of him being the real villain in the story. Knowing what he's done to my family, some would say that because he is a god, he has the right to take life how he sees fit, be he is not a god, he is only a monster.

Why was I remembering this now? What triggered this memory to reappear? I had no idea, but I would need to find answers soon.

My dream was not yet over. Darkness flooded my senses and then I caught a glimpse of something else. It was something oddly familiar, though I knew I'd never seen it before, not with my own eyes.

It was the lost blade of Sazarr—a dagger with the blade of a serpent fang, white and glistening, its hilt forged from some sort of metal with strange welded designs and markings. It was surrounded by darkness, hiding, waiting. Was it calling to me? Was it showing me the way to it? I had no body that I could sense in any place, but rather I was being shown this through eyes that I could not understand. It nearly scared me to death.

I shot upright in bed, panting heavily, one hand over my chest, the other over my forehead, as if my mind had just deceived me. That dream—whatever it was—it had disturbed me and shown me terrible things. I didn't understand it, and I wouldn't, not for a while.

I knew someone else was awake, probably because of me, as I felt the bed shift and heard it creak slightly. "Bad dream?" Will whispered to me. There was concern in his voice.

"Something like that," I whispered back. "I'm fine. Don't worry. Go back to sleep, okay?"

"Are you sure?" he asked.

"She said she's fine," Aerez cut in, apparently awake as well. "Now both of you, shut your mouths and go back to sleep."

I turned onto my side, away from both of them, knowing that Will was still awake and likely waiting for me to say something else, likely contemplating how he thought he could help me. I didn't want his help, not with this. Eventually I fell back to sleep, though not peacefully.

We headed out into town the next day, with the intention to restock our supplies for the remainder of our trip to Frystal. We would leave the horses there, and travel by foot the rest of the way, as they would not be able to make it through the tunnel into the city, and it was too late in the season to take the mountain path. We needed some warmer clothes, especially me, who had never been in such a climate. As eager as I was to see snow, I thought the cold might not make it worth it.

As we made our way through town, I couldn't help but notice that everyone was either on edge or angry or terrified. Nobody seemed at peace, and it made me rather uncomfortable. There was a strange tension in the air, like the townspeople were hiding something, and they were nervous with the guards there, and it made me want to get out of there as quickly as possible.

We passed by a busy square, where a large group of people had gathered. I was surprised the guards hadn't separated them, with as suspicious as they looked. There was a man, middle-aged, dressed in black robes standing at some sort of podium. He was facing the people, like he was about to address them.

I walked closer, mostly because I was interested to see what all the fuss was about, and Will and Aerez followed behind me as we settled into the crowd.

The man cleared his throat, then began. "Far away, in the city once ruled by the ancient but great Havu family, there are whispers of The Lost Daughter's return to the world."

The crowd began to murmur, but I froze in place, entirely shocked. That was not at all what I expected the man to go on about. I would have never expected him to say something like that.

He continued. "The Queen of the Otherealm will make an appearance once more, and she will take her place in this world of cruel and evil men. She will break barriers, she will destroy our enemies, and she will restore this land to its former greatness. Those in power will perish, and those who claim to preside over us will cease to exist. She will set us free. A fight is coming, and people will die, but that is the price for liberation. That is the price for us to live freely. We are no less slaves than those who are chained in Faulton. We must say no more!"

The crown applauded, some of them even cheering.

I looked nervously towards Will, finding that he was already watching me. I didn't know what to think. Then I looked for Aerez, but she was no longer at our sides. I searched the crowd, finding her shoving her way through it straight towards the speaker. I pointed so Will could see, and he was running a moment later, to stop her.

But Aerez was too quick. She reached the man, anger simmering from her. She began to yell. "You have no idea what being a slave is like!" The crowd fell silent. "You have no right to compare yourself to that. A slave would *never* have the freedom to say what you just did."

And even though she had a knife pulled free and poised at him, the man did not look afraid. He spoke to her quietly, but I was close enough to hear. "I'm sorry if I have offended you," he said, like he genuinely meant it. "But in a moment, you will see that I do not have the freedom to say what I just did. In a moment, things are going to get violent, so you should leave before that happens."

"What are you talking about?" Aerez asked the man, but he was already backing away from her, looking into the distance towards where a handful of guards had just broken through the crowd, and were running straight for him. Everyone began to scream, frantically trying to get away.

That man, these people, they were not Sazarr supporters. They were supporters of *me*. They knew that I was alive, and they believed that I was somehow going to help them. To liberate them.

We really, really needed to get out of this town.

Will took me by the wrist and pulled me into a nearby alley, where Aerez was already waiting. We tried our best to stay hidden as people ran by, and as guards chased after them.

"You two should go back to the inn," Will told us. "Keep your hood up, don't let anyone see you. I'll get what we need and meet you back there in a little while."

"I don't think—"

"Karalia, please," he said to me. "You need to go."

I nodded hesitantly and then turned to Aerez, who already had her weapons drawn like she would slaughter our way back to the inn. That did not give me a good feeling.

"Go," Will said again, and we did.

We broke into a light run, doing our best to blend in with the other townspeople. We weren't the only ones running. Others ran past us, shouts and sounds of violence coming from the square where the man had just spoken. A part of me wanted to go back and help him, but I knew he was likely dead by now.

We ran past a child on the street, alone and crying. I tried to help them, but Aerez didn't give me a second to stop. She grabbed me by the arm and kept moving. I couldn't be upset with her; she was only doing her job as my protector.

A woman stepped into our path, not intentionally, but as we approached her, I collided with her body, sending her falling to the ground. I had to force Aerez to let go of me so I could help the woman up.

"Thank you," she said, her voice frail and quiet. She turned to look at me, and then her eyes widened—not with fear, but with awe. When I tried to keep moving forwards, she stepped in front of me to keep me from going. "You're her," she said quietly. "The Lost Daughter."

I took a backward step, terrified that I was so easily recognized. How could this woman possibly know who I was? Aerez let out a sound that was almost like a growl as she raised a short sword and pointed it at the woman's neck.

But the woman was not looking at the assassin, she was only looking at me. "What are you doing here?" she pressed.

"It's not safe—" she reached, as if to touch my arm, but Aerez shoved her hand away. "You shouldn't be here," she finally said.

I shook my head slowly. "I'm sorry, but I have no idea what you're talking about."

"We know what you look like," she said, her voice even lower. "The rebels, they keep copies of your portrait, so they know who to look for."

"What?" I said. "Where would they get—"

"Have you come, them?" she cut in. "To save us?"

"I don't know what you're talking about," I said again. "I am not some savior within the rebel cause, and I have no intention to help you. Whoever you think I am, you are wrong."

None of it made sense. Why would those people think that I was coming to save them? Why were they plotting a rebellion in my name? If I was that easily recognizable, since apparently they knew what I looked like, then we needed to get hidden as soon as possible.

"Do not tell anyone that you saw me," I demanded of the woman. "And take no part in this rebellion. It will only get you killed."

"Nothing can stop it," she said, somewhat hysterically. "There is unrest—too many mixed opinions in our country. War is on the brink."

I had to practically shove past the woman to get away from her. If she didn't want to listen to my words, then it was her own fault if she got killed. Aerez and I continued making our way to the inn, running even faster now.

A few minutes later a group of guards appeared further down the street, so we slowed to a walk to keep their attention from us. They gave us a glance, likely marking us as two women taking a leisurely stroll, and then continued their hunt for whatever it was they were looking for. I assumed that they were rounding up rebels.

A few more minutes after that, we were back in our room, shutting and locking the door behind ourselves, securing the windows, sliding the curtains closed. I sat on the bed while Aerez nervously paced back and forth.

"We need to get out of this town," she told me. "Today."

I nodded urgently. "I have no idea what is happening. This is insane. What do you think that woman meant, that war is coming?"

"I don't know," she said. "But it can't be good."

Chapter 37

It took us a few short minutes to pack all our belongings, and then we would just need to sit and wait patiently for Will to return. We waited, but then an hour passed, and then another and another, and I started to doubt if he was coming back. If he got injured or stopped by the guards, then he might have needed our help.

I knew Aerez was thinking the same thing, and that she could hardly stay in the room any longer. She'd been pacing for hours, and then cleaning all her weapons, and then pacing some more.

When a soft knock sounded at the door, Aerez sprinted over to it, silently, and lurked beside it. Neither of us dared to speak or even breathe too loudly.

They knocked again, just a hint louder that time. "Open up," Will said. "It's me." But there was something off about his voice.

I released the breath I had been holding in, unclenching my fists that had been held tight. Aerez flipped the lock on the door and opened it just wide enough for Will to fit through. He slid inside and then they shut and relocked the door.

I gasped when I saw the blood, covering Will from his torso all the way down to his feet. He held a hand over the side of his stomach, as if trying to stop the bleeding. Whatever injury had been inflicted on him, it was nothing idle. Aerez and I quickly took the supplies from him and set them down, then moved to assess his wound.

Aerez reached him first, already pulling off his cloak and then lifting his shirt, revealing a large gash in his side. It was mostly clotted, but still needed to be cleaned and dressed. Aerez entered the bathing room to search for supplies.

"What happened?" I asked, guiding him towards the bed and forcing him down onto it.

"It's madness out there," he said, and then groaned loudly as he sprawled himself on the bed. I could see him wince as he met my eyes, and I wrapped my arms around his back to keep him steady. "The guards were attacking people—randomly. They were stopping people in the streets for questioning, and one of them decided to pick a fight with me."

I wouldn't dare ask him what was left of the guard.

Aerez emerged then, cloth in hand, as well as some sort of salve I wasn't exactly sure where she'd gotten from. She approached Will.

"Take your shirt off," she said to him.

He tried to smile, but it was filled with pain. "You're not even going to ask politely?" he joked. "This isn't how I imagined undressing in front of you for the first time."

"Oh, please," she said. "I saw you naked when I tried to drown you in that lake, it's nothing to boast about."

He didn't respond to that, but there was still a hint of a smile on his face. Aerez carefully lifted his shirt and then pulled it over his head, pinching it with the tips of her fingers as if it to keep the blood from touching her. It was strange to see her so nurturing. You wouldn't think that someone who was so good at injuring people would be so good at healing them as well. And it was strange that she would help Will, after nearly two weeks ago when they were at each other's throats every moment of the day. I guess a lot could change in a short amount of time; even a friendship could form.

She dabbed him with the cloth, and he squirmed, letting out a hiss of pain. "Sit still, you squeamish coward," she said, leaning over him.

"It hurts!" he exclaimed.

"Well, it's not going to stop hurting if you don't shut your mouth and stop distracting me." She had most of the blood wiped away then. "This is going to leave one horrid scar."

377

"An addition to the collection," he murmured.

"I could make it bigger if you wanted," she crooned. "How about I extend it all the way to your navel?"

"No, thank you."

"Then shut your damn mouth and let me work."

"You know, you don't have to be so mean."

"You don't have to be so annoying."

They continued, on and on, spewing insults at one another. I realized what she was doing before he did. She was taking his mind off of the pain by starting an argument with him. I supposed it was kind, for her to do that.

When she was finished, she applied the salve and wrapped a bandage around his stomach. "All done," she said, and then added with a smirk, "I think you'll live." And when he tried to get out of bed, she pushed on his chest, keeping him down. "You need to rest—for at least another day."

"We don't have that kind of time," he said, looking at me.

"She's right," I told him. "We couldn't possibly travel with you in this condition. Just one night, okay? If you're better tomorrow, then we'll be on our way."

He grunted, then leaned back and rested his head against the pillow, closing his eyes like he could not put off sleep any longer.

I turned to Aerez. "Where did you learn to do that?"

She shrugged. "It's just one of the man skills that you pick up when you have my sort of occupation." I could tell she didn't want to go into any further detail.

"I can go find some dinner for us," I offered.

"No," Aerez said. "I'll go. You stay here and watch Will. I don't want anyone else recognizing you."

"I don't need anyone to watch me," Will said, but Aerez was already out the door and unable to hear him.

Nothing much had changed by the time Aerez returned an hour later. Will was still in bed, resting, and I was sitting in the chair in the corner, staring out of the window, watching chaos unfold in the town below.

"This is all I could get," she said, holding up two loaves of bread and a bag full of apples. It was certainly better than nothing.

She assisted Will by cutting up an apple into slices, and then practically feeding them to him. Finally, he brushed her off, and said that he was more than capable of eating on his own. I didn't say anything, as I knew that wasn't any of my business.

We heard distant shouts come from outside occasionally. We wouldn't leave the room again until we knew we were ready, and until we were sure that we could make it out safely. We wouldn't be coming back, at least not until we left Frystal again, which could be a long time to come.

Will had managed to prop himself up in bed, and even looked a bit better, so I told him about the woman we had run into. How the rebels knew what I looked like and how they believed that I was going to save them.

He didn't seem as surprised as I expected. "The people will believe anything when they think there is hope."

"Hope for what?" I asked him.

"For a better world," he said. "For a better life. One where my family doesn't rule. One where we are free. You heard what that man said in the square—I think that whether you personally motivate their actions or not, a rebellion will happen. It is already happening."

"You knew about this?" I asked.

He gave something in between a shrug and a nod. "I didn't know that they were doing it in your name. It's been going on for longer than I even knew you were alive. But we knew something was happening. We just assumed that they were Sazarr supporters."

"And your father knows?" I asked. "About the rebellion?" He nodded. "What would he do if he thought I was leading a rebellion against him? I could hardly be welcomed to marry your brother then."

He frowned, and looked at me a moment before answering. "It doesn't matter, because that isn't what you're doing. You're not going to the capital, and you're not marrying my brother, so what does it matter what they think?"

There was the fact that his father could have me executed if he thought the rumors were true. That was even more of a reason for me not to go to the capital.

"We left Kraxoth just in time," he added. "I overheard one of the guards talking about an uprising there that happened just last week. Lord Vonhal had to order the people own his own city to be killed."

"Because of me?"

"No," he told me. "They made no mention of you, only Sazarr."

I wasn't surprised at all that they'd finally decided to act. Trona warned us that something was coming, I just didn't expect it to be so soon. But I felt like somehow this all had to be connected—that I was playing a larger part in everything than I even knew. It was hard to believe that there were two separate rebel organizations operating so close to each other.

"How can a rebellion be led in my name," I asked them, "without me even being a part of it? How can they claim that I am going to save them when they have heard nothing from me at all?"

I hadn't expected an answer, so I wasn't surprised when neither of them could come up with one. It didn't make sense—any of it. But I felt that somehow, the path that I was already on would lead me to the answers.

I slept on the floor that night with nothing more than a pillow, not wanting to crowd the bed any further. Aerez slept next to Will. We didn't leave the room at all the next day, and hardly even got out of bed, except for when Aerez slipped out again to scrounge up some more food for us. She had also, somehow, found a deck of cards, so we sat on the bed and played for a while. Will seemed better, or at least better enough to get up and walk around the room a bit, but it didn't seem like he would be ready to leave the following day.

Sometime in the evening, Aerez went to change the bandage over his wound, and I nearly yelled out from shock when I saw his skin. It was completely healed, with no wound and not even a scab, but only a pale scar. It didn't seem like it had happened the day before, not at all. It was impossible... But then I remembered. Will didn't heal like an ordinary person, because of his power. It must accelerate the healing process. That surely was handy, especially because it meant that we would be ready to leave the following day.

Aerez froze when she saw the wound, and her hands began to shake. I waited for her to say something, to comment on how unusual that was, but she only picked up Will's shirt and tossed it at him, silently telling him to put it back on. She held her hands stiffly at her sides and said to him, "It looks better."

Will replaced his shirt, then met my gaze only for a short moment before looking away. "We'll leave tomorrow morning," he told us.

And that was all anyone said about it.

The next morning came too quickly, and I was afraid to see what Will's wound looked like then. I wondered if there was even a scar left to tell of the injury, or if even that had vanished. He was up and moving again, packing up our things, seemingly perfectly healthy. Aerez and I asked him several times each if he was sure he could travel, and he assured us that he would be fine.

I knew our travels were not going to be easy from there on. Things would only be getting harder, both in the physical sense and in the sense that the farther north we traveled, the longer it would take to get back to Mortefine when all of this was over. It would be harder knowing that Nola was waiting for me to save her, and that I was trying everything in my power, and it was still not enough.

It felt like I hadn't even talked to her in ages. I saw her a month ago, but only for a few short hours on Rebirth Day. But before that, she had been gone for months to the capital. I just wished I could have seen her one more time, and that I could have said goodbye to her before I left.

Once we were reunited, I would never leave her side again.

Will, Aerez, and I gathered our belongings and left our sad little room at the inn. We wouldn't be taking horses now, just our own two feet and the boots on them to take us the rest of the way.

We slipped quietly out of town, as dawn had only just begun to approach and most of the patrol guards were still sleeping. But even so early in the morning, they still stood at the town entrance and watched us as we left, though nobody made a move to stop us. Even with all the weapons attached to us, they said nothing.

It didn't take long for us to reenter the forest, and then a short while after that I could see the glistening feathers of Aerez's raven flying overhead. It had been keeping an eye on us, apparently. As usual, I ignored it.

The Capital Road went three ways: East, which is where we'd come from. South, which headed towards the capital. And north, which was the direction we were headed in. It would take us to the mountains surrounding the city, and then we would need to find the tunnel entrance.

There was a sign posted that caught my eye. A warning. It depicted what appeared to be a person, freezing to death, with shards of ice falling from the sky. That did not give me a good feeling.

How serious was it, if they needed to put a sign up to warn people? But Will and Aerez seemed the least bit concerned, which reassured me just a bit.

We continued past the sign, heading north, the sun rising to our right. I could tell the air was colder, and that it would continue to grow colder the further we went.

Not long later, a fleck of something soft fell against my cheek. Then another. And another. I held out my hand, letting a small fleck land on my palm. It was cold, and melted moments later.

"Snowflakes," Will told me.

I looked up to the sky, finding the moment rather magical. The little particles continued to fall from above, through the trees, and at last onto the ground. It almost made me want to cry, for some odd reason.

"Come on," Will said, reaching one hand back for me, and the other for Aerez.

We headed off, one step closer to finding the blade and freeing Nola.

Chapter 38

Four days.

That was all the time we got until the next upheaval presented itself. Four days of peace, and, mostly calmness. Our travels had been going rather well. Nobody had attacked us or tried to kill me. Will and Aerez were more comfortable with each other than I ever could have expected them to be. Every night, we huddled around the fire together and then kept close in the tent to stay warm. Will took up hunting for food, so we went to sleep every night with a full belly.

All was going well, until today.

The road was nothing more than a worn-down path, barely visible because of the snow covering the ground. We could see footsteps that indicated previous travelers, though we did not see the travelers themselves. Will and Aerez were walking ahead of me, not twenty feet away.

One second, I was walking through the forest, passing trees and shrubs at my sides, feeling the crunch of snow beneath my boots and the chill air on my face. And then the next thing I knew, I was surrounded by that all too familiar darkness. Only, this time it wasn't happening as I slept. I was wide awake, walking even, and aware of everything single thing that was happening.

I thought I might have yelled out when I felt myself slipping away, or perhaps I was only trying to, because I caught a glimpse of Will and Aerez before I faded, and their backs were to me, like they had no idea anything was happening. Perhaps they would keep walking forever, and leave me to be consumed. They were there, and then the next moment they were not, and neither was I.

The brightness faded out, so overwhelming that I had to close my eyes and allow myself a moment to adjust. When I opened them, there was nothing but darkness. I reached my hands out in front of me, hoping that I would find Will there, or at least some shred of the forest I had just been walking through, but there was nothing at all.

I stood on two feet and started to run, because maybe if I ran fast enough and far enough, I could get out of whatever hell this was. The ground beneath me wasn't that of the forest—it felt like hard rock, even a bit slippery as I moved over it. And the air tasted stale and rotten. Stagnant. I continued to run, but I knew I was getting nowhere.

"Will!" I yelled, but my voice only sounded muffled, like I was screaming it into a pillow. His name echoed in the distance, and there was nobody to answer me.

I couldn't tell if I was really in this dreadful place, or if it was only within my mind. I seemed to have been sucked out of the world and taken here. Every other dream before was never real, right? It always happened in my sleep, so I never really… went anywhere. But now, it felt like I was someplace else. It was too dark to see, but I could feel my body beneath me, like I was still myself.

I forced myself to stop running—to take a breath and figure out how to get out of this place. I spun around, and around, until I could no longer tell which direction it was that I'd come from, looking for any exit. And then off in the distance, I saw the faintest trace of light. I moved towards it, and the space around me seemed to cave in, growing smaller as I neared. The air grew still, and then my body slammed into something cold and hard.

It was a wall made of rock, cold and moist beneath my hands. I felt water tricking from it, and it took me a moment to realize that the water was not falling down, but up. I rested my palms against the rock and used it to guide me towards the light, droplets of water dancing across my chin from where they arose from the ground.

I continued to walk for a while, never seeming to grow closer to my escape. Perhaps I would be lost in this place forever.

The faintest scrape against rock sounded behind me, which halted me in place. I would have ignored it, if it wasn't the first sound I'd heard other than the dripping of water. I jerked my head in the sound's direction, and found nothing but darkness. I had a strange feeling that *something* was there, watching me.

"Hello?" I dared to say, my voice nothing more than a hoarse croak.

Another scrape against rock, closer that time.

"Is somebody there?" I asked the darkness.

Whatever it was, I could feel it growing nearer. The air warmed, just a bit, like I could feel the warm breath of something release into the air. Then I saw it—those green eyes. Before, I hadn't understood it. I didn't know who those eyes belonged to, but now I think I did.

"Sazarr?"

No answer.

If it was Sazarr, then I must have been... I must have been in the Otherealm. Hell. I was trapped in hell, and there was no getting out.

He slithered closer, and I could hear it now—the slithering. But all I could see were those green eyes, devouring me, watching me like I was an intruder. His black serpent body blended in with the consuming darkness.

I wondered if he knew who I was—if he knew that I was searching for his weapon. There had to be some hint of a man left inside of him, that man I saw in the memory. He wasn't immediately attacking me, so he must have somehow understood that I wasn't his enemy.

I dared to take a step closer, just one step, and then the world before me began to disappear. Sunlight hit me like a blow to the head, and I collapsed, or maybe I had already been on the ground. I could feel cold snow against my cheek and leaves in my hair. And somebody was touching me, steadying me, shaking me like I was dead.

"No," I whispered. "No. I have to go back."

Will had his hands on my shoulders and was staring deep into my eyes like there truly was something wrong with me. *Look at me*, he said. *Listen to me*. But I hardly even knew he was there.

"Take me back," I said, sitting up and fumbling with my surroundings, picking up fistfuls of snow and then slamming them into the earth. I looked at Will then and saw the terror and concern in his eyes. "I have to go back," I said again.

And then I sensed him slipping away, or perhaps I was the one slipping away. I felt my body go limp, and then I felt something else taking control. My head might have hit the ground again, but I wasn't sure, and then just like that, I was back to the Otherealm.

Sazarr was directly before me, as a serpent, not even a foot away from my face, hovering there like a terrifying beast. But I wouldn't allow myself to back away in fear. I got a better look at him then and could see his sharp fangs peeking through his mouth, and the scars along the sides of his skin.

I lifted my arm, slowly, and he lowered his head to me, allowing me to place a hand over the tip of his nose. His skin was cold, and he nearly shuddered from my touch, closing his eyes as if it physically pained him. He let out a heavy breath—a sigh—against my hand. I couldn't help but think of how long he'd been trapped there, and how deprived of touch he must have been.

"I'm so sorry," I whispered to him, not sure why I was saying it. Was I sorry for seeking his blade, and disrupting his life in exile? Was I sorry for what Drazen did to him? Was I sorry that he was betrayed by his friend, the person he trusted most?

I realized then that I was, for all of it. I felt bad for him—for this creature that everyone was supposed to fear.

He lowered his head even more, and then softly nudged me in the shoulder, sending me stumbling back a bit but not enough to knock me down. And for some reason, I smiled, though I knew I should have been terrified. No, Sazarr was clearly not a god, but he was also not the monster that everyone made him out to be. He only seemed like a sad being, in need of my help.

"I want to help you," I told him, rather urgently. "I need to find your blade, but after… I want to come back and help you. Can I do that? Do you even want that? Sazarr, I can't leave you here like this."

He jerked his head to the side slightly, as if he was telling me not to bother. However helpless he thought his situation was, he had to know that he was wrong. He had to know that I would do anything to help him.

"I will try," I promised him. "You've been here…alone…" My voice cracked, and then my eyes grew blurry as they filled with tears. "It isn't fair," I said. "None of this is fair." I tried to reach for him again, but I was being pulled away, and I did not fight it that time.

When Will was next to me once more, tears poured from my eyes. Aerez was next to me as well, holding my hand while she wearily watched me. I was on my knees in the forest, snow dampening my pants, and it was as if I'd been there the entire time, though Will and Aerez knew something had happened.

Will's arm was wrapped around my shoulder. "What happened?" he demanded. "You just… collapsed. You fell over like you had died." His voice was panicked, and I didn't think I'd ever seen him so worried.

"I'm okay," I said calmly, if only to give Will some relief. And as I said the words, I knew nobody believed them. I was not okay, not after what just happened and what I'd seen.

"Why are you crying?" he asked me, brushing his knuckles across my cheek to wipe the tears away. The gesture only made me cry harder.

"I saw…" My voice choked up. "I think I had a vision." It was the only explanation I could give them. I certainly couldn't tell them that I'd gone to the Otherealm, because then they would think that I was insane, but perhaps a vision they could understand.

Will's face contorted even more with worry. He and Aerez looked at each other, and then looked back at me with genuine fear on their faces. They had to know that I was okay.

Perhaps it would have been better to tell them about Sazarr, but then I'd risk freaking them out even more. He hadn't told me anything about the blade—he hadn't told me anything at all, but he also didn't seem to want me to stop looking for it. If anything, it was more of a motivation for me to keep going. Maybe he brought me there to let me know that.

"Why are you crying?" Will asked again.

I turned away from them so they couldn't see my face. "I was just… scared. I'm fine now." Neither of them looked convinced. "What happened when I… had the vision? Did I go anywhere? It felt like one of my dreams, but different. It felt more real this time."

"You didn't go anywhere," Aerez said. "You just fell to the ground and started shaking, like your mind had gone absent. We tried everything to get you to stop, and we thought it worked for a moment there, until you started shaking again. I thought you were dying."

I turned to Will, a sadness filling me. I wouldn't have ever wished for them to witness something like that. It had to be terrifying for them.

"What did you see?" Will asked me. "In your vision."

"There was darkness," I said. "And rock, like I was in a cave. And the water, it came up from the ground."

I realized how insane that sounded a moment after the words left my mouth. They didn't understand, and they wouldn't, however much I explained it to them. I wasn't even sure if they believed me, but I also didn't really care, because I knew it was real. I met Sazarr.

Maybe it was wrong for me to think that I could free him, but I hadn't seen Drazen anywhere, so he likely wouldn't try and stop me. Other than him killing my parents all those years ago, he'd been completely absent from our world.

If I had been going to the Otherealm in my dreams the entire time, then there had to be some way for Sazarr to leave there, since he had contact with the outside world. A curse may hold him there, but curses can surely be broken. The woman we spoke with in Kraxoth, Trona, seemed to think such a thing was possible. She seemed optimistic about what most others would consider laughable. I didn't think she was crazy, but I only wished that I could have asked her more about everything.

Could Sazarr have somehow summoned me to the Otherealm? Could his power have brought me there? If so, I didn't know why he would do that, or what he wanted from me.

Chapter 39

After my disappearing act, we thought it best to take a break before we continued traveling. And I certainly needed it. I needed time to collect myself after everything that had happened, and to sort out my thoughts. I still didn't understand it, and I wasn't sure if I ever would. I wondered if telling Will and Aerez more about it would help.

We walked a short way into the forest, off the road just in case anyone passed by, even though we'd seen nobody since leaving The Crossing. People were scarce out here, and most wouldn't risk the journey with it being so close to winter. There was only a short period of time in which it was safe enough to make the trip, which was about three months ago.

The three of us sat on a fallen log, wiping the snow from it to keep our pants dry. While Will and Aerez were keeping quiet, I knew they were just waiting for me to say something—for me to explain. But I wasn't even sure what to think about it yet, let alone speak of it.

I took a long and deep inhale, holding it for a moment, letting the cold air burn my lungs, before exhaling. Their attention was on me, but I continued to say nothing.

Aerez finally stood and turned to us. "I'm going for a walk," she announced, and it almost seemed like she wanted one of us to go with her, though neither of us moved. She prodded off into the forest, her figure becoming consumed by the heavy tree cover.

I could feel Will's attention on me a few minutes later, but I only remained with my arms crossed, looking off into the distance.

"Karalia," he said to me, placing a gentle hand atop my knee. "Are you going to tell me what really happened, or do I have to beg you for it?"

I turned to him and frowned. "What?" I really didn't want to talk about it, because I feared that he was going to call me insane, and tell me that I'd imagined all of it.

"When you collapsed in the woods," he said, shifting his body further towards me. "Tell me exactly what happened, as you remember it. I don't think you had a vision; I think something else happened. You can tell me." He slid his hand over mine, cupping it gently. "Please."

I let out a low sigh, telling myself that I would not cry again. "I remember..." I started. "I remember walking through the woods. One moment, I could see you two walking ahead of me, and then I was... I was transported into darkness. It was like one of my dreams, but different. I called out for you, for anyone, but nobody was there. At first. I saw a light in the distance, so I followed it, and eventually I realized that something was following me." I paused for a moment.

"What was it?"

"There was a pair of green eyes," I explained to him. "Eyes that I had seen before, in my dreams. I only saw them for a moment, until I was pulled away, and that's when I came back in the middle of it. I wanted to go back to the darkness, I needed to, so eventually he brought me back."

"He?" Will looked utterly terrified. Whether he believed what I was saying or not, I couldn't be sure.

"It was Sazarr," I continued. "I think he was the one that brought me there, like he had control over me somehow. It was so strange, but he was right in front of me, in the form of a serpent. I could sense his pain, and his misery. That's why I was crying, because I saw him trapped there like that, and it made me sick."

"And that's when you came back?" he asked me.

I shook my head slowly. "There's something else," I told him, afraid to meet his eyes. "I made him a promise... that I would try and free him. Not now, but once everything has been settled with Nola. I promised that I would try and break his curse, to get him out of there."

"Kara," Will said, and I'd expected him to be angry, but instead there was something like pity in his tone. "You can't."

"Don't tell me that," I said to him. "Will, this is a promise that *I* made. If you don't agree with it, then that's fine, as I would have never expected your help with it. I know you don't understand, and you don't have to, because I will deal with it on my own. Eventually."

"It's not that," he told me. "It's just… Do you really think it would be possible? To free him?"

"Yes."

He didn't answer, and maybe him saying nothing was better than him calling me a fool. I knew it was foolish, but I didn't care what anyone else thought, because I believed in myself. After I freed Nola, I was sure she would be more than willing to help me with this. Will could run back to his family for all I cared, while I freed the serpent god from hell.

It felt as if everything was starting to make sense. When the seer told me that I would unleash a darkness, perhaps this is what she meant. Perhaps she knew that I would one day come to free Sazarr. And when I did free him, the rebellion might even grow, enough that we could out the false god Drazen.

But perhaps none of that would happen, and I was just a fool for believing so. I guess I would just have to wait to find out.

Aerez returned a short while later, though she didn't care to share where she'd been. She also didn't ask me any questions about what had happened, but I offered an explanation anyways. I told her exactly what I'd told Will, and her reaction was more carefree, like she thought freeing Sazarr was a terrific idea. She would never judge me for making that promise to him, and she wasn't disturbed by any of it either.

"I think we should stay here tonight," I told them. "I just... I need a break from everything."

Will reluctantly agreed, while Aerez didn't seem to care. We cleared a patch of snow from the ground so we could get the tent set up, and then built a fire and sat around it while we ate dinner. We feasted on some leftover meat from the night before. I was ready to get some much-needed sleep, only I hoped that no dreams would come to me.

With every day that passed, the air grew colder and colder, more than I ever thought possible. If Mortefine was the city of heat, then Frystal was destined to be the city of ice. Everyone must be so miserable there, if they had to endure such a thing all year long.

We sat around in silence, though my thoughts were quickly interrupted by the crunching of leaves nearby. At first I thought perhaps it was the raven, but it was much too loud for that. When I looked up, Aerez already had a knife drawn and was holding it up to the darkness.

Night had long been upon us, and all I could see through the trees was slight movement, too slow and careful to be some sort of animal. If it was a person, then they might have seen the fire and been drawn over by it. Maybe they only wanted to get warm, but Aerez would never allow that.

Will and Aerez stood and created a barrier between me and whatever it was, shielding me from the potential threat. I craned my neck to get a look, but there was no point.

I listened as the footsteps grew nearer, until they were right in front of us, and then I heard the whimper of what must have been a man. He let out a shallow yelp, like he was afraid.

I stood then, pushing past my companions to see who it was. I expected more people that had come to kill me, but it was only a lone man. Actually, describing him as a boy would be more accurate. He was tall, almost as tall as Will, but oddly skinny, like he'd never trained a day in his life. And it didn't surprise me that he wasn't carrying any weapons either, save for a small knife attached to his hip. He could have been my age, but was certainly younger than Will and Aerez.

Other than his skinniness, his appearance was unremarkable. He had brown hair and brown eyes, and wore clothes that an upper-class city person might wear. There wasn't a scar nor a callous on his entire body, which suggested not only that he was weak, but wealthy.

He watched us with fear, like he was ready to turn around and bolt at any moment. Aerez stepped towards him, holding a dagger out like she was about to carve up her dinner. I knew she was prepared to do whatever was necessary to eliminate the threat, only I didn't really think this boy was a threat. When he saw the dagger, he started shaking, and backing away like a wounded animal. He was terrified.

"Wait, p-please," he said, cowering behind the hands he held in front of his face as if that would protect him. "Please don't hurt me," he cried.

"Who are you?" Aerez demanded, her voice filled with chilling authority and demand.

"Veeran," he told us without a moment's hesitation. "My name is Veeran Hartfore."

"And what are you doing here, Veeran Hartfore?" Aerez asked, taking another carefully calculated step towards him.

"I-I'm traveling to Frystal," he told us. "I have family there." He looked behind Aerez, towards me and Will, as if we could do something to help him. There was pleading in his eyes, for us to save him from the assassin.

"Where did you come from?" Another step forward.

He trembled as he began to speak. "From The Crossing. My father sent me to go live with my family in Frystal."

"Why?" Another step.

"He… He told me it would be safer there. He was headed to Kraxoth, because he had business to attend to, and he said it wouldn't be safe for me there."

Aerez turned back to us then, a wicked smile appearing on her face. She again turned to Veeran. "What manner of business did your father have in Kraxoth? Because I've heard that the only people that go there for business are thieves, liars, and murderers."

"Well, then he must be a liar," the boy told us. "Because he isn't a thief or a murderer."

Aerez let out a low laugh at that, like she was impressed the boy would say such a thing to her. "Tell me," she continued. "What do you know of this secret rebellion being planned?"

His eyes widened with fear. "No. No. My father wouldn't do that—"

"Do not lie," Aerez said to him, taking another step forward. There was little distance left between them, and with one flick of her wrist she could have greatly injured the boy with the dagger she held.

"That's enough," I finally cut in, walking over to them. Will followed right behind me, and Aerez immediately stepped back a few feet from the boy, turning to me as if expecting her next order. "We won't hurt you," I told the boy. "But only if you tell us the truth."

He looked at me—this boy. He was such a mess. While his clothes were nice, they were torn and covered in dirt. His shoes were worn, like he'd been running for quite some time, and his neck was covered in blood, from a wound that I could not see. Whoever he was, I could tell that he needed our help.

The boy lowered his eyes, like he was ashamed. "My father sent me away because he was going to Kraxoth to aid in the rebellion. He didn't want anyone to know that I was his son, because he didn't want them to come after me if the rebellion failed."

"And what is this rebellion for, exactly?" I asked next.

"I don't know," he admitted. "I've only heard what my father speaks of in secret, but he tells me it's for freedom and salvation. For a better world. I begged him not to go, but he seemed so sure that they would succeed."

"They will succeed with what?" I asked. "What are they planning?"

"They…" He looked at the three of us and paused, like he couldn't bear to speak the words.

"Say it," Aerez hissed at him.

"They are going to kill the Drazos family."

I gasped, and then there was only silence for a long moment. My heart sped up as I took in the boy's words. I looked at Will, terrified of what I would find on his face. It was filled with pure rage and loathing, and I swore that I could already feel a heat radiating from him.

Will clenched his fists at his sides, grinding his jaw as he neared Veeran. Then he grabbed Veeran by the collar of his shirt to keep him in place as he punched him straight in the face. Veeran cried out as Will dropped him and discarded him on the ground, and then he huddled over in pain. Will bent down and punched the boy in the stomach next, which was followed by another scream of pain. He grabbed the boy by his hair and began to drag him away.

"Will," I warned, but I didn't think he'd heard me at all.

"What do they think is going to happen when they're dead?" Will yelled at the boy. "Do they expect the country to magically become a better place? Who will lead us when nobody is left?"

Veeran didn't answer, nor did he try to fight back as Will continued to beat on him. He was weak, which helped me to understand why his father would send him away. Blood splattered from his mouth and into the snow. "They have a plan," he wailed. "They have someone else they would put on the throne."

"Who?" I asked. He didn't answer immediately, so I walked over to Will and bid him to step away from the boy.

"The Lost Daughter," Veeran said breathlessly. "They want to put the Lady of Orothoz on the throne. The Havu daughter that everyone thought was murdered all those years ago. She's alive."

I stopped breathing. I stopped moving. I stopped thinking entirely. I knew Will was watching me, and I felt when he grabbed onto my arm lightly, as if to comfort me, but I only stood there as if I were absent.

"What god do you serve?" I finally whispered to the boy.

Veeran looked at me, the tears falling down his cheeks and mixing with the blood from his nose. "The one true god, Sazarr."

"Step away from him," I told both Will and Aerez. "He's mine."

Aerez shot me a grin filled with pride, while Will just stood there, confused. They both obliged, and stepped away from the boy, coming to join me at my side.

I stepped towards the boy, bending down and offering him my hand. After a moment of hesitation, he took it, and I hauled him up, so he stood directly before me. "Well, Veeran," I said. "I suppose it's your lucky day."

The boy cried the entire night. I supposed he wasn't a boy, not really. He couldn't have been any younger than my nineteen years.

We gave him some food and water, and a cloth to clean the dirt and blood from himself. Luckily, Will hadn't done any serious damage. I would make him apologize to Veeran tomorrow, but now we just needed some rest. We had to squeeze Veeran into the tent with us, and both Will and Aerez refused to sleep beside him, so I got to, with Aerez on the other side of me, and Will on the other side of her.

Even if Will had just found out that people were planning to murder his entire family, that didn't give him the right to beat the daylight out of someone he'd only just met. I never would have expected him to do something like that.

Aerez and I stayed awake for a while, to keep an eye on our new accomplice. She had done well—playing my bodyguard—even if the threat she was protecting me against was as harmless as a puppy. But going forward, I knew the protection she would give to me would be much more necessary, especially since I'd found out that the rebels planned to put me on the throne. What would the king think if he heard that?

The following morning, Veeran had only calmed down in the slightest. He wasn't crying anymore, at least, though I could tell that Will and Aerez's presence frightened him. And when it was time for us to continue traveling, he came right along with us.

"They won't hurt you," I assured him sometime later, after I caught him watching them for about the tenth time in a row. "They listen to me, and I've forbidden them from putting a hand on you."

I could see the cuts and bruises on his skin now, and the swollen parts of his face. I felt bad for letting Will hurt him like that.

"Why are you helping me?" he asked.

Will's eyes flashed to me a moment before I responded, but I ignored him. "Because it's the right thing to do."

"You won't turn me in, then?" he asked. "For being a rebel?"

I knew Will was listening carefully as I said. "Do you plan to act with them when they go to murder the royal family?" Veeran quickly shook his head. "Then I don't see what threat you pose to anyone. So long as you do not plan to join the rebels, then I will not have you punished."

"Whose side are you on?" he asked me.

I turned and looked directly into his eyes, and I noticed how uncomfortable that made him. "I believe only in myself."

He didn't talk much after that, and he kept his distance from us as well. I wouldn't tell him who I was, not then and probably not ever. We would help him make it to Frystal safely, but after that, I didn't really care what he did or where he went. Surely Will didn't want him around, but it was only for a few more days.

Chapter 40

Two more days passed as we traveled through the cold and the snow with our new companion. When we awoke this morning, we could spot snowcapped mountains in the distance, an indication that we were nearing Frystal at last. Within the next day, hopefully, we would make it to the city.

While I cared for our new companion, he seemed to be nothing more than a burden. I wondered if taking him with us was the wisest decision. If we were ambushed, if it came to a fight, he'd likely get in the way. I didn't want any of us to have to put our lives at risk by trying to protect him, though of course, I knew that I would protect him if it came to that. I couldn't stomach the idea of leaving him alone out in the forest. He wouldn't last more than a day without our help.

Although Veeran was helpful, in the way that he shared more valuable information with us about the rebellion. His father, as it turned out, was a general of the rebel cause, and one of their leaders. They were at The Crossing trying to gather supporters, and his father was heading to Kraxoth where the head rebellion efforts were located. While Veeran wasn't privy to much about the rebellion, he did believe that something big was coming, and soon. Not something as big as assassinating the royal family, but something that would take them one step closer to that. He didn't think that his father would have sent him away if it were otherwise.

It bothered me that the rebels fought in both Sazarr's name and my own name, when neither of us were truly involved. They fought for something that essentially didn't exist. And while I did not think they would succeed, they had no clear goal for what would come if they did succeed.

It made me wonder about Mortefine, and about whose side Hiran was on. He was never particularly fond of the king and queen, but surely he would not betray them in such a way. He would never align himself with the rebels, but he might have his own agenda. If he knew who I was the entire time, and if he knew I was alive, then perhaps that had something to do with the rebels believing that I was alive. But that still didn't tell me why he would want the lost blade of Sazarr, or what he planned to do with it.

Hiran was on nobody's side but his own. His agendas aligned with nothing but his own wicked scheming. Surely his reasoning for sending me to retrieve the blade could not be something so simple as to protect his city. He was lying to me, the same way he'd lied to me my entire life.

I would never let the blade slip into his hands long enough for him to try and use it. I would exchange it for Nola's freedom, and then I would find a way to take it back. Especially now that I'd made a promise to Sazarr, to free him. I didn't think Sazarr would be very happy if I took his blade, only to hand it over to someone who intended to use it for evil.

But I honestly had no idea what would happen *after* I freed Sazarr, if I did somehow accomplish that. Perhaps he would wreak havoc on the world and set out to personally destroy the Drazos family. But maybe, hopefully, he would seek a more peaceful life.

Me, Will, Aerez, and Veeran continued on our way to Frystal, trudging through a fresh thick layer of snow that had fallen the night before. It was cold beyond reason, but I forced myself to push through it.

Somewhere up above I heard a familiar flutter of wings, and squinted with the sun in my eyes to see a black raven hopping from tree to tree. It cawed loudly, but continued to keep its distance. As usual, I did my best to ignore the bird. But Veeran didn't know what it was, and I watched as he looked up and took in the bird's presence, but he remained silent, not bringing it to anyone's attention. But then sometime later, after maybe thirty minutes had passed and the raven was still following us, Veeran stopped in his tracks and said to us, "Do you guys see that?"

"See what?" Aerez asked blandly.

"There's a—" He looked up, to where the bird had been moments before, but it was gone. "There *was* a creepy bird following us. A raven, I think. I think it's been watching us."

"I didn't see anything," Aerez said, and I could hear the amusement in her words. She was being cruel, while Veeran was likely questioning if he had imagined the entire thing.

He continued to remain silent, but I had a hunch that the next time the raven showed up, he would start asking questions again. Hopefully he would not be in our company long enough for that to happen.

A short while later we came to a split in the road, one way heading east and the other west. Will said, "We'll need to head east, towards the tunnel entrance."

Veeran looked confused. "We're not taking the road in?" he asked.

Will shook his head. "It's too late in the year, we wouldn't make it through all the snow. It's smarter and faster to take the tunnel."

"But—" Veeran started, becoming a bit frantic. "But we can't take the tunnel!" His voice shook a little as he spoke.

"And why not?" Aerez asked him, teasingly. "Are you afraid?"

Veeran didn't respond, but his answer was obvious enough.

"What's wrong with the tunnel?" I asked.

Veeran was the only one who dared to answer. "They say there are things down there. Bad things. My father warned me not to go that way."

"There's nothing in the tunnel," Will said, as if to reassure me. I wasn't sure if I was thankful for that or not.

402

"I've taken it before at least a half dozen times. We'll be fine."

"What kind of things?" I asked, suddenly growing nervous. Nobody answered me.

We reached the tunnel entrance a short while later, and it was clearly marked, but chained up like we weren't supposed to be going through it. The entryway was wider than I expected, certainly wide enough for a carriage and even more to fit through. But I suspected that no carriage could make it to where we were going.

There was a sign posted, and while it looked a bit worn down, I could still make out what it said: *Those seeking passage to Frystal may enter this tunnel, but beware that it does not keep out the cold, nor does it protect you from anything lurking within the darkness. Enter at your own risk, or travel half a day west to seek the mountain path.*

They might as well have added a sarcastic *good luck* at the end of that, because it felt like they were condemning us to a disastrous fate.

"Where is everyone?" I asked, expecting that we would see at least a few other people who were traveling to or from the city, but we hadn't seen even one person. Nobody answered me.

Aerez said, "We should have taken the mountain path."

Will shot her a frown. "Don't tell me now that you're afraid. You're supposed to be the brave one. We wouldn't have lasted that way, not with the heavy snowfall from last night. This way is much quicker. We'll be out of there in no time."

"But why is the entrance barred?" Veeran asked, his voice shaking.

"Good question," I said, but not one of us had the answer to it.

"If we die," Aerez said, turning to Will, "then it's all your fault."

He gave her a smile that I knew was only to offer some sense of comfort. He pulled the chain free, lifting it enough that we would be able to pass beneath it. "Ladies first," he said to Aerez, gesturing a hand.

She rolled her eyes but walked forwards anyways, entering the tunnel and immediately becoming enveloped by darkness. I followed behind her, with Veeran not far behind me, like he would grab onto me when he got spooked. And then Will at last followed behind us, and I heard the chain clank as he set it back down.

I put my hands out in front of me, unable to see anything but hoping that I could at least feel for where Aerez had gone. But a moment later, strong hands were on me, yanking my arm and pulling me back seconds before I would have plummeted down a very long and steep set of stairs. I hadn't seen them. Will lit a match a moment later, and I could see Aerez beside me, her hands still on me like she thought I was still at risk of falling down the stairs.

"We have to go *down there*?" I said, gasping slightly.

Veeran looked like he was going to be sick.

The stairs had no end that was within sight. They kept going, down and down as if to the Otherealm itself. Will brushed past us and went down first, holding the match out in front of him to illuminate the way. Every time one burnt out, he would stop to light another.

We climbed down, and down, and down, for what seemed like hours. My legs quickly tired and grew weak, and I wondered how much more I could take until I collapsed entirely. And Will's matches would also run out eventually. When that happened, we would either have to find our way through the darkness, or he could do what needed to be done.

A while later, we reached the bottom of those stairs, and were again on flat ground. We must have been very deep underground, beneath the mountains. If anything were to happen, we'd be buried down here.

As a unit, we walked forward, alert for whatever threats that may lie ahead. But it was utterly silent, other than the shuffle of our feet and our heavy breaths. It was as if life itself had ceased to exist.

"It's dark as hell down here," Aerez said, and I almost laughed because of the accuracy of her statement. If I had in fact been to the Otherealm, then I knew that her comment wasn't very far off.

"Actually, I think hell is darker," I told her.

"I guess you would know, wouldn't you?" She let out a low laugh.

Veeran didn't say anything from where he walked behind us, but if I could see his face, I'm sure he would look both confused and terrified.

It suddenly grew dark, and we all stopped and waited for Will to light a match, and I heard him curse quietly as he realized that there were none left. He knew that we couldn't travel the entire way in darkness.

Will spoke from beside me, much closer than I thought he was. "I suppose I have a solution." Nobody said anything, just waiting for him to continue. "Okay. Don't freak out."

"Why would we—" Veeran started, but his mouth immediately clamped shut as light flooded the tunnel. Light from the flame that rested in the palm of Will's hand. "*What is that*?" he said, his voice nervous and shaky.

"Fire," Will stated bluntly.

"But it's coming from… It's coming out of your *hand*." Veeran backed away a few steps, like he would turn in the opposite direction and run away scared.

"Yes, it is," Will said. The small orb of flame floated above his outstretched hand, barely bigger than an apple, just enough to light the way for us. It also heated the air just a bit, which I was thankful for.

I noticed the cocky look Will was giving Aerez, and the smug smile he had on his face, like he was waiting for her to swoon over him. But instead, Aerez said, "Do you think I'm an idiot, *prince*? I know who you are, and I know what ability your family has. Even if I hadn't realized it right from the start, I would have known the day you burnt down that forest."

"Prince?" Veeran gasped. "Who... who are you?" He wasn't asking just Will, but all of us, even more terrified.

"Don't worry about it," Aerez said to him, her voice filled with a razor-sharp edge. "We're helping you get to Frystal, that's all you need to know. You don't get to ask us questions."

Will continued to smile, lifting that ball of flame and sending it closer to Aerez's face. She hissed and swatted it away.

"That could have come in handy before," she said to him.

"I know," I agreed. "I saw it for the first time when he killed the sea serpent that attacked us in the Alanah Sea. I went looking for him, thinking that he could use my help, and there he was, shooting flames straight out of his hands."

Aerez grinned. "I would have liked to see that."

"Maybe you will one day," Will challenged, grinning right back at her. He twirled his fingers around, the flames changing form and snaking around his fingers as if they were alive.

"I have no idea what's happening," Veeran said.

"Me neither," I said, laughing.

Will's flames continued to light the way, guiding us towards Frystal.

"Does it come only out of your hands?" Aerez asked Will sometime later. "Or anywhere else?"

"Just my hands," he responded, and then a moment later he added, "Where else would it come from?"

Aerez laughed softly. "I don't know. Your eyes, your mouth, or maybe even straight out of your ass."

We all laughed then, except for Veeran who was still keeping a safe distance from Will.

"Does the rest of your family have this… ability?" Aerez asked, and I realized then that I hadn't thought about that before. I hadn't thought about the fact that his brother, Prince Daenaron, the man who I was supposed to marry, could have the same exact ability. Or even his father, the king.

Will didn't respond immediately, and a long moment passed before he said, "My father does not, nor my uncle, but my brother does. My late grandfather did as well."

I might have stopped breathing for a second, which made the air feel much colder. I wasn't exactly sure why. I knew I wasn't going to actually marry Will's brother, I had no interest in even meeting him, but knowing that he had the same ability… It frightened me.

"Is your brother's power the same as yours?" Aerez asked, a carefully crafted question regarding the future King of Vatragon. I liked to think that she asked for my benefit as well.

I wasn't sure if Will would tell us, but he finally did after another moment. "My power," he started, "is just a fraction of what my brother is capable of." I couldn't help but note the way Will's eyes shifted to me, as if in warning.

If Veeran knew what we were talking about, he did not let on.

"Why do you keep it a secret?" Aerez asked.

"The people of this country, they don't understand power like that. They know that it is said to come from the gods, but it still frightens them. If we were to openly use it whenever we pleased, it might lead the people to be frightened so much that they act without thinking."

I thought that was fair enough, but Aerez went on. "The people in Meriton have magic, and they don't hide it. They're worshiped for it there. They don't claim that it was given to them by any gods, either, but a token of their own good will."

"Well, this isn't Meriton," Will told her. "I couldn't presume to know what their religion entails, but here, there are only two gods. A god of good and a god of evil. And there's argument enough about which is which. Why do you think there hasn't been any *serpent blooded* for centuries? They would be hunted and killed, because of some foolish religious prenotions. Being feared leads people to act foolishly."

"So you're saying that they hide?" I asked him. "The *serpent blooded?*"

He shook his head. "I'm just saying that there's a reason that people like me would choose to stay hidden."

If there was a *serpent blooded* out there, that would certainly change things, especially with this coming rebellion. But I wasn't sure if that would be a good or a bad thing.

Eventually, we stopped to rest, though we weren't even sure what time of day it was. We found a small alcove of sorts in the side of the tunnel, which was big enough for us all to sleep in.

Will extinguished his flames and I quickly fell asleep within the darkness.

An unknown amount of time later, something dragged me from sleep. I wasn't sure what, but one second, I was asleep, and then the next I was awake. And then a moment later I felt it—a rumbling of the earth. It shook from somewhere far off, strong enough to reach the tunnel and cause dust to fall from the rock ceiling above us.

Aerez awoke a moment later, standing quickly and surveying for the source. But it was very far away from us— very far above us. And for the first time, I was glad to be underground in the tunnel, because whatever it was, it was in the world above us.

A stronger rumble shook the entire tunnel and then everyone was awake. "What was that?" Veeran asked nervously.

Even Will looked worried. "We should go," he told us. And that was enough to get me up and gathering my things. A few short minutes later, we were walking again, Will's flames lighting the way.

A few more hours passed. It might have been more than that, or less, but I wasn't exactly sure. We couldn't have been down there for more than a day.

Will continued to light the way for us, and I wondered if it ever made him tired, using it for so long. I didn't think that I would ever get used to seeing him use the ability—to seeing magic. I went most of my life without even believing in it, but now… anything seemed possible. And if he claimed that his brother was more powerful than he, a part of me was afraid of that. I was terrified to see what his brother would do if I challenged him, and if I refused him.

Will halted directly in front of us, and I could see a set of stairs come into view. It looked exactly like the set of stairs that we had initially climbed down, but this had to be the way out, the way up to Frystal.

If I thought there were a lot of stairs before, there must have been triple that now. We went up and up, the never-ending stairs, my legs burning, my body craving water, and craving rest. All of us were struggling, and I hoped that it wouldn't be much farther.

Eventually, I started to practically drag myself up the stairs, crawling up to freedom like a wild animal. I knew we were close—the air began to smell fresher, and it grew colder.

And then I could see light. It wasn't bright, so I assumed that it was nighttime, but there it was ahead of us—the sky.

And then we were out.

For a second, I reconsidered my initial assumption, that perhaps it was daytime because of the overwhelming brightness that flooded my view, causing me to squint my eyes. But it was only snow—lots of snow. The moon reflected over the white causing a bright cast of light.

We were in the mountains, not far off from where we could see Frystal in the distance.

"Let's go," Will said.

Chapter 41

The city was as badly on lockdown as Kraxoth had been, even more so. The rebellion had clearly made its way to Frystal as well, which was bad news for Veeran's father, who hoped to keep him out of the mess. It was a short walk down a rocky snow-covered path into the city, and while there was no gate to keep invaders out, there were a plethora of guards standing patrol.

I feared they would stop us, the same way that I feared my mission was going to be impossible to continue. There were guards at every corner, a mix of those dressed in Frystal armor and those I could recognize from the capital. I was less concerned about myself than I was for Will, because they might easily recognize him.

Staying hidden needed to become much higher on our list of priorities. I'd tried to do my best before, and yet I was still recognized when we were at The Crossing. Even in the middle of the night, there were guards prowling the streets, stopping drunk revelers as they stumbled their way home.

We thought it was wise to do the same. We made it past them as we entered the city, but once we were on the streets, when a guard came our way, we would pretend that we were so plastered we couldn't even remember our names. I kept my eyes closed and held on to Will's arm, like I couldn't even keep myself upright.

And when they moved past us, we returned to normal, walking at a fast pace through the city and towards safety. The city looked different than I expected. It was well put together and even wealthy. The buildings were finely made, each with its own chimney blowing smoke into the night. Everything seemed more accommodated to the cold—and to snow. Even at this hour, which if I were to guess was probably around three or four in the morning, there were servants outside shoveling snow, clearing the streets for tomorrow's activities.

"Hey!" a guard shouted at us, and I realized then that none of us had seen him walking towards us from down a side street. "Stop right there," he called, shouting loudly despite the silence of the night.

I forced a slight stumble into my step as I turned around, holding onto Will, while Aerez held onto Veeran, though she looked very uncomfortable doing it.

There were three guards striding towards us, hands on the pommels of their swords. They were Frystal men, so they wouldn't recognize Will.

"Yesss?" Will slurred, holding onto me as well.

"What are you doing out at this hour?" the guard demanded to know.

"Uhhh…" Will started, turning to me as if he couldn't remember. "My wife and I," he said, patting my arm, "were out for drinks—with our two friends here." He held up a finger as if he had just recalled the fact.

Out of the corner of my eye, I could see Aerez and Veeran holding onto each other as well, though Aerez's hand was on the inside of her cloak, like she was ready to pull a weapon free at any moment.

"And where exactly is it that you went for these *drinks*?" the guard said, reaching to his side like he was aching to pull a sword free, like he was aching to fight us. Aerez's eyes were locked on that guard's hands.

"I don't remember the name," Will sighed. "Some tavern down that way." He pointed down a random road, and then turned around quickly to another. "No, maybe it was that way."

"And where is your residence?" the guard asked, his eyes locked onto mine, like he expected me to answer him. I lowered my eyes to the ground, both to pretend like I was an afraid girl and so he wouldn't see the color of them.

The guard waited for me to respond, but then Veeran finally cut in. "We live on Saford Street," he explained. "We're neighbors, and we're heading that way now if you would kindly let us pass."

The guard narrowed his eyes on us, turned to his companions, and then finally said, "Go home. No more staying out late, not for a while. We'll be implementing a curfew soon."

Will and Veeran nodded to the guards, and I flashed a wide drunken smile, keeping my eyes squinted as if I were too tired to open them. Aerez continued to frown, though the guards hardly seemed to notice her.

"Goodnight." I waved to the men, sweetening my voice.

We greatly increased our pace after that, moving quickly behind Veeran who led the way towards his uncle's home— which I assumed was on Saford Street, wherever that was. My fingers and the tip of my nose were cold, and I knew that if I didn't get inside soon then I would start to feel ill.

It took no more than a quarter of an hour for us to make it there. Veeran stopped on the street in front of a row of run-down homes, which I wouldn't have thought anyone lived in if it weren't for the candlelight fluttering out of the windows.

He walked up to one of the doors and knocked softly, like he was unsure of himself, or perhaps he just didn't want to wake whoever was inside. But they needed to wake if they were going to let us in. To my relief, a moment later the door swung open, and we were greeted by a tall burly-looking man.

"Who are you," he growled at us, one hand still on the door, while the other was at his side, gripping the handle of an axe. I took a step back without even realizing it, while Veeran stepped forward.

"Um—" Veeran hesitated, clearly nervous. "It's me, uncle. Veeran Hartfore. Your brother's son."

His uncle's eyes widened, and then he seemed to relax a bit. He poked his head out into the street, and then opened the door wider. "Come in, you lot," he told us, and I could already feel the warmth greeting us from within.

A short while later, after the man kindly offered to make us tea, we were all seated around a small kitchen table taking sips of our drinks and eating slightly stale crackers. It was a cozy home, warm despite the frigid outside air. It was evident that children lived there, which was why we continued to speak in whispers.

"Did you get my father's letter?" Veeran asked his uncle. "He's off to Kraxoth—he wanted me to come stay here and—"

"I got the letter," he replied. "It didn't say that there would be others with you." His eyes flashed to the sword at my back, the one at Will's side, and the many blades adorning Aerez's body.

"They're my traveling companions," Veeran said somewhat defensively. "They helped me get here safely. Without them, I think I would have been stranded in the forest."

His uncle looked unconvinced, but he turned to us and said, "Thank you for getting Veeran here safely, but I'm not letting criminals stay in my home. You're just walking targets for those guards to come here and sniff around. I have a wife, and children, I need to think about them first."

"Uncle—" Veeran started.

Will cut him off abruptly. "Criminals?"

I remained silent, unsure of what I would even say, while Aerez sat beside me and grinned, like she was watching a competition unfold. I nudged her with my foot beneath the table, and while it shifted her attention, it didn't wipe the smile off her face.

"We understand," I said. "We wouldn't want to cause any trouble for you. We didn't come here with the intention to stay, we only wanted to make sure that Veeran ended up somewhere safe, and that he would be well off once we parted ways." I stood from the table then, Will and Aerez joining me. "Please keep Veeran safe," I said. "He's a good kid, and I would hate to see anything bad happen to him."

"He's family," the man said. "He's safer here than anywhere else."

I only offered a shallow nod and then walked across the kitchen towards the front door. I did not say goodbye as I left, not to Veeran nor his uncle. The three of us stepped out into the cold city night, again stranded.

Aerez stepped up beside me once we'd closed the door. "What a bastard," she growled. "He left us with nowhere to sleep. He could have at least let us stay the night and then kicked us out in the morning."

I turned to her. "It's not his fault. And I would never put his family in jeopardy like that. We'll find an inn."

"I bet if he knew who Will was, he would have let us stay," she muttered.

"Or he could have just handed us over to the guards," I said. "Or worse, to the ruler of the city." And I wasn't even sure who ruled the city.

"He called us criminals," Will added.

"Can you blame him?" I said. "We show up at his home looking like we've just come back from war—what do you expect him to think? I don't even want to know who he thought Aerez was."

"I would have slept in his bathing room if that was what he offered," Aerez said. "It'll be his fault if I freeze to death."

"Well, then we should get going," I said.

We headed off in search of somewhere to stay, again doing our best to stay hidden.

The sun was already starting to rise by the time we made it to an inn. There was a man sleeping behind the desk inside, no doubt having slept the entire night as any normal person would have. He wouldn't have expected anyone to show up at such an hour, especially not with the guards out patrolling.

414

"We need a room," Will said, his voice louder than usual so that the man would wake.

He almost fell out of his chair, but then he steadied himself a moment later, straightening his tunic and running a hand through his greasy hair. He reeked of liquor, which made sense because of the discarded flask on the floor directly beside him. "Just one room?" he asked, his eyes flashing between the three of us. He grabbed a key from the wall behind him and then slid it across the desk to us. "How many nights?"

"We don't know yet," Will told him, snatching the key and sliding it into his pocket. "How about we start with one week, and I'll come tell you if I need to stay longer?"

The man shrugged and then waved us off. "Whatever you say, but if you stay less than a week, I still expect a full week's payment."

"Of course," Will said to the man, and then he turned and walked towards the long hall of rooms. We followed behind him, and he pulled the key out, revealing a small 9 carved onto the top of it.

I turned back to find that the man had already leaned back in his chair again, his eyes closed and mouth open like he'd been sleeping the entire time.

Will unlocked the door to our room, and we entered. It was warmer than I expected because of a fire that had already been lit in the small fireplace. I wondered if they'd had time to do that just now, or if they always kept the rooms warm even when they were empty. There was a pitcher of water and a plate of fruits that I didn't recognize set out on a small table.

It was certainly the nicest inn I'd ever stayed at, out of my short time of staying at inns. The room was clean, and it smelled nice. The bed sheets were pristine white, the curtains unruffled and midnight blue, keeping out the sun that was beginning to rise. There was an adjoining bathing chamber, that I thought was rather large for an inn, but I wasn't complaining.

I would have explored further if it wasn't for the extreme exhaustion I was currently experiencing. I removed my cloak, then my boots, then my pants and jacket, leaving nothing but my shirt and underclothes. I had not a shred of modesty within me at the moment, and the only thing I cared about was finding sleep.

I slid into the sheets, cool against my bare skin. It was certainly much cozier than the tent we'd been sleeping in. Aerez slid in beside me, her cloak and weapons discarded beside the bed. I was already half asleep by the time Will joined us, cozying up beside me. I thought I might have felt his hand brush down my arm, but I was truly asleep then.

The bed was emptier when I awoke. Will snored softly beside me, but on the other side of him, Aerez was nowhere to be found. I jerked up and looked around the room, still somewhat dark because the curtains were drawn, though I could see enough to know Aerez was not there.

Aerez was gone.

If I were to guess, I would say that it was about midday, maybe just past noon, so it would make sense that Aerez had gone off somewhere, rather than waiting for us to wake, but her absence still made me uneasy.

"Will," I said, shaking his arm softly. He was still asleep when he turned onto his side towards me and reached his hand out, sliding it over my waist as if to hold me. I grabbed onto his hand and threw it off me. "Will," I said again. Nothing. "WILL!" I said for a third time, smacking his face as I did.

He flinched and immediately sat upright, his hands reaching for me like he thought I was the injured one. "What is it?" he said breathlessly.

"Aerez is gone."

He frowned at me, before slumping back down against the pillows, closing his eyes and groaning. "Where did she go?" he asked me.

"I'm the one asking you where she went," I said. "I just woke up and she wasn't here."

"Maybe it's for the best," he muttered. "Maybe she finally decided to leave us alone."

"Will!" I punched his chest. "Don't be a dick."

He sighed. "She probably just went to get food or something, I don't know. I'm sure she'll be back soon, don't worry."

But I didn't believe him, so I got out of bed and dressed, not caring how messy my hair was or how bad I still smelled. I walked around the lobby of the inn in search of her. Nothing. I looked onto the street outside. Nothing. I even went as far as to enter the tavern next door. Again, nothing.

I began to fear that she really had left us—that she took this opportunity to get free of her contract to us and to make sure that she'd never be bound to anyone ever again. If that was the case, then how could I blame her? I certainly couldn't, not knowing her past. But it saddened me—the thought that I might never see her again.

I walked back into the room, unsurprised to find Will still in bed, but now Aerez was there, sitting in a chair in the corner of the room, her feet propped up on the table beside it. Will looked at me as I entered and saw where my attention was, then looked as well, eyes widening.

"What the—" Will sat up. "When did you... How did you..." His attention shifted again towards the open window beside her. "Damn, your good," he said.

"I didn't know you cared about me that much, Kara. I'd been following you around for the past thirty minutes while you searched for me."

"Well, where the hell were you?" I demanded, not bothering to sound kind. "I thought..."

"You thought I abandoned you?" she laughed softly, shaking her head at the same time. "Not yet. I was off gathering information for our little investigation while you two slept through half the day."

"Oh," I said. "And?"

417

"*And*," she went on, staring at me and Will while she remained quiet for another moment, "I found your man."

I gasped softly, while Will looked at her as if he were angry. She just smiled at us, like she was proud of herself.

"I did some asking around," Aerez said. "That was all it took. One word about this *collector* guy and everyone's practically throwing his address at me. They don't seem to like this guy very much."

"Did you ask anything about the blade?"

She shook her head at me. "No. I didn't need to. Someone was more than willing to share with me that they've heard from someone else that this man has it. Apparently, he acquired it nearly fifty years ago."

"Who is he?" Will asked.

"His name is Fenir Camrall," she told us. "He's one of the richest men in the city. He runs some sort of museum where he holds all the artifacts he's collected over the years. They say it's very hard to get an invitation—that only the most elite can grace his presence." She lowered her hand and slid it into her pocket, pulling out a folded piece of paper. "Fortunately, I got my hands on his list of meetings for the day and made a copy of it." She tossed it across the room to me.

I didn't even want to ask or know how she got ahold of that, but I gratefully took the paper. It was full except for a two-hour period later in the day, a few hours from now.

"So," I said, "we go today?" They nodded in confirmation. "Thank you for doing this, Aerez. This is very helpful."

She waved a dismissive hand at me. "It's my job. I'm good at it. It was nothing, really."

Chapter 42

Somehow, more snow had already compiled on the streets since we entered the inn earlier that morning, and had already been shoveled away by workers. If there's one thing I noticed about the city, it was that everything had to look its best at all times. Buildings were finely painted, plants and trees were trimmed, and even the streets remained free of clutter.

And from what I'd gathered from being in the city for less than one day, I knew it wasn't some place I would ever want to live. Aside from the fact that it was too damn cold, and that I'd come to realize how much I hated snow, the people that lived in Frystal were different. They acted as if they knew their city is superior to everyone else, so they behaved accordingly to that. They watched me like they could tell I was outsider.

So, because of that, We kept the hoods of our cloaks securely overhead as we made our way through the city, not wanting to attract the wrong sort of attention. Though I suppose that Aerez had it the worst, as her skin was much darker than everyone else in the city. They were all pale and sickly looking. But to our luck, we made it to our destination without issue. It was a larger, multistory building, with large windows decorating the outside, and a set of double red-painted doors. We approached those doors, which were nearly twice my height, and the three of us waited.

We weren't sure if we were supposed to knock or just let ourselves in, but there was a sign on the door that read *Camrall's Collections*, and then right below it, *Appointments Required*. We would certainly see about that, but it said nothing about knocking, so we pulled on the handle and opened the large heavy doors.

We entered the building, and while I expected something grand, it was nothing more than a small greeting room. There was a skinny man sitting behind a desk, blocking off another set of doors that I assumed led further into the building. He saw us and frowned.

"Hello," I said to him with as much of a smile as I could force at the moment.

"Can I help you?" he asked.

"We were hoping to speak with Fenir. There's something very important that we need to inquire about."

His eyes shifted from me, to Will, and then finally to Aerez. He let out a long, unpleasant sigh and then wrote something down on a notepad. It was too far away for me to see exactly what. "And who, might I ask, are you three?"

"Does it matter?" I asked, again forcing my smile.

The man set down his pen and crossed his hands atop the desk. "Mister Camrall is a very important and very busy man. If you would like to schedule an appointment, then I would be happy to set that up, but it could be months before his schedule allows for such a thing. As I've said, he is a very busy man. But if you're anyone of... *importance*, then he might be able to speak to you sooner. And that would require you to tell me who you are. If not, then I must ask you to leave." He stared down his nose at us like we were nothing more than street rats.

"It is very urgent," I said. "Please—"

"What exactly is it that you wish to *inquire* about," he said.

I didn't say anything, as I didn't think we should have, but then Will told the man, "We are searching for the lost blade of Sazarr. We heard that it was here."

The man might have stopped breathing, and perhaps even started to shake a bit. There was genuine fear in his eyes. "What do you want with *that*?" he spat, nothing formal about the way he spoke to us now.

"That is between us and *Mister Camrall*," I told him.

In an instant, the man's voice had resumed its arrogant taunt. "You will have to make an appointment," he sighed, and then he opened what appeared to be a folder holding documents. "I have… three months from today. How is that?" He raised his brows at us.

I took a deep breath before speaking, willing myself to remain calm. "We don't have three months," I said. "People's lives depend on us finding the blade. Please, it is very important."

He gave me a bored glare. "I'm very sorry, but—"

His words were cut off by a low choking sound. He looked at me with fear and pleading as Aerez pressed a knife to the side of his neck, just beneath his ear. She had moved closer to the man without any of us realizing it, and from the looks of it, she was planning to threaten him to get what we came for. The man could no longer speak—if he moved one muscle, the knife would pierce his flesh.

"You are going to listen very carefully," Aerez whispered into the man's ear, her voice so terrifyingly cold. "You go get your boss, and you tell him that *Tommen Saxthon* sent his best to come and speak with him. Surely you know who Tommen is? You tell your boss that we need to speak with him today, and if he refuses, well, then *my* boss is going to be very unhappy."

She pulled the knife away from him, and while she hadn't cut his skin, it was red from where it pressed against him. The man lifted a hand to his neck and closed it around that spot, as if he too couldn't believe that he was unharmed. He quickly stood from his chair, nearly tripping over himself, and then walked through that set of double doors. We could hear the lock click as he closed them behind himself, likely running away in fear from what Aerez had just done to him.

The three of us stood in complete silence within that small greeting room of a presumably grand building. There were chairs along one of the walls, but none of us dared to sit down. We stayed close to the doors that led back onto the street, and Will stood beside a window, keeping an eye out in case any guards came our way.

I turned to Aerez. "Who is Tommen Saxthon?"

A hint of a smile spread on her face, something like smug pride. "He's my boss. He's got a sort of... reputation. Even here. And not a good one. People who get on his bad side, there's not usually a pleasant outcome for them. I figured this Camrall guy would know who he was. This place has practically got *criminal* written all over it, don't you think?"

"So we're going to gain this meeting by lying to the man?" Will said.

Aerez shrugged. "You'll get over it. Welcome to the criminal life, prince." She winked at him.

"We could have just told him who I was," Will said.

"No, we couldn't," Aerez told him. "That would raise too much suspicion. It's better for him to think that we're a band of nobodies and assassins than for him to know who you really are." She looked at both me and Will.

The doors swung open, and the same man prodded through. He cleared his throat. "Mister Camrall is finishing up with some personal business at the moment, but he has invited you to tour his collection while you wait. He will be ready to speak with you within the hour."

"Thank you," I said to him.

He merely nodded, and then turned to Aerez. "We apologize for any misunderstandings, and we hope that your master will be satisfied with the outcome of this arrangement."

She smirked at him, flashing her teeth. "We shall see."

The man held the doors open for us as we made our way into the room beyond. We walked down a short hall, until we reached a large open space—the gallery. Maybe at one time the building could have been three stories tall, but now there was only one massive room. On the floor there were rows and rows of shelves, all housing different items, and along the walls there were objects mounted to them. There were stairs that led up to balconies and what appeared to be smaller rooms off to the side. We would need to look everywhere if we were to find the blade.

Aerez had already wandered off somewhere when I turned, expecting to find her at my side. She walked down one of the isles, observing a rather large painting. Will was climbing the set of stairs to the left, up to a second-floor balcony with a set of glass cases enclosing what appeared to be jewelry. I walked up the stairs to the right, finding a display holding ancient-looking weapons—rusted swords and battle armor. If the blade was anywhere in the building, this seemed like the place to start looking.

There were daggers, and plenty of them, but none that appeared to be made from a serpent fang. I sighed, unsure of where I should have gone to search next.

But then I felt this… strange feeling within me. It was something similar to the darkness that often dragged me away in my sleep, but also something very different. I could feel the presence of something within the building—something evil and powerful, and something that wanted me to find it. If it was the blade, then perhaps it was guiding me towards it. If it was something else, then I was perhaps afraid.

Without even realizing what I was doing, I started to walk. I moved down isles and rows, taking turns that I didn't know where they led to, climbing up more stairs, finding myself lost even though my body seemed to know exactly where it was going. It was searching.

The building was huge, and I couldn't have possibly found wherever it was I was going if there wasn't this strange tether within me. The pull was strong at first, and then it grew weaker and weaker until I reached what it was I'd been walking towards. I knew when I had found it, but I hadn't expected to find someone else already there.

Will was standing a dozen feet ahead of me, staring down at a case that held what I assumed to be the item my body led me towards.

"What are you doing?" I asked him.

He turned to me quickly, blinking rapidly as if I had frightened him. "I…" he started. "I don't know. I felt…"

I closed the space between us and walked up to his side. "I felt it too."

He stared at me, strangely, like he was recognizing me for the first time. Then he turned back to the glass case in front of him and said, "What is it?"

I turned and looked down towards the case that enclosed two small metallic objects. They were identical in every way except for their contrasting colors. One was orange, and the other green. It wasn't the blade, but it appeared to be something else.

They were rings. And while they looked old and dull, the colors still stood out vibrantly against the fading metal. They appeared too large to be able to fit my own fingers, so I knew they had to have been made for men. I leaned down to get a closer look, and found something carved on the inside of them, some sort of text. It was too small to read.

"I don't know," I said to Will. "This is very strange."

Will reached for my hand, at the same moment a voice interrupted us. "Very strange, indeed," said an unfamiliar man from behind us. His voice was deep, and aged.

I turned around quickly, finding a man dressed in long black robes, his head balding and his face slightly wrinkled. There was something about him that greatly repulsed me.

"I am Fenir Camrall," he said to us. "And you two are?"

"Nobody," I told him. "Two orphans from Mortefine."

He clucked his tongue, seeming almost disappointed by that. "And your other female companion?" he asked. "You two don't seem like the type to work for Tommen Saxthon."

"She's his assassin," Will said. "We're working together… on an investigation."

He nodded, smiling slightly. "I would be happy to answer any questions you may have for me." A pause. "But first I must ask if you know what it was you were looking at just before I arrived?"

We both shook our heads.

"I find it very odd that you observe these artifacts when you have come in search of the serpent god's blade. Yet you have no inkling as to what these are?"

"No," I said to him. "Why does it even matter?"

He sighed. "There is more you do not tell me, but that is okay. I can assume enough."

"We don't know what you mean," Will said.

"These rings once belonged to the serpent and the dragon gods." He paused, giving us a moment to let that sink in. "While they were still mortal, of course. We should go to my office and discuss this further. And grab your little assassin too, I wouldn't want her to miss any of this."

Chapter 43

We followed Fenir up yet another set of stairs and down a hall lined with dozens of windows facing out towards the city. Even from there, I could see guards patrolling below. Fenir pulled a glass key from his pocket, exactly the type of thing I would have expected to see in his collection, and used it to unlock a door at the end of the hall. He opened it and gestured for us to follow inside. The office was larger than our room at the inn, but decorated accordingly compared to the rest of the man's establishment. There was already a servant inside waiting, and when she saw us she got to work pouring tea straight away.

Will, Aerez, and I sat on a long plush couch, the fabric as white as snow, clean and crisp, the cushions so soft that I nearly sank into them. Fenir sat in his own chair behind a large wooden desk. The servant delivered us each a cup of tea, in a small hand-painted mug. The tea was brown in color, but had a spicy smell to it, something that I didn't recognize, so I left mine untouched.

Fenir waved off the servant, who exited through a small side door, and turned to us with his legs crossed, like he was about to deliver us a prophecy. "So," he said, tapping a finger to his chin. "The lost blade of the serpent god. What could you possibly want with that?"

"Well," I started. "We... um..." I wasn't sure if I should have said to truth or come up with a lie.

"You don't know?" he said, somewhat amused. "Let me start by giving you a piece of advice: If you want to create any sort of understanding between us, then you need to tell me the truth. I will know if you lie. So, why do you want the blade?"

"So, you have it, then?" Will asked him.

The man looked displeased. "I'm not rather comfortable telling you three anything until you tell me the truth about why you are here. I can assume enough that you are not who you claim to be, and I won't ask questions about that, but I will warn you that the lost blade is dangerous. I wouldn't share anything with you if I thought you were at risk of releasing that danger."

I thought for a moment. It would have been easy to lie, and perhaps we could have even gotten away with it, but would it be so terrible for me to actually tell the truth? I turned back to the man. "I am the one looking for the blade. My companions are only here to aid in my search. I need it to exchange for my friend's freedom—for her life."

"What?" the man said, as if in disbelief. "You want to *exchange* it? You don't even want to keep it? That is absurd."

"Why would I want to keep something so evil in my possession?" I said to him. "I have no interest in the blade at all other than finding it to save my friend. If it were any other way, I would have preferred the blade to remain lost for all eternity."

"This is perhaps selfish of you, then," he told me, and I couldn't really disagree with him. "So tell me, who does want it? Who has asked for it? Because that is the person that seeks to use it."

"I have no idea what they want it for," I admitted. "But I am quite certain that his intentions are not pure. I hope that perhaps I can stop him before he gets the chance to use it."

"You should hardly be concerned about that," he explained. "If he's any normal man, then he likely will be unable to use the blade. But still, you would need to keep it out of the wrong hands."

"What does it do?" I asked quickly. "What kind of... power... does the blade have? Is Sazarr the one that made it himself? Is that why it is so dangerous?"

427

The man scowled at me. "You ask so many questions, girl, and yet you offer me nothing in return." He had an evil look on his face, like he was scheming a plan to get something greater out of this. "Tell me," he continued, "who are you?"

I was silent for a moment, wondering if I should really tell him, but then I remembered that I'd already decided to tell the truth. "If I tell you who I am, will you give us the blade?"

"If you tell me who you are then I will tell you what you want to know," he said, dipping his head in conformation. "A fair trade, I believe."

I hesitated, but the words came out anyway. "My name is... My name is Karalia Havu, the lost Lady of Orothoz."

The man suddenly became ecstatic, filled with such joy and excitement, a sharp contrast to the old brooding man he had been a moment ago. "Lady Havu?" he crooned. "And where have you been hiding all these years? You know, there are whispers that you're planning a rebellion."

"I am doing no such thing," I snapped.

And then Will cut in, his voice as sharp as a knife. "Tell us about the blade."

Fenir frowned at Will, like he would have him thrown out of his establishment if he said another word. "Very well," he started. "I assume that the blade has some sort of ability. Power, as you call it. Anytime I've ever been around it, it gives me a strange feeling—like I can feel the darkness seeping from directly within it. I've never let myself hold it or even be near it for too long, for fear that it might slip its way into my mind."

"You've never used it?" Will asked.

He shook his head. "Only a fool would dare to try and use it. But when I first acquired it, years ago, I had a little experiment performed. I had one of my servants use the blade to kill another one of my servants. You see, they had both been selling my secrets for some time, so it wasn't an undeserved punishment. Their names were Raj and Hector."

"What happened?" Aerez asked, speaking for the first time.

Fenir leaned back further into his chair. "I ordered Raj to kill Hector—to plunge the blade straight into his heart. And he did. Hector collapsed, and we assumed that he had died, in a way that any other weapon could have done, but we were wrong. He fell over, and then started convulsing and seizing. Black blood sprayed from his mouth—so much blood that he surely should have been dead. We waited for him to die, but he wouldn't. I had to lock him in my cellar and chain him to the wall. The blade prevented him from perishing, but only for a short while. It poisoned him, somehow, and he lived for weeks before I finally put him out of his misery, though by that point he was hardly more than a corpse with a pulse."

"What happened to Raj?" I asked.

"Oh, Raj was dead the second he used the blade," Fenir explained. "I assume that he tried to use it for more than what was allotted, and that the blade took his life as punishment. He fell over and his pulse faded out. I assumed that was the fate of anyone who dared to use the blade in such a way—as a weapon of death."

"So what is the blade to be used for?" Will asked.

"I believe the blade has a purpose," Fenir told us. "But what that purpose it, I am not sure. If it ended up in the wrong hands, to someone with the wrong intentions, then I fear that something dreadful could happen."

"But would it be okay to exchange the blade for my friend's freedom?" I asked.

Fenir shrugged. "I honestly could not say. I do not know what the blade wants or who it wants it from. Tell me, has it started to call to you yet? Does it find you in the depths of night?"

"What?"

"Do you dream about it?" Fenir went on. There was a look in his eyes, like he already knew the answer, like he had expected nothing less. "I believe that you were set on this path for a reason, Karalia Havu. You have such strange eyes, do you know that? They'd never been seen before in your family until you and your brother came along. Tell me, who was your mother's family?"

"I don't know what you mean," I said to him. "My mother is dead, and I have no memories of her. You are clearly mistaken in whatever assumption you think it is you've made."

"I think you know exactly what I mean," he said, laughing softly. "Does the darkness find you even when you do not want it to? Is it always waiting to pull you under?"

"That's—" I was about to tell him that he was insane, and that he was wrong, but he wasn't. He knew the truth, somehow. "How could you possibly know that?" I asked him.

Aerez and Will both turned to me, as if in shock, and watched me like they just realized they didn't know me at all. Fenir continued to smile from where he sat.

"Give us the blade," I said to him. "I've told you everything you want to know, now give it to us so we can be on our way."

He again folded his hands atop the desk. "I do not have it."

Aerez was already out of her seat before the words had even processed in my mind. Will lunged for her, wrapping an arm around her waist and pulling her back to the couch. She let out a sound between a growl and a hiss, while Fenir watched us like we were a group of bickering children.

"What do you mean… you don't have it?" I said slowly.

"It is not here," he said.

"Then where the hell is it?" Will yelled.

"I acquired the blade some forty years ago," he explained. "I had it brought here from Kraxoth, and it stayed in my collection for quite some time. It was a glorious addition, and people traveled from all around the country to come and see it. But one night, nearly fifteen years ago, it simply disappeared."

"Where did it go?"

"I assume back to the serpent god in the Otherealm. It was stolen in the night, straight out of its locked casing. There was no evidence of any sort of break-in, and my guards hadn't seen a thing."

"Well, how do we get it?"

"I have no idea," he told us, rather smugly. "Truthfully, I was relieved when the blade disappeared. I knew it was evil, and I'd wanted it out of my collection for quite some time. It always gave me a strange feeling, and even stranger, I get that same exact feeling from you, Karalia. I do not think it is a coincidence—I do not think any of this is a coincidence."

It almost sounded like he was suggesting…

No. I knew that wasn't possible, and it was absurd even to think such a thing. Whatever he was going on about, he must have just been insane.

But he continued anyway. "To retrieve the blade, I would assume that you need to travel to the Otherealm and find it yourself. But even then, I doubt that the serpent god would so willingly hand it over."

Will and Aerez started to fidget again, while I remained silent. I already knew that such a thing was possible, because I'd gone to the Otherealm many times before. I could wait for it to happen again, and I could ask Sazarr himself to give it to me. But if my physical body needed to actually be there to get it, then it was going to be much more difficult.

"That's impossible," Will said. "We can't *go* to the Otherealm."

"You have no idea what is possible," Fenir said, turning to me again. "There is something strange about you, girl— something that I can't quite understand, but maybe one day *you* will. I must wish you good luck with your search for the blade, and I hope that perhaps it will not remain lost for much longer."

"That's it?" I said. "That's all the help you can give us?"

"I'm afraid so," he said, standing from his chair and moving towards the door. "Now, I must ask you to leave."

He opened the door to let us out, but at the same moment, the man that had been at the front desk when we entered downstairs ran in, slightly out of breath. "Mister," he said.

"There are capital guards at the front door. They say they need to talk to you, and that they don't want to wait. I'm afraid they've already entered the building."

"Let's go," Will said, grabbing me by the hand, Aerez at our side. We walked out of the room and into the hall, turning back to Fenir. "I assume there is a backdoor? Tell us the way."

"Go down the stairs to the second floor, and then take a right down the first hall you see. The door is painted black and white—it leads to the back alley, so you'll have to climb a fence to get onto the main street."

"Thank you," I told Fenir as we were already making our way out.

He offered a slight dip of his head in return, and then called to me, "I'll be waiting for you to change the world, my dear."

I didn't let the words sink in. Actually, I tried to block them out entirely as we hurried down the hall and to the stairs in search of our exit. It took no longer than a minute to find the door. Will pulled it open, and sunlight flooded our view. When my eyes adjusted, I could see a thin set of stairs that led down to the alley below. We went down. While we were inside, the ground had become covered in a fresh layer of snow.

We ran up to the fence, which appeared to be an expensively made metal contraption, meant to keep out thieves. Luckily, there were pieces of wood stacked on the inside that were just tall enough for us to be able to reach the top of the fence and then haul ourselves over. Will went first, standing directly on the other side to help me and Aerez make it over as well.

When the three of us were all on the other side, we ran into the crowded afternoon street, hoping to blend in. But I could hear shouting behind us, from the entrance to the building, and turned to see a small group of guards running straight towards us. People cleared the way to let them pass.

"Stop right there," one of the guards called to us.

Will and I made sure to pull our hoods over our heads and keep them firmly in place, hiding ourselves, if they hadn't marked us already. Aerez kept her hood down, to make sure that she had a good view of the men running toward us as she pulled a short sword free from her side and prepared to unleash it.

She slowed her pace, allowing me and Will to continue forward so she could slaughter the men. The thought made me sick. I heard shouting from behind, both from the guards and from the city folk that had to witness it. When it was silent again, Aerez rejoined us, her sword bloody at her side.

"We need to find cover," she told us, panting. "One of them got away, no doubt to go and bring back others."

"The inn is just up this way," Will said, pointing down the street.

We managed not to run into any other guards on our way back, and a few minutes later we were back in our room, locking and barring the door shut behind us, closing the curtains, and removing our hoods once we knew there was no one to see us.

"We need to get out of this city," I said to them, pulling my long-braided-back hair free from the inside of my cloak.

"We can leave tomorrow," Will said. "Hopefully that will be enough time for those guards to calm down, and then we get out of here as fast as possible."

I nodded, slumping down into a chair in the corner and pulling my boots off. "This is insane," I said, partly to myself. "We can't really *go* to the Otherealm, can we?"

But they didn't say anything—we all had a lot to think about.

Chapter 44

Even though we all knew that it would have been the wisest to stay in our room all night, and to stay away from prying eyes, we ended up going to a tavern next door for dinner... and drinks. While I wasn't particularly in the mood to get drunk, Will and Aerez were, which I knew would likely lead to an interesting evening.

The three of us shared a meal of roasted meat, what I assumed to be pork. The seasoning wasn't something I was familiar with. It was sweet and spicy at the same time, and delicious. We also feasted on potatoes roasted with butter and cooked greens. It was certainly the best meal I'd had in weeks. I had one cup of ale, and it was easy not to go for a second, because I'd never particularly liked the taste of ale. By the time we finished eating, Will and Aerez were on their third or fourth cups, clearly drunk, and clearly having more fun than I was. I would let them have their fun tonight, and tomorrow we could focus again on finding the blade.

It was a rather modest tavern, with no music or dancing, and not even any card games or gambling. Everyone sat separately and kept to themselves, talking in hushed voices. Everyone was also much older than we were, but it didn't seem to be a problem. I just wanted to eat and then go back to our room and sleep. But unfortunately, we did not leave when the meal was over. We stayed much longer than we should have, and certainly long enough for someone to note our presence and report it to the guards patrolling the city. But nobody recognized us, and nothing happened.

I sat there with my arms crossed over the table, a bored expression on my face, and watched the two of them make fools of themselves. Then I watched as the barman refused them any more drinks, and that should have been sign enough for us to head on our way, but again, we didn't.

At one point—and this was something I never thought I'd see—Aerez had crawled out of her seat and found her way on top of Will's lap. It was quite the display, and certainly drew the attention of others in the building. He didn't move her off of him, he just sat there, as if he enjoyed it. They were giggling, and I knew then that they must have been very drunk, because such a thing would never happen if they were sober. Even I almost laughed at how ridiculous they looked.

Aerez began to move her hips over Will's lap, in a way that was anything but innocent. And he seemed to like it. I should have forced them to leave then, but instead I thought it better for only me to go. I watched as Will ran his hands over Aerez's back, even going as far as to slide them beneath her shirt. And then her hands were on his chest, and his mouth was on her neck.

It was time for me to go. They hardly seemed to notice or care that I was present, so it was easy for me to stand from the table and walk out of the building. I laughed quietly to myself, mostly because of the absurdity of all this. We should have been focusing on more important things, like planning for our departure from the city that was supposed to happen *tomorrow*.

I leaned against the outside wall of the tavern, resting my head against the cool brick and closing my eyes for a moment. I heard the door open, but I hadn't expected it to be either of them.

"Karalia," Will said quietly, stepping up beside me. I only opened my eyes when I felt his hand on my arm, as if he would beg for my attention.

"What?" I said, and it came out more harshly than I'd intended.

"Are you okay?" he asked me.

"I'm fine," I sighed, and then pushed off the wall and turned to head back towards the inn.

"Wait," he said, walking quickly to catch up with me. I ignored him, so he grabbed onto me and started to pull me down the alley in between the buildings.

I should have kept walking, and left him there, but I didn't. I allowed him to corner me against the wall, though I knew he would let me go if I really wanted.

"What do you want?" I asked him.

"Karalia," he said, and there was something pained in his voice. "That was… That was nothing. We were just drunk."

"Okay," I said, slightly confused. But then a moment later, I realized what he was saying to me. He thought I left because I was jealous—of what he and Aerez had been doing. I ran my hands over my face, covering my mouth with one to hold in my laughter, but to Will it probably looked like I was upset.

He slid one hand up my arm, and the other he rested on my hip. What was he doing? He pressed our bodies closer together, and I couldn't lie, it made something flush within me, but I knew it was wrong. I knew we shouldn't have been doing that.

He was holding me in place as he stared down at me, directly at my lips like he was intent on kissing them. I honestly wasn't sure what I would do if he did. My pulse quickened, and a thrill of excitement ran through me, but I knew it wasn't right.

"We shouldn't," I whispered to him.

"It's okay," he said, leaning down towards me, close enough to share breath, his mouth only inches from mine.

I let out a soft sound, which he probably heard as motivation for him to continue. He reached a hand up to my cheek and stroked a finger down the side of it, and then pressed his hand against my jaw.

"Have I ever told you how beautiful you are," he said to me.

I tried to turn away, but he held me in place, held my face positioned towards him. "What are you doing?" I asked.

He shifted his hips and pressed them harder into me, spreading my legs and situating his body between them. "Karalia," he said, and it sounded exactly like a plea. "Please… let me kiss you."

I stared back at him, my eyes wide, my expression vacant. "You want to kiss me?" I said, and then he nodded. "Don't you think that's a little desperate?"

He jerked his head back slightly, confused by my words, but he didn't remove his hands from my body. And I hated that part of me that didn't want him to remove them. I wished that doing what he wanted wouldn't complicate things so much.

He leaned down and brushed his lips against mine, as if to test the waters before going completely in. I could feel the tension in his body, from how still he held himself and from the tight grip he kept on me. When I didn't stop him, he leaned down and kissed me again, this time harder, though his lips were still soft and warm, and very inviting.

I tilted my head back as he deepened the kiss. He held onto my head from behind, keeping me in the position he wanted me while our mouths collided with one another. And I opened for him entirely, letting his tongue sweep in as I tasted the ale on his mouth.

I knew it was wrong. I knew I needed to stop it, and soon. It wasn't even what I wanted, but a part of me just couldn't resist what he was offering. I fisted my hands onto his clothes, pulling him towards me and pushing him away at the same time.

We stayed like that for a while, tangled in one another down that alley in the middle of the night. When we finally pulled away, he smiled down at me, so sweetly that it made my heart ache, because I knew that it meant something else to him than it did to me.

"Let me hold you tonight," he said, brushing his lips against mine one last time.

I didn't say anything. I couldn't. I felt so selfish for what I had already done, so surely, I couldn't promise him something like that. I knew I was holding his heart in the palm of my hand, dagger poised to strike it at any moment. I shouldn't have kissed him. I should have even allowed him to drag me down this alley.

He left me standing there alone, entering the inn where he would wait for me to return. I leaned my head against the wall and ran my hands over my face, groaning softly, wanting to scream so loudly that the windows burst. With my eyes closed, I heard a slight shuffling nearby, and I feared for a moment that Will had returned, but it was not him.

It was a woman dressed in all black, an assassin, with a knife in her hand, pointing it towards me as she walked down the alley. I remained exactly where I was.

"Aerez," I said. "Please."

She walked up beside me, and while the knife wasn't pointed at me anymore, it was still in her hand. "You're a terrible person," she told me.

"I know," I said, sighing. "Believe me, I know."

"Why would you do that?" she asked, her voice slightly louder that time. "You treat him horribly. You know he has feelings for you, that you do not return, and yet you still lead him on."

"I know," I said.

"You don't even know," she scoffed, and I waited for her to elaborate. She turned and looked directly into my eyes. "He's in love with you, Kara."

"Love?" I said, looking back into her eyes, realizing then that she had been crying.

"You do know what that means, don't you?"

I felt even more terrible then. I hadn't wanted to complicate things with Will, but I'd just done exactly that. I let him believe that I... that I wanted him as well.

Aerez didn't seem to care that I was deep in thought. "If anyone ever cared for me the way he does for you, I would never treat them like that. You are a terrible person. If there's

438

any decency left in you at all, then you need to end it with him. Tell him that it was a mistake and stop letting him think that he has a chance."

"I've told him that before."

"And your actions just now countered anything you might have told him in the past," she said to me. "You kissed him, and not because you feel any affection towards him, but because you're a selfish bitch." She gripped the knife harder in her hand, knuckles turning white.

"Aerez," I warned.

But then before I even had time to move, the knife was pressed against my throat, the cool blade rubbing against my skin. "You are going to go talk to him—right now. I'm tired of seeing him suffer every moment that you're around."

"He'll suffer even more if I do this."

"Perhaps," she said. "But he'll be grateful of it when he has moved on from you one day."

"Why do you care?" I said. "I thought you hated him."

She pressed her blade harder against my throat. "The two of you are the stupidest people I have ever met." And then she released me, hurrying off into the night, deeper into the city.

I returned to the tavern, only for a short while, long enough for me to down a whiskey or two. When I had gotten my fill of liquid courage, I returned to our room, finding Will seated at the table, smiling as he saw me enter, seemingly a great deal more sober than before.

"Karalia," he said, standing and then walking over to me. He grabbed onto my arms, and I was too stunned by this to even say anything, so I let him continue. "There's something I need to tell you. I know it's probably selfish, but I need to say it, just once."

"I don't think you should," I told him.

His eyes met mine, and he looked confused and hurt all at the same time. I let him guide me towards the table, where we sat down on opposite ends of it, and he waited for me to speak.

"Will," I said quietly. "What we did… it was a mistake."

He nodded slowly, as if he expected this. "Okay," he said. "So, you came here to, what? Make a fool of me?"

"Of course not," I said quickly. "I came here to apologize."

"Karalia," he said sadly. "You must know that… that I love you."

"Stop," I said. "Will, don't."

"It's the truth."

"I know," I said. "And I suppose that I also came here to tell you that I will never love you, Will. Not in the way that you want me to. Could you honestly think that I would share romantic feelings for you? Will, every second I spend away from Mortefine is a reminder that Nola is locked up there. And do you know who it was that locked her up? The man I used to love. So forgive me if I do not return your feelings, Will."

"Do you want me to hate you, then? Is that it?"

"Perhaps that would be better than whatever this is."

I expected him to raise his voice—to get angry and yell—but he spoke with surprising calmness. "Fine," he said. "If that is what you truly want from me, then I do hate you. I hate that I feel this way for you. I hate that I ever lied to you, and I hate that I care for you despite how badly we've treated each other. What I feel for you… it makes me sick. Do you know that?"

"Do you know what makes *me* sick?" I replied. "Your arrogance. Your stupidity. Your blindness. You're just like every other one of your kind, and I want you to stay away from me, okay? Do not pretend like there's anything more between us than this agreement. You can continue to help me search for the blade, and then after I want nothing to do with you. I want you out of my life forever."

"Don't worry," he muttered. "Once we find the blade, I'll be out of your way. I leave you alone again, just like you've always been, right? I'm starting to think your messed up life has been nobody's fault but your own."

I scoffed, though really his words made me want to cry. "That's fine," I told him. "That's great, actually. But let me tell you one more thing, Will. I know I have been cruel to you, but you cannot sit here and pretend like you haven't done the exact same thing to Aerez. I know you're not that stupid, or perhaps I have greatly overestimated you. It's obvious that she cares about you, so why don't you spend your time swooning over her instead. Unless you were only flirting with her to make me jealous, and if that's the case, then I definitely overestimated you."

He watched me for a moment, and I could see the words sinking in, as if I had really struck something. He stood from the table and walked to the door. "I'm sorry," he said. "I told you I was selfish."

I rolled my eyes. "You're too stupid to even realize that I'm the selfish one."

He gave me one last wary glance before walking through the door and closing it softly behind himself. I sat there and listened as his footsteps faded down the hall.

I didn't know where Will went, and I didn't particularly care either. I found myself again on the street outside, just needing some fresh air, and I wasn't surprised at all when Aerez walked up to my side.

"That was… chaotic," she told me.

I turned to her, anger simmering within my blood. "I hope you're happy now," I said. "He's all yours."

I stepped away from her, though I didn't know where I would go, but she grabbed onto my wrist, stopping me in place. "You think that's why I did it?"

"Isn't it?" I said, laughing quietly to myself. "Isn't that the little game you're playing? Pretending you hate him when you're secretly in love with him."

"That's…" she started, choking slightly on her words. "You have no idea what you're talking about."

"I don't really give a shit," I said. "There's nothing wrong with *feeling*, Aerez. Love, or whatever else it might be."

"Don't be ridiculous," she told me. "I am incapable of something like that."

"Whatever," I said. "I'm going out. Do not follow me."

"Kara," Aerez called, and the way she said it forced me to turn to her. "I have sworn to protect you," she said. "I don't want to argue, and I don't want to be your enemy. Please, just come inside."

"I will be back later." I turned and walked down the dark empty street, heading further into the city. Aerez didn't call after me again, and didn't follow me either. I listened to the door close as she made her way back into the inn.

Chapter 45

I had no clue as to where I was going. I followed the sounds of laughter and music, taking me into the entertainment district of the city. While the buildings remained discreet from the outside, I could only guess that on the inside they were bars and brothels and gambling dens. It was such a different atmosphere from what the city was like during the day. Now, it seemed like I might have been able to have a bit of fun, if I wasn't already in a terrible mood. There were no guards there, nobody to stop me, and nobody sober enough to recognize me either.

It's not as if I felt unsafe there. The only people out were those engaging in nightly leisure activities, or those just coming back from a long day's work, not anybody who would try to murder me, I don't think. The people seemed to have no issue at all with the cool air. Some women wore revealing gowns, bearing most of their upper bodies to the cold.

If I had any money, I might have stopped at an establishment and found a way to have some fun of my own—to take my mind off of things. But Will was the one who had been paying for everything.

I continued onward, walking wherever it was my feet would take me. I turned down an alleyway, finding that it was not empty, but occupied by a man and a woman who were engaged in a very indecent act—or at least one that should never occur in public. I gasped and hurried away from them.

I had no idea what any of the buildings were, so I didn't dare to go inside, for fear that I might walk into something even worse than what I'd seen in the alley. Eventually I grew tired and knew that the wisest decision would be to turn around and head back to the inn. I went the exact same way I had before, for fear of getting lost.

But then something strange began to happen. I could feel that familiar tether within me, like it was trying to alert me of something, though I wasn't sure what at first. I tried to ignore it and continue on my way, but it grew desperate, filling my head with a strange roaring sensation. It was eager, for some reason.

I squeezed my eyes shut and tried to shout into my mind. *No. No. No.* But I think I might have shouted it out loud as well, because whatever people had been around were now staring at me like I was insane. Some were coming towards me as if to help, while others fled in the opposite direction.

I needed to get out of there. I needed to find somewhere that I could hide, at least until this was over. If I drew too much attention, then guards might come for me, and realize who I am. If they catch me and neither Will nor Aerez are there to help... that would be bad.

I tried to run. Tried, and failed. After only a few steps, my knees and legs gave out on me, and I collapsed to the ground, right in the center of the busy street. Then I tried to crawl out of sight, running my hands along the brick road, but it was no use. The area was far too large and there were far too many people for me to remain unnoticed.

I continued trying to reach and then spun my head around as if to look out for any guards coming my way, and the movement must have made me dizzy because a moment later everything went black. I passed out—or fell asleep—or something else that I couldn't explain.

I was in my dream-like state when images began to flash in my mind. Everything was gray and dull, and there were clouds in the sky overhead, blocking out the sun. There was a loud roaring in the distance, which I recognize as waves in a body of water, slamming into some sort of land. There was an island, more like a mass of rock, resting in an expanse of open water. I did not recognize the island nor anything else in the vision, but something about it was strangely familiar.

I followed the waves as they slammed into shore, my gaze shifting to the strange structure on it. It appeared to be some sort of cave entrance, with an eerie mist seeping from it, sending a chill through me though I was certain that I was dreaming. I tried to go towards it, or to at least reach for it, but then my surroundings faded again, and I was left with nothing.

When I was able to open my eyes again, I expected to find myself in that dreadfully dark realm, perhaps even with a serpent before me, but I did not. I was lying on the street in Frystal, flurries of snow falling onto me, people standing and staring.

There were at least a dozen people in my immediate vicinity, circling around me, blocking out my view of anything else in the area. They mostly just looked concerned, though I wished that they would have left me alone. One woman, wearing nothing but a wrinkled nightgown, reached a hand down to help me up. I refused her hand and lifted my arms behind me to prop myself up. Then I dragged my knees forward and moved into a standing position.

Some of the people began to back away, while others stayed to make sure that I was okay. A man lifted a hand under my arm, keeping me upright, though I did nothing to shoo him off.

"Thank you," I muttered to the crowd.

"How much have you had to drink?" another man asked me, and I nearly laughed when I realized that he was serious.

Perhaps that would be a better explanation than the truth. "A bit," I said, forcing shame into my voice. "I just got dizzy. I'm fine."

They led me to the edge of the street, and I still could not believe that something like that was happening. Perhaps I misjudged the people of Frystal, because right now they seemed to be very kind and caring, even to a stranger like me. I leaned against the wall of a nearby building and waited as a man went to find me some water, while most of the others had already dispersed.

When he didn't return for a minute or two, I decided that it would be better for me to just head on my way. I pulled my hood over my head and filed back into the crowd, hoping to make it back to the inn before another vision took over.

I saw an island, there was no doubt about that. And while I didn't recognize it, it seemed like I should have. It felt like that was where I needed to go—like *someone* was showing me the way. I needed to tell Will and Aerez about it.

Fenir told us that I would need to go to the Otherealm on my own two feet to retrieve the blade, so maybe that island was somehow connected to that. Maybe there was so much more to this than I ever anticipated.

I quickly made it back to the room, disappointed to find that Will had still not returned. I knew he probably needed time after our conversation from earlier, after he confessed that to me, but I had something more important to tell him. I couldn't have guessed where he'd gone, or when he'd be back, but I hoped that it would be soon.

Aerez was asleep in bed when I walked in, so I pulled back the sheets and climbed in beside her. I knew she was still asleep when she rolled towards me and wrapped her arm around my waist, clinging to me. And while I should have been afraid, I found the gesture oddly comforting.

I forced every thought out of my mind as I attempted to sleep.

Sometime during the night, I awoke to the sound of a door closing, and I cracked my eyes open just enough to see Will entering the room. His clothes and hair were a mess, and he smelled strongly of liquor. I remained awake as he went into the bathing room to wash himself, and as he came out and situated himself on the floor beside the bed, using his balled-up cloak as a pillow. A part of me felt bad for him.

The following morning, he was still in that spot when I got up, sleeping soundly and snoring softly, likely suffering from the first signs of a hangover. Aerez was also asleep beside me, her arm draped now across my chest instead of my waist.

I dressed and grabbed some of the money Will left on the table, then headed downstairs in search of food. Luckily, the innkeeper had some that I could purchase. It was mostly just fruit and a few dried goods, but it would do.

When I returned upstairs, Will and Aerez were awake and waiting for me. They stared at me as if I had done something wrong, and I supposed that they were right.

"Karalia," Will said as soon as I entered the room, like there was something he'd been burning to say, and it could not wait any longer.

I wasn't exactly sure what to expect. I didn't know if they were mad at me, or if they thought I was mad at them, and I didn't really care, either, because we had more important things to discuss.

"I got some food," I told them, setting it down on the table. I turned back towards the bed, and they were both still watching me like I was insane. "What?" I demanded.

Will shook his head, as if deep in thought. "I—" he started. "I want to apologize for last night."

I clenched my fists as my sides and took a deep breath. "For what?" I asked. "*I* should be the one apologizing, not you."

Will looked at me like he wanted to disagree, but then Aerez said, "It's fine. We all said and did things that we didn't mean. How about we just forget about it, okay?"

Will and I both nodded, and that was that. We sat down to eat.

Finally, I decided that it was time to tell them what happened the night before. "I need to tell you guys something," I said. "Last night… something happened. I was walking through the street, and then I had a *vision*. I saw an island, and I think that's where we need to go."

"Shit," Will said, like he already knew what I was talking about. "I was afraid of this."

"You know this island?" I asked.

He gave me a shallow nod. "It's called *Svar*. It's a small island off the western coast of Vatragon, though it's not claimed by Vatragon, nor Meriton or Faulton. Nobody wants it, because it's rumored to be an entrance to the Otherealm."

"How do we get there?" I asked quickly, almost too eagerly.

"You don't," Aerez cut in. "No captain of any ship is stupid enough to sail there. It's far too dangerous."

"We're going."

Will sighed. "I hate to say this, but I think Karalia is right. It's the best chance we have of getting to the Otherealm and finding the blade."

Aerez shook her head and scoffed at us. "I'm sorry, but I will not be going there. I will help you make it to the coast, and help you find passage on a ship, but sailing to Svar is where we part ways. I will not sail to *hell*—that is closer to death than I want to be for a very long time. I did not sign up for that."

Will looked displeased, but I cut in. "That's fine," I told her. "I wouldn't ask that of you—of either of you. I know the risks involved and it would be something that I'm willing to do alone if I must."

"You're not going alone," Will growled. I had to admit that I was a bit relieved by that, because the thought of going by myself terrified me.

I gave him an appreciative nod.

"We leave today," he told us. "Let's take an hour or two to gather supplies, and then we can head for the tunnel out of the city."

About an hour later I was alone in the room, packing our things, while Will and Aerez snuck around the city and purchased some food to bring along with us. They were to meet me back at the room within the hour, and we would immediately depart from there.

I heard a soft knock at the door, which I knew could not have been Will or Aerez because neither of them ever knocked so quietly. And they wouldn't have knocked, anyways, they would have just walked right in. Because of that, I hesitated to open the door, pulling my knife free from my pants and stalking over to it. I slowly twisted the handle, peeked through, and found a familiar face waiting on the other side.

"Oh, hello!" Veeran said, a wide smile on his face like he was surprised to see me, though he obviously came here for a reason.

I released my breath, tucking the knife back into my pants before Veeran could see it and get scared away. "Veeran," I said. "How did you know I was here?"

"Oh," he said. "Um… Can I come in?"

I opened the door fully, allowing him to enter and then slamming it shut again. He hesitantly walked further into the room, sitting down at the small table and turning back to me.

"This is the closest inn to my uncle's home," he told me. "I took a guess and then asked the innkeeper if anyone showed up really early the other morning. He told me what room you were in."

"He shouldn't have given that information away so easily," I said as I walked over to the table and joined Veeran.

"I just wanted to come say goodbye," he told me. "Before you leave the city. You are leaving, aren't you?"

"We are," I said, sighing. "Well, how are you doing? How is living with your uncle?"

He warmed up a bit to that. "It's great, actually," he told me. "He and my aunt own a shop on the other side of town. I'm going to help them run it, along with my cousins, of course, but they're still too young."

"That's great," I told him, relieved that I didn't have to force my smile. "What kind of shop is it?"

"A clothing shop. Apparently, my aunt has a knack for sewing. They're actually very nice clothes. I wish you could have stayed longer so I could have taken you there."

"I would have liked that," I said. "You know, despite what it might seem like, I'm very fond of dresses."

"I believe you," he said, laughing softly. "It would have been quite a sight to see."

"You're a shameless flirt, you know that?" I said to him. "One day, you're going to make some girl very happy, Veeran."

"Thanks," he said, turning away to hide his blush. "So, where are you headed next?"

"Very, very far from here," I told him.

He was silent for a moment, and he turned to meet my eyes, something wary in them. "I know who you are," he whispered. "My uncle... He recognized you when he saw you. You really should be trying to stay hidden better. It's dangerous, especially with all the guards here."

He seemed to note the lack of surprise on my face. He wasn't expecting that.

"You really are her?" he asked me.

"I really don't know what you're talking about," I said. "I'm an orphan from Mortefine. I'm nobody." I knew he didn't believe me, but that didn't matter.

He reached a hand across the table, resting it atop my own and squeezing lightly. "It's okay," he told me. "I... I'm not going to tell anyone. There's not even anyone *for* me to tell. I just... Why do you travel with the prince?"

"He's helping me."

"Can you trust him?"

"I don't know."

"Look," he said. "You know I'm not a part of the rebellion, but I would be if it was to help you. I would come with you if you needed me."

"No," I said quickly. "Veeran, the only place for you is here within this city. Your father wanted you to stay away from the rebellion, so that is what you're going to do. And besides… I'm not who you think I am."

"You are not The Lost Daughter?"

"I am," I said. "But I am not involved in the rebellion at all. I've been in Mortefine for most of my life, without contact to the outside world. I only just learned of the rebellion about a month ago when I was in Kraxoth. Whatever they think my role in this is, they're wrong."

He looked confused. "You… You don't want a rebellion?" I could see the moment his realization set in. "Why would…"

"I may not agree with how King Daemien rules this country, but I am certainly not planning his assassination," I said. "I have no idea who is plotting that or why they are using my name as a cover."

"Does the prince mean to take you to the capital?" he asked, more urgently now. "You can't go there. They'll kill you, even if you aren't truly involved, they will kill you for what the rebels have planned."

"I'm not going to the capital," I assured him. "Will, the prince, he's helping me with something else. He's promised not to take me to his father, at least not yet, not until I decide that it is the right time. But one day, I might have to go there, and when I do, I'll tell him the truth of my involvement in everything."

He let go of my hand and slumped back into his chair. "I'm worried," he said. "How would the rebels know what you look like if you've never even spoken with them? I would understand more if there was someone else claiming to be you, but they have your portrait. They had to have gotten it from somewhere. If you've been in Mortefine all this time, then the rebels must be working from there, too."

"You're right," I said. "It doesn't make sense."

I hardly even knew what to think, but one specific thought kept making its way back to me. Or rather, one specific person. *Hiran.* I never understood his motives in all of this, nor his involvement. It just wouldn't make sense for him to be involved with the rebels, but perhaps he was. Perhaps he was the one that sent my portrait out. But that still didn't explain what he would want with the lost blade, or why he needed *me* to find it.

"Veeran," I said, somewhat urgently. "Promise me that you'll stay out of the rebellion. I know we don't know each other well, and we spent no more than a week together, but I'm worried about you. I fear what is to come, and I don't want innocents getting hurt."

"I promise," he said. "But what about you? How will you stay safe?"

"Don't worry about me," I said, offering a sad smile. "I have more than enough protection."

"And what do you plan to do about everything?"

"Nothing."

We both went silent after that, and I knew that Veeran was thinking hard about what I'd said. I knew that wasn't the answer he wanted, and that he was probably hoping I'd say that I would join the rebels, but that wasn't what I wanted, nor did I believe that it was the best option for our country at the moment. I didn't believe that the rebels would win, so even if I did believe in their cause, I would not join them.

I heard footsteps approach from the hall and had just enough time to turn before spotting Will and Aerez enter the room, their arms full of the various things they carried. Both of their eyes quickly landed on Veeran, assessing any threat he might pose. I merely shook my head at them.

"What is he doing here?" Will practically growled.

"He's come to say goodbye," I answered. When neither of them said anything, I added, "He knows who we are."

Will stared at me like he was angry, which would make sense after last night, but I had a feeling that it had to do with Veeran's presence. He thought I was the one who'd told him.

"I realized it when I saw you use your power," Veeran blurted, I think for my benefit. "I mean, I guessed it. But her... Lady Karalia...she's not that hard to recognize when it comes down to it."

"Very well," Will said.

And Veeran kept going. "I promise I'm not going to tell anyone. I mean, I would love to tag along with you guys and help, but Karalia is worried about my safety. I'm going to stay out of the rebellion. If my father contacts me, I won't ignore him. But if he changes his mind and asks me to aid the cause, I will have to refuse him."

"Smart boy," Will said. "Now, I'm going to have to ask you to leave, because in a short while we will be leaving this city for good, and you don't want to be spotted with us when these guards start sniffing around."

Chapter 46

Veeran offered to walk us to the tunnel, and while I thought it was a bad idea, I couldn't bring myself to refuse him. I could admit that I didn't know him well, but I knew that he was a good person. And I could tell that our parting ways saddened him. He was being forced to say goodbye to people he cared about yet again. Even if Will and Aerez weren't fond of him, I considered him a friend. I always would, and if I ever returned to Frystal, I would know that I could find him as my ally.

We headed downstairs to the front desk with all our belongings and paid the innkeeper what little money we had left. He watched us wearily, the same way he had that first early morning, but said nothing else otherwise. Veeran was still at our sides as we headed for the door and out onto the snow-covered street.

"STOP RIGHT THERE!"

"DROP YOUR WEAPONS!"

As if it were instinct, Will and Aerez stepped in front of me, creating a human shield, while I reached for Veeran, hiding him behind me as if he were the one these guards were looking for. There was a large group of them, more than a dozen, standing with their weapons poised, like they were waiting for us, like they knew we would be there. It was likely that damned innkeeper.

"Veeran," I whispered very quietly, too low for the guards to hear. From where he was standing, they hadn't yet spotted him. "You need to go." But he only clung to me tighter, like he would defend me as well.

"Drop your weapons," they shouted again, a bit quieter that time.

"Will," I said, and he ignored me. "Will, what's the plan?"

We carried all our supplies, and it probably would have been wiser to abandon them and make a run for it, but if we did escape, we would be needing those on our journey.

Will finally turned around and looked directly at Veeran, fury on his face like he suspected the boy was the one who had sold us out. Veeran shook his head quickly. "It wasn't me, I swear it," he said.

"It was probably Fenir," Aerez growled.

"It was *probably* that innkeeper we just paid," I said.

"Shut your damned mouths," one of the guards called. "You four are coming with us, to see the Lady of Frystal."

The Lady of Frystal? Who was she? And what did she have to do with this? I didn't particularly care, because I would not allow myself to be brought to her like a prisoner.

"We'll see about that," Aerez said, mostly to herself.

Again, we didn't move—waiting and formulating a plan. The guards had clearly come from the left, because that's where most of them were standing, and there were fewer to the right, which was luckily the way we needed to go. That was the way to the tunnel.

"Kara," Will said, not turning to me but rather just grabbing my attention. "I believe we are going to have to fight these men. I want you to take the boy and run away as fast as you can. He certainly won't be able to fight, and I don't want you getting hurt in the process. If we get captured, you need to hide somewhere in the city."

That certainly did not seem like a good plan. The two of them couldn't go up against all those guards, not unless… unless Will used his ability on them. Then, I supposed, we might have had a chance.

I grabbed firmly onto Veeran's hand, waiting for the signal for us to flee. Aerez turned around to look at me, and then at Veeran, with such sincerity in her eyes. She reached down to the side of her pants, pulling free a small knife. Then she handed it to Veeran.

"Thank you," I told her, watching as Veeran held the knife firmly in his hands. At least he seemed prepared to use it, if it came to that.

"You need to run," Aerez said, and I knew that was our signal. In the very same instant, Aerez had stepped away from the building and was already lunging for the nearest guard. She hadn't drawn her weapons, and I knew whatever she was doing was just a distraction so Veeran and I could get away.

I tugged onto Veeran's hand, urging him to begin running, but his feet were planted firmly to the ground. "No," I said. "Listen to me." His eyes shifted to me, though they were still filled with terror. "We need to run."

And then we broke into a sprint. I let go of his hand and guided him in front of me, so I could protect him from behind if I needed to. The guards were so preoccupied with Aerez that they hardly even noticed us slipping by. As soon as we made it around the first corner, out of the guards' view, I grabbed him by the arm and pulled him down the nearest side street.

"Veeran," I said, shaking him slightly. "Veeran, you take that knife, and you run. Do you hear me? Protect yourself. Fight, if you need to. I have to go and help my friends."

"I can help too," he said, and my heart nearly burst in my chest.

"Veeran, please go home."

Still, he did not move.

"You promised me," I told him. "You promised that you would leave us and keep yourself safe. Your time with us is over. You made it to Frystal, like your father wanted, and now you need to stay here where it's safe." I put an arm around his back and pulled him in for an embrace. "Go to your family."

Veeran lurched forward, and I heard him cry out, and at first, I thought he was merely sad to leave me behind, but then I heard the footsteps near, and saw the guard running towards us, with a bow in his hands.

Veeran had collapsed onto me, and his hold on me had suddenly gone weak. I pulled back to examine him, and then I saw the blood. There was an arrow protruding through his chest, shot through his back, dangerously close to his heart. He could hardly even stand on his own, but I could see the guard coming near us, loading another arrow, so I carefully set Veeran to the ground.

The guard shot towards us, or towards me, and I ducked out of the way just in time for it to go over my head, hitting the side of a building behind us. I reached for my back and had my sword pulled free in an instant. The guard prepared another arrow, but I was already running towards him. Fangmar wasn't big enough to cut him up the way I wanted to, so I had to be careful about the wounds I inflicted.

He threw his bow to the side when he realized that it would be helpless against me, and instead swung his arms out in attempt to grab my sword. I turned to the side, slicing down his lower arm, cutting all the way from the crook of his elbow to his wrist. Blood began to pour, but the guard continued to reach for me.

I stepped back, though there was little room for me to go in the first place, and when he reached for me again, I swung my sword across his chest. His armor was too thick, and Fangmar too small. I backed away another few steps, but not quick enough to avoid the guard's blow. He didn't try to punch or kick me, but rather grabbed straight for my face, closing his hand around it and then shoving me into the nearest wall. My body and head slammed against it, and I was forced to close my eyes due to the excruciating pain I now felt.

I couldn't see the guard, so I took to swinging my sword out in every direction, keeping him away from me while I was immobilized. Veeran remained silent behind us. When I opened my eyes again, I could see that the guard had gone back for his bow and was loading another arrow. I ran up to him while his back was turned to me, doing my best to stay silent, though I was sure he could hear my heavy breathing.

He turned around to shoot at me, but not quick enough to avoid my sword.

I slid it through his throat, piercing it, and when he stumbled and fell away backward, blood sprayed everywhere. He clutched for his throat, trying to stop the bleeding, but I knew he would not survive that.

I killed him.

I left him there to choke on his own blood and ran back towards Veeran, finding him sprawled out across the ground, his eyes entirely vacant.

"Veeran!" I called, and then I bent down to reach for him, lifting and cradling him in my arms. He was still, and so, so cold.

"Karalia," he rasped, coughing and spitting up blood.

I wiped the tears from his eyes, ignoring the ones that fell from my own eyes. The knife was still clutched in his hand, like even now he was prepared to use it. I pulled it from his grip and set it on the ground.

"Thank you," he said to me. "For... For what you have done for me. For what you can do... for... everyone else."

"Veeran!" I sobbed. "Please."

He tried to speak again, but the words would not come out.

"It's going to be okay," I said, forcing a smile, feeling the tears run down my cheeks at the same time. "You're going to be okay."

"I think..." He stopped crying, and was instead looking up, towards the sky. "I think I'm going now."

"Please," I said again. But I already knew what was happening. It was too late, and there was too much blood. "It's going to be okay," I repeated, and then I bent down and brushed a kiss on his forehead, my final farewell.

And then he was gone. His head fell back, like he had used his last bit of energy to look up at me. There was nothing left within him. He was dead.

This boy, this kind and brave boy who wanted nothing more than to be a part of something that mattered, had been killed by the king's guards. He was not fighting them, and yet they showed him no mercy. They gave him no chance to plea for his life, which I was certain he would have down. He was a kind soul, and he didn't deserve this. All I could think was that… was that it should have been me instead, and not him.

It should have come as a sign to me, that enough blood had been shed, and that perhaps there was no need for further death, but I was vengeful. I wanted to go and fight the guards and kill every last one of them for what they'd done to Veeran.

I lowered his body to the ground and gently sat him against the wall of a building. I couldn't stand the sight of the blood. I couldn't stand the sight of the permanent fear on his face. He'd had such a life ahead of him.

I wiped any remaining tears away as I walked back onto the main street. I could hear fighting nearby, and knew that was where I needed to be, so Will and Aerez would not suffer the same fate that Veeran had. Nobody else needed to die because of me—except those guards.

I quickly came into view of the fighting, watching as Will and Aerez held their own, the collapsed bodies of other guards already surrounding them.

I maintained the grip on my sword firmly as three guards began to move toward me. The first one lunged, his sword aiming straight for my side, where it would have cut right into my stomach if I hadn't dodged the blow. His sword swept past me, clashing with the side of a building, sending shards of brick flying. Before he could recover, I lifted my leg and dug my foot right into his stomach, as hard as I possibly could. He stumbled back, clutching his abdomen in pain just as I landed another kick in between his legs. He collapsed to the ground and huddled over.

Aerez and Will ran over to me as soon as they had the chance, noting the streaks of dried tears on my face. They didn't ask me about it, but likely assumed the truth judging by my state. They positioned themselves on either side of me, prepared to protect and defend with whatever it would take.

A fresh group of guards circled in on us from further down the street, all of them prepared to fight and perhaps even kill us. Aerez wasted no time—she moved stealthily towards the guards, like *she* was the predator closing in on its prey. They didn't even have a second to counter her attacks. And then Will moved as well, taking advantage of the guards being distracted by Aerez.

I knew Will was strong, but I didn't realize the full extent of that strength. He could have long turned them all into ash, but instead he was fighting them the normal way, whether to keep his identity hidden or to show the guards mercy, though I didn't think they deserved that. A guard swung for Will, managing to give him a shallow cut across the underside of his arm, fresh blood welling. But Will was not the least bit deterred by it. He countered, swinging out horizontally and digging into the man's neck with the flat side of his sword. He wasn't intending to kill the man, but he at least needed to immobilize him. Will must have realized that too because a moment later he took his free fist and swung it straight at the man's face, knocking him out cold to the ground. He turned to the next guard.

I shifted my attention to Aerez, who was somehow entertaining several guards at once. They were too large and clumsy to counter her maneuvers, and she was small enough to squirm out of the way every time they attempted to land a blow. She ducked, swung, lunged, sliced. The guards didn't even see what was coming. One by one they fell to the ground, coating the street in red. I couldn't tell if they were dead or only injured, and I didn't really want to know.

I was so busy watching them fight that I hadn't been paying attention to myself. There was a man running toward me, and he carried no weapon other than a large knife. He had a taunting grin on his face. I sheathed my sword across my back and instead pulled my knife free. If he wanted to fight with a knife, then I would as well.

He stepped closer, hissing between his teeth. "I would hate to mess up that pretty face of yours, *whore*."

To my credit, I laughed. "You really think I'm pretty?"

He swung the knife for me, for my neck. I took a large step back and easily moved out of his reach. He grunted, and then swung again. Another miss. He was large and clumsy, and not quick enough to get near me with such a small weapon.

I smiled at him as I lunged and stepped around him, so that I was facing his back. Before he could see where I'd gone, I jumped and brought my hand around the front of his throat. He swung his elbows back to throw me off, so I did the only thing I could think to do and shoved my knife into his back, straight where I thought his heart would be. Though he was a big man, so I couldn't be sure if the knife had landed its blow.

He yelled out in pain, and I let him go so I could step back and watch. When I saw that he was still able to walk, I knew I needed to attack him harder. I lunged for him again, shoving the knife in deeper and twisting it. His blood coated my hands, my clothes, and the metallic smell of it made me want to vomit. He fell to his knees then, so I kicked him as hard as I could, sending his face down onto the brick street.

When I turned back from the man, I found Will watching me while he fought someone else. There was blood dripping down the side of his face, and I could see steam rising from the top of his head, from how hot his body was compared to the cold. He seemed almost unnerved by what I had done, but his face was carefully blank. And when I turned to Aerez, she was grinning at me, like she was proud. I grinned right back at her—satisfied.

They finished off the rest of the guards, for now, before more of them showed up. There were bodies piled around us, from our own doing. I felt as if I were walking through a dream—one where I was the monster.

I tried to stand fully, but my knees felt weak, and I collapsed to the ground. I ran the back of my hand across my mouth, before realizing that it was covered in blood. I looked down and saw a mass of red. My stomach failed me, and I huddled over and retched all over the ground.

Veeran was gone.

I was a murderer.

Suddenly Will and Aerez were at my side. Aerez pulled a cloth free from somewhere and bent down to clean my face. I sat there vacantly, eyes pointed on the ground, unable to formulate words or even thoughts.

"Where is Veeran?" Will asked me.

I began to shake then, and to keep myself from getting sick again I had to clamp a hand over my mouth, shutting my eyes to keep everything out. I wanted to scream. I wanted to run. I wanted everything to end.

"Did he get away?" Will went on.

I only had enough energy to shake my head.

Will slid a soft, careful hand under my arm and slowly pulled me to my feet. They both allowed me to lean on them as we started to walk down the street, toward the tunnel.

"We need to go," Will said.

And he was right, because further down the street was a fresh group of guards making their way towards us. The three of us broke into a run, leaving behind the blood massacre we had created. We would make it to the tunnel, and then out of the city, because I didn't want to think about what would happen if we were to get caught.

Chapter 47

My feet trembled beneath me. My lungs burned. My eyes stung with tears. Rather than the relief that I should have felt after discovering the true location of the blade, I only felt fear and guilt and remorse. I should have been running towards something, but instead I was running away. I was running from those guards like I really was the criminal they thought me to be—like I really was a rebel.

I knew that I should have tried to keep my mind clear while we escaped, and thought about everything later, but it was hard. The image of Veeran's dead body continually flashed into my mind, as if to remind me that it was my fault. I hadn't gotten him away quick enough. We should have kept running, but instead I made us stop, so that I could go back to help Will and Aerez, when they clearly didn't need my help at all. He was gone because of me.

And the men that I killed… That was something else that would surely come to haunt me once all of this settled. At the time, yes, I believed that they deserved to die for attacking us and trying to capture us, but they were only doing their job, as were the other guards that were chasing us now as we made our way to the tunnel.

They were going to catch us. How could they not? We were far outnumbered, and while Will did have an advantage over them, I didn't think he would be playing that card anytime soon. For some reason, he wouldn't. Even if we made it to the tunnel, they could chase us down it, and we'd all be running through the dark where they were bound to catch us eventually. Anywhere we went, they would just keep chasing and chasing us, until they had us.

I didn't understand what they were after. Surely the capital guards were looking for Will, after he lied and abandoned his family, and stole a rather large group of soldiers, and then journeyed across the country with them. That was understandable. But what I didn't understand was what they wanted from me. They couldn't have known who I was, not these guards, but perhaps they only wanted me because I had been traveling with the prince, not because they thought I was a rebel. If we did get captured, I would have to make a very convincing case, and keep my identity hidden for as long as possible.

Will, Aerez, and I continued to run through the city, towards the exit that would take us to the tunnel. I followed blindly behind them, not sure what part of the city we were in or how much longer it would take, but they were keeping us away from the guards, so I didn't question them.

In the distance, I could still hear the shouting, both from the guards and the citizens they were likely barreling through to get to us. We could easily have taken a turn and hidden ourselves somewhere within the city, but we needed to leave once and for all. We couldn't afford any more delays.

I knew we were reaching the edge of the city, as the people and buildings grew scarcer. I didn't recognize any of it, because the first time we'd passed that way, it had been in the middle of the night. But straight down the street we were already on, I could see open space in the distance. We sped our pace. So close.

Having horses right about now would have been very helpful, though we would have had to abandon them when we reached the tunnel.

"Kara," Will said quietly to me as we continued to run. "I need you to listen, okay?" I waited. "I don't think they're after you. I think they're looking for me. So if they catch me, you might be able to get away, and get out of the city."

"No," I said quickly.

"Listen to me," he said, somewhat louder then. "They're never going to stop chasing me. This is likely just my father, angry over my disappearance. I'll be fine. You need to go with Aerez and continue the mission. You know where the blade is, so the rest will be easy."

"I won't leave you," I said, partly choking on my words. "I can't… I can't do it without you."

Aerez continued to run beside us, though she remained silent.

"You can," he said. "You're going to have to. I will do everything in my power to get away from them and find you."

"Will you?" I said, and the words came out a bit harsher than I intended. "Will you do everything in your *power*, Will?"

He didn't say anything, because we'd just run through the city exit, and reached a large open area, with rocky terrain covered in a thick layer of snow. It crunched beneath our feet, slowing us down just a bit.

It was hard to find any path or road through all the snow, and we ended up in what appeared to be a large open field. I could still feel the hard rock beneath my feet, though it was mostly flat. I couldn't see the tunnel entrance in the distance, only more rock and mountain.

Will and Aerez slowed, until eventually we had gone to a standstill. It seemed that they didn't know where we were either. They looked around, for anywhere that we could go, but there was nowhere even to seek cover.

But then I felt something—a shift in the air. The wind began to blow differently, like a storm was coming, though there was hardly a cloud in the sky. And it was warmer compared to what it had been moments before, a great deal warmer. I looked around, up into the sky, but I could see nothing other than my heavy breath blowing out in front of me.

Will slid his hand through mine, and while I thought it was to comfort me, he only shoved me towards Aerez, like he was handing me over to her. He squeezed my hand tightly one last time before letting go.

"You need to run," he said. "Right now."

Before my feet could move, something cracked within the sky, a sound like thunder, and the sun dimmed, as if blocked by something very large. The force of it was so strong that it rumbled the earth, causing my legs to again become unsteady. A strong wind hit me, blowing the hair back from my face. A shadow covered us overhead, and I realized then that something was coming—something was flying straight towards us.

Will again tried to push me away, but I wouldn't leave him there. I wouldn't leave him with whatever beast it was that had come to kill us. It let out a large growl, or more like a roar, screeching so loudly that I had to clamp my hands over my ears. It was a sound that promised to destroy anything that got in its way.

Will's arm wrapped around my waist, like he also understood that it was too late for me to get away and had decided to protect me instead. I gripped his arm tightly as I tilted my head back and looked up to the sky. I saw it then, swooping down towards us. For us.

A dragon.

Its wings extended long enough to cover the entire field, flared out, membranous with sharp claws at the ends. There were spikes along its tail, traveling up its back all the way to its head. And also on that head, were long horns that protruded from its skull—like a beastly crown. Some of its scales were a pale-yellow color, running in lines down the sides of its body, while the rest of it was black. And its eyes... they were the color of fire. They swirled like it, too.

It landed not far off from us, just on the other side of the clearing, its claws digging into the ground and scraping against the rock. It watched us with intelligent eyes, as if to assess us as threats. Will moved me so that he was positioned in between me and the beast, like he would stop at nothing to keep it away from me. And I could hardly protest, because I was terrified.

It watched us, and I could have sworn some strange sadness passed through its eyes, before it tilted its head up towards the sky. A moment later, a thick stream of flames shot from its mouth, meeting nothing but open air, but heating everything else. The hair on my arms reacted, either from the heat or from fear, and I was certain then that I was going to die.

I could hardly think about anything else at the moment, only that I wanted to get as far away from this beast as possible. I knew my body was shaking, and without Will holding onto me, I was likely to collapse at any moment. And I did. I felt my knees hit the ground; the blow softened by the layer of snow. My mind filled with a mess of unpleasant thoughts.

Drazen. Was this Drazen, come to kill me at last?

Tears fell from my eyes as I continued to shake. I couldn't move. I couldn't do anything but sit there like a coward. For some reason, all I could see within my mind was the memory of Sazarr's limbs and wings being ripped from his body. And teeth and claws and shrieks of pain. And blood—so much blood.

I vaguely heard Will yell, "Get out of here. You're terrifying her!" He couldn't have been talking to the beast, could he? He spoke as if he… as if he *knew* it. As if they were familiar.

Will bent down and wrapped his arms around me, offering his comfort. Aerez stood with her twin short swords out, her back towards me as if there was a target I could not see that she was facing. And a moment later, I saw the guards circling in on us, moving in from every direction. They weren't scared of the dragon… they weren't even looking at it. Something wasn't right. Something was very, very wrong.

"You can't fight them," I heard Will say to Aerez, but she didn't seem to care, because a moment later she was running towards them, slicing into them quicker than I could even see.

467

Will quickly set me down and ran over to her. A guards lunged for him, and he was forced to draw his sword and cut down the man. When he reached Aerez, I thought he would continue to help her fight, but instead he was trying to *restrain* her. He grabbed onto her wrists and pulled her swords from her hands, throwing them into the snow. She looked at him, as confused as I felt, and then began to back away.

"You bastard," she growled at him, and then her eyes shifted to me, filled with pity and... sadness. "I'm sorry," she said to me. "But I'm not going to be put in chains because of him. They're not looking for me."

"What?" I said, though it was too quiet for her to hear. She had already turned around and started to run through the snow, back towards the city. The guards made no move to stop her. "Aerez!" I shouted. I couldn't understand why she was leaving me.

Will walked back over to me, and I expected the guards to close in on us, but they only stood there. I again turned my attention to the beast that was in the same spot, watching us, as if waiting for us to make a move.

"It's going to kill us," I said to Will. "We must go. We must run. Why did Aerez leave me?" I was speaking frantically, clearly not in my right mind. I was in shock. I was terrified.

"It's okay," Will said, bending down and running a hand over my cheek. It didn't feel okay. I flinched from his touch, crawling away from him slightly, but he continued towards me. He grabbed onto my arm and pulled me so that I was standing, and then leaned in and whispered into my ear, "He won't hurt you. He's my brother."

Brother...

His *brother*.

I shoved hard onto Will's chest, so hard that he went stumbling back a few feet. "You traitor," I said. "How could you..."

I couldn't even finish the thought, not with the way Will was looking at me. His face was filled with such confusion and anger—because of *me*. I had never seen him look at me that way, nor anyone else. In that moment it made me... afraid of him.

He started to walk away, leaving me there where the guards could swoop in and grab me at any moment. He untied his cloak and discarded it in the snow, and then rolled up the sleeves of his shirt. The dragon, his brother, growled at him, as if he knew something I did not understand.

The guards began to back away, like they were afraid now, and one of them grabbed me by the arm and began to pull me away as well. I didn't even protest—I couldn't. They weren't putting me in chains or cuffs, but only pulling me away as if to keep me from danger—from whatever the princes were about to do.

Will began to yell something at the beast, but I was too far away to hear, and the wind was too loud, like it too knew what was coming. My vision began to blur, but not from tears. I felt dizzy, like something was happening to my mind. Something...

I felt the air warm again, only slightly, and turned towards Will to find flames swirling at his hands, melting all the snow within his immediate proximity. Those flames grew, and then they began to shoot outwards, straight towards the dragon.

But when I looked at the dragon, I found its mouth open, rows of sharp teeth reflecting in the sunlight. And then flame began to whirl within that mouth, and a moment later they were shooting out, straight towards Will.

They were aiming for each other, and their flames collided somewhere in the middle. Snow melted all around. Birds flying overhead turned and flew in the opposite direction. Sweat poured down my body, pooling beneath my clothes.

They were fighting, with flames. It didn't seem like either of them were actually trying to harm one another, but I

469

couldn't tell what their intentions were. I could hardly see either of them through the brightness of the flames, and the black smoke rising as those flames hit the earth. Will was engulfed by it, while I could still make out the large body of the dragon.

I again started to feel... wrong. It felt as if I was walking through a dream, and that none of this was really happening at all. Wouldn't that be a relief? It felt like I had reached the point in a dream where things had gotten so scary that my body awoke all on its own, and that any moment now I would find myself in bed and realize that it had all been in my head.

I again fell to the ground, and I could see the guards standing by, watching me, confusion holding their faces. I felt my body start to shake and my limbs begin to flail uncontrollably. I thought I was dying.

I tried to look for Will, but I didn't even have the energy to turn my head in his direction. I reached out, I tried to call his name. I turned my neck just enough to see him, finding him running towards me, having forgotten the fight with his brother. His brother's flames hit him as he turned away, scorching his skin, and I heard him hiss in pain. He fell over and clutched at his body, trying to stop the burning.

Will.

I wanted to go to him, to help him, but there was something very wrong with me. It felt like I was dying, and my mind was fading away. I tried everything I could to crawl, to move an inch, but something else had taken control of me. Something was pulling me away—taking me far away from this place.

Chapter 48

His brother. I… had no idea what to think of that. I had no idea what to think about anything. I thought Will had betrayed me, and that was why his brother was there, and why he wasn't fighting the guards, but then he fought his brother anyways. They weren't trying to kill one another, but there was certainly some fight for control taking place.

And I couldn't even figure it out, because the darkness had taken me away. My eyes took their time adjusting to the shift in brightness, changing from the sunny mountaintop to a dark cavern. It was cold, and musty, and… all too familiar. I was more aware of my surroundings in this place now than I ever had been before. While it still felt like a dream, I knew with certainty that it was not.

I wasn't sure if I should have felt relieved or annoyed that I had been taken away at such a time. Perhaps I should have been worried, because my body, my physical one, was still in that clearing outside of Frystal, and it likely looked to them like I was dead. But Will would know what was happening. He would know to protect me. We were in the midst of being captured by those guards—of being attacked by a dragon—and this had to happen right now.

Perhaps I could find help, or at least find some way for me to get back to my body.

I ran a hand over my face, surprised to find that all the sweat and tears had disappeared from before. I looked down at myself, and while I was wearing the same clothes, these were clean, not covered in blood or anything else, and my hair fell in soft waves down my back. My body felt strong, if such a thing was possible. I didn't feel at all like I had just been in a fight or been running a great distance.

A sound far off caught my attention, further down the cave. I could tell that I was in a cave, because where I usually saw nothing but darkness, now I could see the walls of the cave, and the trickles of water that rolled up them. It was a wide-open area, and further down I could see that it branched off into other rooms and paths.

I followed the sound, which took me into a smaller cavern, with one candle burning in the corner. A candle? How odd that was, to see such a thing in the Otherealm. And even more odd, there was a... desk, and on that desk were papers and books and jars of ink.

I turned to the other side of the space, and I saw a shape moving within the shadows. I backed up a few steps, mostly out of fear, and my back slammed hard into that desk, rattling the bottles of ink. It was not a serpent that I saw, but something *human*.

"Hello?" I whispered.

Footsteps shuffled, and the shape moved, coming towards me with surprising swiftness. It was... a man. "Do not be afraid," he told me, coming to stand directly in front of me. His voice was deep and rough from lack of use, but there was something about it that I found incredibly soothing.

The candle lit enough of the space for me to see his features. He was tall, much taller than any man I'd met before. He wore nice black clothes, which seemed odd considering where we were, but I guess there was a lot I didn't understand about this place. His hair was long and black, falling all the way down to his waist, nearly as long as mine. His face was beautiful. He had a strong jawline and high cheekbones, thin eyebrows and long straight eyelashes. And his eyes... My breath caught when I saw them. Emerald green, though his glowed in a way that I knew was unnatural. He blinked at me, watching as I stared back at him.

"Who are you?" I asked, and my voice was too unsteady for me to hide how afraid I was. My heart was beating faster now than it had when I'd seen that dragon, because of the power I felt seeping from this man before me.

"Do you pretend to not already know?" he asked, and I noticed the slight accent to his voice, and the way he spoke, there was something almost…old about it. "You know who I am," he whispered. His voice sent a chill through me, though not in a bad way. It filled me with a thrill of excitement and eagerness, and it made me move closer to him without even realizing it.

"Sazarr," I said. "I expected to find a serpent."

He didn't say anything for a moment, but I thought I glimpsed something like a smile cross his face, which was not something I ever thought I would see. He was handsome, there was no denying that, and he appeared to be only about ten years older than me, though I knew that wasn't the truth. His smile disappeared. "Are you alright?"

I met his eyes, imagining that he could hypnotize me with them, imagining that he could do a lot of things with only one look. "I'm… fine," I said. "I'm just very confused. Can you tell me how this is happening? Am I asleep?"

"That is unimportant," he said. "There are other things for us to discuss, and we do not have much time."

"How am I here?" I continued. "Why am I here?"

"Karalia," he said, so tenderly that I nearly fell onto my knees before him. What the hell was happening to me?

"Stop," I said, loud enough for it to echo throughout the cave. "Whatever you're doing, stop it right now or I refuse to talk to you about anything."

He turned his head away, annoyed, and then I felt something shift within me. My body sagged, and I had to lean against the desk to steady myself. But my mind felt more like my own again.

"You smell," he started, his nostrils flaring, "like the enemy. You have surrounded yourself in flames."

"Flames?" I said. "That doesn't seem like such a bad thing compared to this darkness." I looked around. "If you brought me here to reprimand me, then you can just send me back right now, because I don't want to hear it. The reason I smell like flames is because I was about to get devoured by a dragon, if you didn't know."

He kept his mouth shut, though his eyes were still on me. He took me in from the bottom up, staring at my feet, then my legs, up to my stomach, my chest, before finally finding my face again. He took one step toward me, and I refused to move, which made him smile a little.

I had no idea what he was doing, but if he wanted to play, then so could I. "When was the last time you saw a woman?" I asked, and one of his brows raised curiously. "I imagine it's been a very long time, so I will not get angry with you for staring at me in such an intimate way."

"Surely this is not what you wish to ask me about," he said flatly.

"I don't know," I shrugged. "You're the one that brought me here, so I suspect there's something you want to tell me. Or am I wrong?"

"You are correct."

"Well, then let's get on with it. My body is in a very compromising position at the moment, so if I don't get back soon, I fear that they may think me to be dead."

"Why do you say such things?" he asked me, a confused expression on his face. "Do you have a death wish?"

I rolled my eyes. "Look, Sazarr, oh mighty serpent god, whatever, I know you've been down here for a long time, and I'm sure a lot has changed since you've been up, you know, in the real world. But where I come from, men can't just snatch away women while they're in the middle of something and then look at them like they want to devour them, and then scold them for speaking their minds."

"I'm sorry," he said quickly, like he'd already realized his mistake before I'd said anything. "That was... That isn't why I brought you here. You just look very familiar to me. Forgive me for staring."

"Then why don't you tell me why you've brought me here."

"You seek my blade, do you not? And have you not also just been told that you can find it in the Otherealm?"

"Do not trick me," I said. "Can you give it to me?"

His face was carefully blank. "No."

"But it is here?"

"Yes."

"So, then how do I get it?"

"You will have to enter the Otherealm on your own two feet, in your own body. Which is not what this is. There is an island northwest of Vatragon. There, you will find what you need."

That must have been the island I'd seen last night, in my vision.

"Why do you keep bringing me here?" I asked him.

Something like shock passed his face. "You do not know?"

"Know what?"

"Surely you must have guessed it. Haven't you wondered why it's been so easy for you to search for the blade? Haven't you wondered why the serpents keep finding you? Haven't you wondered why I have selected you to help me?"

"Of course I've wondered," I said. "But that doesn't explain how—"

"You are *serpent blooded*," he cut in.

I took a few more steps back, though there wasn't much room for me to go anywhere at all. And Sazarr only continued towards me.

"We are connected," he said. "I sensed your danger just now, so I brought you here."

"That isn't possible," I told him. "There are no *serpent blooded*."

"There never has been before," he agreed. "But there is now. You are my descendant, Karalia. My power has been within your bloodline for a thousand years."

"That isn't possible," I said again. "I thought you were trapped here."

"I am trapped here," he answered sternly. "While I have been granted leave on occasion, it is only in a dreamlike state such as your own. My physical body is cursed to remain here. But that does not stop others from coming to me."

"My ancestor came to you?"

He nodded. "Many people used to come, before they stopped believing in me. They used to think that I could help them—that I could give them a better life. They were wrong. But then one day, a woman came to me, and I knew right away that she was different from the others. She did not cower in my presence, and she did not run away screaming.

"I was immediately infatuated with her, which I hate to admit quickly turned into obsession. She fell in love with me and had no intention of going back to her old life, to the real world, and she stayed with me here for some time. I came to care for her deeply, in the only way that I am capable of. I could never love a mortal, not even one as special as her. She was not yet even a woman when she arrived, and she stayed with me for fifteen years before I sent her away. You see, she was with child, and I knew that she could not have the child here in the Otherealm. And I also had no interest in seeing it once it was born.

"I forced her to go, even though I knew she would hate me forever because of it. I never saw her again, though I heard whispers that she died in childbirth, while the child lived on with the rest of her family. I debated searching for and killing that child, because I didn't want any part of myself out in the world where Drazen could find it. But then I wondered if, perhaps, that child could have been born special, with some sort of ability, as Drazen's descendants had been.

"He was a boy. I watched him grow up, and waited for it to happen, but it never did. Eventually he married, had children of his own, and then passed on. So I watched those children, and again, nothing. On and on it went, children being born, again as disappointments to me. I started to believe that there was nothing special about them at all, until one late fall day when a little girl was born, with golden hair

476

and green eyes, a reminder of the woman from so long ago. I immediately felt something within you, something so different from all the others, and it didn't take me long to realize what you were. I knew you could be the one to help me someday."

My eyes began to fill with tears, yet again, and while I knew they weren't real tears, they felt like they were.

"I watched over you your entire childhood," Sazarr continued. "Though I never interfered. I knew I needed to wait until you were old enough, until you would be able to understand all of this. But then Drazen must have discovered the truth. He must have felt that power within you as well, and he sought to eliminate it. He killed your parents first, because he didn't know which one of them it was that had given the ability to you, but he wanted to make sure that they could not create something like you ever again. And then he came for you, but of course, he failed, and you got away. He thought he succeeded in killing you, which is why I think he stayed away, but if he hasn't learned the truth already, then he will soon, and he *will* be coming back for you, Karalia."

"Why me?" I said. "Why am I the first one, after so long?"

"I don't know," he told me. "I never understood how this magic worked. I thought that perhaps it was a part of the curse, that because my friend bested me, I could never transfer my power onto others."

"But here I am," I muttered, mostly to myself. "I feel like this… like it explains everything. Like me being… *serpent blooded* is the reason that I've been sent to find the blade in the first place. I never knew why, but maybe I do now." I paused, continuing to think deeply. "I meant what I said, you know. That I am going to try and free you."

He closed his eyes, taking a deep breath. "Don't bother. It won't work." Then he turned around, turned away from me and began to walk into the darkness.

I moved quickly, reaching a hand through the surrounding mist, my fingers finding his back. He felt cold, but it wasn't as unsettling as it should have been, "Sazarr."

"Karalia," he said, turning around so quickly that I nearly fell backward again, but his hands reached and grabbed onto my arms, steadying me. "Are you frightened?" he asked, some of the amusement returning to his tone.

"Yes."

"You do not need to be." He lifted a hand towards my face, brushing his fingers down the side of my cheek. "You just need time to get used to everything." He moved those fingers down my jaw, and then down my neck. I saw him lean forwards and I closed my eyes, afraid that he might kiss me, but then I felt his lips brush my ear as he whispered, "Soon, you will be surrounded by enemies. Do not let them know what you are. Let them think that you are weak, helpless, and afraid. We will destroy those who have wronged us. That, I can promise you. If I make it out of this place, the world will not be able to hide from our wrath."

He pulled back, his hand still on my neck, and I stared into his eyes for a long moment. I placed my hand atop his own, and he allowed me to pull it away, but even when it was at his side again, I remained holding on to it. "I'm sorry for what he did to you," I said. "I'm sorry that... that this has been your life. The people are going to learn the truth; a lot of them know it already. They toast drinks in your name and celebrate you in secret. They are planning a rebellion in our names. Drazen is going to burn in hell when we're through with him."

He gave me a promising grin as I continued to squeeze his hand, but then I felt the darkness begin to swirl. I was being pulled away, back to the tragedy unfolding in Frystal, but I was not ready for that, not yet.

"Wait!" I called, and then I pulled so hard on his hand that he came moving towards me, his chest pressing against my own. My breath caught as I said. "I'm not ready to go yet."

He didn't say anything for a moment, and I had the feeling that he didn't know what to say. This was as new to him as it was to me. He reached his free hand up to my hair and twirled his fingers around in it, playing with the soft golden waves. "You look just like her," he finally said to me. "I had forgotten what she looked like, until I saw you here today."

He smiled softly, in a way that I would never have expected the serpent god to appear. It made him look so human, and so vulnerable. Without realizing what I was doing, I lifted my arms and wrapped them around his back. It took a moment, but he hugged me back.

"I will be watching over you," he told me. "I will try and protect you as best as I can, but when you are around them, it's difficult for me to see things clearly, because his power interferes with my own. I know you can save your friend. I have seen how brave and fearless you are. I know you are strong." He hugged me tighter. "But please do not forget me."

"I could never forget you," I said, with the side of my face pressed against his chest. I was surprised to hear a heart beating within it. "There's so much I still need to ask you about. "

"And you will," he said. "Soon."

Brightness flooded my view, and I knew then that my time was up.

There was cold snow beneath me, against the back side of me from where I was currently lying on the ground. I cracked my eyes open, finding the afternoon sun high overhead, bearing down on me, likely burning my skin. How long had I been away? I'd expected the guards to put me in chains by now.

It took a moment for my other senses to return, and I could hear others around me, surrounding me, and I lifted my head just enough to find Will's face peering over me. He was saying something that I could not make out, running a hand through my hair as if to soothe me. His eyes were even filled with tears. My head was resting in his lap as he cradled me like a child, holding onto me as if I had really been dead.

I still could not fathom the fact that I was *serpent blooded*, and that a *dragon blooded*, two *dragon blooded*, were currently in close proximity to me. What would they do if they knew the truth?

I had a feeling that I knew how this situation was going to end, and perhaps Sazarr did too. The guards would capture me, and I would be brought back to the capital, as it was originally intended by the dragon prince. Surely, he only came here to collect me.

I shifted my gaze to the distance, towards the dragon that was now lying down. It looked like a very large puppy, though it still terrified me. Initially, I thought it was Drazen, but now I know that it couldn't have been. It was Prince Daenaron. He was much smaller than the memories I'd seen of Drazen, and their coloring was different. This wasn't the man that wanted to kill me, it was only the man that wanted to steal me away and force me to be his bride.

I knew there was no point in fighting, as I no longer had a chance of escaping this.

I pulled Will's arms from me, nearly swatting him off as I scooted away and then attempted to stand. My body was weak, and I was still crying, despite having calmed down a bit. I probably looked like a fool, but I didn't really care. I'd just seen Veeran die, killed two men, watched Aerez abandon me, spoken with Sazarr, found out that I was *serpent blooded*, and now I had to wait for these guards to restrain me, where they would likely lock me up somewhere.

But the guards hadn't moved, not yet. They were waiting for orders, from… Prince Daenaron.

I met the dragon's eyes, finding him watching me sadly. I didn't hide my anger or disgust, not at all. I stood there and watched him, waiting for something to happen, aware of Will at my back, like he still thought I needed protection.

Then the dragon lifted its head, and then the rest of its body, until it was standing on its arms and legs, stretching its wings out widely. It took a step towards us, and the earth rumbled, another step, another rumble.

I turned to Will, but for some reason he had backed *away*, both from me and the beast. He was retreating to the guards. Was I supposed to join him? Did Daen have that much control over him?

I didn't run or flee in the opposite direction. I remained standing there as the dragon approached me, even as it stood directly in front of me. I shoved my fear away, putting on a face that was not my own, and a voice that I could not recognize. "You are a monster," I said to it, hoping that it could understand me.

It lowered its head to me, so close that I could feel its breath hit me hard enough to blow my hair back. He just... watched me.

"Leave me alone," I said, quiet enough that I knew Will could not hear. "You are a monster," I said again. "And not because you have this... form, but because of what you plan to do with me. You don't even know me, and yet you plan to steal me away. I would sooner end my life than leave here with you."

He was so close, and I could tell he'd heard my word because he turned his head away from me, as if he couldn't even bear to look at me. I waited for him to get angry and turn me to ash. I wanted to see if there was more beast or man within him. But he only backed away, ever so slowly. His eyes went to the guards, like he was giving them some silent command, and they understood him immediately. They were moving towards me in an instant.

Another crack sounded—a loud boom—and I again covered my ears as the dragon launched itself into the sky. The force of air from its wings nearly knocked me over, but I stood my ground, looking up to the sky as he flew away. I was much less afraid now.

The dragon turned back to me, one last time, our eyes locking and holding for a moment before he headed south,

481

over the mountains and away from Frystal. I assumed that he was headed back to the capital.

I didn't say anything as the guards walked up to me and locked shackles around my wrists, and as they took away my sword and knife. They did not restrain Will, though he moved to stand at my side. One of the guards gave me a hard shove to get me moving, back into the city.

"Let's see what the Lady of Frystal has to say about this," one of the men sneered.

Chapter 49

Will and I were led through the city by at least a dozen guards, though I knew there would be more waiting where we were going. Other than the shackles they put around my wrists, they made no further moves to bind us. Will was left to walk freely, which irritated me. If he wanted to, he could injure any of those men. But me, without my sword I was pretty much useless.

The city people watched us as we passed, most of their faces stern and unreadable, though some look rather piteous. I couldn't blame them. They were likely relieved that the guards invading their city had found whatever it was they were looking for. But then I saw a familiar face within the thrall of people, and I went completely still. So still, that one of the guards had to give me a shove to keep me moving.

It was Veeran's uncle. Alongside a short and round woman, with two small children at her side. They didn't know. They were likely standing there in hopes that Veeran might show up, but they didn't know that they would never see him again.

They were standing too far for me to converse with them, and we were walking too fast, but from the look his uncle gave me, I could tell he saw what was in my eyes. He looked down towards the ground, sadly, clutching his wife tighter at his side. When he looked toward me again, I mouthed the words *I'm sorry*, and he gave me a solemn nod before turning and leading his family away.

I was going to collapse and begin weeping again, but a guard shoved the pommel of his sword into my back, causing me to cry out, but it got me moving again.

I was far too exhausted to try to fight or escape. If they locked me up for this, well, there was nothing I could really do about that. Perhaps Will could find some way to help me, though I suspected he was in as much trouble as I was.

We were headed towards the Lady of Frystal's residence, though I had no idea who she was. I would find out soon enough, but I could only hope that she would be merciful with whatever punishment she gave me.

It was a rather long walk, seeming to have taken us to the entirely opposite end of the city, all the way to the outskirts and further down the side of the mountain. Past all the buildings and everything else, far down below, I could see a large building surrounded by snow-covered fields.

I assumed it was an estate, and I had no doubt that was where we were headed. As we got even closer, I could see the massive building made of black brick, with tall windows lined in gold trimming. The yard was barren other than a few frozen shrubs, and in the middle of it was a fountain, long having gone frozen. I wondered if the thing was ever *not* frozen. There was a stone path that led up to the building, the snow freshly cleared, making it much easier to walk on.

The guards opened the large singular door made entirely of glass, though it was frosted so I could not see what lay on the other side. Will walked a few steps ahead of me, and I wisely stayed at his back.

We entered a just as ornate setting as the outside had been, though everything inside seemed much cozier. We passed the entryway and entered what I assumed was a sitting room. There was a massive fireplace in the corner, flames roaring within, heating the room almost too warm for comfort. The room was decorated with pale blue colors. Along one wall was a long white couch, and along another was a table with gold cushioned chairs. The guards led us to that table, shoving me down into one of the chairs, and Will taking up the one next to me. This was certainly not going to be a warm welcome, despite the temperature of the room.

We sat there for a short while until the doors to the room opened and in walked a woman, the Lady of Frystal. She was beautiful, in a terrifying way. Her skin was as pale as the snow that settled outside, and her hair was almost exactly the same color. Bone-white. Her eyes were the darkest color I'd ever seen, so black that I could hardly even make them out, while the whites surrounding them were again the color of snow. Her lips were as red as blood, and she smiled at us as she approached, revealing a set of straight shiny teeth.

I sat there, completely still, as she walked up to the table. I was relieved when she ignored me and instead walked up to Will, but then she bent down, placing a kiss on his cheek.

"Nephew," she said, her voice just as cold as I would have expected. "I've been waiting for you to show yourself."

Nephew?

"Hello, aunt," Will said back to her.

"What—" I hadn't meant to voice my confusion, but it slipped out. Will's hand slid beneath the table, resting atop my thigh, I think his attempt to help me relax.

This woman was the Lady of Frystal, and Will's aunt? I had no idea if I should have been relieved by that, or even more terrified.

She stepped away from us and took up a seat at the opposite end of the table. A servant came and poured us each a cup of tea, and then after, everyone was dismissed from the room, including all the guards.

The Lady of Frystal lifted her cup and took a small sip. "I do apologize for the measures we have taken to bring you here, but the two of you have been causing a lot of trouble lately." She did not sound the least bit apologetic.

Will smiled at his aunt, a sharp contrast to the words that came out of his mouth. "You do not have the authority to *capture* me, nor my companion. She is under my protection."

She let out a cold, low laugh. "Did you think you could prance around my city without me knowing? You should know better than that. What is it that you're up to? Your family has not heard from you in months, and there have been rumors of you being seen in Kraxoth, at The Crossing, and now here."

"Please," Will said, though he sounded very unpleased. "There is something very important that we need to do. You can't tell my father, if he knows—"

"Your father is the one who ordered me to capture you," she snapped. "Why do you think your brother was here? He came days ago, worried sick because you'd been missing. And then you showed up a few days later. You are to be escorted back to the capital, along with your female companion." Her eyes flashed to me, a careless assessing glance. "Who is she, anyway?"

"Nobody," I answered. "An orphan he picked up in Mortefine."

"Then I suppose that will make it easy for the king to punish you." She shot me a look of disgust before turning back to Will. "It's clear that you don't plan to reveal your scheming to me, so you'll just have to tell your father once you return home. The two of you will leave tomorrow, as will the guards your father has sent here."

"Am I your prisoner?" I said to her.

"No, dear," she replied. "You are the *king's* prisoner. Not mine."

I leaned further toward her. "With all due respect, lady, I have no interest in going to the capital."

"You don't have a choice." She shrugged. "The king has ordered this himself. You cannot refuse. Whoever you are, and whatever you're up to, he *will* find out the truth."

"We'll see."

"You are a foolish girl," she said to me, and then turned to Will. "And you are a foolish prince. Did you think your father would not mind such reckless behavior? You injured or even killed dozens of his guards."

"They killed an innocent defenseless boy!" I said, much louder than I had been speaking before. I could hear the guards moving outside of the door, though they made no move to enter. "They hunted us like animals. We were only protecting ourselves."

"Call it whatever you like," she said. "Even if I did believe that you were innocent, I could not go against the king's orders. Perhaps Will can beg for your life to be spared."

She called the guards back into the room, and then had them remove me. They led me up a set of stairs and down a long hall, into what I assumed was some sort of guest room. I had expected a cell. They removed my shackles and then shoved me into the room, locking it behind me.

I waited for something to happen—for anything to happen. Nobody entered the room except for a servant delivering a tray of food, and when I tried to ask them questions, they merely turned and ran from the room, where the door was again slammed and locked in my face. I wanted to talk to Will, but I didn't think that would happen anytime soon.

The windows looked up towards the city, and to the side I could see the sun beginning to set, and that it had also started to snow. At least there was a fireplace in my room to keep me warm.

I knew I was in some sort of guest room. There was an adjoining bathing chamber that I knew I would need to use at some point before we headed off tomorrow, with a tub large enough to fit half a dozen people. There wasn't much else in the main room besides a bed.

I was sitting on that bed, I had been for a while, lost within my thoughts, when I heard some sort of tap on the window. It was so faint that I might have dismissed it as the wind, if it weren't for a second, and then a third tap immediately after.

I jumped up from the bed, ran over to the window, and pulled the curtains as wide as they would go. I held in my scream when I saw a face staring back at me, smiling like they had come to murder me.

To my surprise, the window was unlocked, and I slid it open enough for Aerez to climb through before anyone from the outside noticed her presence. Her usual dark clothes were covered in snow, soaked with it.

"Shit," she said, slipping into the room. "It's cold out there." She shivered slightly, sending flakes of snow falling to the floor.

"Where have you been?" I demanded. "I thought you abandoned me!" I wouldn't ask her how she made it here, undetected, because that was not the part of this that surprised me.

She had a guilty look on her face. "I thought about abandoning you, but I didn't want you to think I was a coward."

"Why did you run?"

She raised her brown, a hint of that usual amusement returning. "Like I said, I wouldn't allow them to chain me up. And because there was an actual *dragon*. I thought it was going to eat me."

"You were scared?" I asked, and she nodded. I could understand that, but I was still angry that she left. "I was afraid too. I... I went away. I can't explain it now, but I spoke with Sazarr. He confirmed that we need to go to that island, to Svar."

"You want to escape?" she asked, like she was already eager to aid me.

"No," I said. "At least not yet. Will and I are to be brought to the capital. On the king's orders. I think I should go and ask for his help. There's... something else I need to do there before we continue the search for the blade. Will you come with us, to Vatragon City?"

She thought for a moment, before meeting my eyes with a smile. "Of course I will. I'd hate to be stuck in this cold shit hole of a city. I'll find you there. Don't worry, I'm good at staying hidden."

"Thank you," I said, and I truly meant it. I leaned towards her and wrapped my hands around her back, pulling her towards me. She was stiff for just a moment, as if in hesitation, before hugging me back. "Aerez, I'm so sorry for everything that happened last night. It was stupid."

"It's fine," she said. "Honestly, I'd forgotten about that. We have bigger things to worry about now."

I pulled away, tears slipping from my eyes.

"Don't cry," she said. "What is it?"

I shook my head. "It's nothing. I just… I thought you left me. I thought I'd never get to see you again or get to say goodbye."

She smiled at me, such a warm splendid smile, and it made my heart warm. "I would never leave without saying goodbye." We both laughed softly, doing our best to remain quiet. "I've told you before that I'm here for you. I'm your friend, and I would not abandon you so easily."

"I suppose that makes me lucky," I told her. "That I have you as my friend."

I closed my eyes for a moment, smiling to myself, taking a deep breath so that I did not cry again. But when I opened them and looked for Aerez, she was no longer there. She slipped quietly through the window and back out into the snowy world beyond. I looked out of the window and saw nothing, not even footprints in the snow. She was gone, but she would find me again, because she'd made me a promise.

As I dreamt that night, I did everything in my power to contact Sazarr. I knew that if I could just speak with him again, I could get the answers I had been looking for. I practically pleaded for him to find me.

But nothing happened.

My dreams were filled with light and sunshine, and even in the shadows I saw none of that usual darkness that I used to slip into so easily. I dreamt of the dragon prince, of flames and heat. I dreamt of the capital, of the king and queen, of what would happen when I made it there. I dreamt of Will and Aerez, of the friends I had come to care for so greatly in such a short amount of time. I dreamt of Nola, and I awoke with tears in my eyes, from the sadness I felt for her.

It was still dark out, very early the next morning, and the house was completely silent. I heard nothing beyond the door to my room, but I was sure there were guards posted just outside. I knew Will slept somewhere beyond, and I imagined him sitting in bed, unable to sleep, worried as well about what was to come.

I didn't know what to think about Will. He was my blood-sworn enemy, but Sazarr hadn't warned me to stay away from him, he'd bid me to get closer to his entire family. I didn't know what Sazarr had planned, but I knew I couldn't harm Will if it came to that. I cared about him too much, even if I wasn't supposed to.

But his brother… well, I thought that I would enjoy harming him, for all he'd done to me. I knew things would get even more complicated when I made it to the capital. He had to have known already who I was, and despite what I'd said to him, he probably still wanted to force me to be his bride.

Things were going to change, very soon.

The following morning two guards came to escort me to the drive of the estate, where about two dozen guards were waiting, all saddled atop horses. Will was there as well, still unrestrained, loading a pack onto the side of a horse.

He smiled when he saw me, though I couldn't bring myself to do the same. Did he know I'd been locked up all night? Did he care? Where had he been?

"I asked them to let us share a horse," he said to me as I approached. "I know you're still not comfortable riding by yourself."

"Okay."

"Here," he said, handing me something. My eyes widened when I saw what it was. He slipped my sword holster over my back, with Fangmar inside of it, and tucked the knife into the back of my pants. "You might need them out there."

"Thank you," I offered.

He climbs atop the horse and then reached down to help me up, and placed me in front of him, sliding his hands protectively around my waist. I was too exhausted to even care, so I leaned back onto him, resting my head against his chest.

"I'm sorry," he said to me. "This isn't—this wasn't how this was supposed to happen. I didn't want this."

"I know," I told him. "It's okay. At least now you can fulfill your original duty and deliver me to your brother."

"I never wanted that for you," he said. "If I could stop it, I—"

"No," I told him, practically shouting the word. "It's… this will be okay. We will deal with it—together. I still have time."

"I am your friend," he told me. "I care for you—in a way that I know you could never care for me. What I said, what we both said… you mean a lot to me, okay? Nothing will ever change that."

I turned around to face him. "Will…" I started. "Have I ever thanked you? For everything you have done for me? You saved my life, more than once. You helped me in ways that I don't think anyone else ever could. I am glad to have you at my side, despite what I might sometimes say."

He smiled down at me, though it didn't quite reach his eyes. "I will always be here for you." And then he placed a kiss atop my head.

Then we headed off. The guards led us through the city, all the way to the opposite end of it where we would leave from. We passed the tunnel, heading further west towards the mountain road. It was covered in snow, deep enough to cover most of the horse's legs, though they were still able to walk through it.

I looked up to the cloudless sky, disturbed to find that a part of me had expected to see that dragon fly by again. That a

491

part of me *wanted* to see it again, if only to satisfy my curiosity.

"What is it?" Will asked me.

"Why didn't you tell me?" I asked. "That your brother can turn into an *actual* dragon."

He hesitated for a moment before speaking. "I know I should have told you," he said. "But it's not really something I like reminding myself of."

"A warning would have been nice. Aerez full-on fled because of it."

"Do you think she'll come back?" he asked, and there was almost a hint of something like desperation in his voice.

I nodded. "She'll be back." And then I told him, quietly so that the guards could not hear, everything about Aerez coming to visit me the night before. I told him everything that we hadn't yet gotten a chance to talk about—everything that had happened when I collapsed in that clearing. I told him where I had gone, who I had seen, and everything we'd talked about.

But I might have left out the part about me being *serpent blooded*. I didn't know what would happen if he knew about that. I didn't know what he would do, or who he would tell. That needed to remain a secret for now.

"You can't let my father know who you are," Will said, referring to me being Karalia Havu. "At least not yet. Daen will know, but he might just keep his mouth shut about it for a little while, if we can convince him to."

"Why would he?"

"When we get to the capital, my brother is going to claim you. He thinks that you belong to him, and he won't leave you alone until you're his. I won't be able to protect you from him, especially not if my father finds out the truth, and if he supports my brother's intentions to wed you."

"I'm not afraid of your brother," I said, though even as the words left my mouth, I knew they weren't entirely true.

"You should be," Will said. "He's never let anyone stop him from taking what he wants. He's a monster. Please, just take this one piece of advice: do not get on his bad side. I can assure you, being his enemy is not a pleasant experience. He will destroy you."

"Not if I destroy him first."

Will didn't know that I already was his brother's enemy, *his* enemy too. They were bringing me into their midst, and I might have been planning to bring damnation to them all. The blood and power running through my veins had been rivals with the Drazos family for centuries.

"Tell me what you're thinking," Will finally said. "You can be honest. You can always be honest with me."

I turned around to face him, finding a look in his eyes that let me know he was not lying. Perhaps I had been a fool all along, to not realize how great of a friend he was the entire time. He had been my protector, my companion, and whatever I needed him to be. He would remain with me until the end. Even if he was my enemy, I still cared about him.

I released a long breath and then turned to face forward again as I started to speak. "I never thought my life would end up like this." Will's only answer was a tightened grip around my waist. "I wasn't the happiest in Mortefine, but I was content. I had a nice home, that I shared with the greatest friend I could ever ask for. But Hiran took her away from me. And it's a miracle that I'm still on two feet today. I could have given up a long time ago. I chose to work with my enemy rather than stand against him—for the people of that city. I let him manipulate me so that everyone else could stay safe. I wanted to give up, but the thought of seeing my friend again is the only thing keeping me going."

Will rested his chin atop my head, letting me know that he understood.

"I didn't ask for any of this," I continued. "I didn't ask to be Karalia Havu. I didn't ask to be betrothed to your brother. I didn't ask to be hunted. I didn't ask to be worshiped. I just wanted to find the blade and save my friend. I wish that it didn't matter who I was. I would have been satisfied living my life as a peasant if it meant that I was free. If it meant that

I could make my own decisions about what to do with my life, who I married, and where I lived. But..." I let out a long sigh. "Unfortunately, none of that is going to happen. Once I find the blade, I won't be able to return to Mortefine and pretend like nothing ever happened. I know what I'm going to have to do, and I won't allow anybody to stand in my way."

Will tensed behind me, like he was afraid of my words, and that sent a thrill of satisfaction through me.

We continued heading south, over the mountains, through the cold and snow. Soon we would begin our descent, down into the cold forest, towards The Crossing, over the Indrun River, and south until we reached Vatragon City. It would take weeks, but at least Will would be at my side, and at least I had plenty of time to plan my next moves.

Then things would change, and there would be a larger game for me to play.

To be continued...

Made in United States
Orlando, FL
27 December 2022

27681732R00280